Twice Promised

Outside the sea raged, thunder shook the foundations of the earth, and lightning threw daylight across the midnight sky. Inside Darcie, the storm was just as great. Desire raged as she snuggled against Zack, writhing against the length of his hard body, drawing her hand across his wide chest. He moaned as she reached his neck and encircled it with her arms.

Mewling in anticipation, Darcie brought Zack's head near to kiss his lips. She brushed them lightly and then moved on to his cheeks and ears, passing on her knowledge of sensual joys learned from him only moments earlier.

Groaning, Zack kissed her deeply, savagely, plunging deep inside her mouth to taste its forbidden sweetness, and Darcie knew her lips would bear the badge of his exquisite assault . . .

TWICE
PROMISED

NANCY
C. KNIGHT

ST. MARTIN'S PRESS / NEW YORK

TWICE PROMISED

Copyright © 1989 by Nancy Knight.

All rights reserved. No part of this book may be used or reproduced in any manner whatsoever without written permission except in the case of brief quotations embodied in critical articles or reviews. For information address St. Martin's Press, 175 Fifth Avenue, New York, N.Y. 10010.

ISBN: 0-312-91464-4 Can. ISBN: 0-312-91465-2

Printed in the United States of America

First St. Martin's Press mass market edition / April 1989

10 9 8 7 6 5 4 3 2 1

Dedicated
In loving honor
of Mother
Who taught me courage in the face of adversity.
And to look back on happy times. Love still blooms
where memories linger and flourish.
A lifetime of work, of joy, of sorrow
makes us capable of coping with tomorrow.

And in loving memory
of Daddy
Who never believed in limitations.
And who taught me to believe in Santa Claus.

Chapter One

"You're as graceful as a peg-legged sailor, Darcie Gaynor," she exclaimed to herself as the wind caught her shawl on the closing wrought iron gate, jerking her backward. She turned and looked at the snagged shawl, an exasperated sigh escaping her lips.

"But, mademoiselle, you're far prettier than any sailor I ever sailed with." A deep masculine voice teased with a decidedly French accent. "I'd wager the Empress Eugénie's jewels on it."

Brushing aside the leaves of a live oak tree that reached across the fence and hung between them, Darcie twisted around, her face flaming with the color of an oleander. She reached back to release the fabric and found the lace edging impaled high on a tapered black spike. She fidgeted with the snagged lace a moment while she tried to think of something to say to the forward stranger. A flicker of anger furrowed her brow as she wrestled helplessly with the lace, and she exclaimed through clenched teeth, "Does Her Majesty know you wager her jewels with such cavalier abandon?"

"Non," he replied, laughing as the breeze that had caused her present problem ruffled the dark curls on his forehead, "but I have no fear of losing such a wager and shall escape the guillotine again."

Her retort froze in her throat as she heard his offhand reference to the guillotine, and she stared half afraid, half curious at the smiling stranger. Frenchmen were common in Charleston, but few would venture to speak to a shipowner's daughter without a proper introduction. Darcie studied him quickly. Far handsomer than Barclay Rhett or Gideon Sanders, he stood a good seven or eight inches taller than she.

She looked back at the gate. There was a three-inch rip in the lace. She stamped her foot with the same impatience that had caused her to rush through the gate. Once again, the brisk wind blowing in from the Ashley River fluttered the lace on her shawl, as if it were flaunting the ugly tear.

She felt foolish dangling like a puppet from the gate, and every retort she considered seemed even sillier than her predicament. Besides, standing here on the street talking with an intriguing Frenchman who spoke of guillotines excited her. His clothes were those of a gentleman and he wore them well on his muscular body, but he seemed to care nothing for proprieties. Though she found his chatter delightful, she ignored his remark because he *was* extremely bold and forward. She responded with the cool voice she should have used in the beginning. "May I help you, sir?"

"Yes, you may, mademoiselle." He stepped closer, and his smile widened. "And, perhaps, I may be of assistance to you." He studied her carefully a moment and then glanced at the snagged lace. A mischievous smile teased his lips. "Tell me, were you climbing in or out when you . . . were, eh, apprehended?"

She looked at the stranger again, her eyes narrowing with anger. His smile bordered on laughter, and his eyes brimmed with mirth. Bristling at his amusement over her situation, Darcie glared at him. This was too embarrassing. She averted her eyes from his piercing gaze, unable to bear his close scrutiny any longer without deepening the scarlet tinge of her blush. "In what way may you be of assistance to me?"

He smiled and slid his arms around her.

"Sir! Unhand me this instant." Darcie wriggled until her hand was free and drew back to slap him. What nerve! She'd never been so astonished by a gentleman's—a *man's* behavior!

He caught her hand with his, pressing her closer to him, and kissed it gently as if they had just been formally introduced. "Be still, you vixen. Do you want to ruin the shawl completely?"

Darcie held her breath and peered into his eyes, wondering what would happen next. He took a step, and she felt the cold iron of the gate through the fine silk of her dress. Even more unsettling than the cold on her spine was the warmth that his body afforded as she hung helpless against him.

Working quickly, he lifted her a little higher and with his free hand released the lace. Gazing at her face, her eyes, her lips, he slowly lowered her until her slippers touched the ground.

Standing so close, Darcie felt that he must hear her heart hammering in her chest. No man had ever been so bold with her. And she had never felt like this before. Her body was warm all over—as if her blush extended from her face to her feet.

"Your freedom, mademoiselle."

"It seems I'm in your debt, monsieur. The wind lifted my shawl as the door was closing, and the wrought iron caught the lace." With his face so close to hers that she could feel his breath like a kiss on her cheek, Darcie looked up. Her sapphire gaze met warm brown eyes fringed with thick coal black lashes, long enough to be inviting, but short of being feminine as was her own flutter of lash. His hand still rested on her waist, and her voice was barely a whisper when she said, "How may I help you?"

"Ah, yes. I'm looking for Mlle. Darcie Jeanne Gaynor, present owner of Gaynor Shipping Company." His gaze seemed to evaluate her, flitting down the length of her slender body, pausing only momentarily to appreciate the tiny circle of her waist and full breasts. "Dare I pray that you are she?"

Darcie suppressed a giggle. Even in their most passionate

moments, Barclay Rhett and Gideon Sanders never spoke so eloquently. Nor did their stares elicit such blushes and palpitations from her. Nervously fingering the soft cream-colored lace of her shawl, she glanced up into his handsome face.

Moments ago, her breasts had been pressed against his broad chest, the length of her body molded against his. It was the most exciting thing that had ever happened to her. In the span of minutes, this man had taken more liberties with her than both Barclay Rhett and Gideon Sanders had through all the years of her acquaintance with them. She knew she ought to be insulted and shocked, but she felt exhilarated. Eyes wide with wonder, she gazed deeply into his warm brown ones and felt as if she were surrounded by some sort of invisible brandied comfort.

The scent of jasmine perfumed the air; the scree of gulls broke the silence of the late summer afternoon; and the sun dappled South Bay Street with shimmering silhouettes of live oak, palmetto, and oleander. Carriages rumbled past on nearby Meeting Street, and wagons lumbered up and down East Bay to and from wharves, stores, and homes. Ships lay in the harbor, others made their ways in or out. Charleston was indeed a city teeming with activity.

A carriage rolled by, slowing as it passed. "Good afternoon, Miss Gaynor."

Darcie jerked away from the strange Frenchman's grasp and saw Barclay Rhett glaring at her from his new vis à vis carriage with the pair of strutting white horses. Her wave was limp as she watched the carriage turn onto Meeting Street.

Forgetting Barclay, she looked back at the Frenchman who had rescued her. Feeling suddenly playful, she countered, "Your prayers are answered, monsieur. However, I must warn you."

"Warn me?"

"Yes. Charity, my mammy, cautions against asking for anything in prayer." Again Darcie stifled a giggle, thoroughly enjoying the look of confusion on the Frenchman's face.

"And why should she warn against asking for something in prayer?"

Darcie could no longer keep a stern face, and a smile erupted showing perfect white teeth peeking through full sensuous lips. "Because the good Lord may give you what you pray for."

The giggle bubbled forth at his look of shock, and Darcie covered her mouth with her delicate fingers, trying to stifle her unladylike outburst. The Frenchman comprehended her meaning quickly and laughed with her.

"Ah, a teasing game, eh?" His smile showed genuine delight at her wit. "Quite a little flirt, are you?"

"My apologies, monsieur." Darcie regained her composure, knowing that Charity was most likely standing at the parlor window listening and watching, already planning the scolding she would issue. No doubt the Frenchman would think she had no more upbringing than a field hand, but she didn't care. After this incident, she doubted if she'd ever see him again. She looked at him thoughtfully. "You don't sound exactly French."

"Mon Dieu, but you are quick," he replied, smiling. *"Ma mère* was *Anglaise*—English—and I spent many months in England with her."

Darcie glanced at a ladybug that lit on her bosom and then at the stranger whose gaze was fixed on the insect. He jerked his chin abruptly as if to pry his eyes from a tantalizing vision. If only she could brush the embarrassing insect away without appearing to draw the Frenchman's attention to her breasts.

She felt the blood creep up her neck and spill crimson color into her cheeks. To cover her embarrassment, she fluttered her eyelashes and smiled. "I am occasionally subject to lapses into the foolishness of my girlhood, as Charity frequently chides. I am indeed Darcie Jeanne Gaynor. And I'm afraid you have the advantage since I have no inkling as to your identity."

"Allow me to remedy the situation." He stepped back, removed his hat, and bowed deeply, clutching his hat to his chest. "Zacharie Etienne Manville at your service, Mademoiselle Gaynor."

"Manville?" Trying unsuccessfully to appear nonchalant, Darcie tugged on the knot of her shawl, drawing it closer about her neck and across her bosom. To her relief, the activity startled the ladybug and it flew away, and M. Manville returned his attention to her face.

"Yes. You have, perhaps, heard of me, after all?" His eyebrows lifted questioningly.

"Heard of you?" She wondered aloud. Could he possibly be related to the owner of Manville Trading Company, whose offices were not far from her father's. The tales her father told of the private war between the Manville Trading Company and the Gaynor Shipping Company were engraved in her mind. Darcie had been raised on stories of how the Gaynor ships rammed the Manville ships, of how cannon fire sank many fine ships, of the valiant crews lost on both sides. A costly private war that had ended fifteen years ago with a pact—a treaty between the two companies. Her smile seemed false now; the frivolous game with the stranger no longer fun. "I'm afraid not, sir. The name is merely familiar to me from the distant past."

Zacharie studied the young woman for a moment. Without doubt, she'd heard of him, but did she know who he was? Who he *really* was? His father had mentioned that the pact was written rather than oral, and that both parties received copies. Damn, but he wished his father had lived long enough to tell him where to find the Manville copy. "Mlle. Gaynor, I am Zacharie Manville of the Manville Trading Company."

Her back stiffened, but she kept smiling, her eyes unblinking. Deep in the folds of her gown, her fingers were clenched into tight fists as she lifted her chin. "I'm delighted for you. Now, if you don't mind, I was on my way—"

"Mlle. Gaynor, I must speak with you before you leave." He caught her arm and stopped her from walking away. "The matter is of great importance."

Darcie sighed. There seemed to be nothing to do but hear him out. He had, after all, rescued her.

"Forgive my manners, Monsieur Manville, but I was on an errand which depends on the timeliness of its completion." She didn't dare tell him that she was on the way to the shops by the wharves to see if the French ship that docked this morning had brought any silks. "Please state your business quickly."

"May we sit for a moment?" Zacharie's gaze settled on the piazza that stretched across the entire front of the house and down the south side.

"Of course, M. Manville. Come with me." Darcie walked back through the gate that had unfortunately caught her before she escaped this man. Regardless of how handsome and charming he was, she wanted nothing to do with anyone even remotely connected with Manville Trading Company. The Manvilles had been her father's enemies—and she was her father's daughter.

Darcie walked up one side of the gracefully curved stone staircase to the piazza and indicated a chair. "Would you like some lemonade, M. Manville?"

"It sounds delightful."

Of course, she thought. *The man has no breeding.* If he had, he would have realized that her invitation issued from good manners rather than from a desire for his company. "I won't be a moment."

Darcie disappeared into the house, silently cursing him for interrupting her errand. She wanted first choice of the silks because of the upcoming St. Cecilia's Ball at St. Andrews Hall, the first major social event of the year, not counting Race Week of course. If she didn't hurry, she'd be the last to select fabric for her gown, and that just wouldn't do. She refused to take what others left.

This gown was especially important since this would be her first ball. She'd been in deep mourning for three years, while other young women her age were flitting from party to ball with seemingly no cares. Despite her deep grief over her father's death, Darcie Gaynor was like any other girl. She'd wanted to go to balls and parties, to have beautiful new gowns and beaux hanging about all the time. For three long years she'd worn black, kept her house as dark as a tomb, and received calls only from her circle of close friends. Here she was at age nineteen, eagerly awaiting her first ball. Yes, this gown had to be very special.

Within moments, she returned with a tray laden with a cool

pitcher of lemonade, glasses, and tea cakes fresh from the oven. "Cook is a wonderful baker. Please try the tea cakes. Cook frosts them with chocolate. Positively sinful."

"Thank you, I will." He selected a tea cake, took a bite, and placed the remainder on a plate. "Mlle. Gaynor, I'm sorry to be the bearer of bad news, but I can delay my mission no longer."

"Bad news?" Whatever could he mean? They'd never even met. How could he know anything about her? "I'm afraid I don't understand."

Zack Manville looked at the woman sitting across the table from him. Her golden hair was drawn into a mass of curls that escaped her bonnet in the back and showed a fringe of shimmering wisps on her forehead. Her lips were relaxed, not frowning nor smiling, just slightly parted and inviting. Eyes the color of the sky over the Mediterranean peered at him, alert and quick, ready to accuse or ready to tease. The slightly angular cheekbones were high and aristocratic, perhaps indicating the strength of character he instinctively felt she possessed.

Zack Manville had been at sea for more than two months, and the sight of this extraordinarily beautiful woman elicited an ache that nearly consumed him. *Ah,* he thought wistfully, *I should not be thinking such thoughts in the presence of this innocent young girl.*

"Mlle. Gaynor," he began, not quite knowing how to approach her with the news of such a disaster. He didn't want to deal with a hysterical woman. "Your ship, the *Gay Dolphin,* has sunk. Much of—"

"Sunk?" Darcie leaped to her feet. The small dessert plate balanced on her knee clattered to the piazza floor and split in several shards of porcelain. "Sunk? That's impossible. The ship was new. The best on the sea. Why, it was . . ."

Her voice trailed off, and she fell back into her chair, shock draining all the vigor from her face. Her lively hands rested lamely in her lap for a change, still and delicate as a china doll's. Before either of them could speak further, the gate creaked and Dalton James, the captain of the *Gay Dolphin* strode toward them. Captain James seemed surprised at the Frenchman's presence, but from the expression on his face, Darcie knew that he had come with bad news. He was ashamed to have to face her, and hung his head low.

Together, Captain James and Zacharie Manville told of the sinking of her ship, of the bloodshed, of the injuries and of the deaths. Darcie was almost overcome with the horror.

As Darcie listened, she peered across White Point Gardens at the Ashley River, seeing nothing. Her delicate hands were clenched into tight fists, the only outward indication of her anger. "Pirates, Captain James? *Pirates?* in 1857?"

"Yes, miss." Captain James shifted his weight, still avoiding her eyes. "We lost ten men as well as the grandest ship known to man."

A fringe of tawny lashes fluttered over sapphire eyes, and for a moment, Darcie's chin touched her chest. Ten men. Lost at sea or killed by enemy gunfire. It didn't seem possible. And the *Gay Dolphin* sunk beneath enemy cannon. "Do you know anything about the pirates? What kind of ship? Who? It just doesn't make any sense to me."

"Aye. It don't make no sense to me neither." He joined her at the piazza railing, resting his hand on the smooth wood. He seemed relieved that she didn't accuse him of neglect. "Why, I ain't seen no pirates nor nothing that looked like pirates since them Frenchies stopped raiding us in '43. Beggin' yer pardon, M. Manville, sir."

Zacharie Manville nodded his understanding. He'd remained silent for the past few minutes as Captain James told of the horrors. Darcie had listened intently to her captain's story, exhibiting none of the theatrics Zack had expected from an American woman who was the gently bred daughter of a wealthy planter and shipper. In fact, she'd shown remarkable spirit and sense of humor, qualities he found lacking in most women. He discovered that he'd enjoyed the verbal sparring that had taken place before he told her of the shipwreck.

"Frenchies?" Darcie whispered, recalling again her father's mention of the private war between the Gaynor Shipping Company and his rivals, the Manville Trading Company. "You don't

think that . . . No, it's too absurd to consider." She glanced at
Zacharie Manville. Why was he really here? Could he be involved, trying to cover his guilt by beating the captain to tell
her the tale?

"Naw, it weren't the same Frenchies. Beggin' yer pardon, Mr.
Manville, sir. Was his ship, the *La Mer Magnifique,* she was the
one rescued us," he reported earnestly. "It was Mr. Manville's
sailors picked us up right quicklike, too. They was right there,
no sooner'n them rascals left us to die. I never seen no lower
scum than them varmints."

"I see." Darcie took a long look at Zacharie Manville. As
Darcie spoke the words, her mind was working. Could the
Manville Trading Company have begun their war again? But
why? They had been at peace since 1843, when a peace pact was
signed by her father and César Manville. And there was business
enough for both companies. However, it would bear looking
into—quietly. She couldn't ask Captain James to do it. He was
apparently in awe of the eloquent Frenchman.

"And, ma'am, I guess you won't be needin' me any more,
bein' as how I lost your fair ship," Captain James began, his
voice trembling with emotion. "I been treated good by Gaynor.
I ain't got no complaints. I'm awful ashamed."

Darcie looked with sympathy at the anguished man standing
before her. "You're mistaken, Captain James. You have a job
with Gaynor Shipping for as long as you wish. I'm confident
that you'll be receiving another commission soon." His look of
gratitude and relief touched her. "Please, convey my gratitude
to the captain of *La Mer Magnifique.* And I commend you for
your valiant efforts on behalf of my company."

"Thank you, ma'am. I'll do my best to please you. I appreciate your confidence." Captain James moved toward the steps
and turned. "Is there anything else I can do?"

Shock still registered on Darcie's face. Remembering her
manners, she smiled and said, "Thank you for your report, Captain James. See to the families of the dead. We will assume the
care of the injured. Tell the main office to call on me if they
have any questions. This is something that cannot await instruc-

tions from my dear guardian Uncle Talbot. My uncle lives in France. He's shown little interest in our affairs here since my father's death. We've been on our own." She looked Zack straight in the eye.

"I'm afraid I must be going, too." Zack stood and walked to the curved staircase. "Good-bye, Mlle. Gaynor. I hope we may meet again under less distressing conditions. I have other business to discuss with you, but I fear it will have to wait until you've recovered from your shock."

"Good-bye." Darcie watched him touch his hat and walk down the steps. "And, thank you, M. Manville. It was kind of you to bring me the news personally. Please, forgive my manners. I'd like for you to join me this evening if possible. I'm having friends over for a quiet dinner."

"I'd be delighted. Should I arrive around seven-thirty?" He smiled and closed the gate behind himself and Captain James.

Shutting her eyes momentarily, Darcie felt the warm sun on her closed eyelids and blanched cheeks, and then she looked toward the street again. The sun was brilliant against a corn-flower blue sky; nothing bad should happen on a day like this. But it had.

Darcie watched Zacharie Manville and Captain James until they were out of sight, and then descended the steps into her garden, the garden that had served as a haven to her since her childhood. Today, she found no real solace there.

The sweet scent of jasmine followed her to a bench where she sat down to think, trying to reason through the facts she'd just heard. Pirates, it was too hard to swallow. And the Frenchman —her father's acknowledged enemy—what part did he actually play in the event?

Tears filled her eyes as she imagined the carnage that had taken place as those brave men defended her ship. Having known most of them since her childhood, she imagined their tan faces beneath the billowing sails of the *Gay Dolphin*. Then she closed her eyes and saw the spilt blood, the open wounds, the anguish of waiting for death to come. She imagined the silence as the ship slipped beneath the Atlantic's unforgiving waves. Tears ran down her cheeks, futile tears of grief, anger, and frustration.

Her mauve-colored silk skirts billowed around her and, without even stopping to think, she rearranged them slightly to assure that her ankles were covered. She dabbed at her eyes with a lace-edged handkerchief. *What a day this has been,* she thought, *what will happen next?*

Restless, she could sit no longer and began to walk through the walled garden past the fragrant pomegranate trees with their lush dark leaves and vivid orange blossoms. When she neared the front gate, she heard the sound of someone walking outside, crisp long steps.

Well, she had no time to dawdle. Cook would have supper on the table soon, and Darcie was expecting guests. However, she could not shirk her duty. Intent on a trip to the dock to assure herself that Horace Jackson, her man in charge of running the Gaynor Company, was arranging for the care of the injured, she hurried up the steps, stopping abruptly when she heard the iron gate open behind her.

She turned and found herself face to face with Barclay Rhett. He removed his hat quickly and smiled. "Good afternoon, Miss Gaynor."

"Hello, Mr. Rhett." Darcie didn't want company right now. She wanted to be alone, to think about the attack on her ship. *Damnation,* she thought. *Uncle Talbot needs to be here. Father never intended for him to run the business from Paris. Uncle Talbot simply must come to Charleston.*

"I heard about the *Gay Dolphin.* Too bad. She was the most beautiful ship I've ever seen." Barclay Rhett walked up the steps, stopping near the top, and stood, one foot on the third step down and one foot on the top step. He rested his elbow on his elevated knee. "I know you must be distraught. I've come to offer my condolences for your crew, and my assistance to you."

"Thank you, Bar." Darcie reverted to her informal nickname for her friend. If she counted anyone as a suitor, it was Barclay

Rhett. They truly understood one another, having grown up so close together. Darcie had no doubts as to his sincerity.

He gazed at her a moment, curiosity carving his face into familiar angles of concern. "I believe I saw a strange gentleman outside your gate when I passed earlier. And you seemed to be," he paused, apparently choosing his words carefully, "deep in conversation."

Darcie recognized the jealousy that characterized their relationship. Even though nothing had been formally declared between them, she knew that Barclay counted on marrying her. She was recently out of mourning for her father, and expected Barclay to ask her to marry him any day now. "Conversation? No, he was merely . . ." her voice trailed off as she remembered Zack's touch, "helping me to dislodge my shawl from the spikes of the gate."

"I see." He hesitated for a moment, as if his questioning might push her too far. "And who was the gentleman? I owe him my gratitude."

"You owe him nothing, Barclay." She fidgeted, knowing that poor Barclay deserved a more complete explanation. "But you'll meet him tonight. I've invited him to dine with us this evening."

Barclay Rhett grimaced and moved back down the stairs. "Fine. Then I'll be off." He turned, green eyes flashing in the sunlight. "I'll see you later this evening."

Glad to be left in solitude for the afternoon, Darcie watched him leave. Without hesitating further, she hurried down the steps and strode out the gate, taking particular care this time that the wind didn't catch her shawl's lace.

She fairly ran along East Bay Street until she came to her late father's offices. She hadn't been there since his death three years ago, so when she stepped inside, memories flooded over her. She remembered the fun times, the days her father allowed her to accompany him to the office, the days when she sat on the high stool before the huge ledger book and entered figures for him.

Horace Jackson now sat on her father's stool, poring over that same ledger. "Hello, Horace."

He jumped with surprise. "Why good afternoon, Miss Gaynor. What brings you here?"

What indeed, she thought. "I've come to assure myself that the families of the men lost will be taken care of, and that those injured will receive medical care."

"Now, miss, what kind of manager do you think I am? I must await orders from Mr. Neville in Paris before I can make any—"

"Horace Jackson, I insist that you do my bidding. Those men served us well for many years." Darcie felt the color rush into her cheeks. How dare this man . . . this employee tell her . . . "Mr. Jackson, I shall personally see that Dr. Rutledge cares for the wounded, but you will pay the bill the instant it arrives. A settlement of five hundred dollars is to be made to the families of each of the dead men. Tomorrow. Not a minute later."

"But, Miss Gay—"

Darcie heard no more. She knew that Horace would do the right thing. Before Uncle Talbot took over, Horace would never have questioned her authority, even though she was a very young woman during the interim between her father's death and Uncle Talbot's letter confirming that he would indeed be running the company from Paris. She would write a letter of explanation to Uncle Talbot, and at the same time implore him to move to Charleston for the sake of expediency, if nothing else.

She stopped by Tradd Street and left word for Dr. Rutledge to see to the injured men and bill the Gaynor Shipping Company for his expenses. Feeling slightly better, she hurried home to dress for dinner.

Early that evening Charity pulled the yellow watered-silk gown over Darcie's hoops and smoothed its twelve-yard skirt. "I cain't see no reason to be dressin' like a peacock for a pauper's dinner. This ain't no ball, nor nothing fancy. Jus' chicken n' dumplin's. You spill them greasy dumplin's on this dress, and next week I be usin' this yaller silk to wash windows."

Charity inhaled deeply and continued her lecture. "Mr. Rhett and Mr. Sanders both is already looking fo' to marry you. How come you don't make up yo mind and git it done? Fo you know it, that Miss Emilie be done hitched up to Mr. Sanders and that Miss Patty be swooning over Mr. Rhett. And you ain't gonna be nothin' but a wore-out bridesmaid with two new dresses and no husband."

Darcie pulled the bodice down a bit, until the picture presented in her mirror suited her. "Oh, hush, Charity. I'm not a cow to be auctioned to the highest bidder. When I marry, it will be for love. Besides, I can't marry without Uncle Talbot's permission until I'm twenty-one."

"If'n you wait for that Frenchie to say anything, you gonna be a old maid fo' sure." Charity pulled Darcie's hair back and tamed the golden cloud into a chignon. She stepped back and appraised her charge. "I bet you is the purtiest gal in Charleston. The purtiest one without a husband, that is."

Darcie stood up. Her waist was small, her breasts full. Her lustrous hair framed an attractive face, although she thought her face was a little too square to be considered beautiful. *No,* she thought, *but I'm attractive enough to attract beaux.*

"Don't be silly. You're prejudiced," she replied, hugging her mammy. Charity had been with her since she could remember. In fact, Charity was one of Darcie's first memories. Her mother had been dead for so many years that she would hardly remember what she looked like if it weren't for the portrait over the fireplace in the parlor.

Taking a last look and pinching her cheeks a bit for color, Darcie descended the stairs, mentally cursing her cumbersome hoop skirts. *I don't know why a body would want to wear these things anyhow.*

Jasper was opening the door. Zacharie Manville entered, removed his hat, and spoke a few words to the butler.

"Welcome, Monsieur Manville." She floated gracefully down the remaining stairs and held out her hand in welcome.

Zacharie took it in his own, and kissed it gently, hardly touching his lips to her skin. "You are indeed a vision, mademoiselle."

"Now, M. Manville," she flirted, fluttering her eyelashes co-quettishly. "You'll take my breath away with such flattery. We here in Charleston aren't accustomed to such eloquent ways."

"Then you should become accustomed to hearing praise, for you are lovely." Zacharie kissed her hand again, this time linger-ing for a moment. He stood erect and looked into her eyes. With little persuasion, he would swing her into his arms, carry her up that winding staircase, and make love to her. Her scent reached his nostrils, a sweet violet scent that seemed to cling to her skin.

"Come, M. Manville. You are the first to arrive." Darcie gestured toward the parlor. "May I offer you a glass of wine before dinner?"

Zack considered her offer and remembered his previous thoughts. Too much wine and he would indeed whisk her up those stairs and into the first room with a bed. "I think not. Maybe after your other guests arrive."

"As you wish." Darcie sat down on the blue brocade sofa, carefully folding her hoops behind her. "I presume you had an uneventful trip, except for your heroic rescue of my crew."

"Yes, mademoiselle. Before I left Paris, I visited with your uncle—"

"Darcie." Barclay Rhett strode into the room, grasped her hands in his, and kissed her on the cheek. "Sorry to be late, but you know Gideon and Patty are never on time."

"Hello, Bar. Allow me to present M. Zacharie Manville, late of Paris." Blushing slightly at Barclay's familiar behavior, Darcie smiled at Zack and said, "M. Manville, meet Barclay Rhett."

Zacharie Manville stood and shook hands with Barclay Rhett. "Good to see you again. You see, mademoiselle, I am acquainted with M. Rhett."

"Yes, Darcie," Barclay explained, with a slight frown. "We met in Paris two years ago."

"Fine. Then you'll have a great deal to talk about, I'm sure." Darcie was delighted to find that her guests were acquainted.

The evening would be such a problem if there were awkward moments of silence when one didn't know what to say to a newcomer. She nudged Barclay, hoping to make him remove the scowl from his face. "You'll be interested in hearing M. Manville tell about his wonderfully heroic rescue of my crew. And, where are Emmy, Patty, and Gideon?"

"They were right—"

"I say, Barclay, chap, you fairly raced up the stairs. Were you stung by a bee or something?" Gideon walked in, looked around, and crossed to Darcie. "Good evening, love."

He, too, kissed her on the cheek, and Darcie blushed again. I'll never know why I bothered to pinch my cheeks. I must look like one of those women who stand around the wharves when the ships come in. "Hello, Gideon. Please allow me to introduce—"

"No introduction is necessary. Capital bit of daring, I'd say, Mr. Manville." Gideon marched across the room and clapped Zacharie on the shoulder. "Like to hear all about it. Beg pardon, I'm Gideon Sanders," Gideon proclaimed. "And, this is my sister, Patty Sanders. Zacharie Manville, Patty."

Darcie watched in amazement as Gideon continued to dominate the conversation. She'd never seen him so animated. As the tale of Zacharie's rescue of her crew unfolded in greater detail, she was astounded.

"And when I heard of your daring—your valiant effort," Gideon fairly gushed, "to think you boarded a sinking vessel, one with the stern already under water, my god, man—what were you thinking?" He glanced at Darcie and then around the room as if he were pausing for dramatic effect. "To board a ship, fair gurgling its farewell, to save the injured sailors."

Darcie jerked to attention. She hadn't realized that Zack himself participated in the rescue. Of course, Captain James had referred to Zack's heroism, but she thought he was speaking generally, about the entire crew.

Barclay slid forward on his chair, not to be outdone by his friend and rival. "And I heard that you carried Captain James off his ship, even though he fought to stay aboard, vowing to go down with her."

Darcie's mouth fell open in shock. She knew it was a captain's duty to go down with his ship, but she'd always considered such heroics as nonsense. She gaped at Zack in stunned admiration. In addition to displaying unflagging courage, he demonstrated good common sense.

"It seems I am indeed in your debt, M. Manville." She crossed the room and took his hand. "I am honored to call you a friend."

"You owe me nothing, mademoiselle." Zacharie stood and looked down into the sapphire depths of her eyes. "It is I who am honored to be at your service."

Darcie felt her face grow warm as he bent over her hand and kissed it for a third time this evening. She felt guilty for having believed he might be involved in the sinking of her ship. He was far too charming and sincere to be a murderer.

"Well, what have we here, boys?" Emilie Rhett swished her scarlet silk skirts and entered the parlor. "A little competition?"

"Em!" Darcie jerked her hand from Zacharie's and swung around to confront her outspoken friend. Face flaming, she said in a calculated even tone, "Allow me to introduce Zacharie Manville, who rescued my crew from the *Gay Dolphin*."

"So you're the hero who's the talk of Charleston." Emilie Rhett sauntered to his side. "I'm delighted to meet you."

"Miss Darcie, supper's ready to be served." Jasper stood at the doorway of the parlor.

"Fine. Ladies, gentlemen, shall we?" Darcie looked from one to the other of the group.

"May I escort you in to dinner, Mademoiselle Gaynor?" Zacharie asked, holding out his arm to her.

"I'd be delighted, monsieur." Darcie placed her hand on his arm and led him to the dining room across the hallway. "Please, call me Darcie. We're friends. *All friends.*" With an emphasis on the last two words, Darcie glared at Barclay Rhett who appeared to be sulking.

"And I am Zack to my friends."

For a moment, Darcie felt herself being swept away from reality, in a swirling brandy-colored whirlpool that was his gaze. Her body tingled as if she'd stepped from a tub of steaming water into a snowstorm, and her knees were as weak as a newborn lamb's. This Frenchman seemed to have a magical touch that left her powerless.

Chapter Two

Darcie's thoughts drifted back to Zack's words before Barclay interrupted them. Zack had mentioned her uncle—undoubtedly Talbot Neville. She wondered how Zack knew Uncle Talbot. Of course, both lived in Paris, so their paths had probably crossed.

"Take yo plate, Miss Darcie?" She sat back as Jasper removed the plate of oysters in front of her, bringing her back to the present. The sheer silk of the summer draperies fluttered, allowing the cool breeze from the Ashley River to swirl about the room, making it a little more comfortable for those dining. Jasper had raised the floor-to-ceiling windows their entire length, the weights pulling the heavily framed glass up into the next floor. All that remained were wide openings and a wisp of silk that invited the air from the river to circulate among the guests.

The table was lovely. In the center were fresh flowers from her garden—rose-colored peonies, pink and rose oleander, and roses. The scent was heavenly as it mingled with the delectable odors escaping the kitchen. Her friends were dressed as if this were a grand social occasion instead of a friendly supper, and

Darcie knew that this was a dress rehearsal for the Rutledge's party later this week.

Darcie had a lot to be thankful for. Her friends were wonderful. The long, lonely days of her mourning were brightened by quick visits and notes of sympathy and encouragement. But nothing made up for her inability to be free. For three years she'd felt imprisoned within the confines of her garden and piazza, for that was as far as she allowed herself to go, except for the few occasions she accompanied one of her friends to church or to a quiet supper. She tried to concentrate on the lively conversation of her friends.

"And, there was Chad. Stuck on a sandbar," Barclay said, laughing heartily. "He was livid. You know how he treasures that boat."

"Chadwick Rutledge is a friend of ours. One who will wager on anything, but most especially the *Charleston Lady*," Darcie explained to Zack who seemed a bit puzzled by the conversation. She felt a pang of guilt. They'd been at the table for half an hour and she'd hardly said ten words to him, although he sat at her right. "He's so sure of himself now, that he wagers the schooner instead of money."

"Sacre bleu!" exclaimed Zack, his eyebrows lifting in surprise.

"We thought he'd lose for sure," Gideon took up the story of a recent race between Chad Rutledge's schooner and another.

"First thing you know, here's Chad tossing things overboard," Barclay continued, raising his dark eyebrows suggestively. "We saw him throw a large chest over."

"You can imagine what we were thinking then! Everybody along the seawall doubled over with laughter," Gideon added, watching Jasper ladle chicken and dumplings into his bowl.

"The absence of all that liquor made the ship buoyant enough to get free of the sandbar, and he won the race, lucky rascal." Barclay sat at the far end of the table from Darcie, watching her carefully.

"But I'll wager that tomorrow he'll be back there trying to find that chest," Gideon said gleefully.

"Too bad. The fish will be having one hell—beg your pardon, ladies—one heck of a celebration at old Chad's expense." Barclay laughed with delight. "That chest rode out to sea with the tide."

Barclay Rhett and Chadwick Rutledge had been rivals for a long time. Barclay had finally conceded that Chad had the faster boat, and now kept this small group apprised of the schooner's successes. Chad was involved in at least one race per week, often two. He spent a great deal of time at the card tables or the cock fights, and no time at home.

The two men were rivals in other areas, too. Both of them had courted Darcie before her father died. During the three years of mourning, Barclay had remained loyal to her, but Chad's name had been linked with almost every eligible woman in Charleston. He wasn't one to sit around and wait on a woman.

That was one reason Darcie felt so guilty about Barclay. She knew he wanted to marry her. He was good and honest and kind—all virtues a woman wanted in a husband—but he was predictable, and therein lay the problem. Darcie wanted excitement. And she'd never find it with Barclay.

Conversation fairly flew around the table as Jasper removed the soup bowls and replaced them with freshly baked egg custard. "Darcie, you've got the best cook in Charleston," Emmy said, spooning another bite into her mouth. "Mmmm. This is heaven. I'd marry a Yankee abolitionist if I could have your cook."

"What a fate!" Patty cried. "In addition to having no sense, those people have no manners and no taste. I'm afraid you'd never find a cook as good as Darcie's in a Yankee household."

By the time they finished supper, Barclay was almost sullen because of being banished to the far end of the table, even though it was considered an honor to sit at the head of the table. Though Darcie realized why his attitude had cooled, she simply smiled and thanked him for helping her at table. When the men retired to the parlor for cigars and brandy, the ladies sat in Darcie's sitting room discussing styles and gossiping.

After a few minutes, they joined the men in the parlor. When

Darcie sat down on the sofa, Barclay almost leaped across the room to take a place beside her. For the remainder of the evening, he never moved from her side. Darcie was beginning to think he'd never leave, but he finally did.

Emmy and Patty were tiring quickly and, as they had to walk home, they insisted that it was time to go. Since Barclay had come with them, he could hardly stay on without them. The grandfather clock in the hallway struck ten as they were putting on their coats and shawls.

"See you tomorrow," Emmy called over her shoulder as she made her way down the staircase carefully. "Early. Or else we won't be done shopping in time to meet Patty for dinner."

Darcie watched her friends leave and turned a smiling face to her remaining guest, Zacharie Manville. "Did you ever see such a prattlesome bunch of people? They always entertain me with the most astounding gossip. I declare, I don't know where they hear it all."

Zack smiled at her attempt at light conversation and responded with the same tone. "A vivacious group. A lively crew if ever I saw one, *ma petite*."

She led him through a window opening onto the side piazza and sat down, shifting the voluminous fabric of her gown before folding her hands in her lap. "And now, Zack, I've been waiting all evening to hear what you started to tell me before we were interrupted."

"Mais oui." Having enjoyed watching her feminine gait as she crossed the room and shifted her skirts as she stepped through the window, Zack listened to the gentle rustling of her gown as she arranged her skirts while he walked over to her. She was totally feminine, and so helpless.

He hated to spoil the atmosphere, but removed the letter from the pocket of his waistcoat anyway. He could keep it from her no longer. "I have correspondence for you from Talbot Neville."

"Talbot Neville?" Darcie took the letter, wondering why her uncle sent a letter by Zack. "Uncle Talbot?" she repeated lamely as she stared at the neat script on the envelope, glad for a mo-

ment's respite from his penetrating gaze. "I . . . Will you forgive me if I read it now? I'm positive that it must be of great
importance. It's his first letter in three years."

"But of course." He moved to a weather-faded wooden chair
across from her and sat down. While she read, he studied her
carefully, secure in the knowledge that her uncle's letter would
maintain her attention. She would make a wonderful wife—
even for the vowed bachelor, Zack Manville.

Now there's a rascal, he thought of her guardian, Talbot Neville, *recalling the rumors of Talbot's debt, of unsavory friends, and of
plots and ploys gone awry.*

His intuition told him that Talbot was up to something, but
Zack hadn't figured it out—yet. He would have to investigate
more thoroughly when he returned to France. His association
with the lovely Mlle. Gaynor would facilitate his investigation.
Zack would have almost unlimited access to the Gaynor estate,
since his engagement to Darcie would undoubtedly be announced at the first appropriate moment.

Zack returned his attention to Darcie, a much more pleasant
occupation. They were promised in marriage, but she didn't
know. She couldn't know. The participants to the pact were
sworn to secrecy, and César Manville had related the details to
his son only after he realized he was dying.

Talbot knew of the marriage pact, but hadn't mentioned it
during his surprise visit to Zack before he left Paris. Zack found
this strange indeed, but kept his suspicions quiet. At the moment, his only problem would be Darcie's reaction. He found
that he cared what she thought of him, whereas, when he'd left
France, her opinion hadn't mattered.

He didn't know what he'd expected—a toothless shrew, an
illiterate wharf woman? Certainly not this lovely Southern belle
with the enchanting personality.

Zack had set out to meet her, to see if she was the kind of
woman he could marry. His father had begged him to honor the
pact, and Zack had reluctantly agreed. Then his father died.
Zack felt honor bound to come to her, to see that she had no
financial difficulties, but marriage? Zack doubted that he could

marry a woman chosen for him, especially now since the driving forces behind the pact were dead.

Her vivacity, her keen mind, her sharp wit, her delicate charm, everything about her seemed perfect, too perfect. And, Darcie was beautiful in addition to her other virtues. Zack had yet to see any seams in an otherwise perfect facade.

The perfect facade dissolved in front of him, and Zack recognized pure rage in the set of her strong jaw, the creases across her forehead, and the narrowing of her lovely eyes. He foresaw a storm coming. When she leapt to her feet, he pretended to be startled by her sudden movement. "Is something wrong?"

"Wrong?" She jerked her chin high. "I won't do it. Do you hear me? I won't."

"I beg your pardon, won't do—"

"I refuse to marry a man I don't love. I won't marry a man not of my own choosing. The nerve of . . ." Darcie gasped for breath. "How can he do this to me? I won't go. I simply won't go."

"I'm sure the news can't be that bad. What has sent you into such a dither?" Zack watched her carefully, trying to assess the reason for her anger. Something had set her off like the discharge of a cannon. Had Neville mentioned that Darcie's fiancé was none other than Zack?

"Oh, but the news *can* be that bad." Darcie inhaled deeply, ordering herself to calm down. "The nerve of that man, to think that he can run . . . can *ruin* my life when he lives in Paris, with never a care for me until now. Never so much as inquiry into my health, nor my circumstances. Why, this is the first direct correspondence in three years."

"Please, Darcie. You'll damage your health." Patting her hand solicitously, Zack led her back to the sofa she'd vacated so abruptly. "Come now, sit here, and tell me all about it."

She jumped up again. "Read it for yourself. I feel like a slave being auctioned."

Zack took the letter, grateful for a chance to see exactly how much her uncle had revealed. Talbot Neville was a notorious scoundrel whose gambling debts were monumental, not to mention his spendthrift wife who cared for nothing but clothes and jewels.

He scanned the letter quickly. Good. Talbot didn't mention that Zack was the intended fiancé. He briefly wondered why, but realized that it made his task easier.

Zack had never seen such a fit of temper in a gently bred young woman. At least by the time they reached France, Zack and Darcie could become acquainted and might know how they felt about each other. Then, *they* could decide whether or not they wanted to marry each other.

Zack always denied any urge to marry. He found women enough to please him without committing to marriage. And, thus far, he'd found none he liked well enough to settle down. Darcie Gaynor was different, and he might find his mind changed.

"If you're involved in this . . . this slave auction, get out of my house this instant! The nerve of you, coming in here like this, worming your way into my regard." Darcie turned on him, suddenly realizing that since he had delivered the letter, he must be in on the arrangement. "Out! He sent you here on this despicable mission."

"Worming? Wait a minute. Please, calm yourself." Zack dropped the letter on the sofa and rose. He strode across to Darcie and looked down at her. He peered down into the depths of her eyes, wondering what she would say if she knew she was to marry him. She seemed to like him a bit—until this moment when she'd turned on him like a shark. "He simply found out that I had business in America and asked me to deliver the letter. *C'est très cruelle.*"

At the very least, he could thank Talbot for remaining silent on the name of the fiancé. For once—perhaps for the first time —he showed good sense.

Convincing Darcie to accompany him to Paris would be difficult, but if she knew that Zack was the man contracted to marry her, she'd never come. And Zack was piling more fuel on the fire with every word. Why didn't he just tell her that she was promised to him?

Judging from her reaction, he didn't know what she'd do if he were honest with her. She might even run away. He'd never find her, for she had too many friends willing to hide her out. He'd have to remain silent until forced to admit who he was. Damn, but dealing with women was a complicated business.

Staring through the blind fury of being manipulated, she glared at him. "Well, *are* you involved? Were you privy to this heinous, devious, damnable, I can't think of a word—"

"Darcie, *s'il vous plaît,* listen to me." He put his hands on her shoulders and drew her stiff body into his arms, comforting her as he might a frightened child. "Until this moment, when I read the letter, I knew nothing of what it said. He never confided in me," he said honestly.

"You mean, he didn't tell you he's . . . he's practically sold me to a . . . to a man who can't woo his own bride?" Darcie leaned her head on his shoulder, gleaning the warmth and strength she felt in his embrace. "I am humiliated."

"Don't be ridiculous, Darcie, we're friends. I swear to you, until now," he whispered into her golden hair, "he told me only that I must deliver the letter and bring you to Paris."

"What am I to do? I refuse to be coerced into such an arrangement. I've been independent too long to succumb to such —oh, I don't know—tyranny." Darcie straightened, realizing that she'd shown far too much emotion in front of a stranger. How stupid of her to lose her temper and shout like a common woman of the street. What would Zack think? She backed away a few steps, blushing furiously. "I apologize to you, Zack, for my behavior. What a fool you must think me."

"I think nothing of the sort." Zack smiled, a genuine smile that touched his eyes with a spark of mirth and raised his eyebrows into devilish peaks. "I know how I'd feel if someone did the same to me. I'd rant and rave for days."

He did understand how she felt. He'd rebelled in much the same way, and only after ten days of coercion by his father did Zack agree to the arrangement.

"You're very kind." Darcie fell onto the sofa, wringing her

hands and trying to decide what she should do. "I believe you, Zack."

"Darcie, think about this. You've said you won't go, but you must." Zack tried to approach her tactfully. He had instructions to bring her to Paris, forcibly if necessary. He had a letter from Talbot for the authorities explaining the situation. "Talbot is your guardian. Until you're twenty-one, you have no choice."

"No choice? How can you talk that way?" Shocked, she gazed up at him, seeing the sympathy in his eyes. He was such a kind man, a considerate man. "You just said we were friends."

"We are friends. I'm exceedingly fond of you, yes, even in so short a time. But," he continued, hating to be the one to draw her back to reality, "Darcie, your uncle can force you to do his will. The law is on his side."

"The law. Ha!" Darcie looked around her parlor, the parlor she'd always imagined as the site of a sweet and wonderful courtship by the man who would eventually win her. How he'd beg for her hand, claim that he couldn't live without her. And then—her first kiss, her first real kiss, full of the want and passion she was saving for the right man. Talbot Neville was destroying her dream with his demand. "The law would never force me to marry against my will."

Even as she spoke the words, she knew they were untrue. A young woman had no power to wield against the authorities, no vote. Not even Darcie Gaynor, daughter of a shipper and planter. She slumped against the back of the loveseat. "What am I to do, Zack? I feel as if I've grown up in a certain mold and now that I'm well formed, I find that I've got to fit another."

Zack sank down beside her, feeling her pain almost as greatly as she. For the first time in his life, he felt protective—protective of an innocent and lovely flower of a girl. His emotions were almost alien to him.

Damn, he thought. *This woman is mine for the asking, mine without asking almost, and yet, if I exercise my right to have her, then I lose her. Careful,* he warned himself, *this is a delicately balanced relationship floating on a tempestuous sea of emotion, and it could sink forever.*

"For now, do nothing," Zack heard himself tell her. "We don't sail for better than two months. We'll do as your uncle asks, and when we arrive in Paris, we'll convince him that this plan is folly."

A glimmer of light began to form into an idea. Zack was right. She would go with him to France and convince Uncle Talbot that he had no right to insist upon her marriage to a strange man. And, what's more, she would refuse to marry the gentleman. Perhaps she could even enlist the aid of her fiancé to help her talk Uncle Talbot out of this silly notion.

Zack looked down at her, knowing she was deep in thought, that her mind was plotting to find a way out of this awful arrangement. Her dark blue eyes stared off into nowhere, and he knew she saw nothing but the vision of her plan. Her luscious lips were parted, as if she might speak at any moment, and Zack longed to kiss her problems away. He imagined their dewy softness under his, opening to permit him further access, inviting him to partake of her innocence. Her golden eyelashes fluttered over the sapphire of her eyes, and he moved closer, unable to resist the unspoken invitation.

The scent of violets wafted to him, tantalizing him further as he gazed at her without her knowledge. The yellow gown hugged her breasts, hiding the treasures that rose and fell with her even breathing. He pictured them, full and ripe in his hands, nipples hardening under his—what was he thinking?

Zack jumped up. "By the sacred ships of the sea, I must go. I have business early tomorrow and can't be late."

Darcie looked startled by his sudden movements. "Must you?"

The perfect hostess, he thought, *she never realized what I was thinking as I gazed at her. Damn, I must be careful around this wench, or I'll find myself bound by marriage under a gun before we leave Charleston.*

She escorted him to the door. "Thank you for your kindness, Zack."

"Think nothing of it," he answered, opening the door behind

him. "I shall call on you again soon, to make you aware of my plans for sailing."

Darcie still looked a little puzzled by his quick departure, but smiled. "Please do. I shall look forward to renewing our acquaintance."

"Good evening, Darcie."

She watched him hurry down the stairs and out the gate. Standing on her piazza, she could see him rounding the corner at Meeting Street as if he were being chased by the hounds of hell. Wondering what she had done that could have precipitated such a sudden departure, she shrugged and went back inside.

Chapter Three

At Mrs. Simpson's sewing shop Darcie looked through the book at the latest styles, trying to select a gown that would make her stand apart, a style a little different from the other gowns that would be worn to St. Cecilia's Ball. In addition, she needed warm clothing for the trip across the Atlantic. Mrs. Simpson could provide anything she would need. She'd have to consult with Zack for ideas about what to buy for the crossing and for the time she would be in France.

Zack. Her thoughts turned to him. What an extraordinary man he was. He'd seen her plight about this ridiculous marriage and sympathized as though it were he instead of she destined to marry an unknown person.

Her eyelids closed, and Darcie could see the errant curls that hung above his expressive eyes, above eyebrows that bespoke his mood. She'd noticed his longing glance—she'd seen enough of them from Barclay and Gideon. She wondered about the gentle caress of his lips on the back of her hand and how they would feel pressed to her lips.

Many times, Darcie had fantasized about the future, about a future with her husband, but never had she done so in such detail as she had last night. Though the night was cool, once she'd gone to bed, and her thoughts had turned to Zack, her body became flushed and hot. She'd lain there imagining him with her until she finally got up, drew on her robe, and went out on the piazza that opened off her room.

There, in the cool fragrant breeze, she'd peered across her yard and into White Point Gardens, watched the lovers walking hand in hand or arm in arm. How would it be to join them? She wanted to feel the touch of a man's lips on hers. She pictured herself walking along the seawall, gazing out at the ships with their lanterns bobbing on the waves, and turning her face to her lover to accept his kiss. The disturbing factor in this fantastic daydream was that the man who lowered his lips to hers was Zack.

Could she really feel this way about a stranger? Especially since the stranger was a member of the Manville family—a dreaded name to her since childhood. Conflicting emotions rose in Darcie. Hatred for the times when her father had been near bankruptcy because of sunken ships and lost cargoes. Admiration for a man who disregarded his own safety to save the lives of sailors he'd never met. Something else, something indefinable within her own body for the way he made her feel when he lifted her in his arms and loosened her lace from the gate.

"I say, Darcie." Emmy said as she shook Darcie's shoulder. "Have you fallen asleep?"

"Asleep?" Darcie repeated dumbly, glancing about the dress shop to see if anyone had noticed her blank stare. "Of course not. I was just . . ." She couldn't tell Emmy about her thoughts. Emmy would be shocked to find that Darcie was thinking such risque thoughts about a perfect stranger. Perfect? He seemed perfect. Too perfect to be real. "I was just deep in thought about my upcoming trip to France."

"Quit brooding about that trip. Be delighted. As I told you on the way over this morning, I would love for somebody to make me go to France. Anyway, I thought you must be in a daze or something." Emmy gazed at her. *"Or something."*

Darcie looked up. "What do you mean?"

"I mean that you are never this distracted when it comes to choosing patterns and accessories." Emmy sat down on the brocade loveseat with Darcie. "Whatever's come over you, love? Dare I believe that you're thinking of my dear brother with such longing in your eyes?"

"Barclay?"

"I have only one brother, ninny." Emmy took Darcie's hand and patted it lovingly. "You know he adores you. And you, well, you like him."

"Like him? Of course, I like him." Darcie stared at her best friend. "Just what are you saying, Emmy?"

Darcie began to feel uncomfortable. She really knew what Emmy was saying, but she didn't want to discuss such private matters here in Mrs. Simpson's sewing shop—or at all. Emmy never kept her thoughts to herself, dear though she was.

For the past three years, perhaps even before that, Emmy had made no secret of the fact that she was vigorously promoting a marriage between her brother and her best friend. She'd often arranged small dinners, carefully placing Darcie with Barclay, and Darcie never objected. Throughout her mourning, Darcie, Emmy, and Barclay had been almost constant companions.

Barclay adored her. She knew it. Since she'd cast off her black crepe, Darcie had avoided being alone with Barclay whenever possible. Until she'd told him about the marriage arranged by her uncle, she expected him to ask permission to speak for her hand.

"Well? What's going on inside your little head?" Emmy persisted. "Are you worrying about this silly marriage contract?"

"Nothing except the trip." Darcie smiled at her friend reassuringly, and tried to steer the conversation away from her arranged marriage. "I'm just a little featherheaded today. I suppose my thoughts are really with the families of my crew who died. I feel so helpless, Emmy."

Emmy stared at her for a moment, as if she didn't believe Darcie. "Oh, yes. I'd quite forgotten the accident." Her eyes widened. "And what about that darling Frenchman? What a dream come true."

"Whatever are you talking about?" Darcie felt the color spring to her cheeks and looked toward the street so Emmy couldn't see that she was blushing.

"As if you didn't know," Emmy retorted. "You know exactly what I mean. Handsome, sophisticated. Daring. Everything a man should be."

"What a silly thing to say."

"Silly, you say. And what's silly about looking out for your future?"

"Future? Emmy! You can't mean that you're interested in Zack." Darcie was astonished. True, she was extremely attracted to him, but Emmy hardly knew him. Darcie hardly knew him!

"Why not?" Emmy asked, flipping the pages of the booklet in front of her. "There's nobody else around here to swoon over."

"What about Gideon? And Chad Rutledge? Emmy, there are many men, handsome men who would die for a . . . for a kiss from you."

The look of disdain on Emmy's face showed clearly how she felt. "Yes, but they're not like Zack. He's so . . . so, I don't know. But there's something different about him. Something tantalizing." Emmy raised her eyebrows suggestively.

Darcie forced herself to inhale deeply, to pause before answering. Who was she to say who Emmy could fall in love with? She doubted seriously that Zacharie Manville was interested in marrying an unsophisticated country girl. He was here on business. Nothing else.

Knowing that if she pursued this conversation or this line of thought much longer, she might say something she'd later regret, Darcie smiled and said, "Em, dearest, if we are to meet Patty for luncheon, we'd better complete our selections."

"I suppose you're right. Still, he's any woman's dream."

"And, as with most men, he'll probably turn into any woman's nightmare after marriage." Darcie laughed and winked at Emmy.

"Maybe," Emmy agreed, halfheartedly. "Maybe."

"Mrs. Simpson," Darcie said as the proprietor of the shop appeared. "I believe I'd like this done in lavender taffeta. With no sleeves at all."

"Fine selection, Miss Gaynor. Anything else?" Mrs. Simpson asked, writing notes on a scrap of paper.

"Yes. The cherry silk. I'd like it made like this one." Darcie flipped to a pleasing sketch of a low-cut sleeveless gown, fairly simple but elegant. Along the hem was a ten-inch ruffle of the same fabric, and along the neckline, a flutter of ruffles.

"Oh, Darcie," Emmy exclaimed. "You'll have the most beautiful dress at St. Cecilia's Ball. I wish I could wear that color."

Darcie smiled at Emmy. "And Mrs. Simpson. I'd like a gold taffeta gown with this black lace over the bodice. You don't have a picture of what I want exactly. Look here." She indicated a sketch. "This sort of overskirt of the same lace."

"Whatever are you going to do with such a gown if you're wearing the cherry silk to St. Cecilia's?" Emmy inquired.

"Maybe nothing. But I'll probably wear it when I go to Paris," Darcie replied thoughtfully. Why bother? She didn't intend to be in Paris long enough to be invited to an affair elegant enough to wear a gown this ornate. But she liked the idea anyway. Damn this trip. It interfered with her whole scheme for her life.

"Oh, and Mrs. Simpson. I'd like another simple gown in navy broadcloth. And a black dress in broadcloth." Darcie thought a minute. "And I'll need a heavy cloak for my trip."

After ordering several sensible items for travel, along with adequate accessories, the girls left the shop. Darcie usually enjoyed shopping for clothes with Emmy, but today she just wasn't in the mood. Along with her irritation about the upcoming trip, she was still concerned about the health of several sailors who were slow to respond to treatment.

As they approached the Charleston Tea Room, they saw Patty and Gideon coming towards them. "Have fun?" she asked.

"Oh, Patty. You should have been there. Darcie selected the most . . . delicious cherry silk for her St. Cecilia's gown. And another, well, you'll just have to wait to see the gold. I can't really describe it," Emmy gushed enthusiastically. "Every man in Charleston will be fighting over her."

"Em!" Darcie scolded, glancing at Gideon to see if he was listening. "What a ridiculous thing to say."

"Believe me, Patty," Emmy continued. "Darcie has an eye for fabric and pattern that puts us to shame."

"Have you ever doubted it?" Patty asked. "Why, even when she was in mourning, she looked far more elegant than any of us. I declare I never saw anyone in mourning look so beautiful. I'm surprised the gentlemen of Charleston realized she was unapproachable."

"Ladies, if you'll stop this silly prattle, we'll go in. I'm quite sure our table is ready." Darcie felt the blush sting her cheeks as Gideon laughed at his sister's remark.

They were seated quickly at a table that overlooked a small garden. Emmy and Patty were discussing the menu when Zack arrived. Darcie's first impulse was to hide behind the server standing at the next table, but Zack saw her and waved.

He strode across the room and stopped beside their table. "Good afternoon, ladies and you, too, sir." He bowed, kissed each uplifted hand, and gazed at Darcie. "What a pleasant surprise to find you here."

"Won't you join us, Zack?" Em fluttered dark lashes at him and smiled coquettishly. "We've plenty of room."

"Oh, I wouldn't want to intrude. I'll just—"

"You'll just sit right down with us." Em glanced around the room. "Oh, Sanders. Please set a place for M. Manville."

The server hurried over and laid out a napkin and silver. Within minutes, Zack was sitting between Em and Darcie.

He looked at her, wondering about the flush on her face. Was she angry because he had intruded? Or was she excited because of his presence? He hoped for the latter.

Darcie sipped her tea, watching him closely.

"M. Manville, when do you plan to return to France? Will you be here for the St. Cecilia's Ball?" Em asked, gazing longingly at Zack.

He looked from Darcie to Emilie. She was a beauty, though not as lovely as Darcie. "I plan to remain here for about one month. As for the ball, I—"

"Oh, you must attend," Em interrupted. "It's going to be the most wonderful evening."

"In that case, I shall be there. When is it?"

Darcie glared at Em as she continued chattering about the ball and all the important people who would be present. "Perhaps Mary Chestnut might attend. I believe she's in town. And, the Rutledges, Ransom Calhoun, the Manigaults . . . everyone in Charleston."

Patty looked at Darcie thoughtfully and said, "This will be Darcie's first ball."

"Your first? Please, Mlle. Gaynor, I do hope you'll waltz with me?" He gazed at her even though she didn't meet his eyes. He could imagine holding her in his arms again, and in fact, had thought of little else since he'd rescued her from the fence. A noise startled him. "Of course, I'd like a dance with all of you. Would it be too presumptuous to ask? Dare I pray that you will?"

Darcie smiled for the first time since he sat down. His reference to prayer must be deliberate. "I must remind you, Zack. Don't ask for things in prayer. Remember, you might get them."

Knowing she caught his reminder, Zack laughed with her. Both Emmy and Patty only stared. Neither of them could possibly know that the reference was to yesterday's conversation, that delightfully free and easy conversation at the fence before their pasts had intruded.

Despite her readiness to be angry with him, she always ended up with a lovely smile on her lips, lips he longed to kiss. And, her eyes sparkled with mirth, a shared secret between kindred spirits. Yes, she would make a man a fine wife.

Chapter Four

Darcie stared through the window onto South Bay, musing about the abrupt changes that had taken place in her life since Zack first freed her shawl from the grasp of the gate. Instead of looking forward to a lifetime of parties, balls, and elegant evenings at the theater here in Charleston, she had no idea what her future would hold.

France. Until a few days ago, it had seemed a faraway romantic place. Now, she hated it—without having ever stood on French soil. And, most of all, she hated Uncle Talbot.

The dark green leaves of an oleander brushed against the window, bringing Darcie's thoughts back to the present. She needed to make a list of items she would need for her upcoming trip. Months, perhaps years, would pass before she'd see her beloved pink and fuschia oleander and yellow Carolina jasmine again, before she could walk through her lush gardens and sit beneath the live oaks, or stroll along the seawall at the High Battery to watch the ships sail in and out.

Sighing, she picked up her needlework, hoping to drive the anger from her mind as she occupied her thoughts and fingers creatively. She didn't want to hate Uncle Talbot, but he'd never been much help to her and he'd never indicated that he even cared about her well-being. At times, she even thought he'd forgotten she existed. He hadn't come to visit since her father's death three years ago.

"Ahem, Miss Darcie, Mr. Manville is here to call on you." Jasper waited inside the doorway for Darcie to reply.

"Thank you, Jasper. Ask M. Manville to wait in the parlor." She placed her embroidery in the workbasket she kept behind the chair by the window. Before she followed Jasper, she peeked at herself in the mirror.

Not a hair was out of place on her daytime chignon. She always pulled her hair back severely and coiled it at the base of her neck. The humidity sometimes reached the saturation point in Charleston, wilting even the most stubborn curls, and Darcie had no time to waste on such inane frivolities.

Her lavender day dress fit well over her slim waist and full breasts and, because of the heat, was sleeveless and cut low without being too indecent for afternoon. Many women still wore long sleeves during the hottest months of summer because of the silly idea about exposed skin inviting illness. Darcie had shocked many a matron—and seamstress as well—by insisting on lightweight clothing which exposed her arms to the gentle breezes of the harbor. She gripped her skirts between her fingers and lifted them so she could walk faster, relishing the cool air that swept beneath the bell-shaped hoops.

One of these days, I'm going to rebel and refuse to wear these silly hoops, she thought. As she walked into the well-ordered parlor, a board creaked, alerting Zack to her presence, and he turned to greet her.

"Good afternoon, sir." Darcie fairly floated across the room and held out her hand. Every Southern gentlewoman learned at an early age to move like a lily pad floating on a pond, and Darcie was no exception, even though her mother had died when she was very young. Charity had insisted that she walk, talk, eat, and sit like a true Southern lady. She had learned that the fragility so often associated with women of her class did not mean weakness, but instead masked a strength that their men were rarely allowed to witness. It was a part of the charm that held males so in awe of them. "What may I do for you?"

"Ah, mademoiselle, how lovely you look." Zack bent crisply from the waist and kissed her hand. "I had forgotten how truly beautiful you are. So cool-looking in this oppressive weather."

"You are too kind, monsieur," Darcie flirted without hesitation, fluttering her eyelashes and spreading her silk fan jauntily. In the past few days, she'd seen enough of Zack to realize that he certainly had a way with women, and she enjoyed their flirtatious banter as much as he appeared to. "Your flattery puts me to the blush, and is certainly undeserved by a plain foundling such as I."

"Plain, indeed, *mademoiselle.* You are . . ." Zack arched his eyebrows thoughtfully and allowed his gaze to travel leisurely up and down her body. "You are a vision, nothing less."

"Sir!" Darcie fell into a fit of laughter, unable to continue the banter any longer. "Welcome, Zack. Come and be comfortable in my home."

Zack waited until Darcie sat down and spread her poplin skirts modestly across the velvet sofa before selecting the chair nearest her. "Ah, *cherie,* your wit and intelligence are unequaled. As is your beauty."

"The game continues, then?" Darcie laughed as a blush crept into her cheeks. Zack's teasing had ended. His last compliment was intended seriously, whether true or false. "I reckon that you, sir, are perhaps the most eloquent flatterer in all of the Empress Eugenie's court."

"I fear that you have reckoned well," Zack conceded, joining in her infectious laughter again. "But, I must protest that my words were spoken in earnest. Flattery sometimes reflects the truth."

"Then I am honored by your kindness." Darcie knew her cheeks were the color of the first flames licking a log in fall. "And, if you continue the conversation in this manner, then I must ask you to leave, for I shall surely be overwhelmed."

"Not another compliment shall escape my lips." Zack looked aghast, his admiration for her increasing as they spoke. "You are an unusual woman, Darcie Gaynor. Most women would listen to my flattery for hours on end—true or not."

Hoping to diminish the scarlet color dappling her cheeks, Darcie tactfully changed the subject. "Tell me about France, about your home, your parents. I know nothing of you, except that you have come to take me with you."

The smile sagged on Zack's face. He'd known she'd ask more questions once they became friends. "My home is the sea, although I keep apartments in Paris and a country house near the Spanish border on the Atlantic."

Darcie nodded. "And your parents?"

"My father died three years ago—the same as your father." Zack paused, then strode to the window, peering across White Point Gardens. Why did he find it so difficult to think of his mother—Madelaine Ortiz? She'd been gone for so many years. At first, Zack would have rather she had died instead of running off the way she did. Now he hardly ever thought of her. "My mother is . . . dead, also," he lied, offering the easy answer. She'd never find out that he'd deceived her about his mother.

"I'm sorry." Darcie recognized the agony that ate away at him and decided that satisfying her curiosity wasn't worth the pain the memory had brought him. "Tell me. What progress have you made toward setting a definite date for our departure?"

"More important, I have yet to find you a suitable traveling companion. I have placed an advertisement in the *Mercury*," he answered matter-of-factly.

"The *Mercury?*" Darcie fidgeted with her fingernails, trying to calm herself. "Why? We have plenty of time. Haven't we?"

"I have tentatively set our date for sailing in three weeks time. I wish to return to France as soon as possible." Zack studied the portrait of Darcie that hung over the grand piano.

"That soon? How can I be prepared in three weeks?" Darcie jumped up. "Why this sudden change of plans?"

"Circumstances have changed," Zack lied.

He couldn't tell Darcie that from information he'd gathered during his brief stay in Charleston, he'd begun to suspect that

Talbot Neville was embezzling funds from Darcie's company, Gaynor Shipping. He was eager to return to France to continue his investigation. In addition, he grew tired of Barclay Rhett— forever hanging about, attempting to best him. "Company problems," he said, hoping to allay further questions.

Darcie couldn't argue with him about his company. She was well aware of the amount of time required to operate a shipping company successfully, and indeed, lack of time devoted to operating a shipping company was her chief complaint about Uncle Talbot. "Do you think we can locate a companion in so short a time?"

"We must. Today and tomorrow, I shall be interviewing applicants at my office. Would you care to be present?" Zack stood and stretched as he waited for an answer and then continued. "After we interview this afternoon, I have a short errand to run before dinner, so I'll bid you good afternoon after the last applicant. Oh, I'll stop by on my way to Barclay's. We can walk together, if you please."

Darcie smiled. Secretly, she thought that he must have stopped by just to ask to walk her to Emmy and Barclay's this evening. Everything else was merely an excuse. He was solely charged with obtaining a companion for her according to Uncle Talbot's letter. However, that fact didn't diminish her glee over being asked to walk with him. "Why, I'd be delighted. I'm honored that you'd walk a simple country girl like me to a social gathering."

"Mlle., it is I who am honored." He stood and clapped his right hand across his heart in mock salute. "After we go our separate ways, I shall count the minutes until we meet again."

Zack strode across the room, clasped her hand in his, and kissed her palm, his lips lingering a moment. Drawing her to her feet, he clutched her hand to his chest and said, "Anything you would ask, I should consider myself duty-bound to do."

Zack's nearness nearly took her breath away but she seized the moment and said, "My heart is torn at the thought of leaving my beloved Charleston and my friends. Don't take me to France."

The magic of the moment faded as Zack realized the seriousness of her request. Not take her to France? He cared nothing for Talbot Neville, but Zack realized that he looked forward to the journey home to France with Darcie at his side. He'd begun thinking of the times they'd have together, taking her to Court, introducing her to the Empress Eugénie.

But he knew that he must be careful. Even though she seemed resigned to the voyage, Zack realized that she might be placating him while she planned her escape. "Ah, *ma cherie,* is the thought of traveling abroad with me so distasteful?"

Darcie stared at him a moment and then decided she had already given too much away. "Oh, sir, how can you think such a thing? Nothing could be further from the truth."

"I'm delighted to hear that." Zack stood and walked toward the open windows. "It's rather warm inside today. Would you like to leave for my office now? Or, if you prefer, I'll interview the prospects myself this afternoon."

Darcie coolly imagined the kind of companion she'd get if she left the hiring solely up to Zack Manville. "Thank you. I'll get my sunbonnet and be along in a moment."

Smiling, Darcie hurried from the room. She enjoyed Zack but regretted that he was in the unfortunate position of being her uncle's emissary.

Upstairs she was thoughtful as she opened the bottom drawer of her bonnet chest, pulled out the white bonnet with the lavender satin ribbons and lace ruffles, and stepped to the mirror over the dressing table. Taking care not to damage her chignon more than necessary, she perched the bonnet on her head and tied the violet ribbons beneath her chin, pausing a moment to find her violet parasol in the bottom of the armoire.

She ran down the stairs until she realized that Zack was no longer waiting in the parlor, but standing at their foot. A little more demurely, she continued down the curved staircase to his side. "I'll tell Charity we're leaving."

Darcie couldn't find Charity at first. She looked in the kitchen, but Cook hadn't seen her. Feeling a little irritated,

Darcie muttered about the black mammy never being around when she was needed.

"I heered that," came a voice from the back porch.

"Charity? What are you doing out there?" Darcie stepped to the door and peered through.

"Tryin' to cool myself off in this heat." Charity sat on a straw-bottomed chair and leaned back against the house. "I reckon the devil done left the gates to hell open and be lettin' out all that hot air. What with you goin off with that Frenchie without no chaperone. I guess you'se gonna ride in a carriage."

Darcie felt a little exasperated. "Of course, we're going to ride in a carriage. It's too hot today to walk all the way down to the wharf."

"First thing you know, my baby be wearin' paint on her face and come in here painted up like one of them no-account white trash women what hangs around down by the wharf liftin' they skirts so's them sailors can see they legs plumb up 'bove the knee." Charity buried her face in her hands and shook her head ruefully. "Lawsy, yo momma gonna raise up in her grave and come after ole Charity. Ain't gonna be no place in heaven fer me. I done let my baby go astray."

"Hush up, Charity, or I won't take you to France. I'm going to do no such thing." Darcie realized that if she allowed Charity to continue, the old black woman would burst into tears and not be worth anything for the rest of the day. She hugged the hunched black shoulders. "I'll be back soon."

Darcie found Zack waiting at the bottom of the staircase staring thoughtfully toward the top. "Ready?" he asked, turning to face her. He pictured her lying across an expanse of white sheets waiting for him, but shook the image from his mind.

"Yes," Darcie answered, and walked past him to the door and grabbed her shawl, wondering what he was looking at. There was nothing of interest upstairs except bedrooms and her own small morning room.

When they reached the gate, Zack opened it and held it for her. "Can't be too careful. Not much air stirring today, but—"

"Thank you," Darcie cut him off. She didn't like being reminded of the embarrassing situation in which he'd found her on the day they'd met. "I'm sure I won't have that problem again."

Zack chuckled and helped her into the waiting carriage. "I hope you don't mind an open carriage. It's so awfully hot that I can hardly stand my coat."

"It *is* rather warm for this time of year." Darcie stared across White Point Gardens to the Ashley River. Usually a breeze blew at all times off the river. All along the peninsula, people built their piazzas on the south side to catch that cooling breeze. It did them little good today. "I've never lived through a hotter summer than this."

Zack nodded and ran his fingers under his collar.

Settling herself comfortably, she slipped her shawl off her shoulders and fanned herself with the hand-painted silk fan looped over her wrist, taking care to position the parasol to protect her creamy white face and bosom. Charity would fall into a fit if a single freckle marred either.

As the horse clopped along on Meeting Street, a gentle breeze stirred among the yellow jasmine wafting a sweet fragrance around them and mingling with the faint musky scent of the streets. Occasionally, Darcie caught the eye of a friend or acquaintance and called out to them, waved, or nodded.

Live oaks towered over the street, their limbs gnarled and reaching as if they could grab her right out of the carriage. Darcie hoped to avoid meeting Barclay Rhett, but as they drove past his house, he stepped through his gate and glowered at them before altering his expression and waving cheerfully. Darcie smiled and returned his greeting, but Zack merely nodded.

She suspected that the two men had little affection for each other, and perhaps, if she and Zack weren't leaving soon, a duel would ensue, well, perhaps not a duel, although the thought excited Darcie. Having been in mourning for so long, the idea of two men fighting over her seemed quite romantic. However, duels must have a winner and a loser. She refused to risk the injury or death of either man. She enjoyed their company far too much.

At last they reached the offices of the Manville Trading Company. The driver called, "Whoa, Mose."

Zack jumped down and helped Darcie. She waited to one side while he handed coins to the driver, and then turned to her. "Let's go in, shall we?"

Darcie lifted her skirts to avoid a puddle and stepped through the door Zack opened for her. Inside, she glanced around. The office was much the same as her father's. The musty scent of ink and old ledger books lingered in the air, teasing her memory.

The windows were thrown open to catch the breeze off the Cooper River, and slight puffs of air fluttered the curls that escaped Darcie's chignon. Without thinking, she pushed the curls back and removed her bonnet.

"Come with me." Zack opened the door to a small office that led off the large reception area. "You may hang your bonnet and shawl in here. We'll wait to see if we have any applicants."

Darcie followed him into the neat office. Behind a desk of black cypress, Zack waited until she sat down on one of the chairs opposite. When she settled her skirts, he sat down.

"Don't mind me. I know you have plenty of work to do." Darcie glanced out the window.

A ship with a tall sail threaded its way into the harbor and set course toward the sea. *In three weeks time, that will be me,* she thought wistfully. *What is to become of me?* she wondered.

She gazed at Zack, intent on examining some papers piled neatly on his desk. She presumed that this was his office, at least while he was in port. Perhaps one of the other men outside in the reception room used the office the rest of the time.

Other than a few papers, a copy of the *Mercury,* and a small globe, the desk was bare. Behind him on the wall hung a large map of the world. Darcie studied it for a while. France seemed so far away. She knew they wouldn't sail directly across the Atlantic Ocean, but would follow the Gulf Stream north and then cut across along the path indicated by the line of small arrows. Zack worked through the stack of papers within minutes.

Zack Manville was a handsome man. Darcie watched him

work, carefully reading the papers and then scratching down notes, occasionally signing a form of some sort. She studied him as carefully as he examined the papers. A smile touched her lips when his dark brows lifted questioningly, when he grimaced aloud. He looked up and caught Darcie staring at him. Flushing, she smiled and glanced away, feeling the warmth of his presence all the way across the room.

Once, he pounded his fist on the desk, crumpled the sheets of paper into a wad, and threw it in the wastebasket. He rose so quickly that he nearly overturned his chair; he paced the floor, never noticing Darcie watching him warily; he returned to his seat and retrieved the offending papers from the wastebasket.

A young man opened the door slightly and poked his head in. "Mr. Manville, sir, there's a lady what says she's here to apply for the position of companion you advertised for."

"Yes. Send her in at once." Zack rose and rounded the desk to meet the lady who entered. "Come in. Please, may I take your shawl and bonnet?"

Darcie studied the heavily clothed woman and realized that she'd never do. Without doubt, the woman would be tyrannical.

The woman gripped her shawl as if Zack were a thug about to steal it. "Thank you, I'll keep it. One never knows who's lurking about. My name is Hildegard Appleby."

"I assure you that you are quite safe, as are your belongings." Zack waited for her to be seated in the chair he indicated and returned to his chair.

"Be that as it may, I'll keep what's mine with me." She eyed Darcie suspiciously. "I was unaware that our interview was to be monitored."

Zack introduced them. Both Darcie and Mrs. Appleby muttered appropriate greetings. Mrs. Appleby seemed as leery of Darcie as Darcie was of Mrs. Appleby.

"Now, may I have your references, Mrs. Appleby?" Zack asked.

Hildegard Appleby stared at him for a moment and then turned to Darcie. The gray-haired woman's gaze took in all of

Darcie, first down and then up her erect frame. She paused as her
eyes rested on Darcie's breasts and then her bare arms. "Sir,
you've introduced us, but I hardly see why I should suffer to
make my application in public."

She glanced up and down Darcie's frame, as if she considered
her to be street trash. She clearly imagined herself above Darcie's
station. "Who is this . . . this young *lady,* and what has she to
do with my interview?"

"Miss Gaynor is the young lady you will accompany, should
you be hired." Zack felt the animosity welling in Darcie as
color spread across her cheeks and decided that Hildegard Appleby would never do. He disliked her already, and so, apparently, did Darcie. This pompous woman would make their voyage miserable. "You will be in her employ. I am merely assisting
her in the interviews."

"Her employ?" Mrs. Appleby's voice cracked as she lifted her
chin in haughty disdain, glaring openly at Darcie. "I'm afraid
you've mistaken my reputation if you think that—"

"And Miss Gaynor comes from one of the finest Charleston
families." Zack stood, his hands clenching into tight fists that
turned white from the pressure. "I'm sorry for taking your time,
Mrs.—"

"Of course, and what a pleasure to make your acquaintence,
Miss Gaynor," Hildegard Appleby gushed, nervously fingering
her gray poplin skirt. Her hair was the color of a band of steel
on a well-worn wagon wheel—dull and gray with a slight tinge
of rust. Her face was tightly pinched into a semblance of a smile.
"I've heard a great deal about you. In fact, Miss Gaynor, I'm
delighted to make your acquaintance."

Darcie seldom revealed her anger, but if Zack didn't throw
this baggage out, then she would do it herself. Obviously the
woman thought that Darcie was Zack's mistress.

"Mrs. Appleby, I'm afraid our interview is concluded." Zack
rounded the desk and stood directly in Mrs. Appleby's line of
vision, preventing the confrontation that he saw about to erupt.
"We have other applicants to see this afternoon. Good day."

"But—" began Mrs. Appleby.

"Good day." Zack opened the door and indicated the way out.

His demeanor told Darcie that if Mrs. Appleby didn't leave immediately, she'd be bodily thrown out. Darcie glared, despising the woman for judging her so unfairly. "It's been a pleasure, Mrs. Appleby."

Zack closed the door and returned to his chair. "I'm sorry, Darcie. Perhaps, you shouldn't—"

He was interrupted by a knock on the door. "Come in."

"A Miss Peabody to see you, sir."

Nodding with resignation, Zack replied, "Send her in."

When Miss Peabody entered, Zack was waiting by the door. He showed her to a chair. "May I take your shawl?"

The woman drew it closer across her breast. "Thank you, no. I'll keep it."

Zack shrugged and sat down. *Another crazy woman,* he thought. *How did I manage to entangle myself in this venture? It would have been much simpler to have allowed Darcie to select her own companion.* But, he admitted his selfishness to himself, he wanted to be sure that the companion she chose would allow him some freedom. *Damn it,* he thought. *I should choose a tyrant and allow Darcie no voice in this decision—to protect my own future freedom.*

He considered their time on the ship. With a little luck, he knew he could lure her to his bed for a sweet interlude at sea. The time would pass quickly. Once they reached France, he'd disappear, out to sea for months aboard one of his ships and lost to her retribution.

Lost to her retribution. Darcie Gaynor was not one to trifle with lightly. Her retribution would not be light, nor would it be sweet. If she felt wronged, Zack had no doubt that she would chase him to the far corners of the earth to exact her revenge.

Ah, sweet revenge. He imagined their lovemaking, lusty and passionate. Most women were lusty once he cracked their shell of propriety. Darcie had no such artifice. She exuded a genuine joy for living, a desire for life to be lived to its fullest, a confidence that she would be equal to any obstacle. Darcie Gaynor was different, and if Zack wasn't careful, he'd succumb to her feminine wiles—if indeed they were wiles.

"Ah, Miss Peabody." Zack forced his attention to the pinch-faced woman sitting opposite him. She'd be a likely candidate for icing down his passions. "May I have your references?"

The middle-aged woman withdrew a folded paper from her reticule and passed it across the desk to Zack. Her eyes never met Darcie's, and while Zack read the neat script, Miss Peabody fidgeted with her bonnet. She clearly considered Darcie to be one of the wharf women and therefore beneath notice.

Zack watched her manner carefully. Yes, she'd be just the tyrant he needed, but was he willing to forego his earlier thoughts completely? He doubted it. "Miss Peabody, allow me to present Miss Gaynor."

Miss Peabody gazed at Darcie and apparently realized that she'd made a hasty decision without foundation. "Oh, I'm delighted to be sure."

Darcie muttered something appropriate and rolled her eyes at Zack's amused expression. He seemed to enjoy torturing her. How dare he suggest that one of these snooty old crones could serve as Darcie's companion?

"Now, Miss Peabody, as I'm sure you're aware, Miss Gaynor has been in mourning for some time and—"

"You have nothing to fear on that count, sir," Miss Peabody interrupted, tucking her hands into the pockets of her black taffeta skirts and continuing to scowl as if something smelled bad. "I am quite strict and will discipline this child as if she were my very own. Why, she'd never so much as step a foot out of my sight and—"

Darcie's eyes blazed with fury. This woman intended to imprison her in the cabin on the ship and Darcie wouldn't see the light of day again until they reached Paris. No doubt the woman would suffer the illnesses of the sea and be indisposed, leaving Darcie to care for her for the entire voyage. "Zack, I'm afraid—"

Zack glared at Darcie and held up his hand to stop her from voicing her rage. "Thank you, Miss Peabody. I'm sure—"

"She'll reach France as pure as she is at this moment." She glanced at Darcie, as if trying to determine if purity were indeed a matter of interest. "I'd stake my reputation on it. I'm a member of the Congregational Church, and anybody who knows me can attest to my—"

"Yes, I'm sure they can. Now," Zack rose and walked around the desk to Miss Peabody's side, "if you don't mind, we have others to interview. We'll be in touch."

When Miss Peabody was safely outside, Darcie and Zack burst into laughter. "What a crone!" Darcie cried.

"Exactly what an impertinent young lady like yourself needs. A firm hand," Zack teased, without a smile.

"If you think I'd venture to step a foot aboard a boat with that old bore, then you've another think." Darcie rose, her full five-feet-seven-inch height drawn up like a snake ready to strike. "If you want a mutiny on your hands, then hire that old war horse."

Zack fell into his chair laughing at the images Darcie conveyed. "All right, little spitfire. Have it your way. I'll cross Miss Peabody off the list, but mind you, if you venture too far out of hand, you'd better beware. I have her references and can easily—"

"Zack Manville—"

"Excuse me, sir, Mrs. Hoskins to see you."

Darcie sank back into her chair, her face flaming. She'd been so angry that she hadn't seen the young man open the door. What a fool she was to let Zack tease her this way.

Almost reluctant to look up, she peered through the doorway past the clerk. At the counter stood another old hag. But Darcie was more interested in the man waiting there. He stared at Darcie, black eyes blazing from a sun and sea-worn face. The scruffy beard indicated that he'd probably shaved upon arriving in Charleston, but not since. He looked like many of the sailors who sailed for Gaynor, particularly the ones who'd been the victims of piracy. Darcie concluded that his ship must have arrived in port about the same time.

"Show her in." Zack's voice interrupted her thoughts.

During the course of the afternoon, Zack and Darcie interviewed several ladies, none of whom were appropriate for various reasons. Darcie felt that she had lived too long without a
firm supervisory hand to succumb to the terroristic attitudes of
these women who were accustomed to ruling their charges with
fingers of iron.

And Zack decided as the afternoon progressed that none were
appropriate because he wanted nothing to interfere with his
growing relationship with Darcie. When they were alone, both
let down their guards and enjoyed the other's company without
the dubious benefits of formality. At least Zack enjoyed Darcie's
company, and she acted as if she liked being with him.

Darcie looked at the latest applicant. This one was certainly
different from the last three or four, and Darcie knew she'd have
little to fear from this woman dressed in her finest fashions.
Darcie was fascinated. She'd never had a chance to see a "woman
of the streets" close up before, not to mention converse with her
in an office. Charity would be livid if she found out.

Miss Smith's scarlet skirts nearly matched her flame-colored
hair. The bodice of the dress was covered in black lace and
exposed far too much of her bosom. Indeed, Darcie felt that
Miss Smith's bosom would pop free at any moment. She crossed
her legs at the knee and addressed Darcie as "hon."

"Y'know, hon," she whispered leaning toward Darcie conspiratorially and winking, "I'm just the sort of companion
y'need along on this trip. Why, y'd hardly know I was about.
You and the handsome mister here could be as friendly as
y'please."

Zack slammed his hands down on the desk. Damned if he
understood why this woman of the streets had appeared to apply
for the job of companion of Darcie. Before he could give any
further thought to the subject, she told him.

"Y'know, luv, I could be a asset on a ship. Y'know, keep the
men, uh, satisfied and happy, get it?" She reared back in the
chair and beamed at Zack, her legs now apart like a divining rod
and her dress hiked up to her knees.

This time, Zack could stand no more. He leapt to his feet.

"My good woman, I'm afraid you've misunderstood this position entirely. Miss Gaynor desires a companion for this journey, not someone who's . . . otherwise employed during the voyage."

"Well, we could muck about sometimes, y'know. I'm a workin' girl, but I ain't wishin' to look at the ceiling all the way across the ocean, meself." She winked at Darcie. "And I ain't opposed to female company neither so long as there ain't too much of it."

Color blazed into Zack's cheeks. "That will be all, Miss Smith!"

The scowl on his face relaxed a bit as soon as he ushered her out. The brassy woman left with a shrug of her heavy shoulders.

"Well, you've thrown out the only candidate that I wouldn't feel constrained by," Darcie teased when she saw the deep lines soften around his mouth and eyes. "She certainly wouldn't have had time to spend acting the tyrant."

Zack disregarded her jest, rose, and started to pace again. "Is there no one in all of Charleston suitable to be a companion?

Amused by his display of disdain, Darcie watched him pacing the floor until she could stand it no longer. "Sir, I fear you'll wear a hole in the flooring and we shall fall into the Cooper River."

"Mlle. Gaynor, I fear you misjudge the awkward position we've been placed in," Zack began, lecturing while his thoughts sped ahead. *What next?* Did he dare take her to France without a companion? And what choice did he have, if tomorrow's crop of old crows was no better than today's? *Damn it all.*

"I suppose we'll just have to postpone our trip."

Darcie's face brightened at the thought. "It may take months to find the right—"

"Mlle. Gaynor, we sail in three weeks time, if I must wear a dress, cap, and shawl all the way to Paris."

Chapter Five

Darcie watched Charity place the curls around her head and then closed her eyes to fully enjoy the gentle touch of her mammy. Zack's face swam before her eyes and she giggled, recalling his statement of frustration. Indeed, Darcie considered him dressed as a woman and thought he'd look rather silly.

"Hold still, Miss Darcie, or yo' gonna go to supper bald as a honeydew melon." Charity tugged a little harder on Darcie's golden curls. "I swear I ain't ever see'd no chile as wigglesome as you."

Darcie's eyes popped open with a pained expression. "I'm sorry, Charity," Darcie replied with a contriteness she didn't really feel. She wanted to dance and sing and shout tonight. And she didn't know why.

Well, she did. But she couldn't admit it—yet. Zack was due here any minute to walk her over to Barclay and Em's house for dinner.

What an afternoon they'd had. She giggled again and felt the resulting tug on her curls—a little harder this time. Charity muttered and continued to arrange Darcie's hair.

Closing her eyes again, she pictured Zack's handsome face

bronzed by the sun. His square chin and jaw served as evidence of the strength she'd seen in him and heard of in his heroic deeds —a true epic hero. She imagined his lips, full and sensuous on hers, and wondered how they'd feel.

Darcie opened her eyes and watched Charity in the mirror. What would Charity say if she knew what Darcie was thinking? She'd be appalled, and Darcie would never hear the end of Charity's sermon.

"I never heard of no young ladies goin' out wif a man dey's never been introduced to," Charity scolded. "It jus ain't fitten. Yo' momma'd whup me clean across Oyster Point wif a yard broom if'n she knowed I let my little kitten—"

"Charity!" Darcie grabbed at a curl Charity was twisting and pulling. "Watch what you're doing."

"Sorry, kitten," Charity answered, dropping down to hug Darcie. "Yo' know ole Charity don't mean to hurt yo' but I—"

"I know. Just finish. They'll be eating dessert by the time we get there." Darcie looked at her dress. The lime taffeta rustled and whispered as she wriggled.

Charity moved back. "How's dat?"

Darcie's gaze met her reflection in the mirror. Deep blue eyes peered back at her, shaded now with flecks of amber and green. Her hair crowned her head like a chain of pure gold.

"It's lovely, Charity. You're a wonder." Jumping up, Darcie turned and dropped a kiss on Charity's cheek. "I don't know what I'd do without you."

"You'd be a sight, that's what you'd do without me. I never knowed a girl—"

"Don't start again." Darcie hugged her. "I've got to go. I'm sure Zack is already waiting."

"Dat's another thing. I ain't never heard of nobody callin' by first names them whut they ain't been introduced to." Charity held a rose-colored crocheted shawl for Darcie to put on. "And, you ain't been—"

"Yes, I have. He had a letter of introduction from Uncle Talbot," Darcie retorted and made a small face at Charity.

"That Frenchie? I wouldn't trust him no further than I could walk on the Ashley or Cooper." Charity started on one of her favorite subjects. "If he was any good, he'd a been here lookin' after my kitten instead of settin' over there lickin' the boots of that Napoleon fella."

"Good night." Darcie closed the door behind her, knowing Charity would continue her speech with or without an audience.

She hurried along the landing to the staircase and descended like a gently bred young lady should, instead of running headlong down them and skipping every other one as she had in her girlhood. Ladies never passed over a step on the way up or down stairs. Of course, Darcie didn't always act like a proper lady.

She met Jasper on the staircase. "Mr. Manville is waiting in the parlor."

Darcie nodded and hurried past. She had no idea where Jasper was headed and didn't care. Zack was waiting.

Before she opened the parlor doors, she inhaled deeply and then exhaled slowly. Craning her neck to see all the way around as well as she could, Darcie checked her skirts to make sure they were settled properly over her hoops.

Feeling dressed as well as any young Charlestonian, she opened the door and stepped into the parlor. Zack stood at a window across the room. Resplendent in a black broadcloth coat and black trousers, he turned to face her.

"Mon Dieu! I never believed you could do it." Zack crossed the room, took her hand, and kissed it. "It's been less than two hours since I left you here."

"And why shouldn't I be able to accomplish what you have done?" She gestured to his natty attire.

"Well, you have . . . I mean, women have to . . . What I mean to say is that, well, you know . . ." Zack fumbled for words. *"Mon Dieu,* Darcie, you have more underthings."

Color sprang to Darcie's cheeks. What a thing to say! She should slap him for having the unmitigated indelicacy to refer to her undergarments, but he was so charming about it that she hadn't the heart.

"Forgive—" he began, dropping his gaze to his hands, but before he could finish, Darcie interrupted him.

She burst into laughter over his obvious embarrassment. "Oh, Zack. I should slap you resoundingly and rush from the room."

Zack looked at her, as if he expected her to do just that. "I deserve no less."

Darcie lifted her chin, narrowed her eyes, and stared accusingly across the delicate bridge of her nose. "You, sir, are a cad of the first water."

"You are absolutely right." He caught the gist of her conversation, her teasing tone, and dropped to one knee. He clasped her hands in his and kissed each one fervently. "Please, mademoiselle, can you forgive me?"

"I should relate the insult to Barclay Rhett," she began, threateningly. "And he would toss you into the Ashley River, post haste."

Zack glanced up at her laughing face and noted its delicate beauty. He loved to see her laugh, and these teasing moments were his favorites—so far. "Oh, please, anything but that." He considered her threat and pursed his lips. "No. You must think of another punishment. I fear M. Rhett would fare worse than I."

Darcie collapsed onto the chair in gales of laughter. She knew that, without a doubt, Zack was right. Barclay would probably end up bobbing in the river, with Zack remaining untouched on the sea wall. "Then you will feel my wrath when I can think of something fitting enough. I shall think on it."

"It will be my most humble pleasure to remain in your thoughts, even for a deed as unworthy as mine committed this evening." His eyes narrowed to slits as he studied her. Arms resting on her lap, she rested against the back of the chair, her chest heaving. His gaze followed the rise and fall of her breasts a moment, the sweetness of her parted mouth as she laughed. He resumed his jesting. "I gratefully await sentencing if the punishment is at your hands."

He turned her hands over and kissed each palm, lingering the slightest moment over each. After a moment, he bowed his head further until it rested on her open hands and the sweet fragrance of violets tempted him to ravish her where she sat.

Still laughing, Darcie lifted his head and cupped his chin gently in her palms. Her laughter subsided somewhat and when she could maintain a straight face again, she quipped, "Well, sir, if you are *that* eager for punishment, then perhaps I shall postpone my decision."

"Oh, you truly torture me with your continued baiting of my adoring soul." Zack tried his best to look contrite, but the laughter touched his eyes and gave him away.

Darcie studied his face. How hard he'd tried to continue the pretense—and how miserably he failed. A face as joyous as his could hardly be considered penitent. Her hands caressed his cheek, and even though he'd shaved earlier today, a touch of roughness greeted her fingers. She imagined him with a beard. It would be as brown as his hair, perhaps, kissed by the sun. Her fingers touched the locks of hair that fell across his forehead, soft and fine.

Her eyes met his. Her mouth parted, as if she felt compelled to say something, but nothing came out. His warm brown eyes engulfed her, invited her into something she couldn't quite understand, but truly wanted to know about. She leaned forward slightly and felt his breath on her cheeks, smelled the clean scent of his soap.

The door rattled and Darcie jumped up, almost knocking him to the floor. "Uh, well, I suppose we must be going. Goodness sakes, we'll be the last ones to arrive."

Caught off guard, Zack steadied himself with his left hand. *Damn!* he thought. *Why now? Why should the damn door rattle now?*

"Of course, you're right." Zack lifted himself off the floor and rubbed his palms together. He walked across the room to place as much distance between them as possible. He gestured gracefully and flamboyantly, bowing and indicating for her to lead the way.

Still a little puzzled by what had happened moments ago, Darcie strode towards the door, as though her decisive movements would cast the vision of Zack's face from her sight. His face had been so close, just inches from hers.

What happened? One moment they were laughing hysterically, and then next, neither was laughing. In fact, she wasn't even breathing.

They strolled down South Bay until they reached Meeting Street and turned. "It isn't far," Darcie said, to kill the silence that gnawed at her.

"I believe I know the place. We passed here this afternoon and M. Rhett was coming out the gate," Zack replied.

"That's it." Darcie's hand was tucked in the curve of Zack's elbow as they walked along and her heart raced. "It's certainly a lovely evening, isn't it?"

"Ah, Darcie, it is." Zack slowed and stopped. "I believe we are approaching his house."

"Next gate," Darcie answered. She regretted arriving at Barclay and Em's so quickly. Zack seemed in a pensive mood, and she wanted a chance to think about the "event" as she began to categorize it. She gazed up at the moon thoughtfully. "Maybe I should talk to Em about it."

"What?"

Startled when she realized she'd spoken aloud, Darcie replied, "Oh, nothing. Just thinking out loud. Um. About a new dress."

Zack stared at her a moment and nodded. "Shall we go in?"

They found everybody else already there. Em had invited several people who hadn't met Zack and so the evening was well along before Darcie had a chance to speak to him again. He seemed to be enjoying himself, and to Barclay's apparent dismay, Zack was the center of attention.

Em had flung open the windows, allowing the sweet scent of her carefully manicured roses to fill the air in the dining room. Darcie's seat was on Barclay's right, while Zack's was on Em's right. A bowl of lovely red and white roses placed in the center of the table prevented her from catching his eye during dinner.

He seemed to be having a wonderful time, and Darcie heard him laugh aloud more than once, reminding her of the "event" that had happened earlier. Em stared at him dreamily, as if she wanted to kiss him right there in front of everybody.

Em kiss Zack? Jealousy welled up in Darcie—a new emotion for her. She'd never known a man that she really cared enough about to be jealous of.

All around the table, the men were talking of states' rights, an issue that had shadowed every dinner and party for several years. Darcie was fascinated usually, feeling herself to be a part of the unwritten history of Charleston. But tonight she was more interested in Zack and Em at the other end of the table.

Barclay nudged her arm. "I say, Darcie—"

"What?" she asked, nearly jumping from surprise and embarrassment for neglecting her dinner partner.

"I said, when do you sail?" he repeated.

"Too soon." Darcie cast a glance Zack's way. He was engrossed in Em's chatter, and could hardly be seen from Darcie's end of the table, further irritating her. She forced a smile for Barclay. "Although we're having a problem acquiring a companion for me. You should have seen the candidates this afternoon. There must have been at least four old crones standing on the edge of open graves. And . . ." her voice trailed off. She wasn't sure whether she should tell Barclay about the other or not. "Well, she was a common woman a, well . . . a woman of the streets."

"What!" Barclay's voice cracked above the murmur of dinner conversation. "Do you mean to tell me that a woman of the wharves applied for the position? That Zack actually allowed her to come into the room with you? Preposterous."

Zack looked at Barclay when his name was called. "Did you address me?"

"Hardly," Barclay answered sarcastically. "How dare you allow some . . . some trollop from the wharves to—"

"Barclay," Darcie began, placing her hand on his arm. She should have known he'd become self-righteous about such a silly incident, particularly when Zack was concerned.

"Leave this to me," he patted her hand. "No gentleman

would have allowed such a woman to enter the building with—"

Zack stood up and glared at Barclay. The malevolence in his eyes silenced Barclay immediately. Zack continued to stare at his opponent. "And no gentleman discusses such private and delicate matters over dinner with guests present."

Barclay glanced around the table at his guests. "Of course, I meant no disrespect, however—"

"However, nothing," Darcie finished for him and whispered through clenched teeth so only he could hear, "Now, be a good boy and eat your dessert."

No further incidents occurred during dinner, but Barclay kept glaring at Zack who completely ignored his host and concentrated on his hostess. Em giggled and laughed during the remainder of the meal, much to Darcie's displeasure. Darcie didn't know which irritated her more—Barclay's closely checked anger or Em's outrageous flirting.

By the time some of the guests were leaving, Darcie wore a scowl almost as obvious as that of the ladies she'd interviewed this afternoon. She felt almost as crotchety as they looked. Em had linked her arm in Zack's as they left the dining room and she stared longingly after him when the gentlemen retired to the library for brandy and cigars.

"I can't understand why men feel they must go off alone after dinner and smoke those horrid cigars that smell up the entire house," Em complained as she stepped into the parlor. Everybody else had left except Darcie, Patty, Zack, and Gideon.

"To escape from busybodies like you," Barclay replied as he entered the room behind her. "Men like a chance to discuss certain matters with other men, and not have to fend off inane remarks from silly women who have no knowledge on the subject, but feel they must address the subject anyway."

"I disagree," Zack countered.

"Oh?" Barclay turned to face Zack. When he continued, his words were clearly sarcastic. "And what do you believe is the reason then, M. Manville?"

Zack winked at Darcie and smiled at Em and Patty. "Why,

so that we may momentarily escape the delightful company of you lovely women and draw a breath, before we succumb to your feminine charms."

"Exactly!" Gideon slapped his knee and laughed. "Well put, Zack."

"Well, I fear I have an early day tomorrow." Zack looked at his pocket watch. "I can look forward to another day of interviewing applicants for the position of companion to Darcie."

"Ugh!" Darcie groaned. "I never saw a bunch of more boring and hypocritical old hags—"

"Darcie!" Patty scolded. "I'm ashamed of you. I never heard you talk like that before."

"You never sat through an afternoon of such distasteful snobbery either," Darcie defended herself. "Besides, they were all so old and cantankerous. Except of course for my personal favorite."

"Now, Darcie, you know that woman was hardly suitable to chaperone—" Zack began.

"Well, she was at least interesting." Darcie rose. She knew it was time to leave. Even though she resented having to interview another crew of applicants, she refused to allow the decision to be made without her.

"Say, Darcie," Em said, enthusiastically. "Let *me* be your companion!"

"You?" Darcie asked, incredulously. "Now why in the world would you want to . . ." her voice trailed off. Zack. Em wanted to be near Zack.

"I'm afraid that's quite impossible." Zack moved to Darcie's side and took her elbow persuasively. If Em came along, he'd never get rid of her long enough to be with Darcie.

"Impossible?" Barclay put in. "I think it's a capital idea. I could go along. Em and I could make the trip, tour France, and return later."

Zack rolled his eyes and turned to face Barclay. Though he didn't want Em along, he *definitely* didn't want Barclay around poking his nose into the Manville affairs—nor into his relationship with Darcie. "Out of the question."

Darcie liked the idea. This way, she wouldn't have to acquaint herself with some ninny who'd ruin her trip. "Oh, Zack, what's so bad about the idea?"

"Well, it's just . . ." What could he say? Barclay had almost called him out over the presence of Miss Smith at his office when Darcie was in the room. If he knew how Zack felt about Darcie, then Barclay would kill him for sure. He might not even wait for a duel. He had to fight this idea. "Darcie, my dear, Miss Rhett isn't old enough to be a proper companion. Your uncle would string me up by my . . . toes if I—"

"Good gracious, Zack. There is absolutely nothing wrong with using Em as my companion." Darcie couldn't understand his opposition to the idea. It made no sense. "Disregarding my feelings on the subject, imagine yourself having to deal with one of those . . . those other applicants for the entire journey. We'd all be daft by the time we reached France."

Zack knew she was right, but somewhere deep inside, he knew having the Rhetts along wouldn't work out. "Darcie, think of your uncle's wishes. As your guardian, he certain—"

"Balderdash!" Darcie cried. "He doesn't care a fig for me. If he did, he'd have come here long ago to see after me instead of waiting three years to send a . . . to send an argumentative, domineering—"

Em drew Darcie into her arms. "Shhh. Now, I'm sure Zack will see this is the best plan, when he's had a chance to think about it. He's just surprised, that's all." She turned to Zack. "You will think about it, won't you?"

As much as he didn't want Em and Barclay Rhett along, he had to admit that it might be his only option. So far, none of the applicants were even remotely appropriate. He took Em's hand and kissed it. "When you ask so sweetly, how can I refuse? I'll think about it."

Darcie glared at him. She was really glad Em had stopped her from allowing her anger to bubble over like that. She needed to learn to control her temper. "Well, it really is time for us to leave."

Barclay's face reddened in anger as Zack took Darcie's arm

and touched his forehead in salute. Gideon and Patty left with Darcie and Zack. Their house was down a block and around the corner on Tradd Street, so they walked together for a short distance only.

When they reached White Point Gardens at the corner of Meeting and South Bay, Zack said. "It's a lovely night. Would you like to walk around the seawall here at White Point Gardens?"

Darcie felt her heart flutter and she knew she should refuse, but couldn't. The night was far too lovely, and she didn't want to leave Zack yet. "Well, I . . . Yes. I'd love to."

Lifting her skirts a little to step over a puddle, Darcie walked along with Zack through the gardens. The moon rose orange over the harbor and laid an undulating path across the Ashley River as they strolled along the seawall. A cool breeze blew across the stone wall and promenade, playfully lifting the ruffles on Darcie's skirts and petticoats.

"Are you warm enough?" Zack stopped and looked down at Darcie. The ruffle across the bodice of her dress caught his attention. The light-colored fabric fluttered over her breasts, first hiding and then exposing the creamy cleavage.

"Oh, yes. The breeze is wonderful after such a hot day." She peered out at a ship's lantern bobbing peacefully in the harbor as the ship lay at anchor. "There never has been a more beautiful sight."

"Well, I must admit, mademoiselle, that you are correct," Zack agreed, trying not to seem overly interested in her breasts. "I have never seen a more lovely sight."

Darcie looked at him. He wasn't even looking out into the harbor. Zack was staring directly at her. Her heart fluttered like a moth in a lamp chimney, and she averted her eyes. "Yes. Artists come from all around to paint this view."

When she glanced up at him again, he was still studying her carefully. Though the moon had turned to silver as it gained full sky, Darcie was thankful the light was so dim that he couldn't see her blush.

Zack took her elbow and they continued their walk. "High Battery is a delightful place. Even I appreciate its beauty."

"Well, it's only been completed for a few years." Darcie hesitated. "It was finished just before my father passed away."

Zack nodded sympathetically. "And your uncle has been at the helm, so to speak, ever since."

"Well, not precisely," Darcie began, delighted for the change of topic. "For the first few months, I kept everything going."

"You? You couldn't have been more than . . ." Zack floundered as he thought better of suggesting an age. He'd been fortunate during the discussion that led to his embarrassment over the subject of her undergarments, he didn't feel so lucky now.

"Seventeen," Darcie supplied for him, knowing that he hesitated out of good manners. Unlike many women, Darcie wasn't so silly as to be sensitive about her age. In fact, she was proud of her accomplishments. "I was seventeen at the time."

"Extraordinary." Zack meant it. He knew that the company had fared better during that period than it had under her uncle's management.

"And, you? How old were you when you assumed control of Manville Trading Company?" Darcie asked, watching a night bird soar over them and land in a tree in White Point Gardens.

Zack looked down at her and then let his gaze follow the bird she was watching. "Twenty. But I had some experience. I had worked with my father for some time. I learned to sail as a boy."

The sound of horses startled her and she whirled around. Coming up behind them on the road that edged the seawall were several of Mayor Miles's new mounted police. There was little likelihood of a fire down here at the Battery, but they patrolled here anyway. The mounted police had been in existence now for about a year, organized to combat the arsonists that had become so prevalent with the threat of secession.

The police officers rode on without stopping. Darcie stared after them. "Mayor Miles believes they'll prevent another destructive fire. In addition to the mounted police, we now have ten fire engines and ten fire companies."

"An excellent idea. In a bustling town such as Charleston, one can never be too careful." Zack paused and stared after the police. "Do they ever catch the arsonists?"

"Seldom. But the fires are caught early enough to be extinguished without a great deal of damage. Most people believe the fires are set by dissatisfied slaves, but there hasn't been a really bad fire since the year after I was born," Darcie added. "I can't imagine why a slave would want to burn anything on purpose."

"Stirred up by all this talk of abolitionists, I suppose," Zack said thoughtfully. "Of course, not everybody is as kind to their slaves as you."

"Well, you may be right."

A fish jumped and the splash attracted their attention. Once again they stopped and peered out across the point where the Cooper River joins the Ashley. An eerie silence descended upon them, a peace and tranquillity that the patrolling officers had disturbed. The Battery was bereft of people except for Darcie and Zack.

The wind picked up and Darcie's shawl nearly blew off her shoulders. Sails flapped on the ship that had just dropped anchor about a hundred yards out, and Darcie heard the call of the sailors preparing the ship for the night.

"Here, *ma petite*, take my coat." Zack removed his frock coat. "I insist."

Without waiting for an answer he drew the black coat about her shoulders. His hands moved to her tiny waist and tugged the broadcloth more snugly around her. "It will go around your waist two times, I believe."

Darcie laughed, a nonsensical laugh born of nervous tension. His hands caressed her waist under the guise of drawing the coat about her, and she couldn't breathe. When she dared to look at Zack, he was staring down at her.

His hands were still about her waist, and her body nearly touched his. In the moonlight she could barely see his eyes fixed upon her, but she felt compelled to look at them. Deep brown, laughing eyes, now serene, bore into her, drew her closer to him, and their bodies touched. Now his hands caressed her back, massaging the tense muscles that held her so stiffly against him until she relaxed, touching her chin to his chest, moonlight illuminating her face.

His embrace tightened, and before she realized what she was doing, Darcie leaned against him, allowing him to hold her steady in the intoxicating Carolina moonlight. He was going to kiss her. She knew it, and she knew she should stop him.

Darcie couldn't. She didn't want to stop him. She didn't want him to stop.

Her lips parted. Darcie knew this kiss would be like no other she'd ever had. Zack didn't do things halfway.

When his mouth finally touched hers, a gasp of pleasure and surprise escaped from her lips. Gentle at first and then building in intensity, his kiss propelled her into a fantasy state from which she never wanted to awaken.

Everything around her became intensified with his deepening kiss. The lapping of waves on the seawall grew louder, more musical, saying, "Kiss me. Kiss me. Kiss me." The scree of gulls lost their discordance and became lyrical, whispering, "Yes. Yes. Yes."

Bathed in the silver glow of moonlight, Darcie slid her arms around his neck, pressing her breasts against his chest, as if she were afraid he'd draw back from her. She wanted the kiss, the night to last forever, forgetting tomorrow, forgetting Uncle Talbot, forgetting her fiancé—

Her fiancé! Darcie was betrothed to another man, albeit one she'd never met, and one she hoped never to meet. She jerked away, flaming with color at her own lack of propriety. How could she have allowed him to kiss her that way?

Zack stared at her, startled by his behavior and hers. What had he done? He'd never intended to kiss her, at least not now, not so soon after they'd met. She'd seemed to be a vision in the moonlight. Dare he blame the moonlight?

Frightened by her contradictory emotions, she stepped back,

out of touching distance. "I . . . I . . . don't know what to say!"

Darcie turned and ran, ignoring the fragility of her slippers. Humiliation rankled within her, and tears of embarrassment stung her eyes.

Zack called after her, even followed for a short distance. But it was Darcie's turn to run as if she were being chased by the hounds of hell.

Chapter Six

Darcie's eyes opened slowly, as though the day were a present to be opened with care. She snuggled beneath the light covers and hugged herself. She'd never before felt so alive, so pretty.

Throwing back the covers, she sprang from the bed and hurried to the window that opened onto East Bay Street. Over the Cooper River, the sun sent shards of purple, pink, and dusky blue to chase the clouds of night away.

"What a glorious day this will be," Darcie whispered, still hugging herself. "Positively glorious."

She closed her eyes and visualized Zack. *He must think I'm an absolute green goose.* Darcie giggled, remembering how she'd run into the darkness last night after Zack kissed her.

What a kiss. Her body still tingled from her toenails to her hair when she recalled the exquisite sensations. She opened her eyes and stared out the window for a moment. The darkness had lifted, and even though Darcie had lain wide-eyed in bed until the early hours of morning, she felt magnificent.

At first, she'd been afraid she'd never see him again. But with the upcoming trip to France, she knew he'd be around soon. And she had raced off wearing his coat. He'd need that.

Whirling about the room, she closed her eyes and visualized him again, his eyelids half-closed as his lips neared hers. What had she looked like to him, she wondered. Did she have the same dreamy look as he? Did he feel the way she did now? She had a million questions and no answers. She was too inexperienced.

She could hardly wait to see him, to see if he looked any different. Darcie knew she wasn't the first girl he'd kissed, and she probably wouldn't be the last. Did the moment mean more to him than the other times? Was it more exciting? Was she different from the other women he'd kissed?

Different? She ran over to the mirror and turned up the lamp. Leaning close, she examined her face. It looked no different to her. Would Zack see any change? Would Em or Barclay?

The house was quiet. She pulled on a wrapper and ran lightly down the stairs to the kitchen. She was very hungry.

The pie safe was closed, but she eased it open, ignoring its creaky protest. Inside she found a half-eaten cherry pie, a plate of cornbread, and two biscuits. Shrugging, she took a thick slice of pie and poured herself a glass of milk from the earthen pitcher covered with a soft cloth.

Hoping to remain undiscovered, she raced back up the stairs to eat in silence. Here she could continue thinking about Zack without interference if anyone else should be up. Darcie sat down and absently ate her pie, pushing the juicy red cherries around the plate and knowing Charity would scold her when she found out.

Zack's face sprang into her mind every time she closed her eyes. She imagined his face just before he kissed her—coming closer and closer, his breath caressing her skin as lightly as a spring mist hovering over the Ashley River.

What would she do when she saw him? She wanted to fling herself into his arms and kiss him again and again. Darcie wouldn't do that, she couldn't. Last night had been a happenstance, a result of the atmosphere, a glass of wine, the soaring Carolina moon and its seductive silver reflection on the water.

Had a single kiss destroyed their relationship? Darcie hoped not. The voyage to France would be long indeed if she and Zack had to be on guard every moment.

She sighed regretfully. The kiss would be her last for a long time.

Somewhere across the wide Atlantic Ocean, a man awaited her arrival. Would his kiss excite her as Zack's had? Did her future husband long for the moment they'd marry and he could claim her as his own?

Was he young? Old? Handsome? "Balderdash!" Darcie exclaimed aloud. "Why didn't Uncle Talbot tell me about him? Anything. Even his name would help. Well, I won't marry him. No matter what I have to do."

There was only one answer to her multitude of questions. Her fiancé must be as old and cross as the women she and Zack had interviewed to be her companion. Darcie's life, her youth, would be wasted on an elderly gentleman who, more likely than not, needed a nurse more than he needed a wife.

Darcie walked to the west window and looked out over Charleston, as much as she could see from there. She loved the port city. It always bustled with activity, and now that she was no longer in mourning, she wanted to be a part of it. There were new people moving here every day, interesting people who gave wonderful parties. She'd listened to Em and Patty describe the social events for too long, and now she wanted to be in the middle of every exciting minute.

She'd wanted to do more than read the books of Mr. William Gilmore Simms who'd written several romances, wonderful novels based on historical fact. He had appeared at several small dinners Darcie had attended, and she'd listened intently to his every word, having read *Katherine Walton* and *The Yemassee* several times. She particularly liked *Katherine Walton* because it was a love story set right here in Charleston—the city she'd been forced to close herself away from—during the Revolution.

Darcie wanted to go to the races. Just out of mourning, she'd never attended the races at the Jockey Club. The events of race week in February had been forbidden to her. However, now that she was out of mourning, she had looked forward to next February's festivities.

What a goose you are, Uncle Talbot, she thought. *You've ruined my life from the distance of thousands of miles.*

Her life wasn't really ruined. France might prove to be exciting, too, she conceded. Especially with Zack around.

The door to her bedroom opened and Charity poked her head in. "I thought it wuz you. Howcum you left that pie safe open? First thing, bugs be crawlin' out the yard lookin' for dat sweet smell." She noticed the empty plate on the floor by Darcie's chair. "And, you et pie for breakfast? What de matter wif you?"

Darcie made a face, got up, and walked over to her dressing table. "Pooh."

"Jus' the same, you ought'n to be eatin' it dis early." Charity opened the door further and came in. "An howcum you runnin' lickety split 'cross White Point Gardens last night like you wuz bein chased by a striped haint? I seen you mysef. An where wuz that Frenchie what took you? Howcum he didn't bring you home?"

Darcie didn't want to answer questions about Zack. Not yet. She picked up her silver brush and drew it through her long golden hair.

"Charity, get my bath ready. I want to send a note to Em and Patty. I want them to come over this morning." She saw Charity's eyes narrow, as if she would refuse to move before her questions were answered. "Now go on. I don't have a minute to spare."

"Tell me everything about St. Cecilia's Ball," Darcie said breathlessly, hoping that Patty and Em wouldn't think she'd gone mad. "I want to know everything."

Patty and Em glanced at each other and then stared blankly at Darcie. Em narrowed her eyes and tilted her head to one side, studying Darcie's face. "Why the sudden interest? You hadn't even considered the ball a real event until now."

"Yes, you've been awfully cool about the ball," Patty added.

Darcie felt her face color. She didn't want to stir their curiosity by appearing to be too interested all of a sudden. "Don't be silly. Just because I refuse to get hysterically involved in it, doesn't mean I'm not interested."

"She's right, Em." Patty shook her head in agreement. "After all she's never been to a St. Cecilia's Ball."

"Yes, but there's something else." Em continued to study her.

Em knew Darcie well, perhaps better than anybody else except Charity. Any minute now, Darcie expected Em to connect the sudden change in her demeanor to Zack. She couldn't allow that to happen.

"I'm going to have a party—a big party. The Gaynor ballroom hasn't been used in years," Darcie announced. "A goodbye to Charleston party."

"Wonderful. I love parties," Em exclaimed happily, moving to the window of Darcie's small sitting room. She held back the heavy curtain and peered into the street below. "I hope you invite the elegant M. Manville."

Darcie ignored Em's reference to Zack. She had to. After last night, she couldn't talk about him—not yet, and especially not to Em who picked up every nuance. "I'll even invite Chad Rutledge!"

Em laughed and returned to her seat. "What fun! I hear he's been a little subdued since he nearly lost his boat."

"Now, Em," Patty chided with a glint of mischief in her green eyes, "you know perfectly well that Chad's been ill."

"Yes. Sick because he almost lost that precious boat." Darcie giggled, setting the last stitch in the napkin she was embroidering.

"You know, Darcie," Em chatted amiably, picking up her needlework and staring very deliberately at the stitches already set. "Barclay's very angry with Zack."

"Why should he be angry with Zack?" Darcie asked and stacked the napkin on top of the others she'd finished. Taking another from the fresh stack, she eyed Em carefully. She didn't want to miss anything. Em often said things in passing that helped Darcie solve a problem with Bar.

Em cut her eyes at Darcie and then said, "He's angry over the little episode with the street woman you told him about last night."

Darcie put down her workbasket so hard the neat stack of napkins toppled over. "What a silly billy he is. I only mentioned it because I found it so amusing. I thought he would, too."

"I suppose not." Em put down her sewing and took a sip of lemonade. She picked up one of Darcie's completed napkins. The neat roses were blush pink on damask, as elegant as any to be found. "I declare, Darcie, you set the neatest stitches in Charleston. I don't know how you do it." She looked up from the napkin. "You should have seen him when you left with Zack."

Darcie flushed and stared at her hands. Barclay's anger had been ill-disguised, but she had chosen to ignore it. She'd also detected the signs of jealousy—once reserved for Chad or perhaps Gideon on occasion.

"He'll get over it," Patty answered for Darcie. "He always does. Remember when Chad gave Darcie the little boat? Barclay was furious."

Darcie looked at the little white boat on the mantel. It had been there at least two years. For about six years, she'd kept it on the mantel in the parlor, but the nasty glances it always got from Barclay finally convinced her that it might actually be in danger. "It's been here so long that I hardly even look at it anymore."

"Well, Bar never forgot it," Em pronounced emphatically. "Gideon took it pretty well."

"He's never been jealous." Patty didn't bother to look up. The argument was an old one. Both girls' brothers adored Darcie and had vied for her attention since they were barely out of the cradle.

"Neither is Bar. He's . . ." Em searched for the right word to defend her brother. "He's . . ."

"Jealous," Patty finished for her. "Too jealous. Imagine how angry he was when Em told him about your upcoming marriage."

Darcie's mouth fell open. "Em! You didn't tell him! You couldn't."

Em averted her eyes and chewed a fingernail. "I didn't mean to, Darcie. It just slipped out."

"Slipped out?" Darcie's voice rose in anger. "How could you do a thing like that? You promised not to tell anyone."

"Really, Darcie, don't make such a fuss," Patty said soothingly. "I'm sure she never meant to break her promise."

Darcie's glare silenced Patty and she turned her rage on Em. "I told you I wanted to tell Barclay myself. How could you? You know how he is."

"I'm really sorry." Em fidgeted in her chair. "Don't be angry with me. I'm so sorry."

"Forget it. It's done." Patty smiled brightly and changed the subject. "What does your new gown look like, Em? Did you select that ginger-colored taffeta you wanted so badly?"

Emilie Rhett ignored her friend and turned her attention back to Darcie. "Say, Darcie, do you—"

Jasper stepped into the sitting room and interrupted her before she could finish her question. "Miss Darcie?"

"Yes, Jasper. What is it?"

"Mr. Rhett here to see you."

"Barclay? At this time of day?" Darcie glanced at Em. "Whatever does he want."

Em averted her eyes. "I'm sure I don't know."

Em was lying—Darcie could tell by the pinched look around her eyes and the controlled tone of her voice. "Well, I'll just go and see. I apologize, ladies, for the intrusion."

Darcie rose and walked from the room. As she closed the door, she hesitated. Inside, Em and Patty giggled as if they were privy to some secret that excluded Darcie. Well, she didn't have time to waste on their foolishness. She knew better than to keep Bar waiting when he was already angry, so Darcie hurried down the stairs. She wished Em hadn't told him about the marriage contract. Darcie had wanted to tell him, gently when they were alone.

Pausing a few seconds in front of the gilt-framed mirror in the foyer, she inhaled deeply. Bar wouldn't be easy to handle if he were still angry. She opened the parlor doors and walked in as if she was ignorant of his emotional state.

"Good morning, Bar," she said briskly as she strode across the room to him.

"Darcie! You look lovely. The petals of the fairest rose pale by your beauty." He hurried to meet her and took both her hands in his. Without hesitating he kissed her gently on the cheek.

"Please be seated, Bar." Wondering about his sudden passionate outburst, Darcie moved to the nearest chair and sat on the rose brocade cushion. Since Zack had arrived, Bar seemed to find opportunities to touch her far more frequently than before. "Em and Patty are upstairs and—"

"Dash Em and Patty!" He turned away from her and stared through the open window. "It's such a lovely day, let's walk in the garden."

"Bar, I have guests upstairs," she reminded him gently, wondering what had gotten into him. He didn't care a fig for the lovely gardens of Charleston.

"Darcie, please come along." He stepped to her side and touched her shoulder, tracing his fingers along her prominent bones. "I've come about a matter of extreme urgency."

"All right." Darcie stood and took Barclay's arm.

They walked through the open window, across the side piazza, and down the steps. Neat rows of brick set out the path that led through the garden beneath an arched trellis covered with wild roses.

They followed the path to the little grotto of live oak trees in the back of the garden and sat down on the stone bench. Darcie waited for Bar to speak, knowing she was about to receive a lecture on propriety. Bar had made no secret of the fact that he didn't like the intimate banter that took place between Darcie and Zack. His jealousy tarnished every thought of Zack with indelible hatred, and nothing she did changed his attitude. To cover his jealousy, Bar usually substituted another problem which could cause a change in her behavior and thereby alleviate the situation.

Bar rose and paced about in the small clearing. He leaned across a low-hanging limb of a live oak and gazed at her for a moment as if he were trying to gather his thoughts. Darcie waited patiently for the lecture. There was no way to hurry his words.

The faint fragrance of jasmine floated on the gentle breeze that stirred the narrow leaves of the live oaks and rattled the swordlike spikes of the palmetto trees. Darcie's patience came to an end. If he didn't know what he wanted to say, then he could come back later. "Bar—"

"Please, don't interrupt me." He bent and walked under the limb, stopping a few feet short of Darcie. His shoulders squared and his chest heaved and fell as he apparently tried to decide how to broach the subject he wanted to discuss. "Darcie, it cannot have escaped your attention that my affection for you has grown stronger over the past few years. I haven't spoken about this before, because of your deep mourning for your dear departed father."

Darcie stared at him in abject disbelief. Barclay Rhett intended to propose marriage to her after all these years! This wasn't going to be just another lecture. She felt the color creep into her cheeks. Barclay knew she would have to refuse because of this silly marriage contract. So why was he asking?

Although she knew that she should stop him before he said something he'd feel foolish about later, she was so stunned that she could hardly breathe. Talking was out of the question.

For many years, everyone had assumed that she and Barclay would one day marry, but he had never hinted that he intended to ask today, particularly since her betrothal was no secret. She thought back over the past few weeks and realized that he had become more possessive, more jealous. But he'd always been like that. Darcie looked up at him as he labored under the weight of his task.

"And, so, Darcie, I wish you to know that I shall endeavor to be as fine a husband as you will be a wife." Barclay knelt before her and took her hand. "I love you, Darcie. Will you make me the happiest of all men and marry me?"

"Barclay, you . . . you have surprised me with your passionate offer." Darcie began to flounder for words. What could she say? "As you may have surmised, I hold you in the highest regard and have always considered you to be one of my dearest friends. However, I fear that I must decline your gracious offer because of a previous commitment made by my guardian, as you know. Of course, I am prevented from forming any liaison on my own."

The lines were deepening around Barclay's mouth and his chin began to jut out. His anger was intensifying, and there was nothing Darcie could do to prevent it. She continued, hoping her gentle words would soften the blow. "I am deeply honored that you have asked me to be your wife, and shall always cherish the memory of this moment, as I do your friendship."

Barclay jumped to his feet and spun away from her. He paced back and forth across the sandy clearing without speaking for several minutes. Darcie began to wonder what he was going to do next, but allowed him the courtesy of responding without interruption.

Finally, he stopped pacing and whirled to face her. "Darcie, you must see that this will never work out. You . . . you cannot marry a man you've never met. Your father and I . . . well, we—"

"My father is gone, Barclay," Darcie reminded him gently. "And my uncle is my guardian, whether I like it or not."

"Guardian be damned! He's thousands of miles away," Barclay exclaimed, pacing back and forth beside the live oaks and azaleas. Suddenly, he snatched a handful of blossoms and shredded them, leaving a pile of bruised fuschia petals to scatter in the wind. "What do we care about him?"

"He manages my business as well as my private life, Bar." Darcie could only answer his objections with calm resolve.

Agreeing with him would only serve to prolong his disappointment.

"And none too well, if the rumors I hear are accurate." Barclay rushed to her side and sat down, taking her hands in his. "Darcie, let me take care of you. I know you and love you. You can't marry a man who cares nothing for you."

"No, Bar. You're right. I can't marry someone I don't love." Even though she wouldn't marry the gentleman waiting for her in France, she still couldn't marry Barclay. But she couldn't tell him that. He had to believe that her commitments prevented their marriage, or his self-esteem would be ruined.

"Then that settles it." Barclay leaped up and stood looking down at her. "I'll see Manville this afternoon and make the arrangements."

"What arrangements?" Darcie gazed at him with much concern. He wasn't making any sense to her.

"I'll book passage on his ship for the trip to France. Em can go along as your companion." He started pacing again. "Yes, that's it. Em can serve as your companion, and I shall accompany you to speak with your uncle."

Darcie rose, feeling the air whoosh out of her lungs. Barclay's ideas were coming much too fast and were totally unwanted. "Barclay, you must see that—"

He drew her close and kissed her hair. "Don't worry about anything, darling. From this moment on, I shall assume control of your life. You have nothing to fear."

"Barclay, you—" Darcie began, but was interrupted by a deep masculine voice coming from behind her.

"I'm dreadfully sorry, but that's quite impossible." Zack stepped into the clearing and strode to join them by the stone bench. "You see, I am Darcie's acting guardian until she reaches France."

"What is the meaning of this?" Barclay stepped away from Darcie and stood between her and Zack.

"Simply that Talbot Neville has passed responsibility for Miss Gaynor to me until we reach France." Zack moved to Darcie's side protectively. His stride brought him within reach of Barclay, but Zack ignored him and took Darcie's arm. "I must say, M. Rhett, that I am appalled that you would ask a dutiful niece to go against her guardian's wishes."

"And I, M. Manville, find her uncle's wishes to be rather ludicrous, considering the lack of care he's shown over the past few years."

Zack privately agreed. Talbot Neville should have rushed to America on the first boat leaving France after he received word of his brother-in-law's death. Leaving Miss Gaynor in the hands of a few servants for three years was inexcusable. "And, I fear, M. Rhett, that the way M. Neville chooses to administer—"

"Administer? What a joke." Barclay threw back his head and laughed. Although the sound that came out could hardly be called a laugh, it was so sharp and piercing. "You probably know as well as I that Neville is ruining Gaynor Shipping."

"If that is the case, it is still of no concern to you." Zack grew tired of this useless bickering. "Furthermore, I feel that you owe an apology to Miss Gaynor for your actions this afternoon."

"Apology? How dare you suggest—"

"Zack! He owes me no apology." Darcie touched Zack's arm. He looked down at her and their eyes met. The world disappeared from around them. The memory of their kiss blasted everything else from her consciousness, and the two stood locked in a warm world of fantasy. It was so vivid. In that moment, Darcie could almost feel the pressure of his lips on hers, could almost smell the fresh scent of his soap.

"Damned if I'll let a fast-talking Frenchman keep me from what's mine." Barclay moved toward the house. "Manville, I want passage on your boat. Em will be Darcie's companion. I shall go to make sure she arrives safely—if you understand my meaning."

"I understand you completely. Far better than you understand yourself, M. Rhett." Zack gazed at him with sad understanding. "You and Miss Rhett shall sail as my guests."

"Hah! I refuse to accept the hospitality of . . . of a gentleman such as yourself." Barclay fairly spat the words and the smile that followed was hardly more than a narrow line below his nose.

"Really? Then, I am afraid that you shall have to find other accommodations." Zack smiled, knowing that he held the upper hand. Barclay wanted to sail with Darcie and would do anything to be on Zack's ship.

"You leave me no choice, sir." Barclay gritted his teeth and glared at Zack. "And, in the future, I'd be delighted if you'd make your presence known, rather than lurking about in shadows and eavesdropping on private conversations." He strode out of the garden without waiting for Zack to respond.

"Delightful fellow," Zack remarked as he watched Barclay leave. "I suppose he means well. He seems to be enamored of you."

"You know that you shouldn't have baited him that way." Darcie tried to defend her friend, but she knew Zack was right about him. He should never have asked for her hand, knowing that she was already engaged.

"He deserved it and more. The idea of his trying to influence a maiden to go against her guardian's wishes is appalling, but quite understandable." Zack smiled at her.

Damn, but women were a complicated lot. Why couldn't she have been someone he could have claimed as his mistress? That would have worked perfectly. Napoleon himself would have turned green with envy when Zack presented Darcie to the Court.

Zack gazed back at her. Darcie was certainly lovely. But, she was different from any woman he'd ever known. The more he thought about Barclay's idea, the better he liked it. However, he'd remain silent on that point until the time was right. He wasn't ready to surrender the tender moments he'd experience with her just yet. "Well, I stopped by to see if you wanted to attend the interviews this afternoon. But, as of just now, that matter has been taken care of."

"This way will be much better, Zack." Darcie sounded as enthusiastic as she could. Even though she liked the idea of having Em along as her companion, she didn't relish the idea of having Barclay, too. His threat to speak to Uncle Talbot would make matters worse for her. "When can I see the compartment in which Em and I shall live during the crossing?"

"This very day," Zack replied. "If you wish, Em may come along, too."

"Em!" Darcie lifted her skirts and strode toward the house. "Come along, Zack. Em and Patty are in my sitting room."

Zack followed her across the garden and up the steps. Above him, her trim ankles tantalized him as she sped onward. *Damn a woman for torturing a man like that,* he thought.

"Wait in the parlor," Darcie called over her shoulder as she raced up the stairs. "Jasper!" she yelled and paused at the landing.

The black man appeared from a doorway and peered up the stairs. "Yas'm."

"See that M. Manville is comfortable in the parlor and bring a pitcher of lemonade and some tea cakes. The ones with chocolate. I'll bring the ladies down to join us."

"Yas'm." Jasper shuffled toward Zack and opened the parlor door. "Here you go, Mr. Manville, sir. I be right back with the lemonade."

Zack watched the servant leave. He was deep in thought over some of the things Barclay had said in the garden. Apparently, it was common knowledge that Talbot knew nothing about running the Gaynor Shipping Company, and that if something wasn't done soon, the company would perish.

That couldn't happen. Zack owed it to Darcie to prevent such a catastrophe. When they arrived in France, he'd speak with Talbot—perhaps give him an ultimatum. If nothing else relieved the problem, then he'd just have to marry her.

Zack considered this idea. As much as he wanted to avoid marital entanglements, the idea of combining Gaynor Shipping and Manville Trading appealed to him. With offices in Charleston and in Paris, the new company would rule the trading seas. People were emigrating to America in droves these days; Manville and Gaynor could set up more space for passengers, expand their services.

Would such a venture be worth giving up his freedom? He looked at the portrait over the piano. His gaze took in every line, every curve, the tiny dimple, the full sensuous lips, the bright expectant eyes. The portrait of Darcie was one of a woman crossing the threshold from girlhood into womanhood. If he did have to sacrifice his freedom, such a woman might make it more pleasant.

He remembered his lips pressed against hers last night and felt a stiffening in his groin. Had she stayed with him, locked in his embrace, for a moment longer, he would have been unable to restrain his emotions. He wanted her, wanted her in the worst kind of way.

You're no better than the scum of the street, he chided himself. *She's a delicately brought up young lady, just out of mourning, with little experience. You can't seduce her and drop her without another thought.*

"Zack. I'm sorry we took so long." Darcie threw the doors open wide and the three girls joined Zack in the parlor.

"Oh, yes," Em purred, lifting her hand to allow Zack to kiss it. "If we'd known you were here, we'd have been down ever so quickly. I do hope you aren't angry with us."

Darcie rolled her eyes and wondered how Em could gush like that. It was so silly.

"Yes, M. Manville," Patty added. "We're delighted to see you again so soon."

Zack glanced at Darcie. She seemed to be irritated about something. Could she be angry over last night's kiss while on the Battery? She hadn't said anything when they were alone, although he knew she was concerned over the little scene with Barclay.

Darcie listened to the light banter among her guests with a little annoyance. Em was infuriating at times. The fluttering of Em's long black lashes almost caused Darcie to groan aloud. How could she be so transparent? If Zack didn't realize what the twit was doing, then he deserved to be saddled with her for life.

For life? Darcie hesitated. She didn't want Em paired with Zack for life. Her stomach turned at the thought. She'd miss the delightful play they enjoyed. She longed for him to kiss her again as he had last night. She longed to feel her breasts crushed against his hard chest.

Her three friends laughed and drew her attention once again. Blushing, she asked them to be seated and hurried from the room to check on the lemonade and tea cakes. She pulled the double doors closed behind her and leaned heavily against them, hoping to shut out the image of Em in Zack's arms.

He wouldn't dare! Was he the kind of man to trifle with her affections and then flee to Em's waiting arms? Did he find Em more attractive? Was her conversation more stimulating? A new sensation welled up in Darcie, flavoring her mouth like bile, and she shook her head slightly to destroy the image of them together, arms locked about each other's waists, their lips passionately open in a breathless kiss that refused to end in her mind.

"You sick, Miss Darcie?"

Darcie's eyes flew open and color sprang to her cheeks as Jasper approached bearing a silver tray laden with sweets and lemonade. "No," she whispered. "Just thinking. That's all."

Jasper nodded, but didn't appear to be convinced. Darcie knew that by this evening the entire household would know of her momentary lapse and would pamper her as if she were a sick child. She straightened. Charity would most certainly dose her with a vile spoonful of castor oil.

Chapter Seven

Darcie dressed carefully for St. Cecilia's Ball. Em and Patty would be arriving at any moment to help with the final preparations. The cherry silk looked wonderful with Darcie's coloring. Her blonde hair hung in ringlets down her neck and had an artful display of pearls pinning it back on one side.

"Gracious, I was right, wasn't I, Patty?" Em asked when they entered the room. "I told you she would have the most beautiful gown in all of Charleston."

"Oh my, it certainly is." Patty ran her fingers along the delicate silk skirt. "It makes me look like a milkmaid."

"You two are the silliest girls in the city." Darcie took her shawl from Charity and glanced once again at her reflection. She did look more vibrant, more alive than usual, although she was just getting used to seeing herself in colors rather than the severe black, white, or gray of mourning. "Both of you are lovely."

They began to discuss the upcoming dance. Darcie listened eagerly, feeling her palms dampen with anticipation. She was secretly glad that Zack had insisted on escorting her instead of allowing Barclay to do so, even though Barclay was incensed. They were going to ride in the same carriage, which did little to assuage Barclay's jealousy. Darcie felt that Zack was tormenting poor Bar every chance he got.

Charity opened the door. "All them gempmum's is in the parlor struttin' like peacocks in they finery. I b'lieve you better git down there 'fore the feathers start to fly."

Darcie agreed. If Barclay's disposition hadn't improved since she saw him last, then the chance of a duel was great.

She allowed her friends to enter the parlor before her as she gave last-minute instructions to Charity for the late supper party. They'd all be famished after an evening of dancing. A light meal of roasted oysters, stuffed flounder, and shrimp gumbo would be well deserved. In addition to her friends in the parlor, Darcie had invited many other Charlestonians to her late supper. With time so short, she hadn't had time to prepare for a true ball, the sort of gathering she really wanted, so this party would have to serve as her good-bye to Charleston.

When Darcie entered the parlor, she heard a gasp. She turned quickly to see who had uttered the sound, but found no evidence to make that determination. Still, she was delighted.

Zack stepped forward and took her hand, kissing it briefly. His eyes met hers, and she understood the admiration conveyed by them. "You look positively stunning."

"Yes," Barclay interrupted, moving closer and kissing her cheek. "Doesn't she?"

The situation was awkward to say the least. Barclay stood with his arm draped over her shoulder and Zack still held her hand.

She disengaged herself from both of them. "Thank you, gentlemen. How good to see you."

Moving easily past them, she extended her hand to Gideon. "It's good to see you, too, dear Gideon."

"You are lovely, my dear Darcie." Gideon kissed the back of her hand gently. "I am delighted to be in your company."

With an air of excitement among the girls and a jealous tension among the men, the party left for St. Andrews Hall. A short trip, to Darcie, who was eager to arrive, it seemed to last forever.

Darcie smiled at Zack and took his arm as they stepped into the throng of people at St. Andrews Hall. At one end of the hall, the St. Cecilia's Society orchestra was playing a lively tune and the dance floor was already crowded with subscribers and their guests.

Placing her hand in his, she allowed him to sweep her around the gleaming floor beneath a chandelier boasting hundreds of white candles. Silks and satins of every color swirled and rustled about her, but she saw and heard only one thing—Zacharie Manville. She tilted her head back and closed her eyes, allowing herself to feel the music as her skirts billowed out behind her, like a rose opening its petals to the sun.

The golden glow of candlelight accented his sun-bronzed skin as they whirled about the ornate hall. Darcie pretended not to see the rage paint Barclay's face a scarlet far more brilliant than the reddest ball gown, and she ignored the look of envy in Em's eyes as she sipped punch on a gilt chair placed along one wall.

The scent of gardenias enveloped her, and she sighed happily. Her first St. Cecilia's Ball was going to be memorable.

When the music stopped, Darcie expected Zack to lead her to the small group of her friends gathered at one end of the room, but he waited for the orchestra to resume playing and they whirled across the floor again. His right hand rested lightly on her back and his face was inches from hers as they waltzed.

Zack was a skilled partner who sensed the rhythm of the music delightfully and led her through the dances one after another. If she could have had one wish, it would have been for the night never to end.

Staring down at Darcie's dreamy face, Zack felt a pang of guilt. He well knew that he should take her to join her friends, but he couldn't abide the barbs he knew would come from Barclay Rhett. Ever since they'd arrived, Rhett had glowered at them from over a glass of punch, spiked no doubt with a stronger brew, perhaps rum, that would enhance his image of himself.

And, Zack admitted reluctantly, he wanted Darcie all to himself. This frock she wore enhanced every slim curve of her body and the color was by far the most becoming he'd seen her wear. Barclay Rhett had every right to be jealous. Darcie was the most beautiful woman at the ball.

He looked down at her again. Her eyes were closed and burnished golden lashes rested on her creamy skin. Her lips were parted slightly, as they had been that night on the Battery when he'd kissed her. He longed to kiss her again, to hold her in his arms and to comfort her, to lift the weight she bore on her slight shoulders to his own, to adore her as she deserved to be adored.

Feeling the discomfort rise in his loins, he realized he was holding her more closely than propriety dictated, but he was powerless to stop. He wanted to crush her to him, to claim her as his own. Her eyes opened, deep sapphire, almost violet dreamy orbs stared at him. Zack realized that they had nearly stopped on the dance floor.

"Ahem," he thought for something to say, anything to cover his embarrassment. "Perhaps we should join the others for a rest. Could I get you a glass of punch?"

For a moment, Darcie couldn't speak. She'd been pressed against him too closely. Embarrassment scattered color in her cheeks. He would think she was extremely forward. "Thank you. Punch would be nice."

They threaded their way to the edge of the floor and slowly walked through the mingling crowd until they reached Patty and Barclay. From the expression on Barclay's face, Darcie knew he was furious.

Patty glanced at Bar and then at Darcie and Zack. "Well, you two certainly look wonderful together on the dance floor. Don't they, Barclay?"

"What?" Barclay looked a bit panicky at the calling of his name. "Oh, yes," he answered with clipped words.

"Oh, I'm exhausted," Darcie said and sat down beside Patty. "Where are Em and Gideon?"

"Dancing together," Patty replied. "They watched you two for a while and then off they went."

Zack looked down at Darcie. "If you don't mind waiting, I'll get us a glass of punch."

"I'll be happy to wait." Darcie smiled and settled her skirts about her. "Isn't it lovely, Patty? I never dreamed of anything so wonderful."

"It's grand. I can't think when I've had such a delightful evening." Patty glared pointedly at Barclay.

"Yes." Barclay stood and smiled a rather snide smile. "It has been an enlightening evening at that. Darcie, would you care to dance?"

"Well, Bar," Darcie began, wondering what she should say. Zack would undoubtedly expect to find her here when he returned with the punch.

"I won't accept a refusal. You've danced with Manville all evening, leaving hardly any time to me." He took her hand and pulled her to her feet. "Come. We'll show Charleston how to dance."

Barclay proved to be a somewhat less skillful dancer than Zack. At first, Darcie thought his lacked of ability sprang from his anger, but she soon decided that he lack the innate grace of Zack, and the smell of whiskey was strong on his breath. But, his conversation soon lightened and his steps were tolerably well placed, and she found herself enjoying herself. She loved dancing—with anybody.

Over Barclay's shoulder, she could see Zack staring at the dancers, trying to locate the two of them on the floor. From the tight line of his lips, she knew he was put out to have returned and found her gone.

Darcie smiled. It wouldn't hurt to let Zack wonder what was going on. He was too confident, far too confident. She straightened her back and stared. Em reached up and touched Zack's face, and he was looking down at her and smiling.

"That Frenchman is infuriating," Barclay said, tightening his grip on Darcie and pulling her closer in his arms. "He has no right to monopolize you as he has. You'd think *he* was your fiancé."

"Now, Barclay," Darcie began, a little irritated that he was

sitting in judgment of the other man. She tried to look over
Barclay's shoulder to see what Em and Zack were doing, but
was positioned so that she couldn't see anything beyond the
whirling dancers. "He's merely doing as my uncle requested
him."

"I don't think so." Barclay swung her around so he could
watch Zack more closely. "That man is up to no good. Why
else would he have accepted Em as a companion for you so
quickly?"

Darcie rolled her eyes. "Perhaps because you gave him no
choice. Or because we could find no other suitable companion
on such short notice."

"Well, I think it's suspicious to say the least." Barclay stepped
on her toe. "Sorry, my dear, I'm not usually this clumsy. He just
makes me so angry the way he hangs around you all the time."

"Barclay, I'm sure this is just as distasteful for him as for
you." Darcie wondered what she could say to placate her friend.
"After all, he was coming here on business and Uncle Talbot
asked him to bring me to Paris, along with all the other problems . . ."

"And, you think he's doing this merely out of a sense of duty
to your uncle?" Barclay's voice rose and he stopped dancing.

Darcie flushed. Several people nearby were staring at them.
"Shhh. You're making a spectacle of us."

Barclay glanced around, glaring at some of the more inquisi-
tive-looking people. "Come on. Let's get out of here for a
minute. It's too hot."

"Barclay, I don't think—"

He didn't stop to listen, but dragged her off the dance floor,
out the front door, and down Broad Street toward King Street.
Darcie looked back at the lights gleaming through the arched
windows of St. Andrews Hall and wondered if Zack would
follow them, and what he would do, if he did.

"Barclay, we must return. The others—"

"Blast the others." They reached the house of Barclay's aunt,
Hilda Rhett, and he opened the gate. "Come in here. We'll talk
privately a moment without that . . . without interference."

"But, Barclay, what will people think?" Darcie hung back, trying to dissuade him from proceeding further into the garden. "Really, we must go back."

"Don't be difficult, Darcie." He pulled her on with him to the little bench in the garden.

At any other time, Darcie would have been captivated by the lovely garden, but at this moment, she was angry at Barclay for his lack of consideration of her reputation. "Barclay, I insist. Take me back at once."

He drew her into his arms. "I have the solution to our problem, Darcie, my love."

"We have no problem, other than the fact that you are no gentleman." Darcie pushed against his chest, and strained backwards to avoid his kiss. "Please, Barclay, stop at once!"

His lips met hers in an unrelenting kiss, hard and long. "There. I've done it. Now we must marry."

"What an absurd idea." Darcie slapped him soundly. She hoped that he could see her face in the moonlight as well as she could see his. She wanted him to see how angry she was. "How dare you drag me out here and take advantage of me like this. Where is your sensitivity? Have you gone mad?"

"I am mad for you, dearest Darcie. When we see your uncle, I will tell him of our indiscretion and he will allow us to marry."

"Even if *he* should allow it, *I* would refuse." Darcie wriggled in his arms, trying to escape. "If you think I'd marry you after this mauling, then—"

"Mauling? After we've made love, you'll not call it a mauling." Barclay kissed her again, holding her head in position with a grip of steel.

Panic rose in Darcie. Made love? Did he intend to make love to her here in his aunt's garden? She renewed her struggle. Her hands were useless against his strength. With a viciousness she never realized she possessed, Darcie bit his lips as hard as she could.

"Damn you, for a feisty wench," he cried, touching his lips

with his hand. A dark stain showed on his hand when he took it away. "Damn. Damn. I'm bleeding!"

"And so you should." Zack's voice penetrated the silence around them. "If she hadn't done such a resounding job of drawing your blood, I'd do so myself."

Barclay mopped at the blood with his handkerchief, but several drops had fallen on his shirt and the spots were spreading in dark circles. "You've an uncanny way of popping up where you're not wanted, Manville."

"And you've a way of taking advantage of my ward when my back is turned." Zack drew Darcie into the protective circle of his arms. Deep lines furrowed his forehead, crinkling his eyes at the corners until they were barely visible. "I forbid you to attempt to be alone with her again. If you persist in this folly, I'll toss you overboard before we're well out of Charleston Harbor."

"Now just a minute—" Barclay began, starting toward Zack.

"You wait just a minute." Zack glared at him with such a menacing look that Barclay stopped without taking another step. "Miss Gaynor and I are returning to the ball. In your present condition, I know she is quite willing to excuse you from dinner this evening."

"Excuse—"

"Good evening, M. Rhett." Zack took Darcie's arm and began walking toward the street. "Come, Darcie, I've a mind to dance the night away with the loveliest of Charleston's damsels."

Darcie allowed herself to be led away. She said nothing to Barclay, not trusting herself to speak to him civilly. Her conversation with him could wait until the effects of the liquor had worn off.

Zack said nothing for most of the walk along Broad Street, but finally stopped about a half a block from St. Andrews Hall. His voice held a quiver of rage that he seldom allowed to show. "Are you hurt, my dear? Did he, well, what I mean to say is, did he, well, you weren't hurt, were you?"

"No," Darcie said, gravely, wondering what kind of scolding she would get for allowing such a breach of etiquette to occur.

"When I think . . . that bastard, beg your pardon, the nerve of him to . . . I can't imagine anyone acting like that, particularly not a Southern gentleman." Zack looked down into her eyes, glittering in the soft moonlight. His fury diminished and his lips softened into a smile.

At first, he'd thought she left of her own accord. He'd raced from the hall intent on chastising her for her conduct, but when he'd witnessed the biting incident, a little of his humor returned. She was a spunky girl who had a strong sense of right and wrong, and he should have known that she wouldn't allow a man like Barclay Rhett to take liberties and go unpunished, even though they were friends.

His admiration for her increased. Many young women would have become hysterical after the scene he'd witnessed, but not Darcie. Her chin was high, and her sense of humor had returned, too. The sparkle had returned to her eye, and the smile to her face. The sweet innocence, her complete lack of guile touched him, and he pulled her close, holding her to his breast as if to comfort a child.

"Thank God, I arrived in time," he whispered against her soft golden curls. "When I think of what might have happened, I'm distraught."

Darcie drew back and looked into his eyes. Her smile was genuine, born of affection for the man she'd known for so short a time. He took his position as her temporary guardian seriously, so seriously that he was condemning himself for allowing this to happen. "You have nothing to fear, Zack. Don't blame yourself. I am to blame for—"

"Dash it, Darcie, you are not to blame." He held her at arm's length and gazed at her in amazement. She was taking the blame for that imbecile's, that reprobate's behavior. "The blame in this matter rests with Barclay Rhett and myself. Him for drinking beyond his capacity to think clearly, and me for not watching you more closely. Rest assured that this will not happen again. I shall protect you."

"Please, Zack, you should understand that for years Barclay has considered me as his future bride." How could she explain the deep disappointment she knew Barclay felt? Even though she didn't love Barclay except as a friend, she realized that he had expected to marry her, and that her father would probably have consented if he had lived.

"Don't defend his actions. He doesn't deserve your loyalty." The fierce lines returned to Zack's forehead and drew his face into a scowl. "I'll be glad when we're rid of him for good."

Darcie realized that reasoning with Zack was as impossible as trying to reason with Barclay. Both men were extremely stubborn, and Barclay was jealous in addition to being obstinate. The trip across the Atlantic should prove interesting at the least.

"Zack, Barclay had, well, been drinking rather heavily." Darcie felt bound to defend her friend, even though his behavior was reprehensible. A cool breeze rattled the palmetto behind her, and somewhere in the distance a nightingale sang along with the music filtering from St. Andrews Hall a few steps away.

Zack gazed down at her. Yes, she would defend Rhett—she was a loyal friend. Zack wondered if she would be as quick to his defense if he had done the same thing. As a matter of fact, he had—almost. Looking at her, with her face turned up expectantly to his, he wanted to kiss her again, to flush the memory of Barclay from her mind.

Suddenly, Zack stared at her. Could she have actually enjoyed the kiss Rhett had foisted upon her? Could she secretly be enjoying his caresses above Zack's? Impossible. He'd felt her response to him that night on the Battery. Anger blew the memory from his mind. "Darcie, I forbid you to be alone with that man again. Do you understand?"

"You . . . how dare you? Just who do—" Anger flew over her like the wings of a thousand crows, black and suffocating, and Darcie stopped her tirade in mid-sentence.

"Now, look. He isn't to be trusted." Zack sought the words to convince her of Barclay's deviousness. "He's, well, Darcie, he's a man, subject to certain . . . tendencies. And you are newly out of mourning and unaccustomed to the ways of men of the world."

"Zacharie Manville, Barclay has been my friend for many years." For once, the scent of jasmine did nothing to improve her mood. In spite of her present animosity toward Barclay, she felt compelled to explain his actions to Zack. Although she didn't love Barclay, she understood his feelings of abandonment. "I have not been as secluded as you may believe, although I have not attended balls and parties. My life has been sheltered during this time, but I'm hardly just out of the schoolroom."

"Of course, of course." Zack hadn't intended to make her angry with him. He merely wanted to warn her and now his good intentions seemed to be backfiring. "Please accept my advice as it was intended. You are a lovely young woman and will be the target of many fortune hunters as well as those of even less savory reputations."

"Zack, please don't worry." Darcie's frown softened into the beginnings of a smile as she picked a leaf absently from the low-hanging live oak sheltering them. "I can take care of myself."

"That's what I'm trying to tell you. You don't have to anymore." He pressed her closer and rubbed his hand gently across her back in an attempt to comfort her. The texture of her silk dress over the firm planes of her back beneath his hands was tantalizing and the scent of violets surrounded him like a soft mist evoking memories of their first kiss. "Darcie, I'm here now and . . ."

Darcie waited expectantly. She began to understand his meaning. He would protect her. He would fight her foes. Zack wanted her to know that she could rely on him, could rest from the weight of having to fend for herself all this time. He must think she was truly helpless. Her smile widened at the serious expression furrowing his brow, and she touched his face with her fingers. "Zack, I . . ."

Her words, too, dwindled off and were whisked away by the evening breeze. Silence enveloped them. The nightingale stopped singing; the palmetto stopped whispering; the music stopped playing.

Darcie and Zack were alone in the street, their eyes locked in wonder. *He's going to kiss me,* she thought, and parted her lips slightly. Her tongue traced along the inside of her lower lip as if recalling the taste of his last kiss, and she tilted her head back further, her eyes never leaving his.

Damn, Zack thought, gazing down at her, studying the glimmer in her eyes and then watching the tiny pink tongue brush lightly across her lip. *I've rescued her from one cad and replaced him with another.* He recalled the resounding slap he'd heard as he approached Barclay and Darcie, and the yelp of pain followed by epithets resulting from her bite. He'd risk either—or both—for the sweet taste of her lips opening to his again.

Without thinking further, he edged forward, pressing her body close to his, imprisoning it between the wrought iron fence behind her and his body. His lips were within an inch of hers, paradise in the oppressive humidity and heat of the city. Beneath him, her lips parted more, a soft sigh escaping through small pearly teeth.

Darcie closed her eyes. She could no longer stand the riveting power of his brandy-colored ones. His breath touched her face, warmer than the erratic breeze that served as the only barrier between their lips. The space closed.

His kiss was like a whisper, tantalizing and exciting, and then it grew more demanding, as if he were unwilling to allow her to merely receive his caress passively rather than participate. Darcie's eyes flew open when his tongue touched hers and caressed the soft recesses of her mouth, and then she relaxed again. Her legs were limp, and she slumped against him, delighting when his embrace drew her completely into the haven of his arms.

Beneath her palms, his face felt at once soft but bristled lightly by the new shadow of whiskers at the end of day. Her hands slipped around his neck and clung, and she snuggled further into the curves of his body. Breasts, high and rounded, pressed flat against his wide chest, and her blood raced through her veins like the ocean rushing around the hull of a ship as it cut through the waves.

His lips left hers, and she felt abandoned as the cool air rasped across her face. A moan escaped from deep inside her as he nuzzled aside her curls and caressed her neck, whispering her name between fluttery kisses.

From somewhere far, far away, laughter splintered the warm space around them, and Zack peered around, startled. He glanced at her, half-expecting her to run as she had just days ago, but she rested her head on his chest as if she were listening to the thundering of his heart.

Darcie couldn't move. Her bones had jelled somehow, and she clung to Zack for support.

Raspy breaths were the only sound now, and he lifted her chin to look into her eyes. His gaze darted back to the entrance to the hall. Two men were standing outside smoking cigars. Beneath the oak's gnarled branches, nearly touching the bricks of the sidewalk, he and Darcie were hidden. Unable to resist, he kissed her again, lightly and lovingly, trying to assure her without words that everything was all right, that they hadn't been discovered.

"Come, love," he whispered and held the branch aside for her to walk by. "We must return or our absence will be noticed."

Darcie was grateful for the cool evening breeze that surrounded her, fanning the bright color from her cheeks. "I'm afraid that our absence has already been noticed. Look."

Zack looked toward the hall. The two cigar smokers had been joined by Em, Patty, and Gideon. The three of them were peering up and down the street into the darkness. "We'll be fine. Don't worry about anything."

She looped her hand around his arm and they strolled along as if nothing had happened. Nearing the hall, Darcie's heart pounded, drowning out the sound of the orchestra in her mind. "Yes, it really is a lovely city by day or by night. However, when the heat is as oppressive as it is now, Charleston is much nicer in the evening, don't you think?"

"Yes," Zack replied, marveling at her lyrical voice and wanting to take her in his arms again.

They reached the steps to St. Andrews Hall and paused.

Darcie pretended not to notice their audience. "And now, M. Manville, I'd like to dance. After all, this is my first ball, you know."

"Of course. How thoughtless of me to keep you." He led her up the steps and pretended to notice her friends for the first time. "Going for a walk are you? Grand night for it."

Darcie smiled and nodded as they walked past. She felt Em's eyes boring into her back and knew that when they were alone, there would be a thousand questions to answer. She wondered what had become of Barclay. He couldn't have come here, not in the condition he was in when he left them. Oh, well, she'd have him to face tomorrow, too.

Somehow, they reached the dance floor, and she melted into his arms. Delighted by the broad expanse of his chest and his extraordinary height, she relaxed, her face hidden from the quizzical stares of her friends and acquaintances.

Dancing was exquisite torment. After their passionate kiss, Darcie could hardly hold herself in position. Their eyes were locked in sensuous silence, a faint smile touching her lips. She wanted to cling to him, to sway to the music, and kiss the night into morning.

"Say, you two." Gideon and Em were dancing next to them. "Don't you think it's time to go? I'm famished."

"Oh, my." Darcie peered at him. "I'd purely forgotten that we were to have supper. I'm sure our other guests will have arrived."

Em glanced around. "Where is Barclay? I thought he went out with you."

Wondering what she could say, Darcie gazed at Zack, her eyes imploring him to extricate her from this uneasy situation. When she saw the laughter lines forming at the corners of his mouth and eyes, she regretted her actions.

"Why, he seemed to have bumped into a low-hanging branch or something. Had a nasty cut on his lip," Zack lied, averting his eyes from Darcie's. He picked at a spot of lint on his sleeve and then looked at Emilie. "You know, these live oaks hang awfully low and at night, it's difficult to see them."

"Bumped into a . . . cut his lip?" Concern etched lines across Em's forehead. "Was he hurt badly?"

"No, not really. He'll recover soon enough," Zack assured her.

Glad that Zack hadn't looked at her, Darcie bit the side of her gloved finger, vainly trying to keep from snickering. The image of Barclay's shocked expression was clear in her mind. She glanced at Em and discovered that her best friend was staring at her, but Darcie couldn't utter a word for fear of laughing out loud at Zack's outrageous lie.

"Cut his lip?" Em repeated. Her gaze slid from Darcie's face to Zack's and back again, and then she laughed. "Well, that should slow him down for a few days."

They arrived at Darcie's home to a houseful of guests. The Rutledges, the Chestnuts, the Rhetts, and others milled about on her piazza or in the parlor. Jasper was circulating among them serving rum punch and lemonade.

Darcie excused herself and made for the kitchen at once. She poked her head in the door and called, "Serve supper as soon as possible. We're starving."

Charity rose from her seat by the back door and opened her mouth, but Darcie didn't wait to listen. Within a few minutes, dinner was announced. Without Barclay, there was an uneven number of guests, but Darcie didn't fret. She asked Gideon to sit at the head of the table in his place.

After the jealousy she experienced at Em's party, she refused to allow Zack to sit that far away. He sat at her right side and made himself charming to all her guests.

"Yes, Dr. Rhett," Zack answered. "We are leaving early next week."

Darcie listened for a moment and caught a smile from Dr. Rhett. Her problems were her own and she wanted no gossip about her after she left, so she offered him an explanation for their sudden departure. "Zack has had some problems that mandate a quick trip to France. Our departure date has been moved forward considerably."

Dr. Rhett nodded. Darcie adored him, having known him for all of her life. He apparently liked Zack quite a bit, for they were engrossed in conversation once again.

Thinking about her upcoming trip, Darcie wondered about seasickness. She had never experienced the dreaded malady—not even in the rough waters they'd sailed through coming home from Savannah four years ago during the storm. Others on the ship, including many sailors, had been disabled for the entire length of the storm.

"Tell me, Dr. Rhett," she asked, when she noticed a pause in his conversation with Zack. "What do you know of seasickness?"

"Not much," he admitted and took a sip of his wine. "I do know that it affects people differently. Some not at all."

"I'm one of the lucky ones," Darcie added thankfully. "I suppose my constitution's like my father's. He never suffered with it either."

"True enough, as he told me many times." Dr. Rhett smiled amiably. "Many people suffer little, while others are miserable. It's impossible to determine in advance who will succumb to the illness."

"What can we do about it?" she asked.

"Not much." Thoughtfully, Dr. Rhett rubbed his chin with his right hand. "Keep the patient comfortable. Feed them thin broths, nothing heavy. I've seen cases where the victim suffers the entire journey, though they're the rare ones."

"I hope we have none of those on board. I'd hate to see someone miserable for the entire voyage," Darcie declared, and wondered how Charity would fare.

"Well, if we have problems of that nature, I have a man who is exceedingly well versed in the handling of such cases," Zack replied. "He's quite good with people."

"Well, at any rate," Dr. Rhett said, nodding to Zack, "most people suffer for a few days only. Some only during turbulent weather."

Though she dawdled with her food, hardly eating a bite of the delicious oysters, she thought supper would never end. The memory of Zack's lips on hers kept nagging at her no matter how hard she tried to stop thinking about it.

Soon, all the guests were gone except Zack. Darcie sunk into a chair in the parlor, fanning herself with the dance program. "Wasn't it a wonderful evening?" she asked, watching Zack carefully for his reaction. She still felt unsure of him. He'd kissed her twice, but what did it mean to him?

"Absolutely marvelous," he replied, suddenly bursting into laughter. "Poor Barclay. He seemed a bit upset when you bit him."

Darcie felt giddy. Everything combined—the ball, Barclay's silly attempt to make love to her, his kiss, the pained look of bewilderment on his face, and Zack's stirring kiss—to make her feel like a child again, giggling over some delicious secret with her friends.

"I swear, I never saw him so shocked." She laughed and laughed, feeling much of the tension flow out with the laughter. "He looked like a little boy who'd fallen from a tree and cut his lip."

Zack nodded, unable to speak for a minute as the image sunk in. "It was worth the booty on one of my ships to witness that moment."

"That's quite a bit," she conceded, laughter wracking her body, and then she sobered a bit. "How about Em? Do you think she believed us?"

"I can't say." Zack rubbed his chin with one hand and peered at her thoughtfully. "Let's hope she asks him if he injured himself in a fall."

"But what if she asks him what happened?" Perspiration beaded her forehead, and she stood and walked to a window. "And what if he tells her the truth—or another story entirely?"

Zack joined her at the window and took her chin in his hand. "Whatever he says, we'll just have to wait and see."

"I know, but Zack—"

"There's no need worrying about something you can't do anything about." He looked down at the worried face, now lined with concern. She was so sweet, so innocent, so dear. He fought the urge to crush her to him, Charity was probably lurking outside the parlor and peeking through the keyhole. "It's awfully warm in here, despite the open windows. Would you like to walk in the garden for a few minutes?"

Darcie knew she shouldn't. Sunrise wasn't far away and she longed for her bed, but she also wanted to be in Zack's arms again. What was happening to her? Ordinarily, she would have never flouted society as she had with Zack. Did it have anything to do with this being her last few days in Charleston?

"Zack, I really shouldn't . . ." she began, halfheartedly, knowing all the while she'd go.

"Come. It'll be the perfect ending to a perfect day." He took her arm and they walked through the open window. They stopped at the edge of the piazza and looked across White Point Gardens. "The sun will be up soon."

Already the sky was lightening from its ebony splendor to satiny gray, and the moon was about to set. The garden was a fantasyland, each tree and shrub seemed all out of proportion and whispered secrets in the breeze that swirled the fragrance of jasmine, petunia, and gardenia all around them.

The brick path was like a dark river flowing through a dense forest as they reached the grotto where Darcie liked to sit in the early morning and listen to the birds. The garden was silent now, except for the occasional chirp of a cricket, the shuffle of their feet along the walkway, and the silken whisper of her gown.

"We leave in three days," Zack said, watching her arrange her skirts on the stone bench, such a feminine thing, something she did without even thinking about it. It struck him that she was a paradox—so feminine and yet so strong. "I want you to know that I won't have much time at first."

"I understand." Darcie wondered where this conversation was leading, but didn't interrupt further. "I'll try not to take much of your time."

"Thank you. I often captain my own ship, although I have a fine lieutenant, my second in command." He paused and gazed at her, marveled at the flattering light on her face. For a moment, he couldn't decide if the light emanated from within or if it were external. Her skin had such a delicate quality, a translucence like the finest silk. Unable to resist, he reached down and touched her face. Impossible as it seemed, it was as soft as he remembered.

Lightning bolted from each of his fingers and spread throughout her body, much like the great storms over the harbor, and her heart thundered in her chest. A knot developed in her throat and she could hardly breathe as he dropped down beside her.

"Oh, Darcie," he whispered, cupping her face in his large, strong hands. "Darcie."

"Yes?" came the breathless reply. Color rushed to her face. She was certain that he could hear the pounding of her heart as easily as she heard the rumbling of old Miss Johnson's round stomach in church.

For a moment, he said nothing. It was as though time had stopped inside the little grotto, and warmth spread over him, enveloped him. His lips crushed hers and he pulled her into the shelter of his arms, pressing his body against hers.

A moan welled up from inside her, and she allowed him to mold her body to his. Gasping for breath, she was powerless to stop him—and didn't want to.

Suddenly, he thrust her back, peering deeply into her eyes, searching her face for evidence of pain or discomfort. "Have I hurt you? *Mon Dieu,* I'm sorry."

Darcie's dreamy eyes opened wider. "Hurt? Uh, no, I—"

He drew her back into his arms. "I don't ever want to see you hurt."

As the words tumbled from his mouth, Zack began to think of his original mission. He recalled her words about marrying someone chosen for her and her vehement opposition when she spoke of a marriage contract. He should tell her, make his— what was he thinking? He didn't want marriage, and besides, telling her would only hurt her. She'd know how badly he'd deceived her, and he couldn't risk the hatred he knew he'd see in her eyes if she found out.

Perhaps he could tell her when they knew each other better,

when she trusted him more, when that scoundrel Rhett was out
of the way. Or maybe when her devious uncle announced the
name of the bridegroom, Zack could feign ignorance. After all,
Talbot had never mentioned it, and he might not be aware that
Zack knew of the arrangement.

When she refused, he could fade away, go back to sea and
forget her. That was it! Then dear Uncle Talbot would agree to
her marriage with Barclay. He would be perfect for her. A man
of her own people, her own ways.

Zack stood up suddenly. "Come, Darcie. It's late. We must
say good night. I can't imagine why we're dawdling here at
dawn."

For a long time after Zack left, Darcie stood on the piazza
outside her room. She'd watched him leave, once again in such a
hurry that he hardly said a decent good-bye. The sun rose,
brilliant red, and sent shards of gold, purple, and pink over
Charleston. It was going to be a fine day.

When she finally returned to her bedroom, she removed her
gown and tossed it over a chair. Her undergarments soon followed and she crawled into bed naked, relishing the crisp, cool
feeling of the sheets against her skin. Charity would be appalled
if she discovered her in bed this way, but Darcie would simply
refuse to arise with her mammy in the room.

As she drifted to sleep, her last thoughts were of Zack's lips
on hers.

"Ain't never seed nothin' like it. A walkin' in the streets all
night like some no 'count wharf woman." Charity slung the
wrinkled silk gown over her arms. "Here it be past ten and Miss
Priss still abed. I ain't never heard of no such."

Darcie lay still and pretended to be asleep. She knew that
Charity was intentionally making noise to awaken her, but she
refused to acknowledge the woman. The door slammed and
Darcie snuggled down under the covers to nod off again into
her pleasant world of dreams and Zack.

"No sir. Ain't never seed nobody but white trash sleep this

late. Wallerin' in bed like a hog in a puddle after a rainstorm."
Heavy footsteps crossed the hardwood floor and were muffled
on the thick carpet. "Get yourself up from here."

Charity reached down and threw off the sheets. "Laws a
mercy, she nekked as the day she come into ole Charity's hands.
Gimme strength, Lawd, my chile done—"

"Oh, hush up Charity." Darcie sprang from the bed and
pulled on a wrapper. "You'd think I'd crawled into bed with a
Yankee."

Tears flooded over Charity's cheeks and she moaned and
keened for a moment. "My chile, my chile. Lawsy, yo' momma
gonna haint me sure."

"I said hush up." Darcie narrowed her eyes and gazed sternly
at the old woman. She tried to think of something to pacify her,
but there was no good excuse. A limp one would have to suffice.
"It was terribly hot last night and you were nowhere to be seen.
I pulled off my gown and fell into bed. Now go get me some
breakfast. I'm famished."

Charity went off muttering, and Darcie realized that the explanation fell short of anything reasonable. However, she didn't
care. She threw back the drapes and stepped onto the piazza. As
dawn had promised, it was a glorious day.

When Charity returned, she bore a tray laden with coffee and
heavy cream, biscuits, and molasses. Darcie ate as if she hadn't
eaten in days. "Charity, lay out something old and ragged. We
have plenty to do this afternoon."

"Yas'm." Charity pulled an old muslin dress from the armoire
and held it up. "It's been a long time since you wore this'n. But,
it'll do."

Darcie sipped her sweet coffee and stuffed down the last bite
of biscuit. "Have you packed?"

"No'm and I ain't gonna." Charity threw the dress on a chair
and crossed her lean arms. "I ain't never rode in no boat, and I is
too old to start now."

Darcie thought that she had seen the signs of rebellion all
week, but as much as she disliked frightening Charity by forcing
her to take this trip, she couldn't face living at her uncle's with

no familiar face. She thought quickly and countered, "You're probably right."

Charity looked startled. Clearly she had expected to elicit a temper tantrum in her young charge.

"Besides, I probably won't need you anyway," Darcie continued when she saw the puzzled stare emanating from old Charity's face. "On the voyage over, I'll have Zack to care for me. I mean, I'll have to dress myself and all that, but Em will help. And Zack will be around for everything else I need."

"Harrumph!" came the sound from Charity's throat. "You don't need nothin' that Frenchie can do for you."

"Still, I guess I'll just have to rely on his judgment." Darcie wiped her index finger through the last drop of molasses and licked it clean. "You know he's acting as my guardian and I have to do as he asks. And, of course, Em will be along."

"Harrumph!" Charity repeated the sound. "She ain't no better than that Frenchie."

"Oh, yes. Sissy is going along," Darcie added, knowing that it was the last straw. Charity would never allow Sissy to do for her "li'l kitten."

"I knows whut you is up to," Charity crossed her arms and glared at Darcie. "You is intendin' to buy that no 'count Sissy, ain't you."

"Of course not."

"You is. Oh, Lawd, Charity been put out to pasture like a used-up mule." Charity's back stiffened and she looked at Darcie with keen black eyes. "You jus' think you goin' off on that boat without me. Well, if that's whut you thinkin', you gotta 'nother think a'comin. I'se goin'. You jus' try and stop me."

Chapter Eight

Darcie sprang out of bed before the first light of dawn warmed the harbor. They were leaving today, and as much as she regretted leaving Charleston, she admitted to herself that she was looking forward to seeing France. The exhilarations of a new adventure teased color into her face—a face paled by a restless night's sleep.

Zack had told her that even though the climate was warm here and it was full summer, the weather in France would be cool. The temperature rarely rose out of the seventies. As a result, Darcie had selected several light dresses for daytime and several heavy, warmer gowns for evening. Her trunks were full of gowns of all description.

This morning she slipped her new navy blue serge traveling gown over her horsehair crinolines and donned the matching cape to protect her against the mists that rose above the harbor this early. She heard the clatter of hoofs on the street and strode onto her piazza. Down on the street, Zack was speaking with the driver of a wagon. Directly behind the wagon, a large open carriage waited, its horse whinnying and puffing.

Darcie peered across the harbor for the last time. How she

loved the moods of the juncture of the two rivers. Early spring mornings, the mist hung like gossamer over the silvery water. On hot, summer days when the sky was cornflower blue, the water glistened and glittered, a faceted sapphire encrusted with diamonds and pearls. In August, tropical storms and hurricanes preyed on Charleston, and the water churned and roared, crashing over the seawall and spilling into White Point Gardens. And there was no place on Earth more lovely than White Point Gardens beneath the intoxicating Carolina moon when it splayed its fairy paths across the harbor, teasing her to come along and dance with the fairies on moonbeams.

Something made Zack look up from where he stood on the street below Darcie's window. He'd felt like someone was watching him and instinctively knew that it was Darcie. Leaning against the railing of the second-floor piazza, she was staring across the water. Caught in the swirling mist, she looked like some beautiful vision from a dream, suddenly left here when he awakened. Her slim waist cried out for his hands to enfold her to him; her wide, sensuous mouth begged for his lips to press against hers. *God,* he thought, *how can a woman affect me this way?*

Suddenly, her eye caught his. A flash of recognition brightened her features and, though he doubted that it was possible, she became more lovely. Her smile engaged her cheeks and dimples appeared as if by magic. *By the sails of my ships, I think she's teasing me,* he thought, unable to will his gaze to move from her.

He heard her lilting laughter, musical and enticing, lofted by the swirls of mist to ring down on the street. He loved to see her happy. She turned to enter the house and paused. Her expression changed to one he was quite familiar with—the teasing and taunting one she reserved for their raucous play—and she lifted her fragile hand to her lips. In a quick motion, she blew a kiss across the distance and disappeared through the window.

Darcie almost danced through the window, feeling lighter than dandelion fluff with anticipation. Charity was opening the door as Darcie turned around. "Good morning, Charity. Are we ready to take to the sea?"

"I'se goin, but I ain't ready." Charity took the small valise containing Darcie's non-clothing items, such as a few of her favorite books, her father's chess set, a bit of jewelry, a small likeness of her father, her mother's jewel-studded purse, Darcie's journal, a small supply of damask napkins, an array of embroidery floss along with her sewing basket, and a few other miscellaneous objects of special interest to her.

"Oh, wait," Darcie called as Charity started to disappear through the doorway. She was glad the bulk of her jewelry had been sent ahead by Horace from the office so that its weight wasn't added to her valise. She had remembered to send a note requesting him to forward her jewelry to the purser of *La Mer Magnifique* late yesterday. Otherwise, she would have ended up in France with the few baubles that she refused to store at the office—regardless of her uncle's instructions soon after he became her guardian. She had reasoned that she had to have some jewelry to wear to parties and she rejected the little voice within that reminded her that she was disobeying her guardian. "Here. I have just one more thing to put in that bag."

"You put much mo' in here, and you'se goin have to git a horse to tote it." Charity placed the carpetbag on a chair and unbuckled its leather fastenings. "I ain't never seed a gal no more spoilt than this'un."

Darcie scrambled through the bottom drawer of her chest and ignored Charity's scolding. There were some of her father's papers hidden away there. Horace had given them to her to carry to Uncle Talbot. She tucked the envelope into the small valise to be kept with her during the journey instead of being stored in the ship's hold.

"Ready," she announced.

"Ain't you goin eat nuthin'?"

"Something light. How about some melon?" Darcie had forgotten breakfast. "Be quick. Zack is here."

"He can jus' wait till my li'l kitten eat," Charity grumbled as she closed the door behind her. "That boat ain't like to go nowhere if'n he ain't there."

When Darcie raced down the stairs, she found Zack standing at the bottom with his right foot perched on the second step. He looked as if he might spring up the curved staircase after her if she dawdled overlong. "Good morning, sir."

"*Bonjour,* mademoiselle." Zack took her hand. "You look lovely this morning."

"Is the weather going to be clear today? I couldn't tell from looking out. There was so much fog."

"A wonderful day. I am looking forward to shoving off. I long to have the sea beneath my feet."

"So, do you walk on water as well as you float about the dance floor?" Darcie teased. Her mood was much too light for serious conversation.

"Having never tried that, I'm not sure," Zack answered, delighted with her quick wit. After all, the sun had not yet risen, and many women refused to be seen before noon. He paused. How could he say the sun had not yet risen? The room glowed with a light that rivaled the sun's. Darcie seemed to emit a radiance all her own. He narrowed his features into a serious expression to continue their banter. "However, if it is your wish, I shall endeavor to walk ahead of the ship to Paris."

So, his mood was light as well. Darcie's mind was quick. "Then perhaps, you wouldn't mind holding a fisherman's line as you walk? I have a strong liking for fresh fish."

"If that is the case, then perhaps you would do me the honor of walking at my side." Zack could no longer maintain a serious facade. Her wit amused and thrilled him. Talking with her was like no other conversation. She was as unpredictable as the sea. Zack looked at the mounting pile of baggage and shook his head gravely. "A bit more than you estimated, perhaps?"

Darcie felt the color rise in her face. She had promised him that she could do with two trunks to be stored in the hold and one for her cabin. "Oh please, Zack, don't be tedious. I know I'm vastly over my estimation. You can't expect me to arrive in

Paris with no clothes to wear. If I came with no more than two trunks, I should be a laughingstock. The Nevilles' poor relation from the wilds of America."

He perused the pile. Even as she had made her promise to limit her number of trunks to two, he had known that it would be impossible. As a result, he had calculated for five and her four would prove no hardship. Em had brought only two. She must have no clothes.

"This once, you are safe. I never met a woman who could travel abroad with only two trunks." Zack smiled inwardly. Guilt was chiseled into her face as if hewn there by a dagger. His words softened the furrows and made him feel suddenly lighthearted. The lovely face upturned to accept his scolding cried out to be caressed, and he touched her cheek with his hand before he realized what he was doing.

"Harrumph," came Charity's voice behind her. "How the boat goin float with all that in its belly?"

Zack's head rolled back with laughter. "Ah, Charity, we'll manage."

They watched as the last pieces were loaded onto the wagon and their gazes followed as it rolled along toward South Bay. "Have we a moment for a cup of coffee against the chill of morning before we leave?" Darcie asked, turning to Zack.

"Most certainly," came his reply and he held the gate for her to enter. "Careful, mademoiselle, I once knew a young lady who nearly hanged herself on the garden gate."

"And, I know of a man who may find his coffee gracing the fabric of his shirt if he continues to remind a certain young lady of that most embarrassing incident," Darcie teased in return. "Although, I understand she has a gentleman friend who would be perfectly willing to sever the offending gentleman's head from his shoulders and post it upon one of the spikes of that very same fence to ward off further—"

"Enough, enough," he cried, holding on to the hand railing of the steps for support. "I can stand no more of this torment. I quake in my boots."

Charity shook her head from side to side and with a "Tsk, tsk," continued on into the house.

Darkness still clung to the city, gray shrouds of fog dancing about the live oaks and palmettos like silk in a whirlwind. The cool mist kissed Darcie's hair and a fringe of damp curls appeared across her high forehead. She stood two steps above Zack, and she looked at him, intent on decrying the value of arising before the fog had dissipated. One glance at his face stopped her.

For once, they could see each other eye to eye and stood shoulder to shoulder. Instinctively, she placed a hand on his left arm and gazed at him. His forehead was wrinkled as if he were deep in thought and his eyes stared straight into hers as if they saw nothing. "Zack? Is something wrong?"

"What?" He shook his head to clear the images that had spun themselves before his eyes like cobwebs of the finest silk, imprisoning his gaze in the sapphire depths of her eyes. Had she not spoken, his arms would have wound themselves around her slender body and crushed her against him as they had that night in the garden. "Oh, no. Whatever gave you the idea that something was wrong?"

Darcie studied him carefully, certain that he had emerged from a dreamlike state upon the calling of his name. "Well, nothing really, I suppose. You just seemed far away. As if you were sleeping with your eyes open."

Zack laughed. "Preposterous. I should be in sad shape if it were true. I'd have tumbled head over heels down these brick steps for certain. And, yet, here I stand wide awake."

"Well, I don't know where you were, but you weren't here with me." Darcie eyed him thoughtfully and suddenly became jealous. "You must have been thinking of some other young lady, perhaps Em? Or could it be some mysterious Frenchwoman who has stolen your thoughts as you prepare to return to your home?"

"Are all American maidens so inquisitive and forward?" Zack tilted his head to one side and considered Darcie as she waited expectantly for his retort. Her smile was tenuous, as if she might be jesting. He really couldn't tell, and said, "There may be need of your valiant knight of Charleston yet, if you persist in torturing me with your jibes. How could you suggest that I would think of another woman while escorting you to coffee?"

Thank goodness, he thinks I was teasing, Darcie mused. Jealousy was a new emotion to her, and she didn't think she liked it overmuch. For a moment, she pictured Em in Zack's arms, dancing about the floor of St. Andrews Hall. A sick feeling welled up in her and she felt her cheeks redden with anger.

How silly, she thought. *Why should I care if Em dances with Zack?* She envisioned Zack touching Em's face, smoothing her hair, and her mouth opened to berate Zack for his infidelity, but she stopped. Infidelity? Darcie had no claims on Zack other than friendship. There was no real reason that he shouldn't dance with Em, or even kiss her if he chose to do so. None whatever —except in Darcie's mind.

For a second, she imagined Em lying on the floor, face dirty and bruised, hair torn out in great fistful, and her dress in tatters. *That would serve her right,* she thought. *Just let her try to take Zack from me.*

Somewhere deep inside, a little voice said, "Zack doesn't belong to you. You belong to another."

The anger whooshed out of Darcie like the gust of a hurricane. *Belong to another.* Belong to another, beat her heart as she gazed at Zack. What was she doing? How could she play the strumpet for a man sent to take her to her future husband? She was a foolish child for allowing her imagination to run wild.

The wharf bustled with activity. Darcie looked about for her trunks, but couldn't see them. Neither could she see the wagon that had brought them. She did see the sailor she'd seen that afternoon in Zack's office when they'd interviewed applicants for a companion and she waved her recognition. His nod was abrupt and he quickly turned back to his task. Abashed, Darcie stared. Why had he been so rude? Then the young blond man, a boy really, standing next to the rude sailor turned to look at her.

A smile split his face and he waved gaily before the other man said something that made him turn away.

Zack was busy shouting orders and barking instructions as he prepared to set sail. Em's luggage had arrived and had been taken into the hold, and now the Rhett carriage arrived.

Barclay sprang down and ran across the gangplank, leaving Em to fend for herself in the midst of kegs of molasses, bales of cotton, casks of rice and indigo, and the swarm of men rolling or carrying them aboard. Em threaded her way among them, trying to avoid being run over by a rolling barrel.

The memory of her earlier jealous vision—Em prostrate on the floor, legs askew, hair a mess—clouded Darcie's eyes for a moment, but she recovered and drew her friend warmly into her arms. "I'm delighted to see you so early this morning. Isn't this exciting?"

"Exciting?" Em asked incredulously. "How about stupid, silly, ridiculous, insane?"

"Now, Em," Darcie began, trying to make up for her own naughty thoughts. "You know Zack wants to get an early start."

"Early?" Em cried. "Does the tide wither away during the morning, so that the ship won't sail? What's wrong with afternoon? Look around. Even the sun has the grace not to rise this early."

Darcie shook her head. Em had never been one to rise early, and therefore had missed the beauty of daybreak over the harbor. She turned to her lifelong friend to chide her for her laziness, but found that she was alone beside the railing, and as she peered across the deck, she realized that Em must have gone below with Charity.

"Miss Darcie!" came a masculine voice from the wharf.

Turning to see who had called her, Darcie spotted Captain James waving frantically and running up the gangplank. As he reached the deck, she strode to meet him. "Captain James, how good to see you."

"Aye, and 'tis good to see such a fair lass as yerself." Captain James removed his woolen cap and clasped it firmly between both hands, nervously fingering the brim. "I've come to thankee again for what you done for an old salt. We sail again on the morrow. T'will be good to have the sea beneath me. I've grown tired of solid ground."

"You owe me no thanks. You're a good captain, one of the best." Darcie smiled fondly. His forehead, above ruddy cheeks, was as white as her petticoats, shaded by the cap he always wore. Captain James had been a favorite of hers for a long time, and of her father's. "I wish you good sailing."

"Aye, and thankee for that. I'll be takin' me leave now. No need to hold up on my account. You've a fine head on yer shoulders and a fine heart, Miss Darcie," he replied, a faint tinge of red touching his already ruddy cheeks.

Darcie reached out and touched his arm. "I know you'll do a good job. You always have."

"That I'll do. Aye, that I'll do," Captain James answered and looked around. "This is a fine ship, a fine ship. You'll enjoy sailing her. And, Manville is a fine captain, a fine man. No finer. Exceptin' yer own dear father."

"Thank you, Captain James."

"As I said, I'll be shovin' off." Captain James turned to leave and walked slowly away. When he reached the gangplank, he waved his cap and smiled. His smile faded and was replaced by a frown that creased his blanched forehead.

Darcie looked up to see what had caused the abrupt change in his expression. She saw nothing, except the sailor she'd seen in Zack's office and strode to Captain James's side, concerned about his health. "Captain James? Are you ill?"

"Ill?" His voice was strained, quieter than usual. "No, Missy. It's just that . . ."

"What is it?" Darcie's gaze followed his. The sailor was gone. Nothing seemed amiss. "Captain James, tell me what's wrong."

"Maybe nothin'. And maybe everything." Captain James motioned to the spot where the sailor had stood. "I may be wrong, but I don't think so. I swore I'd never forget them pirates. That man was one of them."

Darcie stared at him in disbelief. How could it be true? "Perhaps, Captain James, you remember his face from the rescue. Or from the trip back here on this ship."

"Maybe. But, I'm not thinkin' that's the way of it." He studied the empty space on the deck. "No, Missy, that just ain't the way of it."

Chapter Nine

Darcie clung to the handrail long after Captain James had left. She stared out at the harbor, hardly seeing the ships that sailed in and out, hardly feeling *La Mer Magnifique* set sail, hardly noticing the dolphins playing in the wake that followed them. Tears stung her eyes, but she refused to allow them to fall.

"Darcie, do come down to the cabin," Barclay pled.

She didn't even bother to look at him. "Not now, Bar. I want to . . ."

"Then I'll stay here, too." He leaned against the railing and placed his arm about her. "We'll watch Charleston fade in the distance."

Shoulders sagging, she muttered, "Please go below. I . . . I wish to be alone."

"Darling, is something wrong?" He hugged her tightly. "Has that cad done something—"

"No, Bar. I just want to be alone for a while." How could she tell him that for a few moments when Captain James had told her he recognized the sailor, she wanted to die? How could she tell him that instead of that death wish, her heart had hardened and sought revenge.

"I insist. Come below and have some wine." Barclay tugged on her arm, urging her to come with him. "It's just the thing for homesickness."

"Please, Bar. I'll be down soon." Darcie glanced up at him, imploring him to grant her wish without further delay.

He stared at her as if he couldn't comprehend her reasoning, but acquiesced to her demand to be left alone. Looking a little dejected, he squeezed her arm a bit and then walked away.

Darcie watched him until he disappeared down the stairs leading to the cabins and then breathed a sigh of relief. Although she realized that she'd have to go down soon or Em and Charity would be out looking for her, she was glad of the solitude.

Captain James had made a frightening accusation, though he probably hadn't made the connection. If, indeed, the sailor in question had been one of the pirates who attacked her ship, then there was a strong chance that the piracy was committed at the direction of Zacharie Manville. Darcie felt as if she were alone on a vast ocean in a small boat and sharks were nipping at the wood.

Zack simply couldn't be involved in such a scheme. Darcie herself had felt at first that the piracy had been committed by Manville's men, but was now convinced otherwise. He had been most considerate, most kind in his treatment of her—why he'd even saved her ship after routing the pirates. It was impossible. There had to be another explanation.

Even as she considered it, Darcie knew that no other explanation held together so well. Well, she'd use her time aboard ship wisely. At every opportunity, she'd find ways to look around, investigate, ask pertinent questions. She'd get to the bottom of this mystery before she reached France or her name wasn't Darcie Gaynor.

Looking about, she spotted Zack. He waved merrily and moved toward her, stopping here and there to speak with his men. During the time it took him to traverse the distance, she willed herself to act naturally, as if nothing out of the ordinary had happened.

"Well, Mlle. Gaynor, I see that you enjoy watching the water, as I do," Zack said as he reached her side. "There's nothing more satisfying or soothing than peering across an expanse of sea."

"You're right, of course." Darcie averted her eyes from his face and stared at the harbor.

To her left, she could see the workers at Fort Sumter. The fort had been started in 1829 and still lay unfinished. In defense of the builders, she had to admit that the island supporting the fort had to be built from boulders shipped from up north.

She couldn't see James Island from where she stood because of the high sails. Fort Johnson was located there, but she'd never been out that far. Just ahead on the left, she could see Fort Moultrie on Sullivan's Island. One of her favorite authors, Mr. Edgar Allan Poe, had been stationed there for a short time. She suspected that it must be a peculiar place because the mysterious island often served as a setting in his stories. She shivered when she thought of the chilling effect his tales had on her.

And, now she felt that same chill in a more personal way, in her own life. Her suspicion of Zack must not color her attitude toward him. After all, America was built on the promise that all men are innocent until proven guilty. But where did she draw the line? Was the evidence offered by Captain James proof enough? No. It was circumstantial.

Zack studied Darcie closely. Something seemed to be troubling her. A frown played across her face, her mouth was drawn in a line of determination. He opened his mouth to tease her, hoping to relieve her of her worry, but thought better of it. Taking a more serious tack, he began, "Darcie, *mon cherie,* why the frown?"

Caught unawares, her cheeks tightened into a smile. "Frown? I'm sorry. I didn't mean to frown at you."

"Are you ill? Seasick? There's nothing to be ashamed of. Even the most experienced sea dogs such as myself suffer the malaise of the sea on occasion." He touched her shoulder, patting it gently as if she were a child. Even though the frown had disappeared, the smile that replaced it didn't seem particularly happy.

"Ill?" Darcie felt a little guilty. He was genuinely concerned about her, and all she could do was scowl at him. "Not ill, just thinking."

"About what?" Zack leaned down on the handrail and peered ahead at the Atlantic, then looked up at her face. "What's got you so deep in thought that you'd forget to shade your face?"

"Forget to . . ." Darcie stared at him a moment and then pulled her bonnet further down over her face, shading it from the harshest of the sun's rays. "My goodness. I had no idea the sun had come out so brilliantly! I'll freckle for sure."

Zack laughed at her furrowed brow as it changed from deep thought to humorous consideration of her situation. He liked that expression much better. The wrinkles weren't so deep, and the eyebrows weren't so closely knit.

"And just what is so funny, Zacharie?" Darcie scolded. "You know perfectly well that Charity will drone on forever about the condition of my skin."

"You deserve it."

"And why should you say that?" She gazed at him in surprise.

"For damaging such lovely skin," he teased. "And for screwing your face into an ugly crone's. I declare, I thought you were one of those hags on board. The ones who applied for the job as your companion, and by the way, Mrs. Appleby—you remember her? Hildegard Appleby, who applied for the job as—"

"I remember the old witch," Darcie interrupted, recalling the ugly visage of the snobbish old woman.

"She's on board."

"What?" Darcie's eyes widened in disbelief. "Zacharie Manville, if you mean to make me angry, you are succeeding," Darcie shouted, and her fists clenched. "I never heard such—"

"Hold on." He backed away, using his hands as shields against an imaginary attack. "I was merely teasing you about your face. And I'm afraid that Hildegard is indeed on board. She paid for passage after I rejected her application for employment."

"Heavens. What else can go wrong?" Darcie wondered

aloud. "How can you do this to me, Zack? You know I can't abide that self-righteous woman."

"It won't be too bad. You won't have to see her too much," he answered, hoping to tease the cruel lines from her face. "Have you left your sense of humor in Charleston? Think what fun you can have with her. And, by the way, your skin is turning a bit pink."

"No, I haven't lost my sense of humor," she answered in a clipped tone. "Nor have I lost my parasol," she continued, raising her white parasol above her head menacingly. "And, I'm not afraid to use it on scoundrels such as yourself."

He ducked as if he thought she might indeed swing the parasol as a weapon. "I give up. Have mercy on a bedazzled mariner."

"Bedazzled?" She lowered the parasol and stared at him quizzically.

"Well, yes," he answered, daring to step closer again. "Such a lovely maiden staring forlornly at the sea. Certainly an enticing sight."

Darcie blushed, adding new color to cheeks already dappled by the sun. Out of the corner of her eye, she watched Zack surreptitiously. His face, too, had been kissed by the sun, and the new color heightened his rough good looks. Without the formality of society, he'd abandoned his coat and loosened his shirt. A bristling of dark, curling hair protruded at the vee formed by the shirt opening and also told of many days at sea with no shirt, for his bronzed skin extended as far as she could see.

Dark curls danced across his high forehead as he looked down at her, and then rested his arm casually on the railing once again. His lips were teased into a dashing smile that deepened the dimple on his left cheek.

Dashing. Darcie considered the word. Yes, that was the perfect description of Zacharie Manville. Dashing.

She remembered his kisses, and suddenly her legs quivered and turned to jelly. Gripping the handrail, she steadied herself, willing herself to think of something else. Beneath them, the open sea undulated and the sails caught full wind for the first time, jarring her as the ship lurched forward.

Her body was thrown against his, and both of them were caught off guard. Zack caught her and as they righted themselves, Darcie carefully looked down as if examining her skirt for damage.

Damage had occurred, but not to her skirts. Her nerves buzzed with heightened activity; her skin burned from his touch; her blood scalded her face with color. After a moment, she chanced a glance at him.

His face was very near hers, too near. Darcie stepped away, wanting to avoid contact at all costs. "Well, I believe I'll go down to the little parlor for a while. Perhaps there I won't injure myself in a fall."

His breath came in short gasps as Zack realized he'd been about to kiss her again. Embarrassment forced his back to straighten, and he stood as stiff as the mast of his ship, his wide sleeves flapping like a sail. "Yes, that seems the most practical solution. I'll see you at dinner."

Darcie nodded. She dared not speak again, not until she had distanced herself from his reach.

"I'll walk you down." He took her elbow. "Can't be too careful. You'll get your sea legs after a bit."

Darcie steeled herself against her reaction to his touch. Momentarily, she longed for another lurch in the ship's motion, one that would throw her into his arms again, but they made it safely down the narrow wooden steps to the cabins.

As they approached the parlor, Darcie stopped. "Thank you for walking with me. I'm such a burden to you. I don't know how I'll ever thank you. Perhaps, when we reach France, Uncle Talbot might settle a sum—"

Zack jerked to a stop, glared at her, and interrupted her before she could say anything else. "I assure you, Mlle. Gaynor, that won't be necessary. Good day."

Darcie would almost swear that as he turned, he clicked his heels together. Watching him climb the stairs, she felt deflated, as if the air had been stolen from her lungs when Zack left.

Feeling a bit lonely, she opened the door to the parlor. To her surprise, it was empty. She had expected to find Em and Barclay, to say the least. Charity and Sissy should have been there, too.

She shrugged her shoulders, closed the door, and continued down the narrow corridor to the room she shared with Em. Without thinking, she opened the door and strode in.

Wearing nothing but her chemise and pantalets, Em lay across her bunk and moaned. Darcie rushed forward and looked at her friend.

"Why, Em, what's wrong?" Darcie asked, and gazed down at the pale face nestled among the pillows.

"Sick," came the weak reply.

"Where is Sissy?" Darcie glanced around, noting that the room that had been so neat was now cluttered.

Each of the two chairs was invisible beneath their load of petticoats, hoopskirts, a cape, and Em's traveling dress. Her bonnet lay crushed on the floor beside the small table that separated the chairs. "Oh, Em. I'm so sorry. What can I do?"

She picked up the bonnet, straightened it as best she could, and hung it on a nail on the door. Finding a loop in the cape, she hung it beneath the bonnet. Darcie took a minute and put the room aright again. "Now, what can I do? Is it seasickness?"

"Ugh," Em groaned, offering a faint affirmative nod as her only answer.

"Where is Sissy?" Darcie insisted. "She should be here looking after you."

"Sick," Em answered and turned on her side, bracing herself against the side of the ship.

Darcie looked down sympathetically at her friend. Poor Em, she thought. "It'll be over soon. Seasickness comes and goes very quickly, I've heard."

Em roused herself enough to glare at Darcie and then surrendered herself to the comfort of the pillow. Darcie removed her friend's shoes and covered her with the sheet and blanket. "I'll be back."

With two missions, Darcie raced from the room. She scurried

down the narrow corridor to the room assigned to Charity and
Sissy for the trip. She knocked lightly on the door and then
peeked in. Both Charity and Sissy lay prostrate on their beds.
"Both of you?" she asked.

"Miss Darcie, I wish I was dead," came a weak reply from
Sissy. "I ain't never been so sick."

"I tole you I din wanna come on no boat." Charity's meager
figure hardly made a furrow on the sheets beneath her. "I tole
you. The Lawd punishing ole Charity for sompum."

Darcie's lips tilted into a smile. "I suppose you're right. You
must have done something truly awful. Have either of you seen
Barclay?"

Charity fluttered her eyelids and stared at Darcie through
glazed eyes. "Yas'm. I seed him. We was settin' in the parlor.
Miss Emilie, Mr. Barclay, and Sissy and me. All of us took to
feelin' poorly. That man fair turned green and run off like he
was chased by a striped haint. I ain't never seed him move that
fast."

Darcie stifled a laugh. She could picture poor Barclay, rushing off in pursuit of a chamber pot. "Well, I'll check on him.
And I'll be back in a bit. Don't worry about anything. I'll take
care of you both."

Backing out of the room, Darcie fought to retain her composure. Barclay was so formidable in demeanor that the sight of
him racing for the chamber pot must have been hilarious.

Without doubt, Zack would know what to do. Darcie
stopped suddenly on the stairs that led to the deck. They were
into the Atlantic and she hadn't experienced any queasiness at
all. Had she been so wrapped up in her thoughts that she hadn't
time to be sick? Obviously that wasn't the answer. Many seamen
were afflicted by seasickness and they were always busy.

Anyway, she was delighted that she hadn't been forced to
take to her bed. The fresh salt air stimulated her, and the scent—
after the sickrooms below—was welcome.

Off to find Zack, she wandered around the deck a bit. Everything about La Mer Magnifique was certainly magnificent as her
name implied. Above her, the sails crackled and clapped, full of

the brisk Atlantic breeze. The teak deck rose and fell with the undulating waves, rocking her like a mother rocks her baby.

Darcie peered back at Charleston. Now a dim line on the horizon, it seemed a distant memory, and hardly tugged at her heart at all. *I'll be back some day,* she vowed, and hurried on to find Zack.

On her way, she passed the sailor she'd begun to think of as her pirate. She had no reason to doubt Captain James's memory of faces, nor could she find reason to believe that the man's intentions were honest. The leering expression on his face made her hurry on her way, and she ignored the slight chill that raced down her spine when she passed by. Walking down the deck, she felt his eyes on her back and stepped more briskly.

"Darcie!" called Zack. "Come up here."

Turning to see where his voice came from, she spotted him on the elevated bridge. She found the short ladder and started to climb.

"Here. Take my hands." Zack stood above her, reaching down to help. "Come on. I'll pull you up."

Stretching, Darcie held up her hands, and he grasped them firmly. With a swift, smooth move, Zack lifted her to his side. "Thank you."

"You're quite welcome. Come and look from here." He took her arm and led her toward the big spiked wheel.

"Actually, Zack, I came about Em—"

"Oh, I had forgotten about her. I'll send Poule to fetch her." He turned to the other man on the bridge.

"No, Zack, don't." Darcie caught his arm as he started to gesture. "Em can't come. She's sick."

A hint of a smile played at the corners of Zack's mouth. "Seasick?"

"Yes." Darcie remembered the pallor of her friend. "I'm afraid she's quite ill. What can we do?"

"Little, I'm afraid," he replied, rubbing his chin thoughtfully. A grin broke out across his face and he laughed. "Tell her that I've never known a man who died of it, though."

Darcie couldn't help laughing with him. He was so full of

gaity and laughter and fun. She tried to glare at him, but was unsuccessful. "Oh, Zack. Don't make me laugh so. Poor Em is below feeling awful."

"In truth, there is little to be done." He tried to speak seriously, but had great difficulty. "Ask Sissy to bathe Em's forehead in cool water."

"Oh!" Darcie cried. "Em is not alone in her malady. I fear I must report that all my traveling companions are abed with seasickness."

"All?" Zack asked. Astonishment banished his laughter, but the creases at the corners of his eyes returned with a twinkle. "Including the honorable M. Rhett?"

Darcie knew that her answer was sure to bring jubilation to Zack's heart. The rivalry between the two men was great. This disability would be the source of much jest later in the voyage when Barclay recovered. "Yes. Including Barclay. He was stricken first."

After a bout of laughter, Zack finally spoke again. "I'll send someone to tend poor Barclay. For the moment, I suppose you are saddled with the ladies."

"Thank you for your kindness." Darcie started to move toward the ladder. "I apologize for the inconvenience my friends have caused."

"I fear that the inconvenience will be upon you." He strode toward her. "Here. I'll accompany you. We'll find clean cloths and a basin for water. Perhaps we can find some biscuits for them. I don't think any of them will be hungry for dinner."

Darcie spent the next few days tending her friends. Zack assigned Poule to care for Barclay, but Darcie spent a great deal of time with her sick male friend. Barclay wanted none other than her to tend him. She bathed his face with cool water, leaving the other, more noxious chores to Poule.

She moved from one room to the next. Each of her companions wanted to usurp all her time. By the end of the third day, Darcie recalled that she hadn't slept more than a few minutes at a time since they'd been at sea. Her own stomach roiled, and for a moment, she thought she was being attacked by seasickness as well as exhaustion. But, she realized that her stomach wasn't rejecting food; it was *begging* for food.

Of Zack she had seen little. Captain of his ship, he spent most of his time on deck or in his cabin studying the charts. He peeked in occasionally on his passengers, but rarely had more than a moment to offer his sympathy.

Darcie decided to ask for a tray to be brought to her. Poule complied and brought a plate of cheese and biscuits. The smell of the warm biscuits made her mouth water, and she sat down at the small table to eat.

"Darcie?" came a weak voice from the bed.

"Yes, Em?" Darcie jumped up and strode to the bedside. "What is it, dear?"

"What is that smell?"

"Why, it's cheese and hot biscuits. Would you like some?" Darcie asked, thinking that Em must be feeling better.

"Ugh!" Em gasped. "Take it away. It's making . . . me sick."

Guilt struck Darcie full force. How thoughtless of her. Em hadn't eaten in days, and although she must be hungry, food still caused her to retch. Darcie hurried to the table, picked up the plate, and rushed out the door.

Poule was coming out of Barclay's room, and she stopped him. "Poule, please take this."

"But you ain't et hardly a bite, miss," the short, bald man replied, looking at the plate of food. "You go right back in there and eat yer fill."

"No, I can't. Miss Em's still awfully sick and the smell makes her worse." Darcie shoved the plate into his hand. "Thank you for your kindness, but I can't stop right now. I'll get something later."

She returned to Em's bedside and wiped her forehead. "I'm sorry, sweet, but I just didn't think of the smell. I'll be right back. I'm going to check on everybody else."

"Hurry back. I feel so wretched." Em's eyes closed and Darcie slipped out the door.

She ran lightly down the hall and entered Charity and Sissy's room. Charity seemed to be feeling a bit better, but Sissy was as bad as Em. Darcie wiped their foreheads and fluffed their pillows.

Satisfied that they were comfortable for the moment, she turned toward the door. It swung open, and Zack stepped in. From the look on his face, she knew that he was angry about something.

He glanced at the two black faces and nodded to Charity. "I hope you ladies are feeling better." Then he turned to Darcie. "May I see you a moment, Nurse Gaynor?"

From his tone, Darcie knew he was angry with her. "Of course, Captain. I'll be back soon, Charity."

When she followed him from the room, he closed the door. "What is the meaning of this?"

"Meaning of what?" Darcie was astonished at his angry tone. "Zack Manville, if you continue to use that tone of voice—"

He glared at her and snatched her hand. Without saying another word, he ignored her protests and dragged her down the corridor to his cabin. Once inside, he deposited her on a chair. "You will remain here until further notice."

Darcie jumped to her feet. "How dare you—"

"How dare I?" he asked. "How dare you? I refuse to allow you to play slave to four sick people any longer. You haven't slept and you haven't eaten in three days. And, now Poule tells me that even though he brought you food, you refused to eat it."

"I'm sorry for the inconvenience, but the smell of food makes Em—"

"Damn Em." Zack pushed her back into the chair. "If you rise again, I swear I'll tie you in the chair."

"Now Zack, really," Darcie began, realizing that he meant every word. "I shall apologize to Poule. I didn't realize that his feelings were hurt. But, surely you must—"

"His feelings? I don't give a tinker's damn about Poule's feelings." He began to pace the floor between her and the door.

"I forbid you to nurse these people. Your health is much more valuable to me than—"

"My health? I'm perfectly fit." She knew that she was lying. Her muscles ached; her head hurt; her stomach lurched. "Zack, somebody must care for them."

"Poule is perfectly capable." Zack turned to face her. "I will not allow you to continue."

"Zack, you know it isn't proper for Poule to attend ladies when they're indisposed," Darcie answered, trying to point out the error of his plan.

"I care nothing for propriety." Before he could say more, a knock sounded at the door. Zack strode across the room and swung the door open. "Come in. Put the trays down there."

Poule and two other men entered with wooden trays and placed them on the table Zack indicated. All but Poule left. "Anything else, sir?"

"Yes, as a matter of fact." Zack followed the others to the door. "Poule, remain with Mlle. Gaynor. If she attempts to get out of that chair, tie her down."

"Sir, I can't—" Poule began, shaking his head from side to side.

"If I return and Miss Gaynor isn't sitting as I left her, I'll tie you to the mast and flog you myself."

Poule's eyes widened. "Aye, Captain. The miss'll be a settin' there till the devil's teeth are strung around the equator, if I've anything to say about it."

Zack smiled at Darcie and fled the room before she could call him any of the names that were flying from her tongue. She could hear him chuckling down the hall.

"Poule, you know Zack would never harm—"

"I'm sorry, miss. Yer a fine lady. As fine as Eugenie herself." He apologized, hanging his head. "But, I daren't let you move. I've seen that man in a fit of temper, and I don't be wantin' it directed at me."

He was right. Zack did have a temper, and she didn't want it directed at the kind man on her account. She'd behave—until

Zack returned. When they were alone, she'd warm his ears with a few well-chosen words.

She didn't have to wait long. Zack burst through the door with a bundle in his arms and dismissed Poule. When the sailor was gone, Zack placed the bundle on his bed and joined her.

"Shall we eat?" he asked.

"I wouldn't eat with you if you were the last man alive." Darcie jumped to her feet and confronted him. "I've never been so humiliated in my life. And, poor Poule. That man's scared witless—"

"He has a right to be." Zack took her arm and propelled her back to the table laden with food. "My men know I don't make idle threats."

"Idle or not, I refuse to eat with a barbarian." Darcie spat the words at him and crossed her arms indignantly.

"That is your privilege," he conceded. "However, I must inform you that before either of us leaves this room, you will eat or be fed."

"How dare you?"

"Darcie, the choice is yours." He pulled out a chair for her. "Either sit and eat, or I'll tie you in the chair and feed you."

His strength was far superior to hers and Darcie realized that he meant every word. With as much grace as she could muster, she sat down and lifted her fork. With a glare that would melt the icebergs of the northern Atlantic, she began to eat.

The stewed beef was delicious. Darcie ate faster and faster, until she thought she would strangle. Forcing herself to slow down, she ate the boiled potatoes and sipped her wine.

Watching him as she ate, Darcie wondered how she could discover the truth about him, about his part in the piracy of her ship. She didn't want to believe he was involved, had refused to believe it, but the nagging doubt wouldn't subside. She had to find out soon, but there wasn't much she could do right now.

When her glass was near empty, Zack refilled it. "Keep eating. You will faint from hunger and exhaustion if you don't."

Darcie knew he was right, but refused to acknowledge him. The wine sent warm waves through her body and she ate much more than she should have. Her plate was almost as clean as the day it was made.

"Well, you did a fine job of cleaning your plate." Zack peered across the table at her, wondering if she'd calmed down yet. If he'd realized sooner that she wasn't eating or sleeping, he'd have offered another man to help her. Damn her for being too proud to ask for help.

Weariness cradled her in its arms, and she almost slid from the chair as she nodded off to sleep.

Chapter Ten

Darcie dreamed of rocking, of Charity rocking her gently to and fro when she'd been ill as a child. The dream changed and Zack replaced Charity. His arms were around her, comforting her, holding her tightly, and his face near hers.

He peered into her eyes, and his were liquid and warm, loving. Darcie watched his lips, wide and inviting, open as they descended upon hers. The caress of his lips spread throughout her body, suffusing it with warmth and tingles of delight. He drew away, and a chill touched every cell and shivers wracked her body. She called to him, but he was too far away to hear her plaintive cry.

She had to find him—the smell of him was all around her, clean and fragrant. Opening door after door, she followed him, ever mindful of the creeping darkness that seemed to enfold him. Where could he have gone?

Her eyelids opened slowly and she peered at her surroundings in the dim light. Where was she? And where was Zack?

Slowly, from the hidden recesses of her mind came the answers to her questions. The undulating motion of the ship prodded her memory. She was on her way to France with Zack aboard his ship. A further recollection awaited her—she wasn't in her own cabin, but Zack's.

For a moment, she stopped breathing. The dream weighed heavily on her mind. Had it truly been a dream? Reality waded in and she knew she had been dreaming of Zack, the deep recesses of her mind remembering his caresses. She propped herself up on her elbows. She recalled that she had fallen asleep in Zack's cabin after days of nursing her friends through their seasickness.

Exhaustion still cramped her leaden muscles and fogged her mind. Darcie could hardly move. She snuggled beneath sheets warmed by her body and fragrant with his scent and dozed off to sleep.

When she awakened again the room was light. She stretched like a cat after a long nap, flexing her fingers and toes. And then she realized that she wasn't alone.

A lamp swung from a beam above the desk that housed Zack's maps, charts, and books, and Zack sat at the desk. She stared at him for a moment, wondering at his intrusion on her privacy. He had promised that the room would be hers alone until Em felt better.

The sound of gentle snoring broke the silence, and she watched the rhythmic rising and falling of Zack's shoulders as he breathed evenly. Hunched over the desk, he was sound asleep.

Guilt consumed Darcie. She had allowed Zack to talk her into using his room as her own, never considering that he had no place else to sleep. All the other cabins were taken.

Darcie wondered what she should do. A lady could hardly dress with a man in the room. Neither could she run down the corridor to her own room, not while she wore nothing but her nightgown.

Her problem seemed to solve itself. While she pondered her dilemma, Zack awakened. He, too, was stretching, arching his back, and rubbing his spine as if his back ached from sleeping in a cramped position.

Abruptly, he whirled to face her, as if he'd suddenly remembered that she was sleeping behind him. "Good morning, made-moiselle."

Darcie pulled the sheet up to her chin. "Good morning, sir."

He stood and faced her. His shirt was open to his waist, and he stretched again without any sign of self-consciousness. "Did you sleep well?" he asked, striding across the room toward her.

Eyes widening, she clutched the bed linens closer about her and shrank from him as if he meant to do her bodily harm. "Well enough."

"Hah!" he laughed, standing feet askew with his hands on his hips. "You slept like a turtle in the sun. You've been asleep for fourteen hours."

"Fourteen?" Momentarily forgetting her attire, she threw back the covers and jumped up. "I must see to Em and the others. Oh, what must they think of me? I've deserted my post in their hour of need."

"You've deserted no one." Zack eyed her with great interest, his gaze covering the length of her in seconds before settling on the opening above her breasts. She's as lovely in the morning as she is when she's dressed for a ball. The keyhole opening in her white batiste gown exposed little of her breasts to his perusal, but the bit of cleavage he saw invited him to see more.

Wondering why Zack had taken to staring at her so blatantly, she looked down and realized why. The gown was quite thin due to excessive washings, and although it covered her from her chin to her toes, her shape was readily apparent. Ignoring the blush that bloomed in her cheeks, she said, "Would you be kind enough to leave the room long enough for me to dress?"

"Dress?" He wanted to rip the wisp of fabric from her body and leave her standing naked, while she wanted to cover her charms with a half-dozen petticoats and a dress the strongest sunlight wouldn't pierce. Ah, but the nightgown she wore was tantalizing. He could easily see the soft rose color of her nipples through the thin fabric. If he continued to study her, he'd end up ripping the piece of fluff off her and throwing her back on the bed from which she'd crawled moments before. "Oh, yes. If you'll excuse me, I'll see to breakfast. Poule can bring it here."

"There's no need. I'll be dressed in minutes and be off to check on my friends." She fought the desire to cover her breasts and stood proud and erect. Color flooded her cheeks, and her body felt warm all over, as if her blush had expanded to cover every inch of her skin.

"You will not leave this cabin before eating a decent meal." Zack stepped toward her, his most menacing expression chiseled into his face. As he moved forward, she moved backward, almost as if they were dancing.

Darcie was almost frightened by the angry look on his face. He acted as if everything always went his way, as if he were unaccustomed to being defied.

Zack nearly gave in. Clearly, she was afraid of him and he regretted it, but he knew that if she were allowed to continue as she had for the past few days, Darcie's health would be threatened. His strides were longer than hers and he smiled inwardly. Within another two steps, he'd easily overtake her.

Even though he knew she hadn't left the room since he'd insisted that she sleep here, she still smelled of violets. He wrapped her in his arms, nuzzling against her hair and closing his eyes. The fragrance clung to her like a cloud to a mountaintop, even as he clung to her, savoring the memories and anticipation that welled within him.

Stroking her hair, he marveled at its texture, soft and satiny as the purest of silks. Unbraided, her hair had lain across her pillow like a golden halo as she slept, as he knelt next to the bed during the night watching her. Once, he'd been unable to resist touching her, and his fingers traced the soft line of her jaw and caressed her cheeks. She'd stirred, but hadn't awakened, so he'd left her to her peace, but her image had plagued his dreams as he slumped over the desk.

Her hair now hung to her waist in a tangle of curls, the same shimmering halo he'd seen earlier. Damn a woman for braiding and knotting her hair until almost none of it showed. Wrapping it around his hand, he held her closer and peered down into startled eyes that glittered like faceted sapphires of the deepest blue. Unable to restrain himself any longer, he leaned down further and his lips claimed hers in a deep kiss, no longer gentle and sweet, but demanding and passionate.

Darcie's eyes opened wide as his lips touched hers, but closed quickly in response to his kiss. Unlike his other kisses that had begun with a soft caress of his lips on hers, this one threatened to make her faint. Darcie had never fainted in her life.

His tongue plundered her mouth, exploring every part of it with idle proficiency. She felt her breath leave her; her pulse quickened; her hands sought his neck and hung on.

Her breasts were pressed against his naked chest, and all that remained between them was the worn batiste. Embarrassingly, her nipples hardened into tiny orbs, much like the crabapples in Em's yard just after the fragrant blossoms fell off.

After a time that seemed like hours, the pressure lessened and he drew away. He studied her upturned face for a few seconds before releasing her. With a voice that hardly rose above a whisper, he said, "I'll be back in half an hour with breakfast. I think you'd better dress."

Darcie clung to the bedpost for support and watched him go. When she realized that she wasn't breathing, she gasped for air like a woman who'd nearly drowned. Her hands went to her nipples. As her chest heaved, her hard nipples rose and fell beneath her hands. How would they feel when Zack's hands caressed them?

Sighing, she removed her nightgown, dressed, and completed her toilet as best she could without the benefit of Charity's able hands. Once her dress was in place over her hoops and her hair braided and pinned into a neat chignon, she felt ready to deal with Zack.

He returned to find her staring at a map of the world which hung behind his desk, although she saw nothing but his face. She turned when she heard the creak of the door. She smiled, trying to wipe from her mind their earlier encounter. "Good morning."

Zack was a little disappointed. He'd hoped to find her waiting in the flimsy gown for his return. Instead, she wore a pale gown of peach-colored taffeta which rustled tantalizingly as she moved. "You found some more suitable clothing, I see."

"Yes." Darcie blushed a bit and smoothed her gown. Since awakening, she realized how much better she felt than she had when Zack had insisted that she needed food and rest, in spite of her protestations to the opposite. Now, a bit embarrassed because of her behavior, she knew she should apologize to Zack. "Thank you for offering your cabin for my use. I didn't know how badly I needed sleep and food."

Zack smiled tentatively, surprised at her apology. His admiration for her grew considerably. "Well, I'm glad to see you looking better. I was concerned about your well-being."

"I appreciate your concern, but I'm fine now and can tend to my friends," she said, delighted that she'd made the bed before he returned.

"No," Zack retorted, somewhat brusquely. "You are no longer nursing everybody. Mrs. Appleby is tending to Em. Poule is tending the others with help from Charity."

"Charity?" Darcie asked.

"Yes. She's feeling much better." Zack sat down at the desk and picked up a thick ledger. "Breakfast should—"

A loud knock interrupted Zack before he could finish, and Darcie strode to the door. When she opened it, the smell of fresh coffee and bacon preceded Poule into the room. "Come in, Poule. Put the tray on the table."

"Thankee miss." He hurried into the room and placed the tray on the table that served as a dining table, and then looked at Zack. "If'n you don't be needin' me for nothin' else, I'll be gettin' me own breakfast."

"Nothing else now, Poule." Zack turned away and resumed his writing.

"Thank you, Poule," Darcie said, walking to the door with the sailor. "And I appreciate your help with my friends. I can never repay you for your kindness."

"That's mighty decent of you to say, miss, but ain't necessary. I just be doin' my duty." Poule touched his cap and turned to leave.

"Oh, Poule." Zack jumped from his chair and ran across the room. "One more thing."

Darcie looked at him expectantly. "Zack, he's done quite enough for us."

"Not quite," Zack replied. "Poule, if this young lady so much as lifts a finger to resume her nursing duties, call me at once. And another thing. She is to eat three times a day at regular intervals. Bring her meals here. I'm assigning you to care for her."

"Now, Zack, that's not necessary. I can—"

"This is my ship and I decide what's necessary and what isn't." He nodded curtly to Poule who smiled and closed the door behind him. "Shall we eat before those biscuits get cold?"

They ate in uncomfortable silence. Darcie and Zack had been alone many times, but not in a room that's principal furnishings were for the bedroom. Although she refused to look at it, the bed seemed to loom larger than life—at least, larger than any bed she'd ever seen.

"Have you sailed before?" he asked, trying to break the silence that seemed to eat at him.

"Oh, yes," she answered eagerly, glad that he had bridged the angry gap that divided them. "My father often carried me with him on short journeys. Especially to the West Indies. We had such a, well, a wonderful relationship. While he was in Charleston, I went everywhere with him."

"Everywhere?" Zack's eyes widened in surprise.

"Well, practically everywhere," Darcie admitted. "I often visited his office. He showed me how to keep his accounts and books. I kept his journals. Everything."

Zack stared at her in wonder. A girl raised alone by a father whose interests lay at sea should have exhibited some unwanted traits, but in Darcie he saw none. She was utterly feminine at all times, even when her willfulness became apparent. "What of your mother?"

Darcie lowered her eyes. She always regretted having no mother to share intimacies with, to unburden herself to. Her father had been marvelous, but he didn't share the emotions of a woman. "I miss my mother." The words slipped out and mist fogged her eyes as she wrung her hands in her lap.

"At times, I even miss mine," he admitted.

Lifting her gaze to him, Darcie looked puzzled. "I don't understand."

Zack pounded on the table. "My mother was . . . she, well, she didn't give a damn about me or my father."

"I'm sure that's not true, she just—"

Zack glared at her, knowing that she could never understand his mother's shallow feelings. "Oh, *ma petite*, but it *is* true. She never wanted me, never cared for me."

"But, Zack, surely—"

Interrupting her, he continued, "And she hated my father."

Tears welled in Darcie's eyes. True, she longed for her mother's comfort at times, but Zack had been denied that comfort from the beginning it seemed. "I'm sorry. I had no idea that—"

Gazing at his clasped hands, Zack realized that he'd stopped the circulation of blood. His hands were turning deep purple. "You have no reason to be sorry."

"But I am," she whispered, feeling that she understood him better than she had.

"She's gone anyway."

Darcie nodded in sympathy. Both of them were orphans. "I sometimes close my eyes and remember how kind my mother was, how beautiful her smile—"

"I see my mother too often to forget," he admitted angrily.

"You see her?" Darcie gazed at him in astonishment. "She's not dead?"

"Hardly," he declared. "She lives in Paris, most of the time."

"But I don't understand."

"She deserted us." Zack turned from her probing eyes, feeling the old hurt well in him again. He'd refused to admit how much she'd hurt him. "Divorced my father. She married a man of great wealth. One who conveniently died a few years later, leaving her one of the gayest and richest widows in Paris."

Darcie rose and walked to stand at his side. How could she, a mere girl, comfort him, relieve his deep hatred? Touching his shoulder gently, she slid her hand across and embraced him tenderly. She whispered, "Don't let your hatred eat at you, Zack."

He stood and gazed down at her for a moment, knowing he had to change the subject. Too many of his secrets had been voiced here today. "I suppose I'd be wasting my time if I ask you to avoid the sickrooms altogether, so I'll compromise."

"How magnanimous of you," Darcie said dryly and returned to her chair.

"You may sit and read if you like. You may visit, but if you so much as fluff a pillow, I'll—"

"I get the idea." Darcie played with the last bit of biscuit, slowly dragging it through the molasses, and then jumped to her feet and saluted. "Aye, aye, cap'n."

Zack fought to keep the smile from his lips, and walked to the door. He never anticipated that his journey would be easy. Darcie was far too sassy—too sassy for her own good—and sure to be a thorn in any man's side. Her independent ways would be hard to tame, a real challenge for the unlucky man who married her.

Unlucky? He stopped and glanced back at her contrite smile. A man would be a fool to believe that behind that angelic face was a woman who would take orders with the docile complacency of most women. No, she'd be a shrew when angered. But, still, he really couldn't believe that the man who married her would be unlucky. She was beautiful and intelligent, had a delightful sense of humor. And her lips promised more than any he could ever have dreamt of.

Darcie stared at the closed door for a long time after Zack left. His demeanor led her to believe that he was amused by her sudden submissiveness, though she could really determine his emotions from his face. An enigmatic man, he surprised her time after time with his moods. She wanted—no, felt compelled—to get to know the real man who was Zacharie Etienne Manville.

Darcie checked her appearance in the small mirror attached to the door and then made her way to see Em. She dreaded the confrontation she knew would occur if Em suspected that she had spent the night in Zack's bed—albeit alone. Em wouldn't criticize necessarily, but she would ask a hundred questions which Darcie didn't really want to answer.

She tapped lightly on the door, feeling a bit silly for knocking to ask admission to her own room, but out of courtesy for Em's "nurse" she did. A shrill voice said something Darcie couldn't understand and she was about to open the door when it was opened for her.

Opening the door a few inches, Mrs. Appleby peeped out as if she expected to find a sea serpent seeking entrance. Darcie could hardly keep from rolling her eyes. "I'd like to see Em."

"She's sleeping," came the derisive reply. Mrs. Appleby lifted her chin and peered through thick glasses which had slid down her nose.

For a second, Darcie wanted to tell the woman exactly who was in charge, but since Zack had asked Mrs. Appleby to sit with Em, then he should be the one to rebuke her for her obvious insolence. "Then I'll just sit with her a few minutes. I'm sure you have other things to do."

The glare she received for her effort was poisonous, and Mrs. Appleby replied in a steady tone that implied superiority. "I have been hired to nurse Miss Rhett, and nurse her I shall. Until I've been instructed to the contrary, I don't take orders from . . . from the likes of you."

While Mrs. Appleby glanced up and down Darcie's figure, plainly indicating her dislike, color sprang to Darcie's cheeks. The urge to slap the mocking smile off the woman's face was great, but Darcie merely smiled and said, "I see. Thank you, Mrs. Appleby, but this is still my cabin. If you don't step aside, I'll fetch M. Manville and ask his opinion about the matter."

Darcie didn't wait, but pushed on the door a bit and Mrs. Appleby relented. Swallowing her anger, Darcie smiled at the grouchy old woman and crossed the floor to Em's bedside.

Except for her hair and eyelashes, poor Em could hardly be distinguished from the sheets. Darcie felt her friend's head, more from habit than from any medical need. The stench of illness hung heavily in the room and she could hardly breathe, almost retching herself. She turned to Mrs. Appleby. "Where is Poule? Why hasn't he emptied the chamber pots?"

"I wouldn't let a man like that enter the bedchambers of a genteel miss such as Miss Rhett." Her answer, whispered between clenched teeth, was almost a hiss.

The heavy emphasis on "Miss Rhett" provided Darcie with a clue to the treatment she received from Mrs. Appleby. Clearly, Mrs. Appleby considered Darcie to be Zack's mistress and not in the same class with "Miss Rhett."

Darcie said nothing, but shook her head slightly and strode to the small round window. Opening it slightly, she peered out and sucked in the fresh salt air that swirled through the narrow hole. "Keep this window open a bit. I'll be back with Poule."

"That man'll not darken the door of this room," Mrs. Appleby called after her as Darcie closed the door behind her.

What a fool that woman is, Darcie thought and went looking for Poule. She found him in Barclay's room, tucking the sheets firmly under Barclay's chin. "Poule," she whispered and motioned for him to come into the corridor.

"Yes, missy?" he asked, closing the door behind him.

Darcie smiled and touched the old sailor on the arm. "I need your help."

"Anything you say, miss," he said and smiled eagerly, showing a gaping hole where two of his front teeth should be. "I be happy to help."

"Thank you. I appreciate your cooperative attitude." Darcie turned slightly so that she could see the door to her cabin. The slight opening told her that Mrs. Appleby was listening at the doorway. "Poule, go to my cabin as soon as you have a minute and empty those . . ." Darcie hesitated. A Southern lady never mentioned anything so private as a chamber pot to a man. Everyone knew of their existence, but nobody acknowledged them. She swallowed and continued, "Those chamber pots. The room smells so awful that I can't abide the place."

"I'm sorry, missy, but it ain't my fault," he explained. "That ole cur Mizz Appleby, not a pleasant sort I'm a thinkin', practically throwed me out when I went to do just that."

Darcie gathered her strength and lifted her chin. "If she gives you any problems, throw *her* out."

A gasp from behind her told Darcie that Mrs. Appleby had heard her instructions to Poule, and although the old crone would be furious with her, he'd be allowed to do his job. Darcie could hardly keep from laughing at the image of Poule tossing Mrs. Appleby from the room.

She turned to watch Poule as he strode down the hallway like a man on a mission, and didn't miss the glowering look from Mrs. Appleby as she opened the door to admit him. The look she reserved for Darcie was one of pure hatred, but Darcie didn't care. Em would never recuperate in an environment like the one Mrs. Appleby had created.

Darcie had looked in on all her friends. Barclay merely moaned a greeting and nothing else. Charity was considerably better, although not fully restored to her usual quarrelsome self, while Sissy offered a loud snore.

Leaving the servants' room, she closed the door behind and glanced up and down the corridor. She had nowhere to go.

Nowhere, except on deck. She almost ran up the steps and when she reached the top, she inhaled deeply, as if the fresh air could cure all her problems.

"Evening, miss," came a quiet masculine voice she didn't recognize.

Whirling, she found herself facing a young man whose blond hair almost glowed in the moonlight. It ruffled slightly with the breeze. "Good evening, sir."

"The sea's a lovely place," he said, gesturing to the expanse of ocean before them. "And *La Mer Magnifique* is the finest ship at sail."

Darcie nodded. Now that her ship lay at the bottom of the ocean, *La Mer Magnifique* probably was the best.

"Well, good night, miss." He walked away whistling a jaunty tune.

Feeling a bit better, Darcie returned her attention to her thoughts. Everyone seemed to have conspired against her—even God.

Night had fallen some time ago, and the stars were brilliant across the western part of the sky. To the east, storm clouds billowed like black silk over a diamond-studded skirt. As she watched, the dark clouds finally obliterated all the stars and the moon took refuge from the rising storm.

Darcie was so deep in thought that she never felt the first droplets of rain that peppered her, the deck, and the sea. The question "Why" obscured all her senses.

Why had her uncle insisted upon her coming to Paris? Why had he chosen a husband for her? Why was Zack so irresistible? Why was there such a mystery about him and his involvement with the piracy of her ship? One question plagued her like a blister on the bottom of her foot: Why had Mrs. Appleby chosen *La Mer Magnifique?*

But the last "why" question, one that had just occurred to her, confounded her. Why was she falling in love with Zack, a man who had undoubtedly eluded the clutches of many beautiful, and wealthy, women?

Zack found her standing at the railing, staring across the midnight sea. She didn't hear his approach, nor his voice when he called to her. He touched her shoulder gently.

Darcie nearly jumped overboard, he frightened her so badly. Holding her close to calm her, he asked, "What were you thinking about? Were you back in Charleston?"

Commanding her heart to stop racing, she closed her eyes briefly and then looked at Zack. She'd been so miserable, so alone, that she was wallowing in self-pity. Other girls had faced worse.

Love? Had she really fallen in love?

She had compounded her problems by falling in love with Zack. How did she know she was in love? Who could she ask? Certainly not Zack. "I . . . Oh, Zack, what am I to do?"

"What do you mean?" Zack's face registered the surprise he felt over her answer. He'd expected a light retort, a scolding, anything but this plaintive plea for help. "Come, Darcie, tell me what's troubling you."

"Nothing," she quipped, feeling the drizzle for the first time. "And everything."

"My, my, but this is serious." He thought for a moment and said, "Come with me. I think you need a glass of wine."

"I don't need a glass—"

"Ah, but you do." He touched her damp hair and then her chin. He gazed into her eyes and saw misery. Zack's heart was filled with pain far greater than hers, to see her so sad. Her pain was doubled in him.

She looked at him and recognized the compassion. His arms drew her into their circle, and she succumbed to the comfort he offered. His thumb traced the line of her cheek and jaw, while his body shut off the rising wind and rain.

Her body was suffused with warmth, and she clung to him, absorbing the comfort of his protective embrace. With gentle fingers, he tugged at her chin until her upturned face was below his and she felt the warm puffs of his breath on her face.

Zack gazed down at her. Tiny droplets of water sparkled on her cheeks and in her hair, and he felt her shiver in his arms. Her breasts were pressed against his chest, and his entire body stiffened with desire for her as he whispered. "You shouldn't be out here alone in the cold rain."

Darcie stared up at him, and the warmth of her body grew into heat that consumed her wherever his body touched hers. "I just . . ." What could she say to him? "I just wanted a breath of fresh air."

"A breath of fresh air is one thing, but you've been standing here for some time." He held her away from himself and looked at her up and down. "You're as wet as an anchor just pulled from the sea."

Darcie laughed. He always made her laugh, even when she didn't want to. "I feel like one."

Beneath them, the sea was rising. The American clipper ship rode high on the crest of a wave and slid down into a deep valley between two mountains of water. Spray began to fly through the air, dousing them with salty water as the ship pitched back and forth, like a ball between two children.

Zack loved to hear her laugh. "If we stay here much longer, we'll look like two jellyfish washed aboard by the waves."

Darcie felt like a jellyfish. Beneath her, legs that had been as sturdy as the ship's timbers seemed as boneless as a jellyfish. "Careful, you may get stung," she warned.

"Aye, aye, matey," he mocked. "And what a pleasure that'd be."

His laugh was infectious, and they clung to the railing and to each other for support. Wet golden curls matted her forehead, and he brushed them out of her face. Jellyfish indeed. She looked more like a lovely mermaid to him, wet hair considered. Regardless of what she was, or what she looked like, she'd woven a spell around him, the silken lair of a mermaid set to trap an unwary sailor.

Wary or unwary, he was trapped in her spell. At that moment he cared nothing for the wind and the rain that pelted them, for the sea that bounced them. He kissed her. Lips claimed lips, forgetting everything else.

Her mouth opened to his, and the transformation of her bones to jelly was complete. Darcie was within his power, the power of his kiss to sustain her and the power of his arms to keep her from falling. Pressed between the railing and his equally hard body, she clung to him and reveled in the wonder of his kiss.

Problems forgotten, she immersed herself in the ecstasy of his touch as his hands traveled down her spine, tracing the narrow pathway that sent sensations shimmering throughout her body. Feeling the vise of his embrace, she opened her mouth further and tentatively touched his tongue with hers. She felt him stiffen against her momentarily and then he moved away, allowing a rush of cold air and rain to envelop her.

His voice was raspy, gravelly, as if he'd been ill with a sore throat. "Come. We can't remain here in the weather."

Darcie allowed him to lead her downstairs, expecting him to stop outside her cabin, but he didn't. They walked on to his cabin and he paused, almost imperceptibly, and then flung open the door.

Forcing herself to breathe, she looked around the familiar room. Across the way, the bed loomed as large as a mountain in a small lake. Before she could speak, Zack closed the door and left her alone. Puzzled, she stared at the doorway and for her troubles, got only a glimpse of herself in his mirror.

Her problems immediately flew from her mind. She looked like a wet puppy. No wonder he'd left so abruptly. Abashed at having had someone see her in this condition, she immediately set to fixing her appearance. She might be a waif on a sea of trouble, but she could at least *look* like a lady.

Chapter Eleven

Zack leaned against the door. What was he doing?

Darcie was a young woman in his care, one he'd been charged with bringing to France safely. He closed his eyes as he recalled how close he'd come to whisking her off to the bed, unmindful of her protestations.

Damn the sea witch for being so beautiful and vulnerable. He marched down the corridor and stopped outside Darcie's cabin when the solution came to him. Mrs. Appleby. He'd hire her to be Darcie's chaperone for the remainder of the voyage and thereby solve all his problems. That old bat would never allow poor Darcie a moment's peace, but she'd keep him away—and Barclay as well, if he recovered sufficiently to pursue a woman before they made port.

That was the cure to his problems. No more would he pace the deck, his body demanding that he abandon his position and go below to the comforts he knew awaited him in Darcie's arms. The knowledge of that old crone's presence in Darcie's cabin would chill even the most heated of passions.

He rapped lightly on the door. After knocking again, the

door opened a bit and black eyes pierced him from within the dimly lit room. "And what might you be awantin'?"

"I humbly beg your pardon for awakening you, but—"

"Awakening is it?" Mrs. Appleby drew herself to her full height. "Be ye accusin' me of abandoning me post to sleep? Full awake I was by the sweet miss's bedside, poor dearie."

Poor dearie, indeed, he thought. "No. No, you misunderstand me. I've come . . ."

Why had he come? In spite of his desire to provide Darcie with some protection against his amorous intentions, he couldn't foist this old crone off on her.

"I reckon you be comin' to draw me across the grid for sassin' yer . . . that little tart." Mrs. Appleby crossed her arms and scowled. "Well, it be no more than she deserved, bustin' in here and disturbin' the young miss, openin' them little windows to let the night air choke my sweet lady, and settin' that viper Poule on me. Why she sent him in here with the miss abed and all, and—"

Zack gaped at her for a moment and refused to listen to any more. "When Mlle. Gaynor visits Mlle. Rhett, I expect you to treat her as well, no, *better* than you treat Mlle. Rhett. Mlle. Gaynor is your employer, not Emilie Rhett and not me."

"I assure you that—"

"No. I assure *you* that if you disobey her, if you make her uncomfortable in any way when she visits Em, then I'll . . ." Zack couldn't think of a punishment fitting enough for this opinionated wretch. "I'll toss you to the sharks for their supper, if they can swallow a morsel as bitter as yourself."

Hatred gleamed in Hildegard Appleby's eyes. "If you think I'll lower myself to her level, why I'd sooner *be* a shark's supper."

"Suit yourself," Zack replied, glaring at her. Why had he ever allowed her on his ship? "In the meantime, Miss Gaynor is in my cabin and desires fresh clothes. Because of your acid tongue, she preferred the storm above to the warmth of her own cabin. If I've made myself clear, you'll find her toilet articles and a nightgown and take them to her immediately."

"I'd sooner—"

Zack shoved the door open and thundered into the room. "On second thought, I'll take them myself."

He found a wrapper, her brush, soap, and various other articles he thought she'd want. From a small nook, he took a silk day gown he'd seen her wear in Charleston, a shawl, and a cape. She'd not go lacking because of this old hag.

When morning came, he'd instruct Poule to remove her luggage and wardrobe from her cabin. Darcie could use his own cabin until Attila the Hun had left, if and when Em recovered from her bout of seasickness.

By the time Zack returned to his own cabin, scowling with anger for the insolent Mrs. Appleby, Darcie had settled herself on a narrow divan with a book, after unpinning her damp hair to allow it to dry. Clad in her own nightgown, she was surprised that he had returned so quickly. She had expected him to remain at the wheel for the duration of the storm. When he burst through the doorway, she jumped to her feet and her hair swung to her waist in a waterfall of curls.

Taking a look at the load in his arms, she cried, "Dry clothes! My brush! Oh, thank you, Zack."

She reached up and kissed him lightly, like a little girl giddy with the joy of receiving a present. He dropped the clothing over a chair and placed the toilet articles on the table where they had eaten their meal.

Without thinking, he drew her into his embrace and clung to her. A woman as sweet and innocent as this didn't deserve the wrath of Mrs. Appleby. Damn the woman for her haughty bigotry. Ever since the interview, she'd thought of Darcie as Zack's mistress, as was evidenced by her lack of respect.

Guiltily, Zack acknowledged that it was his fault. He wanted to make it up to Darcie, but didn't really know how. Nothing he could do would convince Mrs. Appleby that Darcie wasn't his mistress, and the more he protested, the more firmly convinced she'd become that she was right.

He ran his fingers along Darcie's spine, tracing the tiny even bumps down past her waist. Blood thundered in his head, filling every part of him with desire for her.

"Darcie," he whispered into her hair, wrapping great handfuls about his fist, and tilting her head back to accept his kiss.

Zack's mouth descended on hers with a ferocity previously unknown to her. He seemed to need all of her, to touch all of her, to kiss all of her, to possess all of her.

The thin gown between them was nothing, a wisp that he could rip away easily. Zack knew he should restrain himself, but after all, Darcie was his intended, even though she didn't know it yet. He wanted to tell her, to tell her as he introduced her to love, but he held back, realizing that she'd be furious with him for not telling her sooner.

Deep inside Zack realized that Darcie meant more to him than any other woman ever could. She had touched a nerve in him, hidden away, protected from the grasp of conniving, greedy women, but vulnerable to one woman alone. He didn't want to think about the consequences of that discovery.

For now, he'd make love to her. This would be the most memorable night of their lives. Other women, other conquests meant nothing now as he peered down into glittering pools of cobalt fringed with long golden lashes. Color flowered in her cheeks and he felt her go limp in his arms. Startled a moment, he thought she might have fainted, but she merely slumped against him for support.

He nuzzled her ear, kissing its lobes lightly, nibbling, tracing a sensuous trail from her ear to her eyes with his tongue. Light kisses feathered her eyelids and his lips moved down to hers, moist and soft, awaiting his kiss.

Darcie's body went limp. Unable to hold herself erect, she gave her well-being into Zack's care and succumbed to, welcomed his kisses. She lifted her head to allow him free range of her face and neck. Along her ears and cheek, a little trail of fire, like a fuse on a stick of dynamite, sped on its way to her eyelids where he barely brushed them as they closed. The tip of her nose tingled with his kiss and then her lips melded with his in a desire born of weeks of restraint. Their kisses, heretofore playful and sometimes deep, were nothing compared to this.

Feeling oddly buoyant, Darcie smiled inwardly. For the first time, she confronted her own emotions. Without ever realizing the peril of doing so, she had fallen in love with Zacharie Manville. No other man had affected her in the same, vital way as he did. With a glance, he lifted her spirits, sent her reeling into the world of passion that she'd only heard about in whispered conversations. Within her heart, love that had begun as a tight little bud now blossomed full and wonderful.

The kiss consumed their entire bodies. She felt the pressure growing on her left breast and realized that his hand had closed over its fullness. Color sprang to her cheeks in response to his thumb brushing her nipple, a hard pebble beneath the flimsy fabric.

Zack lifted her in his arms and strode across the room as if she weighed no more than a gull's stray feather. Depositing her on the bed, he noticed her eyes—wide and frightened. Kissing her gently and whispering soft words, he tried to reassure her that he wouldn't hurt her, but she clung to him.

Darcie knew he was going to make love to her, and she knew she wouldn't stop him. Never in her entire life had she felt as alive as she now did, in his arms, with his hand cradling her breast. Strobes of lightning shot from each point where he touched her and she felt the glow of desire warm every cell of her body.

She wanted him as badly as he wanted her. He would be gentle, he had whispered. He wouldn't hurt her. In her heart, Darcie recognized his promise as false, but she trusted him anyway. He didn't want to hurt her, but he would. When a woman lay with a man for the first time, pain was inevitable.

Somehow, Darcie wanted to convey to him that she didn't object to his lovemaking, but she didn't know how to respond. Without experience to provide her with knowledge of a man's pleasure, she simply rested her hands on his chest and enjoyed his caresses.

His cheeks were scratchy against hers and soon her blush was heightened by tiny abrasions. Color stained her swollen lips as they begged silently for his kiss.

Darcie hardly remembered anything of those moments except for his warm presence and the shower of tiny kisses with which he covered her face. Her skin tingled from head to toe, but the most delightful sensations emanated from her face where his kisses and caresses were concentrated while he was occupied with his clothing.

There was nothing between them except the thin fabric of her gown. His hands roamed up and down her stomach and he pushed her further back on the bed and lay down beside her.

Darcie soared like a sail, free to fly on the wind except for Zack's hold on her. In the dim candlelight, she could see his face suffused with color. He peered down into her eyes, as if asking for the permission she refused to voice.

How could she answer? She snuggled her body closer to his, writhing against his length and drew her hand across his wide chest, stopping to tease the tiny buds of his nipples.

He groaned and smothered her with more kisses, his body half across hers pushing her deep into the feather mattress. His hands stole around to her back and slid down to her buttocks. Darcie arched in surprise, bringing her into direct contact with his swollen manhood.

Throbbing against her thigh, the evidence of his arousal stiffened when she moved even slightly. Then she realized that he'd completely removed his shirt. Heady with excitement, she brushed her fingernails across his chest, leaving fine pink lines embedded in his golden tan. Her fingers toyed with the springy black curls that covered his bare chest and ended in a dark line below his navel where his pants obscured her view.

He moaned as she traced the line of hair down to his waist, splayed her fingers and lightly brought the nails back up to his nipples. His muscles seemed to ripple from her touch, and she reached his neck and encircled it with her arms.

Mewling in anticipation, she drew his head down to kiss his lips. She brushed them lightly and then moved on to his cheeks and nibbled his ears, passing on her knowledge of erotic joys learned from him just moments ago.

Groaning, he held her hands out beside her, preventing her from touching him at all, and kissed her deeply, savagely, and Darcie knew her lips would bear the badge of his delicious assault.

Knowing that she might still be frightened if he should do something she didn't expect, Zack carefully slid one arm beneath her neck and caressed her stomach with his other hand. He kissed her deeply, thrusting his tongue between her teeth and plunging it inside her mouth to taste the sweetness.

In one motion, he stripped the gown from her body. Ever mindful of her naivete, Zack continued to hold her and kiss her, occasionally reassuring her with tender words. His hand now hovered over her naked stomach; his eyes gazed at her heaving breasts.

When he kissed her again, he rested his hand on her stomach and massaged gently, moving his hand in an ever-widening circle. He could hardly restrain himself.

Still poised with his body half-covering hers, he moved down slightly, feathering kisses on her neck and chest until he reached her breasts. Slowing down when he reached the gentle rise of cleavage, he tantalized, taunted, tracing his tongue all the way around first one and then the other of her breasts, gradually decreasing the figure eight until he stopped on her left nipple.

With his tongue, he teased the hard nipple until it became like a rock, a pebble on a warm beach. Beneath him, she writhed and struggled to get closer, but still he held her hands and tormented her with his passion.

Outside the sea raged, thunder shook the foundations of the earth, and the lightning threw daylight across the midnight sky. Inside Darcie, the storm equaled the one outside. Desire raged, blood ravaged her veins as it thundered through on a course set by the lightning sparked from her heart.

Darcie had never felt this way, but Zack seemed not to notice and continued to tug and suck at her breasts, nipping occasionally and holding them between his teeth and moving from one to the other. The undulating waves of passion lifted her higher and nobody existed in the world except the two of them. Zack teased her masterfully, bringing her desire to the level of his and he sent it past, careening down waves of uncharted waters.

When he sensed that all her inhibitions lay shattered about her, he began to work towards lifting her into rapture. He traced a line with his thumbs from each nipple down to her navel, and spanned his hands to encircle her tiny waist. Caressing her buttocks, he moved her slightly to accommodate his ministrations and continued.

Darcie's emotions sailed on. Flying high before a brisk wind, she was on the edge of tranquillity one minute and on the verge of ecstasy the next.

Zack trailed his fingers down further, seeking the light tangle of hair that grew over his objective. Her quiver sent excitement zinging through him like an arrow toward its target. He kissed her again and again, hardly taking, nor giving her time to breathe.

Taking the feminine moans that occasionally erupted from Darcie as encouragement, Zack played with the springy growth and noticed the way she wriggled in response. Closer and closer he came to her sexuality until his fingertips detected a bit of moisture. Inhaling deeply, he showered kisses on her face and claimed her mouth once more, edging his fingers to the center of her passion.

Brushing across it lightly, he began to stroke her systematically, holding his own raging emotions in check. Never had he shown such restraint—even with a virgin.

Darcie's eyes sprang open. Zack had touched the most private part of herself. She struggled to rise, to end this masquerade she'd allowed herself to become embroiled in. How could she do this? What would he think of her?

And then she didn't care. The fire that he'd started with his kisses flamed to a new life, fueled by this new sensation.

The scent of him filled her, surrounded her, and stimulated her. She realized that she hadn't been breathing. Sucking in breath after breath of his clean scent, of his slightly spicy soap, her passion renewed itself.

She caught the fragrance of leather, of oil, of the salt air, all mingled with his scent and it enveloped her in a delightfully sensuous world of Zack. Every inch of her body sang beneath his touch as his hands wandered over her skin. Forcing her eyes open, she saw him looking at her body and color flooded her cheeks. His movement had stopped and he simply stared.

He glanced at her and kissed her deeply, allowing her senses a chance to rest before a fresh onslaught of sensations. Raising himself slightly, he held himself over her and positioned himself between her legs, all the while feathering her face with kisses or whispering sweet words in her ears.

Suddenly, he lay between her legs and his swollen manhood pressed against her soft moistness. Her breasts were pressed flat by his chest, her body pinioned to the bed by his.

Moving ever so gently, he kissed her, cupping her face in his palms, and then his hands wandered downward to caress her breasts. He slid his hands beneath her, cradling her buttocks in his hands.

His hips were writhing on top of hers, grinding his manhood against the entrance to her femininity. He raised up slightly, and peered down into her frightened eyes, and whispered. "Trust me, Darcie."

His mouth swooped down on hers and his tongue lunged into her mouth, plundering its tender recesses wildly. The pressure on her lower body increased as he pressed down on her, and then he jerked her buttocks toward him with both hands and plunged inside her.

Darcie's eyes flew open and she cried out against his mouth. For a few moments, his hips lay still against hers, and his kisses deepened while he caressed her left breast with gentle fingers. And then the fire that had been nearly doused by the stab of pain in her lower stomach flickered to life.

"Relax," he whispered, and nibbled at her earlobe.

After a minute, his hips began to move rhythmically against hers, and hers started keeping the same pace. The stabbing pain that had stunned her just moments before subsided and became no more than a stinging sensation she found curiously exciting.

Her body became light and free, jerking of its own will and she kissed his neck, tasting the slight salty flavor of his perspiration as she clung frantically to him. Deeper and deeper he thrust into her as her passion heightened until she no longer knew who she was and no longer cared. His clean spicy scent now combined with the fragrance of the candles and with the salty air coming through the porthole, and another aroma mingled with those. At first she couldn't define it, but she decided that it must be the scent of their bodies coming together—and their perfume intoxicated her into a near frenzy of motion.

Zack slowed a bit, allowing her to catch her breath, and then plunged on, bringing her to the brink of something she'd never known. Deep inside her a tingling began, and it spread until all her cells sang with her furious passion. A low moan, almost like a purr, erupted from her as her head thrashed back and forth on the pillow before he captured it with his hands and held her motionless beneath him, kissing her face all over and then her lips.

His lips caressed her a moment and then crushed them as he arrived at the precipice with her. The rapture was prolonged for a few seconds before it began to subside, ebbing and flowing like a low tide.

Zack continued to kiss her, though he slid off her to allow her to breathe. He'd never experienced an intimacy quite like this one. Even though she'd been virginal, she'd responded with a passion he'd never seen in a woman—not even the false passion of a hired woman.

He smoothed her hair away from her face and noticed the moisture. He continued to caress her, whispering gentle words in her ears as he nibbled and played, bringing her down slowly. Knowing that if the experience moved *him* as it had, then it must have had quite an impact on her.

Darcie had achieved the gratification he'd hoped she would. How would she react? Would she hate him forever or cling to him like a vine?

Tears welled in Darcie's eyes. She'd found true happiness, a moment in time that she would treasure always with a man she'd never forget.

But it couldn't happen again. Darcie was promised to another and she knew without doubt that no man wanted soiled goods. She'd have to tell him, whoever he was, that she was no longer pure.

Gazing into Zack's eyes, she saw that he didn't understand her tears. He never would. Men were seldom afraid to take what they wanted from a woman, but never wanted the woman they married to have experienced pleasure at another man's hands. Now she was condemned to a life alone, but she didn't regret what she'd done. At least she wouldn't have to marry some old dotard.

Even as they'd started, she could have stopped him. Something within her refused to allow her to do so. Something inside her demanded that she experience this pleasure with Zack, and she lacked the will to deny it. No, that wasn't exactly right. Darcie had a will of iron. She'd allowed him to take her with her blessings. She'd never offered even token resistance. She'd wanted him as badly as he wanted her.

Darcie startled herself. Did this moment make her the same sort of woman as Miss Smith—the wharf woman who'd applied to be her chaperone? Darcie couldn't picture herself strolling along the dock, hiking her skirts for any man's eyes.

If she never experienced intimacy again, she wouldn't care. Zack had satisfied her for a lifetime. And her love fluttered in her heart like a butterfly over a meadow of clover.

Zack had other plans for her. Aroused once again, he began to caress her in earnest, kissing and fondling. He knew that once he got up from her bed, she might never allow him near her again, especially after she'd had a few days to consider the implications of their lovemaking.

He'd seen the glistening in her eyes and known it was due to tears, but she hadn't cried openly. Was she disappointed?

Startled, he drew back and stared at her. There was no doubt that she'd been moved by their experience. Even now, her eyelids were half-open, as if she didn't understand why he'd pulled away.

Why the tears? He kissed her again and again, until her breath came in short gasps and she returned his caresses and kisses. She seemed to be urging him on, encouraging him to continue as she writhed beneath him once again.

And then Zack forgot her troubling tears. Her moans fueled his passion, as did her gentle touch and the tracing of her fingernails down his chest. Her fingers played with his nipples and with the thatch of hair on his chest.

He rolled over, and made Darcie straddle him. He closed his hands over her breasts and she slumped forward.

"No, Zack. This isn't proper." She found that her voice was little more than a purr.

Zack raised her chin. "Trust me, Darcie. I . . . you, can, well . . ." his voice trailed off. There were some things he couldn't say aloud to her, not yet.

He thrust himself inside her, reveling in the velvety feeling of her. For a moment, she seemed a bit puzzled, but accepted his whispered instructions. With a bit of prompting, she mastered the skill and rhythm required to control their motion, and Zack was soon lifted higher and higher by her gentle movements.

Darcie looked down at Zack. He wanted her to determine their progress this time. She rocked slowly, feeling awkward as she moved above him. He filled her, and the pleasure of her motion consumed her.

Closing her eyes, Darcie imagined herself astride a stallion and rode accordingly, pressing her knees into his side and moving her hips in an easy rhythm. His moan stopped her and for a moment she thought she might have injured him in some way.

Zack wanted to control her again, wanted her beneath him, accepting his thrust and parrying with hers. Rolling her over, he planted butterfly kisses all over her face and shoulders, wooing her as he had the first time.

Heaven, Darcie thought. *I've gone to heaven.* With her eyes closed, she envisioned them on clouds of rapture-laden silks and satins. Every aroma heightened her pleasure; every kiss became a treasure to be remembered forever.

For one night in her life, she lived and experienced life as she never had and never would again, but nobody could rob her of the love that bloomed in her heart.

Chapter Twelve

When Darcie awoke Zack was gone. Leaping from the bed, she peered out the small window and looked at the brilliant sky. The storm had passed, and the sky was as blue as the cornflowers that grew in her garden.

She danced over to a small table where she found a pitcher of water and a bar of soap left for her use. As the sun was high in the sky, she quickly washed and dressed, feeling that everybody would wonder where she was this morning.

She gazed at her face in the small mirror and wondered why there was no change in her appearance. Her heart soared like the gulls that rode high on the wind above waves swollen with love. She hadn't felt so good in years.

Guilt drained the joy from her eyes and she slumped into a slatted wooden chair. Her act—or her lack of action—had changed her life irreparably. No longer was she a maiden, riding the golden crest of innocence and frivolity.

Today, Darcie Jeanne Gaynor was a woman—a tainted woman. Nobody knew except her and Zack, but that didn't change the facts. The secret wonders of marriage were no longer mystical; she had delved into their joys without benefit of vows spoken.

Love had not entered into the act from which she had derived so much rapture. *Well,* she thought, *only one of us has considered love. The other merely enjoyed the fruits of her love.*

One night's pleasure ransomed a lifetime. She'd sipped the nectar of love willingly—would she now become its slave? Its victim?

She refused to allow herself to fall into the doldrums. Her life would continue, and she had things to do.

Opening the door, she ran into Zack. "Oh, good morning." She couldn't look into his eyes, and felt the color tinge her cheeks. Wondering why she acted so foolishly, she thought again of last night. She certainly hadn't shown any embarrassment or reticence then.

Zack said nothing, but drew her back inside the door and into his arms as the door closed. Tilting her head up so he could look into her eyes, he kissed her gently. "Good morning, love. How . . ."

What could he say to her? A man didn't inquire of a lady whose virtue he'd stolen, whether she enjoyed herself or not.

He decided to kiss her instead. Lowering his lips to hers, he found them as delightful as ever and deepened the kiss. She responded as he'd hoped and he held her tightly, bending her head backwards with the pressure of his caress.

The color in Darcie's cheeks blossomed. Zack's kisses took her breath away, and she clung to him for support. His hand massaged her breast, and she found that she longed to take him to her bed once again.

A loud knock interrupted them. "Breakfast," he whispered, releasing her.

Darcie moved across the room as Poule entered with a tray. "Mornin', missy."

"Good morning, Poule," she answered breathlessly. Praying that he wouldn't remain to talk, she smiled shyly. Could he see a difference in her this morning? Was she to be plagued for the rest of her life wondering if anyone could see the change in her?

"Thank you, Poule. That's all for now." Zack dismissed him without further delay. Damn the man for standing about and gawking at Darcie.

The man that married her would spend his life fighting off such stares and fawning. He watched as the older man left and then turned to her, noting the high color of her cheeks. Zack knew of no way to lessen her embarrassment, but he could eliminate her confusion and insecurity.

He strode across to her and took her in his arms, offering the comfort and solace of his embrace. After dropping a light kiss on her forehead, he led her to the table. "Breakfast is getting cold."

Darcie nodded. She didn't know what she'd expected, nor did she know what he expected of her. Did he think she'd fling herself into bed once he'd come back into the room? Or did he plan to ignore their evening together, pretend it had never happened?

They ate in silence. When they had finished, Zack cleaning his plate and Darcie playing with her food, he excused himself.

"I've got some things to attend to, but I'll see you for the noon meal." He stood up, walked to her end of the table and kissed her lightly.

She watched him open the door to leave. Tears clouded her eyes, and, hungering for some recognition of mutual feeling, she called after him, "Zack!"

He spun and looked at her, smiling as he did. "Yes?"

"I . . . well, I . . ." her voice trailed off. What could she say? She dared not ask if he hated her now that he'd conquered her, although she thought he might. After all, she hadn't put up a fight.

He returned to her and pulled her to her feet. Lifting her gently, he carried her to the bed and laid her across it. Lying down beside her, he reached down to kiss her soundly. He knew she was insecure, uncertain of how to act.

"Don't worry, *ma cherie,*" he whispered. "You are lovely this morning. I wish I could remain here with you all day, but duty calls."

Darcie clung to him, hating herself as she did. His kisses stirred her, reviving the passion hovering beneath her tremulous smile. "I know. I'm just . . ."

"You're just a beautiful woman who shall haunt me while I'm away." He kissed her again, wishing that he could stay, but knowing he could not. If there were no other passengers, he'd closet himself with her for the remainder of the voyage, but he owed his guests a rapid, safe trip. "I'll be back as soon as I can slip away."

"Don't trouble yourself for me. I'll be fine," she lied, wondering what she had really expected him to say. He had never claimed to love her, had offered no evidence of love. "I'll read."

"I'll look in on Em and tell her you're not feeling well," he added, knowing that facing her friend might be troubling her. "And I'll tell Charity that you're doing some correspondence for me."

"Oh, would you?" She felt a bit better knowing that her meeting with Charity would be postponed for a while. "Thank you."

Zack left her with a smile on her face. Her excitement returned as she considered her first foray into the grown-up world of making love. He had been considerate of her, she was sure. She'd overheard many tales of horror told when nobody thought she was listening.

Overall, she thought that making love was wonderful. Darcie liked the way she looked this morning, mature and wise. Did that difference really exist?

Darcie could stand the confines of the room no longer. She found that every time she looked up from her book, her gaze strayed to the bed and she pictured Zack there beckoning her.

Action was required. Checking her appearance as she opened the door, Darcie smiled and strode out.

She looked in on Barclay first. He was still in the throes of his malaise. Sissy was no better, but Darcie spent a few minutes with Charity.

Charity felt a bit better, enough to comfort Sissy, but not

enough to notice any change in Darcie. After a few minutes, Darcie moved on.

At Em's door, she glared at Mrs. Appleby and strode past without a word. Em's eyes opened a bit and she tried to smile at Darcie. Darcie patted her friend's hand and fluffed her pillow a bit. As Em's eyes closed again, Darcie left the room. She didn't want to converse with Mrs. Appleby at all.

The sea called her. Had Darcie been a boy, she'd have been a sailor for sure. During her father's lifetime, she'd traveled a little with him and found that she thoroughly enjoyed the sea.

Though she was not experienced by any means, he'd allowed her to help him in his calculations and had even let her take the helm.

"Halloo! I say, halloo down there," came a masculine voice from above.

Darcie looked up and spotted a young sailor she'd seen on several occasions. He held himself securely with one hand and waved his cap with the other. Smiling, she waved back. He seemed so cheerful that his greeting brightened her day considerably.

Knowing that she shouldn't be keeping him from his work, she walked on a short distance and stopped to look at the undulating blue-green water. Some distance from the ship, she spotted a school of dolphins playing about in the waves and watched them for a time.

Zack found her standing at the railing again. "I didn't think you'd stay in your room very long."

Darcie smiled, marveling at how much easier it was to talk with him since that first awkward meeting after they'd made love. "You're right. I felt the call of the sea."

"I'm glad." He rested his elbow on the railing and studied her. She seemed to be happier than she was when he'd gone in to see her this morning. Perhaps she'd resolved the problems that were confronting her. "Would you like to stroll about the deck with me?"

"Oh, do you have time?" Darcie looked up at him, startled

by his suggestion since he'd already warned her that he would be busy most of the day. "I don't want to impose."

"You're not imposing." Zack took her hand and tucked it in the crook of his arm. "I always have time to promenade around the deck with a beautiful woman."

They strolled around the deck several times. The fresh air was wonderful and Darcie was glad of the exercise, until she spotted the sailor Captain James had warned her about.

He was watching her closely and she stopped walking. "Zack, who is that man?"

"What man?"

"The one over there by those kegs of rice," Darcie answered, trying not to point.

Zack glanced at the sailor. "He's Pierre Le Blanc. Why do you ask?"

"No reason," Darcie lied. She couldn't confront Zack with her suspicions until she knew more. "Has he been with you for very long?"

"With me?" Zack considered her question. He couldn't understand why she took such an interest in the man. "I suppose. Actually, he works for me a while, when I need him, and when I don't, he doesn't."

"I see." Darcie moved on. She didn't like the way the man looked at her. His eyes seemed to be sizing her up, calculating the risk. "What's for dinner? I'm starving."

Zack laughed. He felt the same way. After a night as marvelous as last, and a morning as trying as this, he was ready to settle down for a meal with lovely Darcie. Actually, he could skip the food and have Darcie instead. "Soon. I'm hungry, too. We'll stop by the galley and hurry Cook."

Darcie found Cook to be a delightful Frenchman whose sense of humor rivaled Zack's. They spoke with him a few minutes and then returned to Zack's cabin to await their meal.

Zack sat at his desk and made calculations, stopping frequently to examine his charts and maps. The ship's log was a thick book bound in leather, and Zack removed it from its compartment in the desk.

Watching him open it and begin to write, Darcie was glad to find out where he kept it. The log book might provide a clue about the piracy of her ship—particularly if Zack were involved in any way.

Since she had nothing to do, she scurried down the corridor to her cabin, and without knocking, hurried in and found her basket of needlework. Mrs. Appleby glared in open hatred, but Darcie ignored her and peeked at Em who was still sleeping.

When she returned to Zack's cabin, she settled on a chair near a small porthole and took out her embroidery. Tucking a cushion behind her back, she felt much better having her hands doing busy work. Counting the neat stitches and following an intricate pattern kept her from thinking about last night. And, if she didn't think about it—she didn't get flushed and warm all over. After a while, she felt that she was being watched and looked up.

Zack was staring at her. "Is something wrong?" she asked.

"Wrong?" Zack smiled, sheepishly. "Uh, no. Nothing's wrong."

"Then why were you staring?" Darcie placed her needlework on her lap and gazed at him. He was a handsome man in a rugged sort of way. Deep eyes the color of brandy in a cut glass decanter, hair like the centers of the black-eyed susans in her garden, a mouth wide and sensuous, dominated his sun-bronzed face of smooth planes and square jaw.

Darcie discovered she wasn't breathing. Looking closely at him as she had been took her breath away.

"Actually, I'd rather not say," Zack admitted.

What kind of nonsense was this? He stared at her as if her hair had turned green and then refused to say why. Fresh color dappled her cheeks, and she glared at him. "If you refuse to answer, then I shall—"

"Hold on. Don't get so upset." Zack held up his hands as if to ward off the daggers sent by her eyes. "It isn't that bad."

"Well, apparently it is, if you won't admit to your thoughts," Darcie retorted, regretting her sharp tone. After all, he'd only been looking at her and she was just as guilty as he, for she'd been looking at him, too.

"Promise you won't become angry?" he asked.

"I already am." Darcie narrowed her eyes, trying to convey her anger that was ebbing almost as quickly as it had come.

Zack smiled and then tried to appear serious. "I just find that it is, well, I think that, now don't take my—"

Darcie interrupted him, waving a hand in disbelief. "You act like a little boy caught sitting in the apple tree trying to deny that he'd been eating apples."

"Oh, that it were so simple." Zack tried not to laugh. He knew she was having as difficult a time as he, but gave her no reprieve. "Alas, I was stunned by the beauty of a maiden so fair at such a simple chore."

Darcie studied him for a moment. At least a part of his answer was true, she thought. "Aye, sir, but you wouldn't find the task so simple were you to try setting stitches in a ship rocking as this one does."

Delighted to have been let off the hook, he laughed. *"Ma cherie,* I'd have a difficult time setting stitches were the sea as frozen as the highest of the Alps."

Laughing, Darcie picked up her needlework again. Plainly, he didn't intend to tell her why he had been staring. Maybe someday he would.

Soon Darcie heard footsteps in the corridor and jumped up. Running lightly to the door, she glanced at Zack, who was immersed in his books. Before she reached the door, a knock sounded, and she swung the door open.

Poule stood there with a tray balanced on his shoulder. "Cook sent this special for you, miss," he said.

Zack looked up and smiled. Everybody, it seemed, adored Darcie. Everybody except Mrs. Appleby.

After he placed the tray on the table, Poule excused himself. Darcie quickly set the table, feeling as if she would starve if she waited a second longer for the aromatic meal. Cook had promised her a French dish, and if the smell was any indication, it would be delicious.

Chicken with wine sauce, served with crusty bread, was the main course. A fine onion soup was the appetizer.

Darcie could hardly wait for Zack to sit down. They ate in silence as she savored the delicate flavors. He watched her with interest, although he didn't neglect his own meal. For dessert, there was a tart made of a flaky crust with a strawberry jam center.

"That's the best meal I've eaten in a long time." Darcie pushed back from the table and rested her hands in her lap. "Too bad Em's feeling too poorly to taste it."

"I don't think Em will be getting any of this," Zack replied and pushed away from the table, too.

Darcie gazed at him, wondering what he could mean. "Why not?"

"I believe Cook made this meal especially for you." He stood and stretched. "Everybody else gets something much less spectacular."

"But, why?"

"Because, *ma cherie,* nobody else feels up to eating it. Such rich food . . ." Zack paused, staring at their empty plates. "On queasy stomachs would—"

"Never mind. I understand." Darcie could visualize only too easily the results of such a meal. Picking up her embroidery, she settled in her comfortable chair by the window again, peering restlessly out for a moment before resuming her sewing. "Well, pass my compliments on to Cook. And my thanks."

"Consider it done." Zack strode across the room and glanced at his calculations before looking at Darcie again.

If she knew what he'd been thinking a while ago, she'd be furious with him. Zack whirled and studied her for a minute, watching her eyes slowly rise from her work.

Sapphire eyes met brandy-colored eyes. Darcie felt the breath knocked out of her from sheer anticipation, from remembering how it felt to be in his arms, to feel his caresses on her body, to feel him inside her. Fresh color crept into her cheeks as they continued to stare at each other.

"Now what?" she asked, determined to find the answer this

time to his stares. "Why are you staring now? I'm beginning to feel like a stage actress."

"Actress?" He came abruptly back to the present. He had been imagining her in bed again, naked and flushed, warm and soft against his skin. "I apologize. I didn't realize I was making you uncomfortable."

"Uncomfortable doesn't describe how you've made me feel," she whispered, feeling her body temperature rise, or so it seemed. Every part of her warmed under his gaze. Her hands quivered and she stuck her finger. "Ouch!"

Zack looked startled a moment and then rushed across the room. "Darcie, my darling, are you hurt?"

Grabbing her hand so he could look at her injury, he knocked her needlework into the floor. Both of them reached to pick up the basket at the same time and their heads banged together.

"Ouch!" she repeated, snatching her hand back from him and sucking her injured finger as she bent over once again. "I'll get it."

"No, I shall retrieve the basket." Zack rested his hand on her shoulder to prevent her from bending over and then knelt beside her, placing the basket on the table. He took her small hand in his and looked at her injured finger. A tiny sphere of blood appeared on the tip and he brushed it away.

Kissing the end of her finger, he said, "Kissing makes it better."

A little startled by his tenderness, Darcie mumbled, "Kissing. Yes. Always makes it better."

Zack reached for her face and cupped it between his large hands, wincing when he touched her. "Ow. *Sacre bleu.*"

"What is it?" Darcie whispered.

"Blister. From a rope," he replied, caressing her face gently.

"Let me see." Darcie took his hand and looked at it. A nasty blister had formed on his palm near the thumb. Bringing his hand to her mouth, she kissed his blister. "Kissing makes it better."

"Yes, it does." Zack reached around her and drew her close to him. He gazed at her for a moment and then kissed her lightly on the lips. "It certainly does," he added.

Darcie gazed at him, caught once again in his web of passion. Her lips tingled where his had been; her skin sizzled where his hands rested. He closed the distance on them and kissed her again, more urgently, like a starving man devouring his first meal in weeks.

A knock at the door interrupted them before they got any further. Zack leaped to his feet and strode to the door, a thunderous look on his face. He swung the door open and said, "Well, what is it?"

Poule stood sheepishly at the door, glancing past Zack to Darcie. "Mister Rhett wants to see Miss Gaynor."

"Tell him Mlle. Gaynor is eating," Zack replied for her. "She'll be along when she has time."

"Aye, aye, cap'n." Poule disappeared from the doorway and Zack slammed the door.

Darcie broke into a fit of giggles and hid her face from Zack's scowl. He raced across the room and jerked her to her feet, pulling her into his embrace. "Funny, is it?"

His mouth swooped down on hers and the breath left her body. She clung to him, massaging his shoulders and back, reveling in the pleasure of his kiss. All thought of Barclay fled, and Darcie found herself responding eagerly to his caresses.

Zack drew back and gazed at her. "There, that should hold you, you little clown."

"Clown, is it?" Darcie asked, her voice barely audible. She stepped back from him, out of the way of his wandering hands, the hands that had the power to drain passion from her like syrup from a maple tree.

Zack smiled. Damn, but she was feisty. It was a shame he had to leave. All the time he was on deck, he'd thought of nothing but her. Now he was faced with leaving her again, and he dreaded the idea. "We'll have to continue this little discussion later. We need to talk about . . . well, *ma cherie*, we'll talk. I have to go—"

"Go?" Darcie asked and then wondered why. The ship

wouldn't run by itself and he had duties to attend to. She watched him move slowly toward the door, as if he were reluctant to leave. Darcie sat down and tucked the pillow more securely behind her back. "Zack?"

"Yes." He turned to see what she wanted.

"Tell me why you were staring this morning." She couldn't go on without knowing. He had to tell her, or she didn't know what she'd do—throw a tantrum, maybe. But, he'd only smile that lovable smile of his and laugh at her. "You must tell me, it's making me crazy."

Zack looked at her. So, his stares disturbed her. In what way, he wondered. What could he tell her other than the truth that she'd believe? Nothing. "Promise you won't get mad?"

"You get no such promises from me. You were staring. You have to suffer the consequences." *There,* she thought, *that should show him the right of the matter.*

Knowing that she would likely be upset if he told her the truth, but more upset if he didn't, Zack began, "Darcie, *ma cherie,* I was staring at you because you're so lovely."

"Zack, you already said that—"

Interrupting her, he continued, "And because I marvel at the difference in you."

His answer puzzled her enough that she couldn't tell if he was being honest or not. "Difference?"

"Oui." Zack started walking toward her again, drawn by the insecurity in her face as she listened to his reasons. Damn her for being so curious. "Yes, difference."

Warily, she watched him, thinking he might be up to some trick to keep from explaining his actions. "You sound like an echo. Tell me what you mean."

Zack sighed. She'd stop at nothing less than the truth. He paused and gazed at her, her chin uplifted, her eyes glittering with the light of the lamp. He wanted her again, here and now. Damn the ship and damn Poule for interrupting them before.

"I'm waiting."

"Darcie, I was marveling at the change in you," he blurted, knowing that he'd end up regretting it.

"Change? What change?" He was getting more obscure all the time, and Darcie thought she'd never understand.

"Yes. The change, the difference in you . . ." He gulped, hating himself for being such a cad as to think such things. "The difference in you from last night, uh, in bed to this morning while you were sitting—"

"Ugh!" Darcie jumped to her feet. "Why, you disgraceful, hateful, squirming eel! How dare you take advantage of me and then mock me about it!"

Darcie knew she wasn't being fair. She'd been just as willing a partner as he. And moments ago she'd been ready to repeat their experience. "What a low-life, mongrel—"

Zack laughed. "Whoa, I get the picture. I'm sorry, but—"

"Sorry? Sorry?" She almost hissed. "Why, you . . ."

She couldn't think of anything horrible enough to say. Anger flew all over her. She felt used, abused, absolved of her own guilt. Frustration grated on her and she reached for something to throw. Her hands grasped the pillow that had yielded comfort to her back, and she flung it with all her might.

Zack ducked, still laughing. His laughter made her even more furious. She reached for a pewter plate and would have thrown it, but he caught her arm first and wrenched the plate away.

Drawing her, fighting and scratching, into his arms, Zack gazed at her, the laughter now vanished like the mist from the morning sea. *Damn if she isn't a little spitfire,* he thought, twisting her arms behind her to protect his already scratched face. He crushed her to him, kissing her as deeply and soundly as he'd ever kissed her, perhaps more so.

Anger had drawn scarlet into her cheeks and fire into her eyes, exciting him greatly. Longing crept into his loins as he released her hands and pressed her buttocks, finagling to get her body firmly against his. His kiss lingered, becoming more loving, deeper. He was consumed with desire for her.

Feeling her go limp in his arms, Zack smiled inwardly. Temper and passion often went hand in hand, and if her recent show of temper was any indication, her passions would be unequaled by any woman he'd known. The evidence he had so far, one night of splendor, proved his theory.

Darcie felt nothing except Zack. Her body sizzled with heat from his touch and his kiss and she wanted him never to stop. Deep inside her, a quiver began and radiated outward, leaving no cell untouched. Molding her body against his, she clung to him and tried to return his passion.

Finally, he drew away. "Darcie, my darling, *ma cherie,* I hate to leave you, but I must. Poule will be looking for me."

Darcie gasped for breath as she sat down on the chair. How could she answer? Should she ask him to stay, to finish what he'd started? No, she was far too proud for that, so she merely nodded, not trusting herself to speak.

As the door closed, she picked up her needlework. Working on the intricate pattern, she felt some of the tension leave her and soon had escaped from the haunting memory of her night with Zack.

Darcie tapped on the door and waited. Not wanting to disturb Charity if she was resting, the knock was hardly audible. But the door swung open and Darcie was greeted by Charity's smiling face.

"How are you?" Darcie asked, hoping that Charity had completely overcome her illness.

"I'se a whole lot better than Sissy, but I ain't ready to dance at St. Cecilia's yet neither." Charity ambled back to her chair and dropped into the seat.

"Well, I'm delighted to see you up and about." From over in the bed, Darcie heard Sissy snoring softly. "How is Sissy doing?"

"She ain't no better. They ain't nothin' whut goes down whut don't come up," Charity said and grimaced. "I ain't never seed nobody that sick and live."

"Remember, according to Dr. Rhett, most people recover within a few days." Darcie dropped a kiss on Charity's head. "Let me know if there's anything I can do for either of you."

"That Mr. Poule been right helpful. He save ole Charity a

lotta work." Charity nodded her head, her black eyes narrowing, and studied Darcie. "He say you sleepin' in that no 'count Frenchie's cabin. Howcum you do such a thing? I knows you got better raisin' than that."

Darcie hadn't really expected Charity to have a good enough grasp of the situation to scold her—yet. She couldn't tell Charity the truth. The old woman would die of mortification if she knew Darcie had slept with Zack. "Now Charity. I must sleep somewhere. Zack is seldom in the room at all, except when he needs to look up something in his log book. When Em recovers, I can sleep in my own bed. I have enough problems without you scolding me about something I have no control over."

"It jus' ain't right. It ain't," Charity grumbled, pointing a spindly finger at Darcie. "Yo momma gonna torment me to my grave and then after I'se dead."

"Oh, Charity. She's not going to do anything of the sort." Suddenly, Darcie wanted to escape. She wanted to be out from under Charity's scathing eye, out of the way of her penetrating stares. "I'm going to check on the others. I'll be back later."

Darcie didn't wait for an answer. She hurried out the door and closed it behind her, feeling that if she'd stayed another moment, Charity would have perceived the truth and not even hell would have restrained her.

Em might be feeling better, she thought and scurried down the corridor to their room. When she got there, she started to knock, but didn't. She opened the door a crack and peeked in. Em was lying on her bed, but her eyes were open.

Darcie strode in, ignoring the glowers of Mrs. Appleby. "Em, darling, how are you? I've been so worried about you."

A wan smile appeared on Em's face. "I'm going to be fine soon. I hope."

"I hope so, too. It's dreadfully boring without someone to talk to." Darcie pulled a chair up next to the bed. "Would you like for me to read to you? I brought some books. I even have my copy of *Katherine Walton* with me."

"Darcie, do you really like Mr. Simms's books?" Em asked, gazing at her friend.

"Of course I do. I think he's wonderful," Darcie retorted. She grew tired of people criticizing Mr. Simms when they hadn't even read his books. "I adore them."

"Well, maybe later. I just want to sleep." Em closed her eyes. "That's all I want to do. If I'm asleep, I don't retch."

Darcie pulled the sheet up and fluffed Em's pillow. "I'll stop by later and see you. I'll bring a book then."

Em nodded but didn't open her eyes as Darcie left. *That's two out of three,* she thought, as she walked down the hall to Barclay's room and rapped on the door.

Poule opened the door quickly, as if he'd been alerted by her footsteps. "Lovely to see you, miss. Mr. Rhett been askin' for you every time he wakes up."

"Is he awake now?" she asked, peering past Poule into the room. She could hardly see the bed from here, but saw some movement.

Before Poule could answer, Barclay called, "Yes, yes, come in. Come in. I've been waiting for you."

Smiling at Poule, she said, "I'll sit with him a few minutes if you want to get a bite to eat."

"I already et. But I'd be glad of a spell away from this cantankerous—"

Darcie didn't allow him to finish. She knew what a baby Barclay could be when he was ill. "I know. Go along. I'll call if I need you."

Stepping into the room so Poule could leave, Darcie found a chair and brought it closer to the bed. She sat down and flashed a smile at Barclay. "So, how do you feel?"

"Like the very devil has taken residence in my innards." Barclay grimaced and gripped his stomach. "I swear there's knives in the food on this ship, or at least my belly thinks there are."

Darcie laughed. She didn't want to make him feel worse, but his description of the food was hilarious after the fine dinner she'd had. "I'm sure that Cook is giving you something especially designed to make your illness easier."

"Hah." Barclay shook his head. "I'd be willing to bet that

that slimy Frenchman is putting something in the food to make me sick."

"Barclay! How can you say such a thing?" Darcie was stunned by his accusation. "Zack has shown every kindness to you and Em on this trip. Why, he's assigned Poule to watch after you and Mrs. Appleby to watch after Em. I'm ashamed of you."

"Still defending him, eh?" Barclay sighed and played with the edge of the sheet. "Darcie, he's bad for you. You don't know men. You don't know how they—"

Darcie jumped up. "Barclay Rhett, how dare you. I refuse to stand here and let you cast aspersions on my—"

"Wait a minute!" Barclay exclaimed, leaning up on one elbow. "I meant no disrespect to you. I just feel—"

"Keep your feelings to yourself. I won't listen to you malign him anymore." Hurrying to the door, she cast one last glare at him. "When I come back, see if you can act like a gentleman for a change."

Darcie flew out the door, angry with Barclay, but more angry with herself for allowing him to needle her like that. She ran into Zack and they both nearly fell. "Oh, Zack, I'm sorry. I wasn't looking where I was going."

"No damage done. I have something for you to do, if you don't mind." He took her arm. "Come with me."

Poule came along behind them and stopped before he opened the door to Barclay's room. He called to Darcie, "I see you had to leave, too."

"I'm sorry, Poule," she apologized.

"Can you take over again?" Zack asked his man. "I have something for Darcie to do, and need to speak with her about it."

"Sure thing. I've got the little rascal under my control." Poule smiled wryly. "He sasses me, I don't give him no wine nor rum. He's right smart fond of them, so he behaves."

Laughing, Darcie and Zack waved to Poule and continued on down the corridor. He opened the door and they entered his cabin. Darcie realized that she didn't feel quite so uncomfortable as she had the first time she'd come here.

Zack closed the door and gripped her arm to prevent her from moving out of his reach. He drew her into his arms and kissed her.

When he pulled away, Darcie said, "I thought you had something for me to do."

"I did say that, *ma petite.*"

"Well?"

"This is what I want you to do." Zack held her close, lifting her off her feet and pinioning her between him and the wall. "I haven't been able to concentrate on anything this morning, you witch."

Darcie smiled and fresh color bloomed in her cheeks. She had thought of little else, too. "Why, sir, how can you call me that? I am innocent of all charges."

"Innocent? Everything about you has beckoned since I left you." He kissed her neck and nibbled at her ear. "I can't put you out of my mind."

"I'm sure I don't understand." Darcie leaned her head away, so that he had plenty of room to caress her neck. Each touch sent sensations zinging through her body and she couldn't have stood, even if he put her down.

"Mais oui, I believe you do." He touched his lips to hers. "You've bewitched me and you know it, vixen."

Feigning hurt feelings, she screwed her face into a Southern simper and fluttered her eyelashes coquettishly. "Sir, how can you say such a thing. I am wounded that you think I—"

He kissed her into silence. "And, you talk too much."

Chapter Thirteen

Darcie strolled around the deck, drinking in the cool evening air. Zack had long since returned to his duties, leaving her to her own devices.

Love bloomed in her heart and she hardly knew what to do next. Too many things prevented her from allowing it full sway. Somewhere in the recesses of her mind, tucked away to spoil the pleasure of her newfound happiness, was the ugly memory of Captain James's words about the sailor, implicating Zack in the piracy of her ship. Lurking there to ruin her joy, rankled the memory of her uncle's letter and her betrothal.

Life is so unfair, she thought. For the years she'd been in mourning, adhering to tradition more closely than most modern women, one thing had helped to preserve her sanity—that one day soon she'd be free to dance and flirt freely, and to marry the man of her choice.

All of this was denied her now. Willingly she had lain with Zack and tasted the pleasures of love. In doing so, her betrothal to the unknown man of her uncle's choosing had been removed as a block to her happiness. A second, perhaps worse, obstacle had taken its place. She had fallen in love with a man who had sampled the pleasures of many women, a man who would belong to none—and one who probably had ordered the attack on her ship.

And she was no longer fit to marry another. As the betrothal to her uncle's choice of husband must be broken, so must be her ambitions for a happy marriage with a man of her own choosing. No man wanted a woman whose bloom of love had been plucked by another.

Darcie stopped and leaned on the railing, burying her head in her hands. Willingly, eagerly, she had succumbed to Zack's charms, knowing that in doing so, she had sealed her fate. Her future now lay in a different direction. But which direction offered the most satisfaction?

Tears stung her eyes and she peered out to sea, witnessing the unremitting changing of the ocean's surface. Turmoil roiled within her, first accusing, then soothing. She alone held the reins of her future. Uncle Talbot could do nothing for her now. She would speak with him upon her arrival and rid herself of the guilt that plagued her. He would be left to console her waiting bridegroom while she returned to America.

Darcie would obtain passage on the next of her ships bound for Charleston. Barclay would be disappointed, but he would be free to choose another. Charity would not understand, nor would Darcie offer reasons for her behavior. Shrewd Charity might very well guess why Darcie would spurn the proposal of a man who had been selected for her by her uncle and at the same time refuse the hand of the man who all Charleston thought she would eventually marry.

For the remainder of her life, Darcie Gaynor would control her shipping line and remain a spinster. Never again would she experience the rapture she'd found with Zack. Miss Smith's image came to her mind as Darcie stared straight ahead, seeing nothing, and she knew that she could never live like the wharf women of Charleston. Her only option was to spurn the attentions of all men entirely. A tear spilled across her eyelid and traced a cold, silvery trail down her blanched cheeks. She patted it with the edge of her shawl.

Spinsterhood, that's what she was reduced to, and she had nobody to blame but Darcie Jeanne Gaynor. Life in America offered little gaiety for spinsters, but she would have her pride and freedom of sorts, in the Charleston she loved so dearly.

She smiled wryly at her own attitude toward women who never married. She, Em, and Patty had often conjectured about them and the reasons for their spinsterhood, frequently bursting into fits of giggles. Darcie would be laughed at, too, and perhaps someone would remind the other misses that Old Miss Gaynor had been rumored to have been betrothed to a French gentleman. Giggles would bubble forth, and another would say something like, "Old Miss Gaynor? Who would have that old crosspatch?"

Darcie straightened. She had selected her path, now she must tread courageously upon it.

Gazing into the sparkling depths and storm-swollen waves ruffled with foam, she mused that nothing should be that beautiful when she was so miserable. Refusing to succumb to self-pity, she strode along the deck, basking in the early morning sunlight and the cool breeze crackling the sails sharply, confident that the fresh air and exercise would make her feel better.

"Darcie, wait," Zack called, hurrying along behind her. Her hips swayed gently as she moved surefootedly toward the bow. *Mon Dieu,* he thought, *she is a passionate beauty, intelligent, and a good sailor. What more could a man ask for?*

He stopped short. What more could a man ask for? Zack glanced at Darcie. She was watching him quizzically with her head tilted to one side.

Striding towards her, he called, "Ah, good to see you taking the air."

Feeling the weight of her recent decision concerning him— and all men—Darcie averted her eyes. "Yes. It's a lovely day."

Zack noticed the chill in her voice and said, "I have something to discuss with you. Let's go below and have a cup of tea."

Now is the time to tell him of my decision, she thought. Zack would help her once they reached Paris. Her return to America would be much sooner than she had originally thought.

When they reached his cabin, Zack strode to his desk. He fumbled with some papers for a moment, while Darcie settled on her favorite chair.

"Darcie, *ma cherie*," he began. "In view of our . . . well, ahem . . ."

Sitting as straight as the masts of *La Mer Magnifique*, Darcie stared at him. What was he saying to her?

Turning his back to her once again and resting his palms on the ladder back chair that stood at his desk, Zack closed his eyes. *Why does she have to look like that?* How could he force the words he had to say from his mouth? Mon Dieu, but he wanted to take her in his arms and toss her upon the bed.

Darcie's gaze dropped to her idle hands. So, the time had come. Zack was ashamed of her and what she had allowed him to do.

He faced her once more, fighting to still the furious pounding of his heart. "Darcie, last night has changed—"

A fierce beating on the door interrupted him before he could finish his sentence. *All the better,* Darcie mused. *I couldn't take his pity.*

Damn! Zack flew to the door and swung it wide open. Poule was standing outside with his hand raised as if to knock again. "Yes? What is it?"

Poule seemed to recognize the unspoken threat in Zack's clipped words. "Sorry to be troublin' you, sir, but there be a dead man—"

Darcie jumped to her feet and echoed, "Dead man?"

Zack glanced at her and said, "Don't fret, *ma cherie*, I shall investigate and return shortly."

Investigate. The word rang in Darcie's ears for several minutes after Zack closed the door. A dead man—here on Zack's ship. Who could it be?

Darcie paced the floor, wringing her hands and wishing she'd never stepped foot on this boat. Investigate. The word continued to haunt her.

She stopped and whirled to face Zack's desk. This was the

perfect time to investigate Captain James's accusations. Zack would be gone for several minutes at least.

Dashing across the room to his desk, she looked at the cubbyholes and drawers. Where had he put the ledger?

She found it quickly enough in the last section on top. As she looked through the pages for the dates around the time of the attack on her ship, she paused here and there to glance at his entries. It was a common ship's log, relating the events of the voyages of *La Mer Magnifique*.

The neat script told of gales, of doldrums, of hunger when food spoiled, of thirst when water was contaminated, of days when nothing happened except the rising and setting of the sun and the flapping of sails. Most of the entries were short and factual and boring.

The entries concerning the discovery of Darcie's ship under attack were not so short, nor were they boring. Scanning the lines of script, she searched for any reference which might connect him with the attack.

There was none. Taking a deep breath, she started over and read from the beginning of the paragraphs relating to her ship. Tears fell freely as she read of the death and injury to her men, of the destruction of her fine ship, of the malevolence and cruelty of the attackers. According to the log, not much of the bounty was taken. It seemed that their mission was to destroy.

She read, "I've never witnessed such senseless destruction. According to Captain James, the 'pirates' were after papers rather than loot. He reports his Ship's Log was stolen, along with a parcel of papers en route from the Charleston office to the French office. What these papers were is not known."

Papers? Why would pirates want papers?

"A few other stolen items are listed below."

Darcie read the list. It made no sense either. The manifests, the old ship's log, the Captain's private journal, personnel records, and a few miscellaneous items. A small cache of jewelry was also taken, along with money being transferred from the Charleston office to the French bank.

Jewelry? Why was there jewelry aboard? There were no passengers listed on this trip.

Darcie returned to the log. "A small cache of jewelry—personal possessions of the owner—was taken."

Personal possessions of the owner? *Darcie's* personal jewelry? The jewels that Uncle Talbot had insisted be kept at the office for safety?

Darcie bowed her head as grief flooded over her. All her important jewelry was gone.

Why hadn't Horace said something when she instructed him to send it, along with a few books and papers, to Manville's offices? Nothing made sense to her. Her mother's diamond fleur-de-lis earrings and pendant, a garnet set of little monetary value but of great sentimental value since it had belonged to her maternal grandmother, a tiara of rubies and diamonds—everything that her uncle had requested her to store at the office. All the jewelry she had expected to wear in France was gone. She was left with little more than a few trinkets that she had saved because she had refused to part with them. A great feeling of emptiness almost overwhelmed her.

Sniffling, she sat back and closed the book. Zack's vivid description put the picture of the violence clearly into her mind and she wanted to eradicate it. The *Gay Dolphin* had been the pride of her line, but the jewelry had been her mother's legacy to her.

Voices in the hallway frightened her. Shoving the journal back into its place, she stood and tried to calm her emotions. Zack would never understand why she was prying into his private papers.

She strode to the window, patting her hair nervously. When a knock sounded on the door, Darcie jumped so hard that she almost fell over a chair.

"Can't be Zack," she muttered, wondering who was at the door. She paused a moment and then swung the heavy wooden door wide open. "Yes?" she asked with relief, when she saw Poule at the door.

"Miss Gaynor, Cap'n says to tell you he'll be awhile yet," Poule reported. "Be there anything you want?"

"Uh, no. Thank you, Poule." Then she remembered Zack's threat about meals and work. "Well, yes there is. When the noon meal is prepared, will you have mine sent to me here?"

"Sure thing, miss." Poule saluted and strode away.

Darcie closed the door and leaned against it. Deciding that she had no time to waste, she returned to her search. *Zack is so methodical,* she thought. *I'd better be extremely careful about replacing things in the exact spot he left them.*

With that in mind, she pulled another book from the shelf. It was another ship's log, the one used prior to the one which Zack used on this trip. The last entry was several months before the attack on Darcie's ship and so it provided no further information for her.

She calmly slid the log back into its spot, carefully adjusting the cover so that it was perfectly even with the current log. She opened another ledger and found it to be Zack's private journal. She stared at it for a moment, feeling guilty for prying into his private thoughts. She read an accounting of her meeting with him and was as amused by the situation as he seemed to be. His written report of the incident was hilarious.

Warmth flooded over her as she read of the change in his feelings toward her, of his growing attachment. Blushing, she read of their first kiss, of the effect it had on him.

Sitting back, she closed her eyes and remembered his kisses and the delicious feeling of love and tenderness returned. How she savored those moments when love seemed to be a rosebud awakening to the sunlight.

This journal seemed to contain the man's thoughts. She flipped backward through the pages and dived into the report of the attack on her ship, this report far more personal than the cut-and-dried one in the ship's log. Once again, tears sprang to her eyes.

Well, she sniffled, you've read enough about that to know that he's not going to implicate himself in writing. Darcie scanned the first pages of the ledger and found neatly written anecdotes from his days at Court and of the last days in Paris before his trip to Charleston.

The handwriting changed. It became more stilted, as did the words. He referred to a meeting with Madelaine Ortiz and her two stepchildren. His words were hate-filled, almost vindictive, as he described the party and her behavior. Darcie leaned forward and studied the passage, wondering what the woman had done to make him hate her so badly.

Well, it had nothing to do with Darcie Gaynor, nor did it relate to the loss of her ship. She would have to find other means of proof. Sighing, she placed the journal back on the shelf beside the others.

Starting at the left, she opened, examined, and closed several small drawers finding nothing more than a man's knickknacks. When she reached the drawer second from last, she found a handkerchief. She looked at it curiously. None of the other drawers contained clothing.

It was then that she felt the lump. It was hard and small, no larger than a bean seed. She unwound the white linen and gasped aloud at its contents.

Sparkling merrily in the center of the handkerchief was one of her earrings—the fleur-de-lis, a part of the jewelry that had been listed as stolen during the attack on her ship.

Fighting the impulse to steal the earring back, she wound it back in its nest of linen and closed it inside the drawer. Well, she had her proof. Where would Zack have gotten the earring, if not as his part of the booty for attacking the ship?

Nonsense, she told herself. *He couldn't have been responsible.*

Tears that had fallen so freely for the sailors she loved, for the loss of her ship and jewels, now refused to purge her of her feeling of betrayal. Zacharie Manville had robbed her of a part of her heritage, and then had taken the only thing that was truly hers alone—her virginity.

Misery consumed her. Bitter gall rose to taint her mouth, still tingling from his kisses. Her body ached from his ruthless behavior as if he had physically beaten her.

* * *

When Zack returned, she was sitting on her favorite chair once again, with her needlework untouched in her lap. So deep in thought was she that she hardly noticed the opening and closing of the door.

He stood there for a moment, enjoying the tranquillity of the scene—until her eyes met his. The lovely sapphire sparkle had disappeared, and in its place was the dull sheen of eyes tired from crying.

Forgetting the tragedy, the useless killing he'd just come from investigating, Zack rushed to her side and knelt beside her. *"Mon Dieu,* what has happened to make you cry? Are you ill?"

Darcie saw him clearly for the first time. He was as handsome as ever. Windblown curls fell across his forehead. His smile had been erased by a frown of concern that creased his cheeks and forehead. Lips that had the power to vault her into the delicious depths of passion were as talented at lying.

For a moment, she didn't speak. She couldn't.

"Darcie, my darling, speak to me," he pled. "Tell me who has caused this misery and I will personally thrash him."

Closing her eyes in a vain attempt to compose herself, Darcie inhaled deeply. For the past hour she had fluctuated between confronting him with her discovery, or continuing to play his game to see where it ended. She still had not decided what to do.

Her fingers somehow found his brow, caressing it as they drew the capricious curls aside. She stared at her hand, as if it were an alien thing or operated under its own power. Jerking it back, she cuddled it in her lap willing it to stop tingling.

The frown softened on Zack's face. "Oh, my darling, what has happened? I've been gone but little over an hour."

Darcie realized that he was genuinely worried. She was adding to his problems. He never would suspect her of spying on him, and probably had no reason to believe that she might be looking for evidence to implicate him in the attack on her ship. He probably thought she was coming down with a case of seasickness or vapors.

A determined man, he shook her gently, thinking that she was in some sort of stupor. The lines were etched into his forehead once more. "Darcie, speak to me. Tell me what has happened."

Sighing softly, Darcie lifted her chin and nodded. She'd have to tell him something or he'd never leave her alone. "It's really nothing, Zack. Don't fret."

"How can you say it's nothing?" He grasped her chin and forced her to look into his eyes. "I know you well enough to know that something disastrous has happened."

She found her curiosity returning and decided that a diversion would release her from his inquiry. "What of the . . . the dead man? Is he really dead?"

Zack hung his head. A young man—almost too young to become a sailor—had died senselessly. His "accident" appeared to be murder—cold, calculated murder made to resemble an accident. "He is dead."

"Who is he?" she asked.

"A young man. Carson Dupuis. I doubt that you know him." Zack answered simply, feeling the weight of the boy's death squarely on his shoulders. The culprit would have to be found. The boy's parents must be notified. Both distasteful events for Zack to manage, but he would.

"What does . . . did he look like?"

Zack stared at her a moment and knew that her concern didn't rise from morbid curiosity, but more from genuine caring. "A slender blond fellow. Tall. He worked—"

"I believe I've seen him. Very young. Younger than I?" Darcie felt sick. Indeed she had enjoyed watching the young man climb among the sails, wave happily at her.

Zack nodded. "Yes. A little younger. Handsome lad. Now, Darcie, back to the subject. I haven't much time."

"I don't understand." She walked to the porthole and peered out, allowing the fresh cool air to wash over her.

Striding across the room, Zack turned her to face him. "I shall deal with the culprit as soon as I determine who he is. For now, you stay behind locked doors in this cabin. *Mon Dieu*, but you have a way of diverting my attention. Tell me your problem."

Stalling until she could think of some excuse, she muttered, "Forget it. It's my problem."

"See here, Darcie," he began, "If something is troubling you, I want to know about it, and it would be obvious to the blindest dog in France that something is wrong."

Darcie chewed her lip. Time was running out for her. She had no doubt that before long Zack would beat the truth out of her. A man that could order the destruction of a fine ship and care nothing for its crew, had no heart. "Really, Zack, it's a personal thing. I don't want to discuss it."

She rose and walked to her workbasket. Daintily, she placed the napkin she'd been holding on top of the others and smoothed them with her fingertips.

"Darcie, I thought we were friends. We've often . . ." Zack paused and tried to think of the key that would cause her to open up and tell him her problems. *She's probably run out of some color of thread or something silly like that,* he mused. Then he thought again. Darcie wasn't a cabbagehead. She had good sense. He didn't know what was wrong with her, but he knew for sure that it was serious. He continued talking in soothing tones. "We've often spoken of things that wouldn't be considered quite proper. I've felt that we could talk about anything. Now, tell me what's troubling you."

"Can I get something for you? Tea? Hot—"

"The truth," he retorted, getting a little exasperated with her for her stubbornness. "Damn a woman who won't accept a man's help," he mumbled.

"Excuse me?" Darcie had heard the word "damn" and knew he was becoming angry. She couldn't come up with anything to tell him, so she still evaded the question.

Suddenly, Zack's expression changed. His gaze sought her face and examined it minutely. *It couldn't be,* he mused. *She couldn't be upset over the implications of our making love. She didn't seem unduly concerned at the time.*

That must be it, he concluded and smiled. She had no way of knowing what he intended to speak with her about. The solution to her problem was at hand.

"Darcie, my darling," he said, pulling her to her feet. "Come with me."

She drew away, holding back for fear that if he touched her, all of her resolve would melt. Having decided to become a spinster, to avoid close contact with all men, had changed her outlook. The burning sensation of his hand on her arm, the tingles that shot from the spot, reminded her of Zack's power over her. She balked. "No, Zack. We cannot continue this reckless game."

"Game?" He whirled to face her. "Game? What game?"

Darcie gulped. She'd known it wouldn't be easy to cut off the relationship, but she hadn't expected the tears to well behind her eyes, her heart to pound, her lungs to burn. "We must stop this . . . this right away."

"This *what?*" He gazed at her, his dark eyebrows arched quizzically as his fingers tightened on her arm. "Whatever do you mean?"

"I mean that I am moving back to my room." There, she'd said it. "I mean that Mrs. Appleby can move back to hers or jump overboard. I don't want her in my cabin." She looked at him for some indication that he comprehended her meaning and found the glowering stare evidence enough. His temple throbbed with his obvious anger, and she rushed on to prevent an outburst from him. "I admit that I haven't behaved quite properly and deserve your ire, but please understand that this . . . this liaison cannot continue."

A nerve in his eyelid twitched and his eyes narrowed. At any moment, she expected steam to shoot from his ears. "Now, Zack, be reasonable."

"Reasonable? Is that what you call it, Darcie?"

"Certainly. I don't see—"

"You don't see? *Mon Dieu*, but you are a cabbage-headed little ninny." He swung around, leaned against the desk, and glared at her as he spoke between clenched teeth. "Why the sudden desire to end our friendship? Has M. Rhett recovered enough to satisfy your passionate nature?"

"Satisfy my . . ." Darcie stared at him, aghast that he would use such coarse references and speak so angrily. "Wait, Zack, I—"

"You wait. I've spent too much time and money bringing you to France to lose you to a clam-brained, rum-drinking, Charleston aristocrat," he retorted, clenching his teeth against the expletives that threatened to follow.

He led her to the worn brocade sofa and motioned for her to be seated. This wouldn't be easy, but when he looked into her expectant face, he decided that it would be much easier than he had ever thought possible. "Darcie, my beloved, it cannot have escaped your attention that my feelings for you have . . . well, that I have . . . well, that we . . ."

"Zack, listen—"

"Please, don't interrupt." He paced a moment before her and his thoughts returned to the morning when he'd witnessed Barclay's eloquent proposal with such pity. Now he was himself in need of that same emotion. His thoughts were so tangled, his emotions so scrambled, that words escaped him. "What I'm trying to say is—"

"Zack, do not speak to me out of misplaced feelings of pity and—" she began again, only to be waved off as he strode back and forth on the faded carpet.

"Please, I cannot think if you continue to interrupt." He stopped pacing and gazed down at her. She looked so fragile at the moment, so delicate and uncertain, her eyes wide and liquid. "My thoughts crowd my tongue and I find speaking difficult for the first time in my life."

A smile teased her lips, the first he'd seen since returning to his cabin. Uplifted, he forged on. "Darcie, *ma cherie,* it cannot have escaped your attention that my affection . . . my admiration has greatly increased during the short time we've been acquainted."

He knelt beside her and, taking her hands in his, brought them to his lips in a fervent kiss. "I realize this is sudden and you are totally unprepared for my declaration. And, of course, it is totally improper, since I have not spoken with your uncle. However, I feel that under the circumstances—"

Her smile froze and she jerked her hands from his. "The circumstances? Just what circumstances?" Her voice lifted, becoming higher and louder. "You have taken . . . my virtue, which I assume you now refer to as 'the circumstances,' and out of pity or some other misplaced emotion, you wish to assuage your guilt by making an honest woman of me?"

Taken aback by her outburst, Zack stared in disbelief. He was trying to place her beyond the bounds of gossip, to assure that her integrity was never questioned, and the shrew had the audacity to—"I assure you that I speak not from pity, but from true affection."

"Affection? Ha!" she spat back at him.

He reached for her hands and although she sought to keep them from his grasp, he captured them. "I . . . I love you, Darcie. Make me the happiest of all men and marry me."

Chapter Fourteen

Darcie could hardly believe the words that tumbled from Zack's lips. He'd said "I love you" for the first time. For several days, she'd moped about, wishing to hear just those words, knowing that even if she heard them, she'd have to reject his proposal.

She was gratified to hear him say he loved her. The words sang in her heart as she gazed at him, memorizing the moment, for it would be her last proposal, the last declaration of love made to her. Darcie's heart ached with longing as she withdrew her hands and stood up. Walking out of his reach, she closed her eyes and sighed. Life was so unfair.

"Your proposal is . . . most unexpected," Darcie replied, stalling for time. How she wanted to say yes! How she wanted to forget the implications, the evidence against him concerning the attack on her ship. She could no more say yes to his proposal than she could forget his crime.

Zack's gaze had followed her and he now stared in disbelief. Moments ago, she had been distraught over their intimacy. He had presented the solution to her problem, a happy one. "Unexpected? How can this be so?"

Darcie closed her eyes, willing herself to be somewhere else. How could she tell the man she loved that she could not, would not marry him? She hung her head and fingered the fine silk of her day gown. "You know I cannot marry you. Please—"

"But you can!" Zack exclaimed, reaching for her arm. The silky texture of her skin sent sensations throughout his body and he felt his desire for her renewed. He would never tire of this woman. He considered her for a moment, recalling the way her eyes sparkled when they made love, when he kissed her. "And I feel that you—I *know* that you have strong feelings for me as well."

Darcie could hardly deny her feelings. Only a few hours before, she'd lain in his bed and shared his passion. *Passion's promise holds little weight during the stark light of day,* she thought. *I love a man who is my enemy. No, not love. It's nothing more than lust. Infatuation with passion.*

Breathing deeply, Darcie felt her skin turn to stone, her eyes granite, as she turned to face him. She didn't like to lie, but lie she must. "I used you. Perhaps as you've used many women before me."

"Used? Whatever can you mean?" he asked, his eyebrows arched and his forehead wrinkled with concern as he fidgeted with his open collar. The conversation was certainly a puzzle to him. He'd begun by asking her to marry him. How the discussion had shifted to his previous conquests, he couldn't understand.

How she wanted to comfort him. Zack looked so miserable, as if he were on trial for a murder he didn't commit. Darcie hadn't thought he'd take it so hard, her turning him down. Why the sad countenance? "By used, I mean . . . oh, you know what I mean. I allowed you to seduce me so that I could escape a marriage contract."

A smile played at the corners of Zack's mouth and his lips tilted a little. Wrinkles of delight appeared at the corners of his eyes and on his forehead as he began to laugh. *"Mon Dieu,"* he exclaimed. "I thought you intended to reject my proposal. You are caught in your own trap, mademoiselle."

Wondering what he could mean, Darcie picked up a ribbon from the small table she used as a dressing table and twisted it between her fingers. He wouldn't allow her to turn him down gracefully. "I don't know what you mean. What trap? I certainly didn't intend to trap you or anybody else into—"

"Ah," he cooed, stepping closer and turning her to face him. Her lovely upturned nose fascinated him as did her sapphire eyes. Indeed, her beauty and sensitivity captivated him, imprisoned him as bars of steel could not. "You may not have set a trap intentionally, but I fear you have ensnared us both, *ma cherie.*"

"You speak in riddles. What do you mean?" Darcie grew tired of the tension that seemed to be growing between them. She wanted to rid herself of this task and return to the room she should have shared with Em.

Zack slid his arms around her, despite her attempt to dislodge them. Drawing her close he kissed her forehead and held tightly to her struggling body. "Why do you fight me? You derive as much pleasure as I from our union."

His words stopped her struggle—almost more effectively than the strength of his grasp. "Union? We have no union."

"Ah, but we do, *ma petite,* we do." He kissed her eyelids.

Darcie felt herself melting in his arms. She had to do something, break away, put distance between Zack and herself, or their discussion would be at an end and she wanted to finish it now. "No, Zack. We do not. We . . . we were friends. And, now, we—"

"And now we are lovers soon to be wed." Zack caressed her hair, inhaling deeply of the lush scent of violets that hovered around her. "Not soon enough, however."

For a moment, she let her cheek rest on his chest to absorb the strength she needed to go on. "No. We shall never marry."

"What a ridiculous statement. Of course, we shall marry." Zack held her back from him and stared at her, his gaze stripping away the mask he perceived she wanted him to see. "What nonsense is this?"

Deciding to take the easy course, Darcie lied. "I cannot marry you because I am betrothed to another. I would not betray him further."

"Betrothed?"

"I am betrothed by my uncle if you recall the contents of his letter," Darcie explained, although she knew that he remembered the letter as well as she.

"Balderdash," he exclaimed. "That betrothal means nothing. You have said you cannot marry a man not of your choosing. You shall marry me."

"Please, oh, please, don't make this more difficult," she pled. "I belong to another, to a man who will never claim me because of my actions. I can never be wed."

"Never be . . ." his voice trailed off in confusion. "Whatever does that mean? We'll be wed as soon as we arrive in Paris. As soon as your trousseau is selected."

Trousseau. What a fanciful term for the loneliness that would accompany her to her death, instead of the profusion of dresses, capes, petticoats, hats, linens, and gowns she might have chosen under different circumstances. "Let's not speak of that which isn't to be. Zack, I cannot marry you, nor can I marry any other."

"Why not? You must answer," Zack demanded, combing his fingers through his black hair. "I insist upon an explanation."

"I am betrothed to another. I cannot marry him. I shall explain my predicament to my uncle and the betrothal shall be called off." Darcie closed her eyes, unwilling to allow Zack access to her inner being through those sapphire windows. "And, because of my shame, I shall marry no man."

"What a ridiculous notion." Zack realized that he would have to inform her as to the identity of her affianced. "Darcie, I have something to tell you. Something I should have told you about the moment we met."

"You mean when you rescued me from the iron grasp of the gate?" she asked, attempting to lighten the tone of their conversation.

Zack laughed and put his arms around her. At least she didn't slap him for his intimacy. Perhaps they still had a chance. "Well, yes. Mayhap, that would have been the most opportune moment —when you were secured against escape from me."

"Then bolt the door if your words have such import to make you feel the need to imprison me," she retorted.

Zack shook his head. Many times during the past few days he'd considered just that. Locking her in his cabin seemed the best solution to many of his problems. He didn't want her in Barclay Rhett's room, nor did he want her nursing the ladies who had been so ill. Now that their conditions had improved, he found that he didn't want her strolling about the deck. Frequently, he'd noticed the stares of his men. The months of loneliness sailing the ocean caused men to do strange things. He didn't want Darcie to become a victim as had the Dupuis boy, albeit in a different way.

"I have no wish to imprison you, although the need may arise," he teased, attempting to follow her lead in lightening the weighty conversation. "I merely wish to converse with you about a serious matter. I apologize for procrastinating."

"Pray, continue," she teased. Now that the conversation seemed to have drifted from the serious note that earlier threatened to cause an argument, she felt at ease. One of the things she liked best about Zack was his light banter.

His face immediately sobered as he looked at her. Steeling himself against the onslaught of anger that was sure to come, Zack unfurled full sail and began. "Darcie, the letter from your uncle notified you of a previously arranged engagement. I haven't told you all that I know about that situation."

Stunned at the strange turn of conversation, Darcie sank into her chair and stared at him. "Do you know him? My betrothed? What is he like? Is he old?"

For a moment, he wondered how he could have been so foolish. What made him tell her that he knew anything? He could have acted surprised in Paris and she would never have known the truth. "I . . . yes, I know . . ."

Darcie leapt to her feet and placed both hands on his shoulders as if to shake him like a rag doll. "Come on. Tell me what you know. Don't hold anything back."

Inhaling deeply, Zack continued. "I know him well. He's—"

"Is he handsome? Is he kind?"

Zack removed her hands and pressed her back into the chair. "If you will sit calmly, I shall tell you all there is to know about this character."

"Character?" she asked, her voice dropping with her enthusiasm. He must be unsavory or decrepit. Why did she care anyway? She had already told Zack that she would never marry him—no matter who he was.

"Please, don't interrupt." Zack crossed the room, pulled out a chair, and placed his booted foot on the seat. Leaning down on his knee, he rubbed a bit of dust from the Hessians before looking at her again. *"Maintenant.* Darcie—"

"Land's sakes, Zack. Just tell me about him," Darcie said with a slight edge of irritation to her voice.

For safety's sake, Zack glanced at her and her immediate vicinity. There seemed to be nothing she could throw that would injure him severely, so he began. "He's fairly young—"

"Younger or older than you?"

"My age." Why didn't he just tell her and get it done? "He's tall, handsome—or so the ladies say. He's—"

Darcie looked puzzled. "Then why a marriage contract? I don't understand. Is he an ogre?"

Zack's head snapped up and he gazed at her. "I don't think he's—" He stopped. If he continued this much longer she would be more angry than ever. *"C'est moi."*

"I beg your pardon?"

"I said—"

"I heard what you said. Translate. I don't think my French lessons—"

"It is I, Darcie." He gazed eagerly at her eyes and saw the dawning of truth in them. At first a smile flitted across her lips and her eyes sparkled with joy, but then an angry frown drew the corners of her lips down and her eyes bore into him. "I am your betrothed."

"You?" The full meaning of his words blasted her into full-fledged anger. "You knew. All this time you've deceived me.

You're a rotten, low-down cowering ninnyhammer if you think you can—"

"Darcie, wait!" Leaping to his feet, Zack realized that the worst sequence of events had materialized. Darcie was far angrier than he thought she would be. His conduct was below the standards of any low-born peasant and he deserved every word of her ire. "Please, understand. I didn't want to—"

The realization of his reasons for keeping the truth from her burst into her mind like a fire igniting paper soaked in coal oil. "You knew all along. You knew! You came to America, you came to Charleston to . . . to look me over like chattel."

"Wait, Darcie. Calm down a bit," he spoke soothingly and found that his words infuriated her further.

"Calm down? Hah!" she screamed, jumping to her feet. "I am the one who's been looked over like . . . like a slave for your choosing and you tell me to calm down? How dare you even show your face to me?"

Zack shrank back from her as she raced across the room to confront him. He grabbed her wrists to keep her from hitting him, if indeed that was her intent. "Come now. I never thought of you in that regard."

"Let me go. Let me go and get out of my sight. I never want to see you again," she shrieked, fighting with all her power to free her hands from his grasp. "I ought to call you out myself."

Realizing that until she calmed down, he would never be able to explain his actions to her, Zack retreated. Actually, he ran. After loosing her wrists, he charged for the door and was out before she could react.

Fury flamed in Darcie's cheeks and as she paced the worn Aubusson carpet, her hands shook as if she were stricken with palsy. "Oh! How I hate that man. All men. None of them are worth notice."

A knock interrupted her tirade and she stopped. "Who is it?"

"Barclay," came the reply. "May I come in?"

"No. Leave me be or suffer the consequences."

The door opened slightly and she could see his pale face peek through. "Darcie, my darling, what is wrong?"

"I asked you to leave me alone. Go," she replied curtly.

He opened the door further and stepped inside. Glancing around, he seemed to take in the entire room at once. "Please, let me speak with you."

"Barclay," she began. "I am in no mood to talk. Unless you want the full force of my rage, leave quickly."

Barclay smiled, stepped beyond the range of the door, and closed it. "Now, darling, tell me what's wrong."

"I'm warning you."

Striding across the room shakily, Barclay was at her side in a moment. He enfolded her in his weak embrace. "Come now. What can be all that bad?"

In her present state, Darcie couldn't talk about Zack's revelations. She wanted to be alone, to consider the implications. Her mind was spinning with thoughts and theories and her heart was pounding. "I'm not going to discuss this with you."

She softened her visage, although she had to work at it. "I'll see you later. You look like you might enjoy a stroll on the deck."

"Ugh!"

"Don't be hasty. The fresh air will do you good." Darcie stepped out of his embrace. "Now, be a good boy and go away. I promise I'll see you soon. I . . . I just want to be alone."

"Look, Darcie, I've been sick for days. This is my first chance to speak with you without an audience. Come on, give me a few minutes," he begged.

"I can't, Barclay. Not now. Please don't ask again," she answered, praying he wouldn't continue to plead. "I'll see you for supper."

The two dull coals of his eyes brightened. "All right. I'll go."

He turned and walked out the door, pausing for a moment to gaze at her before closing it. "I . . . I'll see you soon."

Darcie dropped onto the sofa, curling her feet beneath her in an unladylike manner. She didn't care. Right now, she wanted to cuddle up and try to figure out why Zack had deceived her. If he had lied to her about one thing—the contents of the letter from her uncle—then he would have no scruples about lying *period*.

A liar is the worst kind of man, her father always said. "A man that will lie to you, will steal from you," were his exact words.

Why, oh, why? Darcie may have been able to discover evidence that cleared Zack of his involvement with the attack on her ship, but he *had* admitted to lying. Tears wouldn't fall, although she felt that crying would lift some of the burden from her weary shoulders.

Her excitement about the Paris trip had faded and dimmed until it hardly glimmered on the horizon any more, and had in fact been replaced by deep regret. Could love be cast away so quickly and hate take its place?

Wondering why life had to be so complicated, she stretched out and rested her head on the plump pillow lodged against the arm of the sofa. Her eyes closed and before long she fell asleep.

Darcie heard voices, one growing louder each time it spoke. Her eyelids were heavy, sealed shut with the salt of tears unshed. Slowly, they opened a little, and through the sliver of her eyelashes, she saw Zack standing at the door as if he were blocking the way.

"She is sleeping," Zack whispered.

His voice was so low that Darcie hardly heard him. Barclay seemed not to care if he awakened her.

"I want to see her, no, I *demand* to see her."

"If you wake her, you'll wish that you were still seasick," Zack whispered again, through clenched teeth. Why did this fool persist? "I'll tell her you were here."

Barclay stood his ground. "I want to see her. What have you done with her?"

"What have I—" Zack's voice raised with each word. "Now see here, you—"

"No. *You* see here. You know it isn't at all the gentlemanly thing to be in a lady's bedroom." Barclay stood full height, which regretfully fell a good three inches below Zack's. "And, if the lady is sleeping, then your breach is doubly an infringement."

"This lady's bedroom, as you choose to label it, happens to be my cabin. All of my logs, journals, maps, and charts are here. I apologize if it offends your Southern sensibilities for me to be here, but I haven't the time to debate the issue." Zack leaned forward as if to emphasize his words.

Barclay gulped and continued, "I'm sure your intentions are of the highest possible, but I demand to see her nonetheless."

"Your demands are beginning to irritate me." Zack glared at the American, but never moved.

Darcie listened behind closed eyelids. She didn't want to speak to either of them. Feigning sleep seemed to be the best way to avoid both gentlemen, although Zack might stay to work, which would present further problems.

She hadn't intended to fall asleep. But the rest had made her feel much better. Zack's lies didn't seem quite so horrible, though they irritated her like freshly starched petticoats. Why didn't they go outside to quarrel?

"See here, Zack, I intend to look at her if I have to resort to fisticuffs with you," Barclay threatened.

Zack shook his head. "If you choose to do so, I'm perfectly willing to teach you a lesson. However, to prevent your loud-mouthed boasting from waking her, I shall allow you a peek. If you do anything to disturb her, I shall gladly feed you to the fishes."

Through the lace of her lashes, Darcie watched as both men approached the bed. Zack's eyes were on Barclay and he stood at the ready, as if he expected the American to pounce on her.

Forcing herself to remain calm, she breathed regularly and kept her body rigid. For several moments, they peered at her, and Darcie thought she would have to move or scream from the tension.

She could see them through her lashes as Zack reached for Barclay and began to pull him away. Relief swept over her and she sighed.

Both men whirled around to look at her. Apparently, each of

them wanted to talk with her and would be delighted for her to awaken. They waited a few seconds and then moved toward the door.

Heavens, she thought, *how much longer must I remain in this position?* Her leg muscles were beginning to cramp.

"She promised to have supper with me." Barclay turned to look at her once more.

Noticing the way Barclay's eyes drifted down Darcie's sleeping frame and came to rest on her exposed ankles, Zack moved to stand in his line of sight. Barclay couldn't see Darcie at all unless he leaned to one side or stood on his toes. Sensing the anger rising once again in the pale man, Zack smiled and said, "I believe she'll miss supper tonight."

Darcie heard the door close and ventured a look. Exerting extreme caution, she peered through heavy-lidded eyes.

Zack stood inside the door and was turning to look at her. "He's gone. You needn't pretend any longer."

Opening her eyes slowly, she propped on her elbow. "Thank you for not giving me away. How did you know I was awake?"

"I'd been watching you for some time and saw the slight movement of your eyelids when you peeked at us." Zack moved across the room and took a chair. Lounging easily, he slung one leg across the chair and watched her rise to a sitting position.

Darcie breathed deeply and glared at him. "Why are you here?"

"This, if you recall, is *my* cabin. In addition to sleeping here, I work here." He picked up a cup from the desk behind him and took a sip of tea. "Would you like something? I'm afraid I have only tea and biscuits, but they're filling."

A quick denial of her hunger sprang to her lips, but Darcie stopped before she allowed the words to be voiced. She really was hungry, even though she didn't want to eat with Zack. Upon considering the situation, she decided that she'd rather eat with him than with Barclay who would be full of questions. "Thank you, I believe I shall."

Zack turned around and poured a cup of tea. He gathered

several biscuits and placed them on a small plate. "Oh, there's cheese, too."

Gratefully, Darcie accepted the plate and began to munch on the cheese. She didn't know why she was so hungry, but she was. As she ate, she watched Zack. He selected first one book and then another, making brief entries in them before returning them to their positions. Her face flushed, she was terrified that he'd notice that one of them was out of place or a page was turned back, but he didn't say anything.

After a few minutes, he stood and faced her. "Are you ready to finish our discussion?"

Darcie almost choked on the biscuit she was eating. The raspberry jam was so delicious that she'd been concentrating on it rather than Zack. "I beg your pardon?"

"I asked if you were ready to talk." Zack pulled his chair across the room so that he was facing her, too close for her to bolt and run without being caught.

"I have nothing else to say on the matter," she retorted and spread more jam on her biscuit.

Zack exhaled and glared at her. Her reasons for rejecting his proposal were still foreign to him and she refused to discuss them. What could he do? Bribe her? A thought occurred to him. "I suppose I might consider dropping my claim to you, if you could provide me with a good enough reason."

Darcie was shocked by his statement. "What do you mean?"

Aha! he thought, *we make progress.* "If you can convince me of the need to do so, I might break our contract."

"What contract?"

Zack watched her as she tried to appear calm, sipping her hot tea slowly. "Our marriage contract, of course."

The cup rested against her lips and she stared at him. "You wouldn't dare try to enforce the contract—if indeed there exists such a document—knowing how I feel, would you?"

"Most certainly," he confirmed, beginning to enjoy the conversation.

"But why? What possible reason could you have for forcing

me into a marriage neither of us wants?" Darcie asked, astonished by his attitude.

"My dear, surely you are aware of how many conniving mothers of boring daughters there are in the world," he explained, leaning forward on one knee so that his face was close to hers. "I tire of the game. I want a wife."

"But you as good as said you came to Charleston to look me over, to see if you could deal with me," Darcie said, staring incredulously at his warm brown eyes. Dash it, why did he have to be so handsome? "If any woman will do, why did you bother?"

"There is the mistake in your thinking," he replied, nodding as if he'd solved a puzzle. "Not just any woman will do. Only you will do. Marry we shall, upon our arrival in Paris."

Chapter Fifteen

Darcie's mouth gaped open in surprise. Zack didn't make any sense to her. If he wanted a woman who would prevent eager mothers from descending upon him at every opportunity, then why bother with coming to America?

Her anger returned. "I'm going back to my room with Em. I'll take my meals there. Until we dock at Calais, I don't wish to see you again."

She stood—upsetting her plate of biscuits and jam—but didn't pause. Her belongings could be gathered later. Without another word, she marched toward the door, fully conscious of the effect her exit was having on Zack.

When she reached the door, she found it locked and had to spend a few seconds trying to open it. In the space of that time, Zack crossed the room and pulled her into his arms.

"Not so fast, little one."

His lips swooped down on hers and he drew her closer into his embrace. Her flailing arms were stilled by the steel bands of his hands and arms capturing her against him. Fighting was useless.

In a few moments, his lips left hers and she suddenly felt cold and alone. Gazing up at him, she saw the anger in his eyes and became frightened. This man could be dangerous if he lost his temper.

Breathing jerkily, she gasped, "Good-bye Zack," and ran out the door.

When she reached Em's room, she slipped inside without knocking. Mrs. Appleby sat by the window knitting and jumped when the door banged open. "What's—"

"I'm reclaiming my room, Mrs. Appleby. Gather your things and be off." Darcie didn't even bother to cover her disgust at finding the woman in the room. Why must she always appear when Darcie wanted to be alone?

Over on the bed, Em's eyes opened. "Darcie, I'm delighted to see you."

Rushing past the astounded Mrs. Appleby, Darcie hurried to Em's side. "I'm glad to see you, too. How are you?"

"Fine," Em answered. "I was just napping. I'm still a bit weak in the knees."

"We'll soon remedy that," Darcie retorted and turned to Mrs. Appleby. "Well, Mrs. Appleby, is there something else you needed?"

"I thought . . . I mean, I figured that you'd . . . that Captain Manville and you would . . ." her voice trailed off into silence.

"How wonderful. What an eloquent speaker you are, Mrs. Appleby." Darcie smiled venomously at her adversary. She knew perfectly well what Mrs. Appleby thought. "I'm sure you have other things to do."

Hidden behind Darcie's skirts, Em smiled. Darcie caught her eye and winked. Both of them felt the same way about the old crosspatch.

"Harrumph!" came the reply, but the door closed and Mrs. Appleby was gone.

"Oh, I thought she'd never leave! Honestly, Darcie, I think she made me feel worse than the seasickness," Em admitted.

Darcie pulled a chair over by the bed. "Well, I'm glad she's gone." Without sitting down, Darcie glanced at the door and wondered if the old biddy was there listening. "You know, Em, I've been to see you several times. At first, she wouldn't even let me in."

Reaching for the door knob, Darcie continued to talk. "Then I forced her to. I think Zack said something, too."

She turned the knob and wrenched the door open. Mrs. Appleby had been leaning against the door to hear them and fell into the room. Both girls broke into laughter as she regained her feet and slunk away.

"Well, have you recovered fully?" Darcie asked as she closed the door and crossed the room.

Em shook her head. "Not quite. But since you chased off that old crone, I'm beginning to perk up a bit."

Darcie laughed as Em got out of bed. Selecting a gown, she turned to Darcie and said, "Let's go to the dining room for supper. I've had enough of this room for a while."

"Oh, Em, let's not." Darcie had to be careful. It wouldn't do for Em to know why Darcie was reluctant.

"I refuse to eat here. This place still smells like a sickroom even though Zack's man has done his best."

Agreeing, Darcie thought that perhaps Zack wouldn't be at table. She hurried down the corridor to find Charity to help them dress. With Charity in tow, she returned and found Em sitting in the chair before the dressing table.

"Oh, Darcie, Charity, how wonderful," she exclaimed. "I'll feel like a princess when I've bathed and changed clothes."

"Me, too," Darcie admitted.

In less than record time, they were ready. Darcie's apple-green taffeta gown boasted ten yards of fabric—the latest in fashion. Its flounces were more than a foot deep and were gathered with bottle-green, velvet ribbon sprigged with tiny bouquets of pink flowers. The patent leather slippers gleamed brightly, but couldn't be seen beneath her expanse of skirts and lavish petticoats.

"By all the oyster shells in White Point Gardens, I doubt if I can remain erect throughout supper with these heavy crinolines," Em said, drawing them beneath her as she sat down.

"If you're feeling poorly, we'll eat here," Darcie reminded her.

"To the dining room it is." Em stood and shook the flounces on her yellow gown. "I can't stand this prison a moment longer."

Darcie took her hand and they slid through the doorway. Charity laughed as they left the room giggling for the first time on the voyage.

They found the dining room and paused a moment. "Have to look like a lady, you know," Em whispered.

"Don't worry." Darcie took a quick inventory to see how she looked. "I don't think anybody here will notice."

Em entered the room first. Darcie noticed the smile on her lips when the dimples appeared on the cheek closest to her.

Oh, no. Zack must be here, she thought.

She was right. The moment they stepped through the door, Zack rose and strode to greet them. Two places were vacant at the end of the table where he had been sitting.

"Ladies, what a pleasure." Zack reached for Em's hand and kissed it gently, and then led her to a chair. He turned back to Darcie. "Miss Gaynor, I'm delighted that you could grace our meal with your presence."

Short of being rude, she couldn't jerk her hand from his lips even when he lingered over her palm overlong. The scent of him wafted to her nostrils and obliterated every other smell. The clean fragrance took her back to their shared intimacy as if she'd never left his cabin.

As he led her to the seat at his right, Darcie's astonishment propelled her forward. Her reaction to his touch, to his presence in the dining room, seemed to make her own animosity fade. All of her anger, her doubts, disappeared when they sat down.

Zack was a delightful host. Their party, made up of Em, Barclay, Zack, Darcie, and another young couple, was in high spirits.

Zack and Barclay verbally fought to keep the girls' attention, and while Darcie tried to remain impartial, she found herself once again enraptured with Zack. If that was his plan, then he succeeded, she thought.

"Well, now that you've attained your sea legs, what do you think of my ship?" Zack asked Barclay.

Barclay sipped his wine and stopped to think for a moment. "I must admit it's one of the finest I've sailed, perhaps the finest."

Zack smiled at Barclay's praise. "When you feel up to it, come to the wheelhouse and give her a try. You'll find me there almost any hour."

"That's kind of you, sir, and I accept your invitation. And," Barclay added, "my compliments to your chef. I'd no idea I'd been missing such delicacies as this extraordinary fish. A fine sauce, too."

The smile on Zack's face broadened. He knew that Cook had spent hours preparing supper tonight, especially for those who had been so ill. "It's a white wine sauce. Cook is a talented man. Can do anything in the kitchen."

Em and Darcie agreed heartily.

Zack turned to Darcie and his gaze searched her face for some clue as to her feelings. He hoped that she had calmed down, that her adamant refusal of his proposal wasn't final. "Darcie, my dear, I believe you left a book in my cabin. You may pick it up any time. Oh," he added, "I've a splendid library. You're welcome to choose what you will to entertain you for the remainder of the journey. You, too, Miss Rhett. Barclay, if your taste runs to literature, then you're invited as well."

Darcie was spared having to answer. Both Em and Barclay eagerly accepted Zack's offer and neither appeared to notice how quiet she was.

Nothing escaped Zack's notice, however. While Em flirted quite outrageously with him, Darcie remained silent. His attempts to include her in their conversation sadly failed and he decided that she was still angry with him. Sometime before the end of their voyage, he would find her alone and speak to her. Letting her brood seemed to be the best way to handle her—for now.

Marveling at his skill at making everyone feel welcome, Darcie watched him during supper. The curl of his lips when he smiled fascinated her, especially when a dimple formed on his left cheek. At times she caught him staring at her as if he wondered what was happening in her mind. His attitude sometimes made her feel like he knew.

Darcie was certain that he couldn't know that she'd discovered his secret identity. She suddenly realized that if she were allowed the time, she might discover other evidence which connected him with the attack. How could she accomplish that without risking her own emotional well-being? His offer of the use of his library presented one possible answer.

He caught her staring at him. Their eyes met and lingered for the first time during the entire evening. The overt invitation in his gaze seemed to melt away her resolve, and even though she'd found concrete evidence of his complicity in the crime, his warm eyes made her doubt her own findings. How she wanted to believe him innocent, if only it could be true.

Darcie turned to Em and found her staring. She wondered if putting to sea stripped one of one's manners. Em had never been so blunt. Then Em's gaze moved from Darcie to Zack. Feeling a blush stain her cheeks Darcie glanced at Barclay who was deep in conversation with the gentleman on his left.

It really wouldn't do for Em to discover how Darcie felt about Zack. Could their emotions be so obvious?

For her to preserve her sanity, Darcie knew she must keep out of Zack's way, and never see him when Em was around. She had to find a way to maneuver that.

When supper was over, she strolled back to the room with Em and Barclay. The young couple that had joined them disappeared; having recently been married, they wanted to be alone.

Alone. Darcie wanted to be alone, too. She wanted the time to search Zack's room further, to explore her own feelings. *La Mer Magnifique,* a large vessel, still provided no extra space for her to hide from Zack.

She felt that her life had become a case of opposites. Her desire to search Zack's room put her in direct opposition to her need to avoid him. Her own recently released passions were the opposite of her own standards of conduct. The man with whom she had fallen in love was the opposite of her needs and desires.

For some time, Darcie paced back and forth until Em said, "Whatever has gotten into you? You're acting like a woman who's being tickled by an ostrich plume from the inside."

Darcie grimaced. She had hoped that Em wouldn't notice how fidgety she was, but she should have known better: Em noticed everything. "I'm sorry to disturb you. I feel so confined."

Em smiled and patted Darcie's hand. "You've had the run of the ship alone for the past several days. It's no wonder you feel boxed in. Why don't you go for a walk?"

"Oh, I couldn't do that," Darcie replied, wondering if she could get away alone. She didn't want Em to realize what she was doing either. "Not on your first real day out of bed."

"Sure you can. I insist." Em smiled and looked around the room. "Besides, I'm really tired."

"Then I'll just sit here and read," Darcie declared, determined not to provide any opportunity to be alone with Zack.

"What will you read? I believe Zack said your book was still in his cabin," Em retorted. "Pick something out for me, too. I'll start it in the morning. For now, I want to sleep."

Darcie helped Em undress and tucked her into bed. For a while she sat there, wondering what she should do and then decided that doing nothing would be impossible.

She circled the deck twice. Zack was in the wheelhouse, but didn't appear to notice her. *He must be really busy,* she thought and considered herself safe for the moment.

Hurrying down the stairs she swept past her own cabin and Barclay's before stopping at the door to Zack's. Without bothering to knock, she scrambled inside and closed the door behind her.

As Zack had said, her book lay on the table by the window where she'd left it. Turning up the lantern so she could see better, she decided to take some of her other belongings. She picked up the book, along with her workbasket and brush. To-morrow, she'd find a way to search his cabin further. But for now, she was too worried about running into him to linger.

Racing for the door, she dropped her book and stopped to pick it up. When she finally reached the door, it opened before she ever touched the knob. In the dim light, she saw the puzzled expression on his face as he pushed his way inside and closed the door. "I . . . I came for my book. And my workbasket."

She held the two items up for him to see. His gaze fell on her hands and then returned to her face. His deep-set eyes glimmered like brandy in the flickering light of the lantern and Darcie felt her resolve melting away, but was unable to will herself to move.

"I see," he answered flatly. "I didn't think you'd take your things so quickly."

His words disturbed her. What did he think she intended to do? "Did you think I'd stay here with you openly when there was no reason? We are the talk of the ship now."

"We are to be married soon."

"And that answers for an unmarried woman and man living together in the same cabin?" Darcie was aghast at his continued belief in their marriage. "And, I have told you. I cannot marry you."

Zack gazed at her, feeling a surge of desire at the flash of sapphire in her eyes as she debated with him. So close—she was close enough for him to touch, and yet, he dared not. He didn't want her to run, not now. Darcie was an honorable woman with an extraordinary sense of obligation. If she hadn't, then she wouldn't be on this ship now. "We are betrothed. Will you break our contract? Have you no honor?"

His taunt pained her. Her father had taught her honor above all else. Southern women are bound by honor, as are Southern men. A true Southerner never shirks his or her obligation. She could almost hear him speak the words as if he were here with them.

In this instance, Darcie's highly prized honor opposed her

scruples. Could she marry a man she suspected of piracy, of murder?

Another thought occurred to her. Why would Zack attack her ship if he intended to marry her? It made no sense. Nothing made sense anymore.

"Honor? You speak of honor?" She lifted her chin and gripped her books so tightly that her knuckles turned unnaturally white. "Has anything associated with the two of us been honorable? Have you been honest with me? Did our intimacy without the bonds of matrimony constitute an honorable act? Where is *our* honor?"

"Darcie, there are many reasons why I didn't tell you of our betrothal at first." Zack stepped forward and caught her free hand in his. He strode to the sofa, half-dragging her along behind him, and when they reached it, he pulled her down beside him. "I couldn't walk up to you and state my name followed by the fact that we were betrothed, could I?"

Hearing the facts succinctly put, Darcie couldn't argue with him. He would have sounded silly and she would have thought he was insane. She tried to pull her hand from his grasp, but had no success. "Go on."

Zack's grip turned to iron to prevent her from withdrawing her hand. He had to explain before she escaped again. "And, when you read your uncle's letter, I couldn't say anything then either. You would have thrown me out. Besides, since your uncle didn't name me as your betrothed, how could I?"

Darcie nodded. He was right, absolutely right about every point he made. "Zack, I understand all of that, I think. You must understand that . . . everything has changed for me so suddenly. I'm . . . I need some time to think."

"What's so hard about saying yes to me, Darcie?" he asked, beginning to wonder what was wrong with him—for two reasons. First, he had never intended to get married and now here he was practically begging this woman to marry him. Second, why was she refusing? Any number of women would jump at the chance to marry him.

What could she tell him? That she thought he was a thief and a murderer? That she'd been rifling through his personal belongings looking for evidence to string him up? "Please, just give me some time, Zack. I can't say yes or no right now. I just know I have to have time to think. Time alone."

"Have it your way, *ma petite*, have it your way," he whispered, leaning closer and inhaling the fresh scent clouded around her hair.

His kiss didn't surprise her. She'd known he would kiss her before his lips touched hers. His mouth touched hers, barely dusted hers with the scantiest of kisses, but his arms held her tightly.

One by one he wrested her belongings from her hand and dropped them on the sofa beside him. When her hands were free, he kissed her again, this time really kissed her. Darcie felt her response to his kiss deepen as his tongue slid between her teeth and teased hers.

"Zack, no, please don't," she whispered, or thought she whispered, against his lips.

After a moment, he drew away. "Why not, *ma cherie?*"

"This isn't right. We shouldn't be . . ." the sound of her voice dwindled off as his lips claimed hers once again.

Pulling back, he gazed at her, peered deeply into her eyes. He wanted her so badly that he ached from his need, but he held himself in check. "Darcie," he croaked. "I think you'd better return to your room."

Flushed from head to toe, Darcie snatched her belongings from the sofa and ran for the door. "Oh, I forgot Em's book."

She hurried to the shelves and picked out *Pride and Prejudice*. That ought to keep her busy for a while.

Before Zack had recovered enough to say anything else, to call her back, Darcie disappeared through the doorway. Feeling somewhat elated because he had made some progress, he stood and stretched. It would be a long night.

Darcie declined to leave her room for meals. Without doubt, Zack would be furious. Em, however, was having the time of her life. She reported to Darcie about every meal, every scrap of conversation, and every bit of gossip.

For the remainder of the voyage, Darcie avoided Zack as though he had the plague. Thankfully, he seemed content to give her the time she needed to think about their changing relationship—or their lack of relationship. So assiduously did she avoid him, that she didn't go outside her own room except when she knew for a fact that he was occupied elsewhere and not likely to disturb her. Of course, that meant abandoning her quest for evidence against him, but it meant that she didn't have to succumb to his great magnetism, thereby forgetting her quest altogether.

On one of their last nights out, Darcie waited until the night shift had come on duty to walk. The fresh salt air whistled through her hair as she walked along the deck, knowing Zack would be asleep by now.

Em thought Darcie had gone daft and refused to walk with her at such a despicable hour. Darcie didn't care. She wanted to feel the wind and spray of the ocean in her face once again before they docked at Calais.

The sails crackled and hummed in the brisk wind that sped them toward France. In a matter of hours—sometime tomorrow afternoon—they would make port. After unloading their personal belongings, they would be on their way to Paris in a private coach.

She'd miss the ship. Darcie had become fond of sailing again, and this might be her last voyage for a long time. Sailing was on the way out. These days ships operated by steam engines were being built which could cross the Atlantic in much less time, just over two weeks. When a way could be found to use less coal—it took thirty tons for the trip—sailing would die as a means of shipping.

Peering off the bow, she wondered how soon she would be able to see Calais. Now that the end of the trip was near, she found herself hungry for fresh fruit and vegetables and meat. As the ship slid down the crest of a wave, she smiled, knowing that in a day she'd feel solid ground beneath her feet again.

"Good evening."

"Oh!" Darcie jerked around and found herself face to face with Zack. "You scared me."

He propped his elbows on the railing and stared out to sea as she had been doing. "My apologies. What are you doing out here at this time of night?"

Cat's foot, she thought. *Why wasn't I paying attention?*

Turning to look at Zack's profile, she leaned against the rail and tilted her head back to see him better. "Apology accepted, kind sir. What brings you out among the night creatures?"

"Night creatures? Here?" he questioned. "Are you naming yourself a night creature? A vampire, perhaps? Mayhap I should protect the tender flesh of my neck."

"Mayhap you should, but not from the bite of a vampire," she agreed. "Perhaps the thug that killed dear Mr. Dupuis."

Darcie failed to mention that she had herself considered doing the job when she found her mother's earbob in Zack's possession. Well, she relented to herself, she wouldn't kill him. She loved him too much.

"That's a tragedy unsolved," he agreed. "And no clues."

Darcie remembered the young man and his jaunty smile and wave. "It's a sad thing, too. He was a nice boy."

Zack looked at her pensively. "Did you know him?"

Shaking her head negatively, Darcie answered, "No. But, I'd seen him on several occasions. He seemed a nice sort."

Still gazing at her, Zack scratched his chin. "Do you remember the man you asked me about during our first few days out? You pointed a man out to me on deck."

A little tremble shot through Darcie's body. Her criminal! The one Captain James said was one of the pirates. "Yes. What has that to do with Mr. Dupuis?"

"I'm not sure," Zack admitted, shaking his head. He'd noticed her trembling and wondered why. The night air was cool, but he'd never seen her actually shiver. "Are you cold? Take my coat."

Darcie stilled his hands as he started to remove the coat. This time her body quivered from the contact with Zack's hands—

not the cool air and not the murder and not the pirate. "I'm not cold. It's . . . it's the murder. That's all. But why do you ask me about that mean-looking sailor?"

Zack stood attentively, gazing at her as if she knew something. "Why do you call him mean-looking? Has he done anything or said anything that—"

Immediately on the defensive, Darcie wondered why Zack should find that statement interesting. Many people were mean-looking; many were sweet-looking. And he hadn't really *done* anything to her. "Nothing. I didn't mean to imply that he had behaved unseemly. I was referring to his scruffy beard, dark eyes, and constant frown. But you still haven't answered my question. Why do you think he's connected with Mr. Dupuis? They don't seem like two who would travel together for long."

Zack studied her. Something about the man interested her and she wasn't willing to tell him what it was. He knew Darcie well enough to know that he'd never force her to tell him anything she didn't want him to know. Maybe if he told her a little about his suspicions, she'd confide in him. "My feelings exactly. When I hired the two of them, they seemed to be together. And they'd sailed together before."

Darcie's eyes widened. Could it be that he didn't know the two men were on the pirate ship? Should she tell him what Captain James said? Or would she be relating a fact he already knew. "You're jesting. Have you questioned him about the murder?"

Was it simple curiosity that drove Darcie's fascination with the murder, he wondered. She didn't appear to be the kind of woman whose interests ran to the morbid. "I have questioned him. He informs me that he knows nothing."

"And you believed him?"

"Why would I not believe him? He had no motive, no more opportunity than others on board." Zack was surprised by Darcie's vehement question. It was as if he'd given her a piece of a puzzle that confirmed her suspicions. *Dash it,* he thought. *Why won't she confide in me? Why doesn't she trust me?*

Darcie shivered again. She felt that she was close to learning the truth, so close, but unable to prove her theory. Zack obviously wasn't telling her all he knew either. If only she could trust him.

"Come below, Darcie," Zack said finally. "It's getting too cold for you out here."

Nodding, she allowed him to lead her to the stairs. "I should get back to my room. I know Em will be wondering about me."

Zack laughed. "If she isn't already asleep, which I believe she must be. Otherwise, she'd have been looking for you by now."

Wishing she had the courage to curse, Darcie merely rolled her eyes. Zack would let her get by with nothing this night. Ever since he'd joined her at the bow, she'd known he wanted to talk to her. Avoiding him had postponed their final confrontation until this moment.

Without delaying further, she walked down the corridor with him. He opened the door to his cabin and stepped aside to allow her to enter first. Glancing over his shoulder, he followed her into the room and shut the door behind him. For some reason, he felt uneasy.

Darcie crossed the room and sank down onto her favorite chair, having ruled out the couch because Zack would have joined her for sure. "Well, what is it?"

Trust her to get right to the point. No delightful banter to ease into the conversation, he mused. "You have yet to answer my proposal."

Sighing, Darcie closed her eyes for a moment gathering her strength. "I have told you no on numerous occasions. My answer is still no."

"You have told me no, true enough," he conceded, dropping onto his knee in front of her.

Dash it, she thought. *Why won't he disappear gracefully? Why do I have to lie to fob him off?* "Zack, I don't know how else to tell you. You refuse to accept my reasons. I cannot marry you."

"We shall see," he answered, gazing deep into her eyes as if he could read her soul and discern her true reasons for rejecting him. He stood and drew her into his arms, smiling as they rose. His lips found hers and fanned their pent-up passion into a blaze that would linger through the night. When he released her, he whispered, "Escape for now, *ma cherie*, for we'll be together soon enough."

Chapter Sixteen

When *La Mer Magnifique* brushed the wharf and bumped to a stop, Darcie was standing at the railing. After months at sea, she was eager to walk on solid ground again.

Solid ground, she thought. *That's what I need to cast this misplaced love for Zack out of my heart.*

The last weeks of the journey had been trying. Staying out of Zack's way had proved difficult, and she had tired of the game. Now she faced a few more hours with him in a carriage and then freedom.

Weary from the long arduous trip from Calais to Paris, none of the group was good company. Zack had insisted upon dropping Barclay and Em at an inn before seeing Darcie to her uncle's house.

At last standing before Uncle Talbot's door, Darcie breathed freely. Zack would be gone forever within a few minutes. She glanced up at him and felt a catch somewhere deep inside. The precious moments she'd spent with him on the voyage were treasures to her far more valuable than the jewelry she'd lost during the piracy of her ship, but she dared not trust him because of the evidence against him as a thief and a liar.

Life stirred within the house in response to her knock and the door opened. A jovial-looking butler answered the door and escorted them into the parlor.

"I will tell monsieur that you have arrived, mademoiselle. Please wait here." Back erect, he strode away and closed the door behind him.

Darcie moved to the hearth and rubbed her hands together before the fire, while Charity huddled near the door. Turning slowly, Darcie tried to warm the chill that seemed to penetrate all the way to her bones. When she faced the room once again, she found Zack staring at her.

Disturbed by his intent gaze, she asked, "Is something wrong?"

Shaking his head, Zack strode to her side. "Darcie, *ma cherie*, we have arrived at a turning point in our lives. Soon——"

"Ah, Darcie, how good to have you with us safe at last." A slender chesnut-haired woman rushed into the room and threw her arms around Darcie. "Oh, my dear, we have been so worried about you, ever since poor Charles passed away. But never you worry. Everything will be . . . how you say it? Wonderful. Everything is to be wonderful now we are together, no?"

Darcie smiled at her, recognizing the features that were so similar to her mother's. "Aunt——"

Aunt Margot interrupted her before she could continue. "Balls and parties. Oh, but Paris is so gay. I have planned——"

"*Mon Dieu!* Margot, give the child a chance to breathe."

Over Aunt Margot's slim shoulders, Darcie saw a man enter the room. *Uncle Talbot,* she guessed.

"Hello, Darcie, dear." He kissed Darcie's cheek and hugged her slightly. "And Zacharie. How can I ever thank you for bringing our beloved Darcie to us? You will remain for luncheon?"

Darcie glanced at him, hoping for a positive response. Now that she was here with her family, she found that she didn't want him to leave her. Aunt Margot was a dear, but Darcie felt out of place, penned in by the sudden rush of devotion from people she hadn't seen in years and hardly remembered. Her eyes were pleading when her gaze met his.

Zack looked at Darcie. Although he realized that Talbot's invitation sprang from good manners rather than a sincere desire for him to stay, Zack pitied Darcie. Alone for three years without the benefit of guidance from a responsible adult, she had done remarkably well. And, now, a "doting" uncle clasped her to his bosom under the guise of attending to her well-being.

The affection with which Talbot had greeted his niece was as false as the proffered dinner invitation. Still, Darcie alone had the power to keep him. Her eyes, those luminescent sapphires, begged. How far should he make her go before he gave in and stayed?

With three pairs of eyes directed at him, Zack smiled at Darcie and then turned to Talbot. *"Merci.* How kind of you. I should be delighted to dine with you."

Margot placed her hand on his wrist and beamed at him as coquettishly as any Southern belle. *"Bon!* I'll see to the arrangements. Gautier!" she called and strode toward the door. "Ah. There you are. See that another place is laid for luncheon. And then take mademoiselle's bags to her room."

She watched him disappear and turned to face the threesome. "Talbot, darling, see that M. Manville has a place to make himself more comfortable. Darcie, dear, come with me. Oh," she stopped as if noticing Charity for the first time. "This must be the marvelous Charity. I'll send Mme. Marie to take care of Charity at once. A treasure such as she must be pampered."

With a grateful smile for Zack, Darcie followed her aunt and winked at Charity as she passed. Charity would have preferred to come with Darcie, but Mme. Marie had arrived at the door.

"Marie, here is our beloved Darcie. She has brought her wonderful Charity with her. Please make her comfortable in the servants' quarters and acquaint her with our staff and home." She beamed at Darcie. "I will have the pleasure then of taking care of my Darcie."

Both Darcie and Marie murmured appropriate greetings and then Darcie watched the older woman take Charity away. Confident that her friend was taken care of, Darcie returned her attention to her aunt.

"Your room is the last on the second floor *à gauche* . . . on the left," Aunt Margot prattled on as they left the parlor. She waived gaily at Zack and Talbot before taking Darcie's arm. "I'm delighted to see you, my darling. You can't know what a fearsome worry it's been, you across the way alone. I've told Talbot many times, begged him actually—" she stopped outside a door and opened it. "Ah, here we are. I've had this room redecorated just for you. I hope you like it."

Darcie walked in and whirled around. "Oh, Aunt Margot, it's lovely."

Tracing a golden acorn on the white poster bed, Darcie tried to settle down. This was a dream room, one imagined for a princess. All mauve, blue, and white, the accouterments were splendid and Darcie could hardly wait to be alone. She felt curiously at home here, safe.

Margot kissed Darcie's cheek and hugged her tightly. "I've longed to have you with us. I . . . we . . . Talbot and I have but one child, the boy Simon. Do you remember him?"

Thinking back almost fifteen years, Darcie pictured a gangly boy a year younger than herself. "Yes, I think so. It's been so long."

"Too long, my darling." Margot pushed Darcie back and peered up into her eyes. "I hope you don't mind if I treat you as the daughter I never had."

Tears sprang to Darcie's eyes. Aunt Margot had always been a love. All of her letters spoke of a deep affection for Darcie and her father, and although she thought that Aunt Margot was a little silly, she liked her already. Uncle Talbot was another matter. His greeting, while intended to display a warmth of affection, did little to melt the ice she perceived there.

Men seldom show their affection, she thought. She smiled warmly at Aunt Margot. "I would be honored."

"Bon," Aunt Margot replied and hugged her again. "I've planned a party for you. A lovely party and I've invited all the

best people. Friday night will be your launch into French society."

"That's wonderful, Aunt Margot, but—"

"Ha! We'll hear no buts on this matter. You must rely on me." Margot released Darcie and surveyed the room with a smile of accomplishment. *"C'est belle, non?"*

"It's lovely. More lovely than—"

Margot interrupted before Darcie could continue. *"Oui. Now—"*

A knock stopped her from completing her own sentence. She strode to the door and swung it open. "Ah, Gautier. And Mimi. *Entrez.*"

She stood aside while the two servants and a third she didn't call by name brought in Darcie's bags. She turned to Darcie and said, "Mimi will be your personal maid."

"But I have Charity and—"

"Yes, the wonderful Charity. She will be at your disposal as well." Margot nodded to Mimi. "However, our Mimi is quite talented at styling the hair and will serve you during your stay. She speaks fluent English. In fact, most of our servants do. We have many English and American friends."

Mimi placed the trunk she had carried up the stairs by the armoire. "Glad to make your acquaintance, miss. I'm delighted to be in your serving."

"In your service, Mimi," Margot corrected.

Blushing, Mimi curtsied and smiled shyly. "In your service, miss."

"I'm delighted as well, Mimi," Darcie replied. The young woman looked eager. It would be almost a holiday for Charity with Mimi's help, although Charity might become a little jealous.

Gautier and the other man left and Margot walked to the door. "Luncheon will be in one hour."

Darcie looked at Mimi and smiled. The next few days would be busy and she would meet many new people. A flare of excitement grew in her and she said, "Well, Mimi, we'll get on well, I'm certain."

Nodding, Mimi said, "I took the liberty of requesting a bath for you, miss. After your long journey, I know you—"

"Oh, Mimi. I'd love a bath." Darcie squeezed Mimi's hand. "Oh, we'll get on famously."

"*Oui,* miss." Mimi looked at the trunks and gestured to them. "Which contains the gown you wish to wear?"

Darcie didn't care about gowns. At the moment, her concern was for a bath. In the months at sea, she hadn't had a chance for a real bath. "Anything," she answered and then stopped. "Oh, they're all wrinkled from being packed. Don't worry about them."

"No problem, miss," Mimi replied, opening the nearest of the trunks. She lifted a white satin gown trimmed in deep blue velvet and laid it across a chair.

Darcie watched for a minute as her new maid lifted gown after gown. "Oh, those gowns are all for evening wear. Try the next case. The one with the silver buckles."

Mimi opened the other case and found a light blue woolen with pagoda sleeves. "Oh, this is lovely, miss."

The gown was one of Darcie's favorites. Its rich froth of lace in the sleeve accented Darcie's small hands and was one of her newest gowns. "I think that one will do, Mimi."

After a brass tub was placed in the corner near the fireplace and filled with steaming water, Mimi arranged an Oriental screen for modesty and helped Darcie to undress. Stepping into the water, Darcie couldn't contain herself. "Ah, this feels marvelous."

"I'll get the blue wool pressed immediately and these others will soon follow. What will you wear this evening?" She pulled a cord hanging by the bed. While Darcie bathed, Mimi continued to remove gowns from the trunks. A knock sounded and Mimi carried the gown to the door. "Bridget, see that this gown is pressed and brought back here immediately. Mademoiselle wants to wear it."

When Darcie heard the door close and knew that Mimi had returned to her task, she called, "This evening?"

"Oh, yes. Madame has planned a small dinner party in your

honor. Just a few close friends." Mimi chatted while she worked. "If you are ready, I shall rinse the hair."

"One moment more, please." Darcie lingered a bit longer and then knew that she'd have no time to dry her hair if she didn't get out of the tub. "Mimi! You may as well go ahead. I'd like to sit here all day."

"You'd soon look like the prunes." Mimi laughed as she poured hot water over Darcie's head. "Mademoiselle is far too lovely for that."

Reluctantly, Darcie rose and allowed Mimi to dry her off. Feeling refreshed, she donned a robe and sat down in front of the fire to dry her hair.

"Please, allow me to do," Mimi requested. "I can do hair good."

Darcie handed the pretty girl a brush and enjoyed the luxury of having someone fix her hair again. She closed her eyes and thought of Zack somewhere downstairs. Or was he? She didn't know where he had been taken to freshen up. His face swam before her closed eyes and she felt warmer all over. Their intimacy was past, but Darcie still longed for his touch, a touch she would never feel again.

"Bon. It is lovely," Mimi pronounced and backed away to look. "It is still damp, but we will complete a more elaborate style later. If we do not hurry, you will have to eat off a tray in your room."

Darcie stepped into the parlor and hesitated. Zack and Uncle Talbot were chatting by the fire. Long legs sprawled before him, Zack continued his tale. "And that's when we arrived."

"Such a shame. My finest ship." Talbot Neville shook his head gravely, and then noticed Darcie.

"My ship, Uncle," she reminded him, and was delighted when Zack jumped to his feet and beamed at her as if she'd rescued him from a conversation that he disliked.

"Of course, of course. I was . . . speaking figuratively. Of course, it's your ship," he corrected anxiously, leaping to his feet. "Come in, my dear. Margot will be along any moment with Simon."

"Je suis ici," Margot called from behind Darcie. "Darcie, love, here is your cousin Simon."

The slender boy kissed Darcie's hand. "A pleasure, mademoiselle. We are overjoyed to have you with us at last."

Darcie smiled at his fervent greeting. He seemed a little immature for his nineteen years, but nonetheless, sincere. "How do you do?"

Gautier stepped inside the door and announced, "Luncheon is served."

Simon took Darcie's arm and led her from the room, leaving Zack to escort Margot. Talbot lagged behind as if he were eager for the meal to be over before it had begun.

Simon said nothing during the meal, but Margot's delightful chatter and gossip kept them all amused. "I have so many plans for you, my dear. We'll be the hit of the season in Paris. So many people are already eager to meet you."

"Aunt Margot, I've traveled a long way and—"

"Certainly you have. You must spend the afternoon abed." She turned to Zack. "We're having a small dinner party this evening, very intimate. We would love to have you with us."

"Madame, I—" he began.

"I won't accept a refusal." She smiled and touched his arm. "After all, we can't have you rush off after bringing our dear Darcie to us, now can we? I insist."

"Thank you for your kind invitation. I accept." Zack lifted Margot's hand to his lips. "How could I refuse such a lovely invitation from the loveliest of France's hostesses?"

"Margot, for the love of the hour, the man's hardly touched his luncheon," Talbot barked from his end of the table. "Have the decency to let him complete one meal before foisting our company on him for a second. Have you considered that he may have other plans?"

Blushing, Margot fluttered her eyelashes and frowned. "Oh, dear, I apologize if I have embarrassed you or put you in an awkward situation. I'm just so happy to have our Darcie with us that I forget myself."

"No harm done, madame. I have grown quite attached to Miss Gaynor during our acquaintance." Zack gazed at Darcie a moment. "I hope that she is agreeable."

"Oh, yes." Darcie could hardly breathe beneath his intent gaze. What could he mean by his statement? Did he plan to ask for her hand during the meal?

Before she could think further on the matter, Gautier interrupted them. "A runner from the Lion's Gate, madame, with a message for you."

"Bring it here." Margot took the small envelope from his hand and opened it while the others watched.

Darcie recognized the script as Barclay's and wondered what he was up to. Perhaps something had happened to Em.

"Ah, the young gentleman from Charleston. M. Barclay. He and his sister wish to call tomorrow afternoon." Margot studied the letter further. "Gautier, is the runner still here?"

"Yes, Madame, he awaits your reply."

"Good. Bring me a fountain pen and paper." While he was gone, she said to the others, "I'll invite them to Darcie's party on Friday. Until then, I believe she'll be quite busy getting ready. We have much to do."

"Margot, perhaps we should discuss this. I mean, we don't know these people and—"

"Talbot, I'm astonished at you." Margot looked up from her paper. "How can you even suggest that we should snub Darcie's friends who cared enough to escort her all the way to Paris?"

Talbot didn't answer, but sat at his end of the table and glowered. Darcie couldn't understand what objection he could possibly have to her friends, nor to Zack for that matter. Although he treated Zack well enough, there was some strange undercurrent between them that made no sense to her. *Oh well, men were strange,* she thought.

When Margot finished the note, Gautier disappeared. She nodded. "I'm delighted that you have friends with you, my darling. How long do they plan to stay in Paris?"

"I'm unsure of their plans, Aunt Margot." Darcie didn't know how long they intended to stay, but wanted to keep in touch. She hoped that by now, Barclay's ridiculous idea about asking for her hand had been forgotten.

After luncheon, Zack took his leave. Darcie said good-bye and allowed herself to be led upstairs by Simon. Outside her door, he kissed her hand once again and clicked his heels together smartly before striding down the hallway.

Inside, Darcie closed the door and leaned against it. Weary from her journey, she suddenly felt that she could hardly walk the distance to the big bed.

"Are you all right, miss?" Mimi asked.

Darcie started and her eyes flew open. "Oh, Mimi, you frightened me. I thought I was alone."

"I was arranging some of your lovely gowns in the armoire, mademoi—I mean, miss."

"Mademoiselle is fine." Darcie walked to the dressing table and sat down. "Darcie is better. We're going to be friends. Please call me Darcie."

Mimi's eyes widened with fear. "Oh, no, miss. Master would beat me and then throw me into the street for such disrespect."

Darcie grimaced. "Well, I wouldn't want that to happen."

"Not I either, miss," Mimi answered, shuddering at the thought. "Here. Let me help you undress. What you need is rest."

"No, Mimi, I must see to my unpacking and—"

"Done. Look around. All your pretty things set about like they was belonged here."

Darcie laughed. "Not was belonged. Say, 'like they belonged here.' "

"Oh, miss. My English is frightful is it?" Mimi hung her head. "I works so hard to make it well."

Pitying the young woman, Darcie patted her arm. "You speak beautifully except for an occasional lapse."

"Well, miss, could you help me?" Mimi asked shyly. "I don't mean to take your time, but when we's here, if you could sort of set me right."

"I'd be delighted," Darcie agreed. "If you'll be my friend."

"Oh, I could do that. But, I couldn't be your friend if anybody is about. That wouldn't be proper." Unbuttoning Darcie's gown, Mimi smiled. "I like you, miss. You're a fine lady."

Hair braided, Darcie climbed into bed to rest. Once she had lain down on the soft mattress, she closed her eyes only to find that Zack's face seemed to be painted on her eyelids. Sleep came quickly, but lacked the peace she needed.

Nightmares ravaged her, as if she were transported to a space between time. There she found Zack—a Zack who wasn't the Zack she knew, or thought she knew. Several times, she dreamed that she had discovered the true Zack, but was disappointed when he unmasked and she realized that he was Uncle Talbot. And then Zack kissed her, not the passionate, loving kiss she expected from him, but a cruel and punishing kiss that she shrank from. A priest stood before them and a marriage ceremony began. When the priest finished the ceremony, he lifted her veil and Darcie discovered that she had married Uncle Talbot instead of Zack!

She screamed. Her shriek echoed through the unfamiliar hallways of her dreams and she was alone, but for the reverberation of Uncle Talbot's laugh.

Darcie sat up abruptly, perspiration running between her breasts. Her hands were clenched into fists and her teeth ground on each other.

Realizing that she was alone in her bedroom, she lay back down and breathed deeply. Her heart thundered in her chest, almost like the sound of Uncle Talbot's laughter in her dream.

She could lie abed no longer. Nervous energy built up in her and threatened an explosion if she didn't release some of the tension.

Until Mimi returned, Darcie really had nothing to do. She wanted to dress quickly and walk outside, work off some of her nervous energy. She already missed the freedom of her life on board *La Mer Magnifique* more than she'd ever dreamed possible.

And she missed Zack. While on board ship, she always knew he was near enough for her to get a glimpse of. Here at Aunt

Margot's, that chance would be rare, since Aunt Margot appeared to be the hovering type. Darcie would hardly get a moment alone for herself, much less time alone with Zack.

A light tapping startled her and she ran to the door. "Who is it?" she asked, glancing down at her muslin pantalets. She couldn't open the door until she slipped on her dressing gown.

"It's Mimi, miss," came the reply.

After tying the sash of her gown, Darcie breathed deeply and opened the door. "Come in, Mimi."

Mimi strode past her carrying a silver tray. "I brought a little something to help you through the evening until dinner. It's just a biscuit and tea."

Darcie smiled at her new friend gratefully. During lunch, she had been so conscious of a strange overtone between Zack and Uncle Talbot that she hardly touched the marvelous food.

Later, while dressing for dinner, Mimi told her about the guests. Madelaine Ortiz, madame's best friend, would be present with her two children, Gabriella and Nicholas, who were about Darcie's age. The Fouchers were also invited. Their sons, Pierre, Didier, and their daughter, Estelle, would also come.

Darcie perked up immediately at the mention of Madelaine Ortiz. Zack had mentioned her with a great deal of animosity in his journal. Wondering if he knew Madelaine was invited, Darcie smiled. It would be nice to see him uncomfortable for a change. He seemed to delight in making others ill at ease during social occasions.

Taking Mimi's advice, Darcie chose a creamy silk gown lavish with Mechlin, gathered with tiny artificial violets at the wrists and flounces. Over her bare shoulders, she swung an embroidered shawl of crepe de chine with a deep fringe. Mimi brushed and twirled and curled Darcie's hair until it reflected the dancing flames in the fireplace. Finally, she parted it and drew it into a violet ribbon and placed the curls to one side of a bunch of violets.

"Oh, Mimi! Can that be me?" Darcie whispered, afraid of breaking a spell. "I look . . ."

"You are beautiful." Mimi smiled and leaned close. "Your beau, that M. Manville, will be . . . will be, I don't know, will be groveling at your feet."

"Zack? Believe me, that man would never grovel." Darcie laughed at the image of Zack that Mimi envisioned. No, he was far too proud. Besides, he had no reason to grovel. He could have any woman he wanted.

The smile faded from her face. She had no jewelry to wear. Anger pressed fresh color into her cheeks as she studied the near-empty jewelry case. Her amethyst brooch would be lovely with the gown, but she had no place to pin it. She looked at it longingly and sighed.

"A beautiful piece, mademoiselle. You have another ribbon? We pin it to the ribbon and tie around your neck." Mimi opened a drawer in the dressing table. "Voila!"

Watching her pin the brooch to the creamy velvet ribbon, Darcie began to smile again. It would be the perfect touch.

Feeling pretty once again, Darcie headed for the stairs. She knew that Zack had arrived a few minutes ago and that others were waiting with her aunt and uncle. After hugging Mimi impulsively, she hurried down the stairs.

At the door to the parlor, she paused, made sure that her gown hung smoothly over the crinolines, and strode through the door. She wanted to appear confident and at ease, but her heart was thundering and her knees felt like currant jelly.

"Ah, here is Darcie." Margot hurried to her side and looped arms with her.

She pulled her toward a tall, thin man with a mustache that covered his entire upper lip. Beside him stood a small woman wearing an expensive silk gown with several rows of flounces. Had the woman been younger the gown would have been appropriate, but on a woman her age, it merely looked frivolous and silly.

After introducing the Fouchers, she drew Darcie toward their children. Pierre looked much like his father without a mustache and had been chatting amiably with Darcie's cousin Simon. Didier, a year younger according to Mimi, resembled his mother. Poor Estelle took after her father and Darcie doubted that she'd ever land a husband, but greeted her warmly. They were close to the same age and Darcie had no real friends here.

Madelaine Ortiz hadn't arrived yet and had he known she was coming, Zack would have refused the invitation—no matter how insulting it seemed to the host and hostess. He stood by the fire, fuming as he thought of the predicament he'd gotten himself into over the little tart now flirting with the silly Foucher boys.

Let her have her fun, he thought. *Our time will come.*

Darcie felt that someone was staring at her and turned. Uncle Talbot seemed to be glaring at her for no reason. Blushing profusely, she excused herself and hurried to his side. "Uncle Talbot, have I done something wrong?" she whispered.

"Wrong. Not exactly." Talbot Neville appeared to force a smile to his lips. "But look at Simon. He wants to talk to you and you ignore him."

"Ignore him? Uncle, he's my cousin. I was speaking with our guests," Darcie explained, wondering why he thought she should spend time with her cousin when she had all day tomorrow to do so.

"True enough, but don't neglect poor Simon. He's not well, you know," Talbot whispered, as if passing on a confidence.

Darcie turned and stared at her uncle. "Not well? What do you mean? What's wrong?"

Talbot shook his head gravely. "I'm afraid he's very ill, although he would never tell you himself. So proud. So . . . fond of you."

The astonishment that registered on Darcie's face drew Zack's attention. What in the devil had Talbot said to upset her so? Whatever it was, Zack decided to stop it before poor Darcie wept all over that lovely gown. "Talbot," he said as he approached them. "Are you attending the Christmas Ball at Versailles?"

"Ball? What are you saying?" Talbot's face flamed with color at the unexpected interruption.

Zack could hardly keep from laughing out loud. Talbot was

clearly unaccustomed to interference from outsiders. "I believe the Empress is giving a ball to celebrate the season. Are you invited?"

"Well, I assume, I mean, we . . . excuse me. I see Margot trying to get my attention." Talbot strode quickly to Margot's side.

Watching the episode, Darcie looked at Zack with eyes brimming with questions. Had he noticed how uncomfortable Uncle Talbot was making her and intentionally stopped the confrontation? From the quivering of his chin as he tried to keep from laughing, she surmised that she was correct.

Her eyes met Zack's and he winked conspiratorially at her as they moved back to the fireplace. Too bad the room was full of people or they could really laugh about his second "rescue" of Darcie. For a moment, she wished they were back in America where they were free to laugh and tease without observing the strict rules of society.

Gautier entered the room and announced that the other guests had arrived. Margot scurried to the door to greet her guests, and Zack stared with interest as he propped his elbow on the mahogany mantel.

Feeling a surge of curiosity for the woman Zack so evidently hated, Darcie turned her attention to the new arrivals. A tall, slender woman adorned in brown silk trimmed with beige lace surveyed the room. Her gaze came to rest on Zack and her expression changed from one of haughty disinterest to one of surprise.

"Zack, darling. How came you to be here?" She strode across the room and threw her arms about him.

Bending stiffly, Zack kissed her cheek dutifully. Darcie surmised that the woman must be one of the women intent on having him for a son-in-law, for behind her trailed a young woman and a young man, both gushing with thanks for the invitation to dinner and to the upcoming ball.

Zack stood erect again and stared at the woman with open animosity. "Madelaine Ortiz, allow me to present Mademoiselle

Darcie Gaynor, recently of Charleston in America. Darcie, Madelaine Ortiz—my mother."

"I'm so very pleased . . ." Darcie's voice trailed off and her gaze transferred from Madelaine Ortiz to Zack questioningly. She clearly remembered his telling her that his mother was dead and later confessed to his lie. She tried to recover as gracefully as possible. "So very pleased to make your acquaintance, Madame Ortiz."

"Miss Gaynor, how charming you are." She smiled at Darcie and then turned to Zack. "And I see my son is quite taken with your charm."

"Now, Mother—"

"Zack, darling, don't be tiresome. I've repeatedly asked you to call me by my name." Madelaine Ortiz tapped his arm with a delicate ivory fan and smiled at Darcie. Her hair was as black as Zack's and curled high on her head. Feathers studded with jet and rubies were tucked into the front curls and matched the cut of those on her necklace and earbobs. Her black silk shawl sparkled with black stones as Madelaine turned to study Darcie. "We're delighted to have you with us, my dear. Don't let this naughty boy scare you away from polite society. He's by far too independent for a man."

"Really, Mother, I—" Zack received a sharp look from Madelaine, and continued, "Madelaine, must you tout my shortcomings so soon after making the lady's acquaintance?"

"Ah, here's my delightful Gabriella." Madelaine pulled Gabriella into the group. "Darcie, my darling, I want you and Gabriella to be special friends."

After a few moments of polite conversation, Darcie realized that Gabriella possessed none of Madelaine's flair for conversation. She seemed totally ill at ease, even with her brother. Darcie looked at her. There *was* a resemblance. And, then Darcie recalled something she'd read in Zack's journal, something about Madelaine Ortiz and her two stepchildren.

Glancing from one to the other of the family, Darcie could easily see the resemblance between Zack and his mother. Gabriella lacked any of the fine features that made Zack handsome and Madelaine beautiful. A long narrow face, overlarge nose and mouth, and wide, deep-set eyes made the poor girl almost comical. It was really too bad, her slight figure was attractive, but her face would serve to drive away many suitors.

Madelaine stared thoughtfully at him and then faced Darcie, as if she hadn't noticed Darcie's close scrutiny of Gabriella. "He's a proper beast. Don't let him bully you, my dear."

"Madame Ortiz, I—" Darcie protested.

"You must call me Madelaine as well. We're going to get on well, you and I." She glanced at Zack and back at Darcie. "I was but a babe myself when this great hulk was born. An incurable wanderer like his father. The woman that tames this one will never have peace."

Darcie's eyes met Zack's. She knew exactly what Madelaine Ortiz meant.

Chapter Seventeen

It was the night of the ball. Darcie and Margot had spent the past few days consulting with the kitchen and housekeeping staffs, receiving cards of acceptance to the ball, and visiting the milliners and couturiers of Paris.

Margot declared that Darcie's wardrobe was inadequate, even with the extra gowns ordered especially for this trip. American styles were always behind the fashion trends, and no respectable woman dared to be considered unfashionable.

Darcie didn't really care. She had no plans to remain in Paris after she spoke with her uncle about breaking her engagement. Since her arrival, she'd been kept so busy, as had he, that they hardly had time to speak more than pleasantries.

During these busy days, Darcie had little chance to think of Zack until bedtime. She hadn't seen him since the evening his mother had warned her about him. Zack seemed displeased with Madelaine's offhand remarks, but Darcie had been delighted. Prepared to dislike the woman he so obviously hated, she had been pleasantly surprised.

Ever since Zack had told her that her arranged marriage was to be to him, she'd considered it privileged information and had mentioned it to no one. And then Madelaine had made such a point of telling Darcie about Zack's wandering spirit. Having been the daughter of another such spirit, Darcie could understand. She, too, felt the tug of the sea. Her arrival in landlocked Paris had taken its toll on her own spirit, and she knew that it must be doing the same to Zack.

Silly girl, she scolded herself. *While you're in Paris, enjoy yourself. You won't soon get this chance again.*

Tonight was the night of the welcome ball for her. Even as she daydreamed, preparations were being made. Silver and china were being readied; festive decorations were being hung and placed all about the house; scores of fancy dishes were being prepared by Cook down in the cavernous kitchen.

Aunt Margot had last-minute errands to run. Uncle Talbot was nowhere to be seen, having declared last night at dinner that he had no tolerance for such busy work. Darcie and Simon were alone in the house, and she hadn't even seen him this afternoon.

Feeling almost left out, Darcie took off her day gown and lay down across her bed to rest. Although she wasn't sleepy, she had nothing else to do.

The excitement of her arrival, meeting all the new people, and the upcoming ball took its toll. Darcie soon fell asleep.

Her eyes sprang open. Someone had called her name.

Sitting up, she rubbed her fists in her eyes to rid herself of the last vestiges of sleep. She swallowed hard, trying to alleviate the cottony feeling in her mouth.

"Wake up, miss. It's time to dress." Mimi was standing beside the bed shaking Darcie's foot.

Looking around, Darcie realized that the sun was setting. How long had she slept? She swung her feet to the floor. "Oh, Mimi, why did you let me sleep so long?"

"Madame said you needed rest. You were not to be disturbed." Mimi moved to the bath. "It's good that you washed your hair this morning. If you wish to bathe quickly, the water is ready."

"Have I time?" Darcie strode to the window and looked out.

The sun would disappear in thirty minutes, and she felt as sluggish as if she'd worked all day in the fields. "I'm so tired."

"A nice warm bath is what you need to set you right." Mimi tested the water with her fingers. "Here you are, nice and warm. Just the thing."

Darcie allowed herself to be pampered. Mimi scrubbed her back, taking care to keep her hair dry. "Now, miss, don't you feel better?"

"Yes." Darcie stood and waited while Mimi wrapped the hearth-warmed towel around her. "Has my gown arrived?"

"Oh, yes. It's the most lovely gown I've ever seen." Mimi turned her back and busied herself arranging the brushes, pins, and other paraphernalia on the dressing table while Darcie pulled on her long white muslin drawers and corset. "Let's see about your hair. I have a grand idea."

Darcie sat down at the dressing table and laced her fingers while Mimi began to brush her long, pale gold hair. Piling it high on Darcie's head, Mimi pinned it and laced a strand of pearls through the curls, finally hiding the catch with an artificial ivory-colored rose.

"There. How do you like it?"

Darcie smiled. She felt like a princess. "It's lovely, Mimi. Thank you."

Then Mimi helped Darcie arrange her new whalebone-reinforced crinoline and several freshly starched muslin petticoats with flounces. She lifted the new ballgown over Darcie's head, listening intently to the rustle of taffeta. "This gown even sounds pretty."

"M. Worth says taffeta is all the rage in gowns this year. I fear he's terribly expensive, but Aunt Margot would hear of nothing but the best." Darcie popped her head through the bodice of the gold taffeta gown and waited while Mimi smoothed it around her and fastened its numerous buttons. "Well, how does it look?"

"Oh, the Empress herself would be envious of you tonight." Mimi looked around. She found a tiny ivory-colored bud from the artificial rose and clipped it off. Within minutes she had attached it to a piece of gold velvet and secured it around Darcie's neck. "Oh, but you have the color for this gown. Nobody else will be as beautiful."

"Thank you, Mimi." Darcie slid into her new kid slippers and pulled on the matching ivory gloves that reached above her elbows. Taking one last look at her reflection, she moved towards the door. "Is it time to go down? Should I wait?"

"I go and see." Mimi disappeared through the door.

Darcie paced before the bed. Excitement surged through her. Tonight was her real introduction into French Society. Her name had brought her easy acceptance in Charleston, especially after the Charleston socialites found her so charming, but France was different. Her knowledge of French ways was limited, though she spoke the language tolerably well. She stopped in front of the mirror and found a pale face reflected there. Pinching her cheeks, she sighed.

What if everyone hated her? What if they found her American ways brash? What if they found her ugly? *Oh, you can find ways to criticize yourself all day, goose,* she chided herself.

Mimi swung open the door and stepped inside. "Miss, madame is looking for you. Guests have begun to arrive."

Darcie hurried to the door and followed Mimi to the landing, pausing only long enough to hug her friend briefly. She had delayed her entrance long enough.

As she reached the bottom of the stairs, she straightened her shoulders and lifted her chin. A quick glance at the ballroom door confirmed that Aunt Margot was indeed already greeting guests.

Noticing the stare of her latest arrival, Margot's gaze followed his and settled on Darcie. "Ah, and here is my darling now. Darcie, come quickly."

Darcie strode as quickly as possible to her aunt and smiled during the introduction. From the expression on the guest's face, Darcie would make a hit with the gentlemen of Paris.

When he moved on, Darcie whispered, "Sorry to be late, Aunt. I fell asleep and could hardly rouse myself."

Margot kissed her niece's cheek. "You have nothing to fear,

my dear. Nobody of importance has arrived. Ah, here are the Fouchers. You remember them, of course, Darcie."

"Yes. How delightful to see you again." Darcie smiled with genuine warmth. Even though the Fouchers were quiet, they were friendly faces. "Pierre, Didier, and Estelle. I do hope that we can chat later on."

Estelle took her hands and smiled, showing perfect white teeth. "Oh, Darcie, your gown is exquisite."

"Thank you. I'm glad you like it." Darcie blushed, noticing the slight signs of wear on Estelle's gown. "How lovely you look tonight."

"Thank you. I . . ." Estelle turned and glanced at the ball-room door. "I see you have other guests arriving. I hope we have a chance to get to know each other."

Darcie felt sorry for the younger woman. This event either didn't qualify as important enough to purchase a new gown for Estelle, or the family was strapped for money. When Darcie considered the sum that her own gown must have cost, she could easily understand their reluctance. After all, Zack had mentioned a ball at The Tuileries for New Year's Day. Perhaps their clothing allowance would be used then.

Margot introduced Darcie to so many people that she could hardly remember the names, much less associate the names with faces. She looked for Zack. He hadn't arrived since she'd been greeting their guests and Darcie hadn't seen him before, so she assumed that he was either late or not coming. Missing him already, she glanced at the throng around the punch bowls. Many handsome men were already laughing and slapping each other on the backs jovially. This promised to be a fun party.

"Ah, and here is Madelaine." Margot turned to Darcie. "You will remember Madelaine. And her lovely daughter, Gabriella. Oh, the handsome Nicholas lags behind."

"Of course, and how are you this evening, Madame Ortiz?" Darcie took the older woman's hand and smiled with genuine fondness. "I am delighted to see you again."

"And I you, my dear. You are positively lovely." Madelaine turned to Margot. "You must pay that man Worth a fortune. I tell you he never suggested anything so stunning for my Gabriella."

"The gown is his design entirely. He made it in so short a time, I accused him of selling us a gown made for another," Margot whispered. "But he said that the mademoiselle and the fabric fairly cried out for each other, and I saw the bolt of taffeta myself. He never before hurried a gown for anyone that I know of."

Darcie blushed. M. Worth had fawned over her for a long time, taking almost an hour with fresh sketches while his assistant measured her and then showed several bolts of cloth.

"I assure you, I shall scold him unmercifully when next I see him," Madelaine confided, still staring at Darcie. "Although, I must admit that the golden color of the taffeta is perfect for her."

"Madame, I—" Darcie began, hoping to divert some of the attention given to her gown to poor Gabriella.

"Madelaine, dearest, *Madelaine,*" Madelaine Ortiz reminded Darcie. "You make me feel positively ancient."

"Oh, I don't mean to do so," Darcie apologized. "Madelaine, I merely wanted to say that Gabriella looks lovely in her white silk."

"Gab . . . Oh, yes. Worth made that gown." Madelaine turned to glance at her stepdaughter. "Such vivid coloring. He said the soft white would make her look less of a . . . less animated."

Smiling, Darcie reached for Gabriella's hand. "I think you look quite lovely. Quite. And your hair is wonderful."

"Oh, do you think so?" Gabriella reached with her other hand and patted a curl. "My Beauchamps is a marvel."

"She certainly is. That's quite an intricate style," Darcie continued. "She must have had you at her mercy for hours."

Gabriella lifted a gloved hand to her mouth and giggled. "All day. I fairly perished before she would let me eat luncheon."

The girls laughed while Margot and Madelaine looked on, pleased that the two were getting on so well. It was clear to

Darcie that the ladies had conspired to make the two girls friends and were clearly delighted with their apparent success.

"Well, my dear," Madelaine began and kissed Darcie's cheek. "I hope to have a nice chat with you later."

"I look forward to it," Darcie replied. She squeezed Gabriella's hand and smiled. "I have promised Estelle a few moments. Will you join us?"

"Oh, yes. I like Estelle," Gabriella's eyes glittered as she turned to scan the room. "Where is she?"

Darcie glanced around the room until she spotted Estelle's brown silk gown. "There." She pointed to a chair near the French doors. "I'll join you as soon as my aunt releases me."

After greeting the ever-slowing stream of new arrivals for several more minutes, Darcie concluded that Zack didn't plan to attend. She felt a bit cross with him for promising to come and then breaking his word. But in addition to being cross, she also felt alone, deserted. For the past few days she'd missed him more than she cared to admit.

"Thank you, my dear, for standing so long without complaint," Margot whispered to Darcie and hugged her. "Here, go along with Simon and dance."

"Aunt, I—"

"Shall we, cousin?" Simon stood erect before her, looking as always a bit self-conscious.

Darcie schooled her features to prevent the grimace and moans that threatened to erupt from showing. It wasn't that she didn't like Simon, but he seemed such a child. *There you go again,* she thought. *Comparing every man to Zack. Remember that Zack is a thief and a liar. Smile.*

The smile that teased her lips meant nothing. She allowed Simon to whirl her off onto the dance floor and they joined the other dancers.

Simon danced technically well, although she felt as if she were dancing with a student who had learned the steps and ignored the music. The ballroom was festive, with an array of costly flowers imported for the occasion contributing their delightful fragrance to the aura of the dance.

Darcie closed her eyes. She could almost imagine herself back in America, walking in her lovely garden with its profusion of blossoms in spring. The image changed slightly and she saw herself seated on the stone bench with Zack at her side. Laughing at some frivolous remark, his head was thrown back and his eyes half-closed.

Feeling a tightening in her stomach from her memories, she opened her eyes. Simon was gazing at her as if he wanted to ask a question, but had decided against it.

Probably can't talk and dance at the same time, she thought uncharitably. Looking over his shoulder, she scanned the crowd for Zack's face and was once again disappointed. *Why am I disappointed? I should be glad to be rid of him.*

The music stopped and Simon followed her from the floor. She headed straight for Madelaine and Gabriella who were chatting with Estelle. When she got near enough to escape from Simon, she turned and smiled at him. He looked so uncertain, like he knew he should do something else and couldn't remember what it was.

"There you are, darling. We were hoping you would join us," Madelaine said as Darcie approached them. "I do wish to get to know you better."

"And I you, Madelaine." Darcie seated herself on a chair between Gabriella and Madelaine. "I do so want to make friends while I'm here."

"While you're here?" Madelaine gazed thoughtfully at Darcie for a moment. "I thought you were going to stay. I understood from Margot that you were moving here, I mean you are betrothed."

"Staying?" Darcie echoed. Aunt Margot would think that she was staying. After all, Uncle Talbot had arranged this marriage and they had no reason to believe her new husband would be eager to run off to America with his new bride. It wouldn't be fair to Aunt Margot and Uncle Talbot for her to tell her plans to someone else before she told them. She crossed her fingers. "Oh, of course. I . . . I wasn't aware that anyone else knew of . . . the betrothal."

Madelaine leaned forward and winked conspiratorially. "Ah, but for a few close friends, your secret is kept."

Darcie smiled and wondered how many "close friends" knew.

"Mlle. Gaynor, may I have this dance?"

Darcie looked up into the deep blue eyes of Pierre Foucher. His smile was warm and inviting. "Yes, thank you."

Rising and placing her hand in his, Darcie glanced back at Madelaine. She found the older woman staring at her as if she'd revealed some dark secret.

Pierre danced much better than Simon. They whirled about the floor and talked of her stay in Paris.

"I'd be honored to show you about, if your aunt permits, of course," he offered.

"You are most kind. I'd be delighted." Darcie's answer was almost mechanical. So great was her disappointment in Zack's absence that she hardly paid attention to anything around her.

Pierre's lips turned up almost all the time, so Darcie couldn't tell if he was smiling or not. He seemed to have two permanent dimples in his cheeks directly below his huge blue eyes.

"You dance splendidly, mademoiselle." His eyes followed the direction of hers.

Darcie hadn't meant to be rude, but Barclay and Em had just entered the ballroom. Em was attired in the yellow silk that made her look ill.

When they reached the closest point in the room to the new arrivals, Darcie sighed. She'd longed to see Em and Barclay ever since Zack deposited her at Aunt Margot's house. "Pierre, I hate to seem ungracious, but I see that my dearest friends have arrived and I do so want you to meet Emilie Rhett."

Pierre gazed in the direction she indicated and led her from the floor. Reaching her friends, Darcie flung her arms around first Em and then Barclay. "Miss Emilie Rhett and Barclay Rhett, allow me to present my new friend, Pierre Foucher. M. Foucher, Emilie and Barclay Rhett."

Em's eyelashes fluttered and she smiled winsomely at Pierre as the music ended and people began leaving the dance floor. "Oh, sir, I'm delighted to meet you."

"And I you, mademoiselle." To Darcie's amusement, Pierre bowed over Em's hand and kissed it ardently. When he stood erectly again, he bowed to Barclay. "And you, sir. A pleasure."

"I'm honored, M. Foucher." Barclay returned Pierre's half-bow.

The music began again and Barclay beamed at Darcie. "Will you dance with me, Darcie?"

Before Darcie could reply, Pierre took Em's hand and they joined the group on the dance floor. "Certainly."

She placed her gloved hand in his and they followed Pierre and Em. Barclay danced beautifully, guiding her expertly around the floor. Darcie thought back to the St. Cecilia's Ball, when Barclay had nearly dragged her off the floor and out of the building. Zack had come to her rescue then.

But there was a difference tonight. Barclay wasn't in his cups as he had been then. His steps were sure and elegant as they whirled around with the other dancers.

"How good it is to have you in my arms, my darling." Barclay tightened his hold ever so slightly.

Darcie, wrenched from her reverie, smiled and replied, "Yes. I agree. I was getting a bit homesick for someone who speaks English with no accent."

Barclay laughed. "I'm afraid the Brits would disagree with you there. They think Charlestonians have an abominable accent."

"True," Darcie agreed laughing with him. "But give me an American accent any day."

When they neared the French doors, Barclay danced her through them. "Is there a garden here?"

Darcie shivered. "Yes, there's a garden. But, Bar, it's awfully cool out here."

"Don't be difficult, Darcie." Bar kept walking, almost dragging her along with him. "Let's find a place to sit. I'll give you my coat."

Struggling to keep up with him, Darcie almost tripped. "Do slow down. Why are you running?"

Barclay looked back over his shoulder. "Because I don't want to be interrupted by a certain Frenchman who has the irritating habit of turning up when I want to be alone with you."

Darcie giggled. So, he remembered Zack's interruption at the St. Cecilia's Ball. "If you're referring to Zack, he isn't here."

He stopped so short that Darcie stumbled into him. "Not here? I should have thought he'd be the first to arrive."

"To be honest, I haven't seen him since the day of my arrival."

"Nor have you seen me since then. My note to you asking for permission to call was rejected quite nastily as I recall." Barclay's petulant tone made him sound like a small boy who'd received a spanking.

Staring at him in the chilly moonlight, Darcie thought back over the notes she'd received since her arrival. She'd seen nothing from Barclay except a note to Aunt Margot. There had been nothing personal. "I've received nothing from you. Nothing at all."

Barclay spun around. "I sent you a letter several days ago requesting permission to call. I must say, you need to see a doctor. Your reply was very blunt."

"Again, I tell you that I received no such missive and sent none in response to the one I didn't receive." How very odd that he'd sent a letter to her that hadn't been given to her. "I must assume that my aunt opened it by mistake and answered it without discovering that it was directed to me. But I can't imagine Aunt Margot being rude."

Music streamed out of the windows, apparently opened to allow fresh air to reach the dancers. Such a throng of people could make a room stuffy very quickly.

"Bar, I think we should go back. Aunt Margot will wonder what has happened to me," Darcie said as she glanced back at the pale glow of golden light pouring from the huge windows. "After all, I am the guest of honor."

"Darcie, I refuse to return until I've had a moment with you." Barclay stopped before a stone bench and spread his coat for her to sit on. "Pray give me a bit of your time."

"All right," Darcie conceded. "Just a moment, though. I must remind you that I have a guardian here and that my conduct must remain above reproach."

"I never thought you'd turn into such a prim and proper miss." He eyed her suspiciously. "Or is it that you find M. Foucher more romantic?"

"Barclay!" Darcie jumped to her feet and stamped her foot. Arms on her hips like she was scolding a child, she glared at him. "How dare you accuse—"

Barclay jerked her down beside him and into his arms. His lips silenced hers even though she continued to struggle.

Darcie freed her mouth from his and fought to escape his embrace. "What right have you to—"

Holding her tightly, he interrupted, "I have every right. I am to be your husband. I intend to speak to your uncle tonight. I refuse to be held at arm's length any longer."

"I'm afraid you will be disappointed." Darcie pulled one of her arms loose. "As I have told you repeatedly, I cannot marry you."

"Do you think I care one whit for a betrothal that exists only in the mind of an old man? Mark my words, he will see the sense of my suit and we shall be wed."

Darcie closed her eyes and unconsciously willed Zack to appear. When she opened her eyes, she half-expected to see him standing before her. She was disappointed that the yew remained a yew, and she and Barclay were still alone. "Regardless of whether I marry the man of my uncle's choosing, I shall not marry you, Barclay. It is impossible."

"It is not impossible. You have been promised to me for years." Barclay tightened his grip and spoke between clenched teeth. "I shall not be denied."

"Promised to you?" Darcie spat. "You speak nonsense. Who made such a foolish promise?"

"Well, your father did. Sort of." Barclay floundered for words. "I mean we had an understanding."

"Barclay, my friend, my dearest friend, my father made no such promise." Darcie tried to think of something comforting, but found that everything seemed either too trite or too harsh.

Barclay didn't want comfort. He refused to see clearly on this issue. "Please, Barclay, don't . . . don't make matters even more uncomfortable."

"Darcie, you know as well as I that people . . . that everybody in Charleston expects us to marry." Barclay kissed her again. "You have nothing to fear, my darling. I shall take care of this matter and we shall return to Charleston post haste."

How could she reach him? He seemed to be convinced of his own argument. "Barclay, if you have any regard for me, do not press this issue. Return to America. I'll provide passage on one of my ships for you and Em."

"We shall marry here, of course," Barclay continued, ignoring her pleas. "I—"

"No, Barclay."

"You have a nasty habit of interrupting, darling." Barclay kissed her roughly. "We shall work on that. In the meantime, I will brook no further argument concerning the matter."

"You'll brook—"

"As I said, the discussion is finished. I do not intend to be denied. We—"

From behind Darcie came a deep voice that sounded as if it were chiseled from stone. "Won't be denied? What must I do to convince you that Darcie's refusal is final?"

"Manville!" Barclay leapt to his feet and glowered at Zack.

"Zack!" Darcie jumped up and ran to him. "Zack! Oh, I thought you weren't coming."

"I'm sorry, *ma petite.*" He tucked her securely under his arm and cuddled her close to him. "I was detained on business."

Barclay reached for Darcie's arm, but his wrist was caught in the steel grasp of Zack's hand. "Loose me, you devil. How dare you interrupt again."

"How dare I?" Zack questioned, never flinching in the face of Barclay's anger. *What kind of fool would act like this?* he wondered and then looked at Darcie. *A fool such as myself,* he answered, recalling that he had intended to say almost the same words, albeit a little more romantically. Dark eyes narrowed, Zack spoke through clenched teeth. "I'm sorry you're ill. If you wish, I'll make your excuses to your hostess and you may leave without returning to the ballroom."

"Ill? Hah!" Barclay barked. "It is you who will be ill if I—"

"I'm sure your headache has prevented your thinking clearly." He released Barclay's hand and enfolded Darcie deeper into his arms.

"Headache? I have no—"

Zack interrupted, "You will if you remain here a minute longer."

"If you think I'm going to turn tail and run like a scared rabbit, then—"

"I not only think it, but I demand it." Zack's voice became considerably louder. "If you wish your nonexistent headache to become reality, remain with us."

"Are you threatening me, sir?" Barclay asked, with a sneer in his voice.

"I assure you that was no idle threat."

Apparently, Zack spoke with such vigorous animosity that Barclay thought better of challenging him. Darcie watched with Zack as Barclay strutted off angrily.

When Barclay had disappeared, she looked up at Zack. "Once again, I owe you my gratitude."

"You owe me nothing." Zack kissed her forehead and held her close. He'd have to warn Talbot about Barclay. Something in the young Charlestonian's brain seemed to have deteriorated. "It is an honor to defend you against such cads of the first water."

"Oh, he's just disappointed, that's all." Darcie sat down and realized that Barclay had left his coat. "He'll be back for this, I'm afraid."

Zack nodded. "With a cooler head, I suspect."

Darcie laughed in agreement. "What a delight it is to see you even under such trying circumstances."

"Congratulate the boy for his persistence." Zack dropped down beside her. "My, but this bench is cold. Whyever would he bring you here?"

"I can only guess." Darcie snuggled into his embrace, telling herself that she did so only for warmth.

"I'm surprised that the temperature out here didn't cool his ardor," Zack said dryly, gazing down into Darcie's eyes.

Beneath the moon, her hair shone like gold with little ivory droplets of dew. He looked more closely at the droplets. *Pearls,* he thought, studying her upturned face. "How lovely you look. I must say that French fashion becomes you."

Without awaiting a reply, he kissed her. For days, he'd stayed away, hoping to forget the sweet taste of her lips on his, the intoxicating scent that surrounded her. His late arrival tonight had been due to his decision to avoid her rather than the business he'd claimed needed his attention. He found that something drew him to her like a magnet. He could not stay away.

"Darcie, my darling." His voice was a croak. "I adore you."

Drawing back to look at him, Darcie gulped. Her memories, however vivid, compared as a shadow to the man. Blood racing through her like flames lapping at logs soaked in kerosene, she leaned against him briefly to catch her breath. When she looked up, she was smiling. "I see that our icy throne has done little to cool *your* ardor, sir."

"There is little that will cool my ardor where you are concerned, miss. You have kindled in me a fire that burns hotter with each passing moment," he parried, taking her cue. "I fear that more than a cold bench will be needed to douse that flame."

They spoke no more. Darcie hungered for him as he hungered for her. The emptiness deep within her seemed filled with joy to be in his arms once again, despite the constant avowals to the contrary spoken to herself within the past days. She put aside her fears and suspicions and cherished the moments with him.

"Darcie!" Uncle Talbot's voice broke the silence from behind her. "Zacharie! What is the meaning of this?"

"Uncle!" Darcie leapt to her feet, feeling the flood of icy air swarm around her. "Let me—"

"Come with me." Talbot grabbed her hand and dragged her with him. "You should be ashamed of yourself."

"Uncle, if you'll let me—"

"Return to our guests. I shall speak to you later." Talbot paused outside the French doors that led back to the ballroom. "I am astonished at your behavior."

Zack trailed along behind them, wondering why Talbot seemed so upset. Within days, the banns would be posted announcing their betrothal. Talbot had every right to expect proper behavior from Darcie, but his indignation seemed misplaced and unfounded under the circumstances.

Face aflame with color, Darcie peered across the ballroom floor. Madelaine's eyes were riveted on her. At first, Darcie thought Madelaine might be angry, but she seemed a bit amused by Darcie's ungraceful entrance behind Talbot.

Once inside Talbot left her side with one last glowering look. Determined to appear as if nothing had happened, Darcie edged her way around the dance floor, heading for Madelaine who seemed to be an island of tranquillity in a stormy sea.

"Whatever was wrong with Talbot?" Madelaine whispered as Darcie sat down. She took Darcie's hands in hers and gazed deeply into her eyes. *"Mon Dieu.* Your hands are freezing. Has that naughty son of mine been exposing you to the elements? I'll have—"

"Did I hear you speak my name?"

Darcie looked up into Zack's laughing eyes and felt comforted. Her embarrassment seemed to disappear as he took her hand from Madelaine's. "Dance with me, my darling."

Rising without speaking, Darcie allowed him to lead her to the floor. Surely Uncle Talbot could have no objection to her dancing with Zack. In his arms, the world seemed to fade away into nothingness. They were alone, alone dancing and whirling about a floor populated with phantoms of others. The music pulsed in her blood and Darcie laughed with Zack and threw herself into the rhythm.

They hardly noticed that the music had stopped until Darcie heard her name. "Darcie?"

She looked around and saw Uncle Talbot beckoning her from the stand at the east end of the room where the orchestra was set up. Zack shrugged and escorted her to her uncle. Hand-ing her up the steps, Zack gazed at her lovingly, giving her courage.

Beside Uncle Talbot, Simon stood uneasily. He peered at Darcie around her uncle and raised his eyebrows slightly, making him appear even more silly. Venturing a glance about the room, she saw Madelaine and Gabriella with Estelle and smiled to them as if to answer an unspoken question. She didn't know what Uncle Talbot was about.

Talbot Neville held up his hands for silence. "Friends, I am pleased above all else to make this announcement."

He peered at his guests. Darcie's gaze followed his and she saw that every eye in the room was on him expectantly. Looking up at him, she saw a tremor of a smile play with his lower lip. *Why doesn't he say what he has to say and be done?* she wondered and glanced at Simon who appeared to be angry over something. *Perhaps he knows what Uncle Talbot intends to say.*

"My friends," he began again, beaming at his audience. "You've met my lovely niece, Darcie Gaynor, late of Charleston. I hadn't intended to make this announcement so soon, but recent circumstances dictate expediency in the matter. I wish to announce, I am delighted to announce the betrothal . . ."

Talbot paused dramatically, and Darcie recognized the sharp intake of breath as being hers. Her eyes sought Zack's. The smile that played at his lips was one of victory it seemed. He had told her of their betrothal, had used it as an argument to convince her to marry him as soon as they reached land, but she had doubted him because of his other lies.

And now, before she could stop Uncle Talbot from telling the world that she and Zack were to be married, he was going to do so. Why, oh, why hadn't she told Uncle Talbot of her decision not to go through with this silly arrangement? Now her own mortification would be complete. The questions would follow her back to Charleston instead of being quelled before the words were uttered.

Talbot smiled at his niece, catching her arm and hugging her. "I wish to announce the betrothal of my niece to my son, Simon."

Chapter Eighteen

Too stunned to speak, Darcie's gaze flew to her uncle's jubilant face. Marry Simon? She looked at him, standing slightly behind her uncle's beaming figure. The blush on his face was so apparent that he appeared to be burned by exposure to the sun. He knew!

Why hadn't she spoken sooner? Darcie felt as though she would die of mortification.

Zack! She scanned the crowd for his face. Astonishment had carved lines across his forehead and radiated from his tightly closed lips. He'd lied to her again.

Glaring at him for lack of a better target for her anger, she noticed that he had turned white with fury. For a fleeting moment, Darcie suspected that Zack had been surprised because he truly expected Uncle Talbot to link her name with his instead of Simon's. Her anger subsided somewhat. *He really believed we were betrothed*, she thought, wondering how he could have imagined such a thing to be true under the circumstances.

Had Uncle Talbot hinted that he would consent to a marriage between Darcie and Zack? She turned to her Uncle. He was studying her carefully. Before she could speak, Simon took her hand and kissed it ardently.

Feeling nothing but revulsion for her cousin, she glared at him. All around her, people began to applaud. Surely they didn't think Simon a suitable match for her? Barclay made his way to the orchestra stand, but Talbot waylaid him before he reached Darcie.

Simon nearly dragged Darcie off the other side and onto the dance floor. "Dance with me . . . my dear."

Darcie glared at him. He must know how she felt. "Simon, you can't allow Uncle Talbot to manipulate us this way. We've no regard for each other, except as . . . cousins."

"On the contrary, my dear, we shall deal famously together." Simon dragged her forward, forcing her to the center of the floor.

All around, people parted and allowed them to pass. Some shouted best wishes and congratulations. Once at the center of the room, he placed his arm around her and began to dance.

Darcie wanted to melt into the floor. Humiliation curdled her stomach, and she thought she would retch before the dance ended.

Zack was among the first to reach them when they finally stopped. He took her hand and kissed the gloved palm. "Best wishes, my darling."

Unprepared for the abject animosity flowing from Zack's demeanor, Darcie felt faint. Nothing was right; the world seemed to have tilted the wrong way, abandoning her to the wiles of men. Numbness almost overwhelmed her and she hardly realized what was going on around her.

"I . . . thank you." *How silly I sound,* she thought. *I should slap him resoundingly for lying to me again. And yet I feel as if I've lost my best friend.*

The warm reassurance she had sought from Zack's eyes wasn't there. There was nothing to see except a glazed steel glint that was cold and hard and unforgiving.

And then he was gone, swallowed up by a crowd of well-wishers and curiosity seekers who mobbed around her and Simon. Darcie was alone in a crowd of more than one hundred people.

The evening wore on. Darcie danced and danced, trying to put the memory of Zack's eyes and rigid features from her mind. Somehow, every man she danced with lacked the grace and skill Zack possessed on the dance floor, lacked the wittiness of Zack's conversation that delighted her so much, lacked the gentle touch of Zack that sent sparks skittering across her skin. No matter how hard she tried not to do so, she compared every man to Zack and found them all inadequate—particularly Simon.

Her emotions finally caught up with her and she realized what a predicament she was in. Uncle Talbot would be furious. Simon would be embarrassed—and probably blush for days. Aunt Margot would be hurt.

Darcie spotted an elderly gentleman headed her way and she turned to Madelaine. "I'm afraid I must excuse myself."

Eyeing her carefully, Madelaine said, "Oh, yes. It's been a long evening. Let's retire to the powder room for a moment's peace and tranquillity."

Madelaine took her arm and steered Darcie past the elderly gentleman with the paunch who had come to ask her for a dance. Leaving him gaping in their wake, Madelaine hurried her along and up the stairs.

"Where are we going?" Darcie asked, a bit puzzled that Madelaine had avoided the downstairs convenience.

Madelaine pulled her on up the marble stairs. "Avoiding the crush of ladies who will undoubtedly be gossiping in the downstairs powder room. Where is your room?"

"There," Darcie pointed and followed Madelaine into the small parlor set aside for her use.

Madelaine closed the door and turned up the lamp, then strode across to the fireplace. "Good thing Talbot isn't too cheap to keep a fire. I'm freezing. All those buffoons who insist upon opening windows in December are beyond my comprehension. A more addlepated gaggle of geese I never saw."

Darcie laughed and gestured for Madelaine to sit down, although by the time the gesture had been made, she was already seated. Sitting on a mauve velvet chair beside the fire, Darcie stared into the flames. By morning, everyone in Paris would know she was betrothed to Simon.

Madelaine's skirt rustled, and Darcie turned to look at her. "My dear, you were gazing at that fire so intently that I thought you'd fallen asleep with your eyes open."

"I'm sorry," Darcie apologized. "So much has happened in the past—"

"Yes," Madelaine interrupted. "Hasn't it? Somehow, I feel that you were unaware of the nature of your uncle's announcement tonight until he actually made it."

Darcie fidgeted with her skirt, enjoying the soft whisper of taffeta upon taffeta and wondering how much she could trust Madelaine. Needing a friend desperately, Darcie felt like pouring the whole truth out to her, but she was Zack's mother. "I, well, I suppose I was. I admit I was a bit surprised that he made the announcement tonight."

"Then you knew of the betrothal?" Madelaine touched Darcie's arm. "Come, my dear, we're friends. Trust me."

Trust me. Zack had said that more than once to Darcie. At the moment, she felt that she could trust no one, not even herself. "Not exactly."

Madelaine edged forward on the chair. "Oh, do tell. I love a good romance."

Laughing nervously, Darcie shook her head. "It's nothing like that, I can tell you."

"Well then, darling, leave nothing out. I insist." Patting Darcie's hand, Madelaine slid back on the seat as if she was prepared to remain right there until she'd heard everything she came to hear.

"Everything is so confusing. I . . . I just don't know where to turn." Darcie withdrew her hand and stood. Sighing, she moved closer to the fire and stared at the glowing coals and the pumpkin-colored flame dancing along the top of the fragrant pine log.

"Now, Darcie, sit down here and tell all." Madelaine patted

the chair and pulled it a little closer to her. "Come on. How can I help you if I don't know what the problem is?"

"Help? Do you really think you can?" Darcie ran her fingers along the cold marble mantel and felt the chill through her gloves. A pine knot popped as she sat down, still wondering how much she should tell Madelaine.

"Of course, I can," Madelaine stated flatly, as if there were no reason to question her on the subject. "I can do anything I decide to do, once I set myself about a task."

Hope rose in Darcie—briefly. There were too many complications to her problem for Madelaine to solve. "I think only a fairy godmother can help me."

"Come now, it can't be all that bad."

Darcie shifted in her seat. "I really don't think I should talk—"

"Nonsense," Madelaine interrupted. "Now, I'll help. You were unprepared for the announcement tonight."

"Correct."

"Ah, yes. It was a complete surprise to you."

"Not exactly. You see," Darcie began and sighed. Zack's face swam before her eyes and she turned to Madelaine. In Madelaine's face, Darcie could see Zack's features, softened a little in the feminine form, but every bit as striking. "You see, Zack came to America on business. My uncle sent a letter by him and instructed Zack to bring me to Paris. In the letter, Uncle Talbot stated that he had arranged a marriage for me. He mentioned no names."

Madelaine settled back in the chair and studied Darcie. "You are a lovely young woman and must have a sizable dowry. Why should he arrange a marriage for you? And with his son?"

"I don't know. I presume you know that Simon is adopted." Trying to gauge Madelaine's reaction, Darcie glanced at her. "I have no, well . . . Simon is . . . we're too different."

"Anyone with a feather for a brain can see that." Madelaine tucked a cushion more securely behind her back. "Rotten chairs. I wouldn't have these dainty uncomfortable things in my sitting room. Why don't you tell Margot to get you something decent to sit upon?"

Darcie laughed. Of all the responses she'd expected from Madelaine, this one was totally unexpected.

"Now. What shall we do? We must insist that Talbot drop this silly notion of your marrying that weasel-witted Simon."

Silently, Darcie agreed that Simon was weasel-witted, although she thought of him as a ninnyhammer, but she couldn't allow Madelaine to broach this subject with Uncle Talbot. "Oh, please, Madelaine, don't talk to Uncle Talbot. He'll be furious with me if he thinks I've given away family secrets."

"What about Zack?"

Color bloomed in Darcie's cheeks and she jumped up. Moving closer to the fire so Madelaine couldn't see her blush, Darcie thought about Zack. *What about Zack? Why do I love him? He's proven himself untrustworthy and devious. His kisses thrill me, his touch sets music to ringing in my heart. I love him. I can't love him.* Darcie argued with herself. Behind her, she knew that Madelaine was waiting for an answer. "I . . . I don't know what you mean."

"Of course you do." Madelaine came to stand beside her. "I am not blind. I saw the way you looked at each other."

Darcie whirled to face her. "What do you mean? You can have seen nothing. There's nothing to see. You are imagining this."

"Ah, such a protest. You have nothing," Madelaine whispered, placing her hands on Darcie's shoulders, "nothing, to fear from me. Your secret is mine. The hour is late. I must think about our problem. Come with me."

Realizing that an argument would result in no gain, Darcie followed Madelaine out of the sitting room and down the hallway. Determined to make one last effort, she stopped Madelaine on the landing. "Madelaine, please, do not make matters worse. Let me handle this my way."

"Oh, posh, I'll have this figured out faster than it will take Talbot to . . . well, I'll find a way." Madelaine leaned over the railing. "Many of the guests are already gone. Margot won't notice if I leave a little earlier than usual."

When they reached the foyer, Margot was standing by the door. "Oh, honestly. My feet feel as though I've carried Versailles all the way across France."

Madelaine ignored Margot's complaint. "My head is splitting, my dear. I think I'll go home and put it to bed. Darcie, be a darling and find Gabriella."

Darcie sped off in search of Gabriella. With Madelaine in a meddling mood, Darcie wanted her out of the house as soon as possible.

When Darcie returned with Gabriella, Madelaine was standing next to Margot studying the girls' return. "Margot, I do believe our Darcie is a delightful surprise. I expect to see her often in the near future. Perhaps for tea tomorrow."

"Madelaine, as you well know, I have appointments tomorrow afternoon," Margot complained. "How about another day?"

Madelaine watched Darcie approach. "Margot, darling, that's perfect. I'll send my driver for her. She can spend the afternoon with us instead of alone."

Chewing her lip, Margot gazed at her friend as if she suspected her of something underhanded. "Well, I don't know if I should—"

"You don't know?" Madelaine sounded exasperated. "You sound like I'm a thief instead of your best friend. Why shouldn't she have some fun?"

"No reason, I guess," Margot conceded and put her arm around Darcie as the girls reached them. "Darcie, my darling, Madelaine is going to send for you tomorrow afternoon. You can have tea with her and Gabriella if you wish. Won't that be lovely?"

Darcie's gaze travelled from Margot's face to Madelaine's. At first, she thought they had schemed together somehow, but one look at the strained expression on Margot's face told Darcie otherwise. It seemed as though her aunt were trying to convince her to reject the invitation without saying so. "How delightful that sounds. May I go, Aunt Margot?"

Sighing almost imperceptibly, Margot smiled. "Yes, of course, you may." Her expression changed slightly as she looked at Madelaine. "Madelaine is my very dearest friend."

Lying in bed some hours later, Darcie could not fall asleep. Her mind was filled with the image of Zack's murderous glare, as if he suspected her of convincing her uncle to allow her to marry Simon. Zack had probably lied all along. He had never been betrothed to her, but had used that lie to persuade her to make love to him after she had decided to end their relationship.

After tossing and turning for several minutes more, she raised her hips and straightened her twisted nightgown. Sleep still eluded her, and in spite of her attempts to clear her mind of her problems, Uncle Talbot's pronouncement began to trouble her.

Uncle Talbot had refused to discuss the betrothal at all. She knew that when she rose, he would be gone, and tomorrow would be wasted except for the visit to Madelaine's house.

The moon cast a rectangle of golden light on the floor and on her bed. Wondering why life must be so complicated, Darcie strode to the window and peered out at the lovely gardens in the long shadows of the moonlight. *Beautiful,* she mused, *but not so lovely as the path of moonlight on the Ashley River. I wonder what the evenings are like along the banks of the Seine. Oh, why didn't I just stay home?*

Darcie didn't know how long she'd been standing there when a noise distracted her. Thinking that someone else must be up and about she turned and found Zack standing in her bedroom.

"What are you doing here?" she demanded.

"Shhh." He strode across the room and took her in his arms. "Do you want to wake the entire city?"

"How did you get in here?" Darcie fought the urge to throw herself into his arms. "I know Gautier locks all the windows and doors. He's such a ninnyhammer that he always double checks to be sure."

"Locked up tight, you are, my dear."

Darcie almost melted as his arms encircled her waist and drew her against him. "Then how do you come to be here?"

"I never left." Zack lifted her easily and carried her to the bed. "I was so angry after Talbot betrayed me that I had to speak to you. Alone."

"What is there to say?" Shifting on the bed to move slightly out of his arms, she pushed against him to no avail. "You'd better get out before someone hears you."

"If you'd be quiet, my darling, nobody will hear anything except your gentle sigh and sweet moan of satisfaction."

Glad she hadn't turned up the lamp, Darcie blushed furiously. "Zack!"

"They'll think you're dreaming of your betrothed," Zack said dryly, drawing the covers over her legs.

"You're in your cups." Darcie pressed her hands against him and tried to slide backwards out of his reach. His strong grip prevented her from having much more success than her last attempt.

Zack kissed her. "I am not. You accuse me falsely, mademoiselle, and I am wounded that you would think such a thing of your devoted servant."

Although she tried to stifle it, Darcie's giggle bubbled forth. "You're mad. You must leave at once. We've been caught, well, we were . . ."

Laughing quietly, Zack pulled her close to him. "We were kissing. That's all."

"That's enough. I've no doubt that Uncle Talbot will—"

"He'll do nothing, Darcie. Something is wrong here. I don't know what it is, but I intend to find out." Zack pushed her back against the pillows and kissed her. "But I don't want to think about him now."

"Now, Zack, be reasonable," Darcie whispered, half-hoping he'd ignore her pleas. Beneath him, she felt alive and loved and in love. She wanted to forget all her problems and the strife associated with Uncle Talbot.

The thin batiste of her gown was as nothing between them. Zack slid under the covers with her and hungrily kissed her

again and again. "Darcie, I adore you. You cannot marry this
. . . this child."

Darcie hardly heard him. Her mind sailed as free as a gull
before a rising wind and his kisses sent her higher and higher.
Roving over her body, his hands nipped and teased until she
could stand no more. "Please, Zack."

Without further delay, Zack slid into her, lifting her hips to
meet his thrust. Muffling her groan with kisses, he plunged his
tongue into her mouth and plundered its tender recesses. Zack
wanted the moment to last forever—and to end exquisitely in
the same instant for them both. Judging her reaction, he moved
slower and then faster, guiding her towards satisfaction as surely
as a rudder guides a sailing ship.

For Darcie, everything was an explosion of sound, color,
scent, and touch. She, too, wanted their lovemaking to last forever. Now, as at no other time, Darcie felt secure. Nothing
could take away these moments of rapture she'd experienced
with Zack.

Tears sprang to her eyes as she realized that this would be her
last time, that her passion would forever be sealed away. After
tonight, she would have to reject the advances of every man.
With Zack, her body betrayed her will, but it could never
happen again.

"Darcie, my darling, what's wrong?" Zack stopped and
wiped at her tears. "Why are you crying?"

Speaking was impossible. Choked in her throat were all the
words of love she wanted to say, if only once. But in her throat
they had to die, for she couldn't bring herself to say them to a
man she could never marry.

Kissing her eyes, Zack whispered sweet words to her and
gradually her tears subsided. Their last lovemaking took on a
sweet poignancy for her. She decided to make this time the best.

Tracing swirls across his chest, Darcie turned slightly and
kissed Zack softly. He seemed to recognize her need to express
her feelings without speaking and responded by holding her
closer. The kiss ended and she lifted her head a little. Looking
down into his face, lighted only by the strong moonlight, she

studied him, memorizing every line, angle, and plane—every detail. Her memory would have to serve for the remainder of her life.

As Darcie studied Zack, he watched her. She stared intently, although he thought she might not realize what she was doing. A smile played across his lips. "Are you capturing my soul with those lovely sapphire eyes?"

"Capturing?" Color warmed Darcie's cheeks. "I'm . . . I was just . . . forgive me. I didn't mean to stare so rudely."

Zack laughed and cuddled her close. "You seemed to be in a dreamlike state. Is something wrong?"

"Wrong? Well, no," Darcie lied, knowing full well that *everything* was wrong. She was about to make love to the man she loved more than life, while her fiancé lay asleep a few doors away.

Darcie straightened her shoulders and grimaced. Her fiancé. She was betrothed to a man she hardly knew, but one she despised for his weaknesses. At every turn, he cowered beneath his father's will without protest and refused to speak against this farce of an engagement even though he knew she didn't love him, and never could.

"Don't scowl so." Zack caressed her back and played with her hair, inhaling the wonderful fragrance that always clung to her. "You make me think my caresses displease you."

"Oh, *no,*" she answered quickly, and smiled. "Your touch is far from displeasing, as I'm sure you well know. I am certain that many ladies could give testimony to your, shall we say, more pleasing qualities."

"Aha, so that is the reason behind the ugly face!" he joked. "For a moment, I thought I'd found my way into Mrs. Appleby's house."

Darcie glared. With mock anger, she grabbed a pillow and stuffed it over his face. "Apologize at once!"

Zack easily overpowered her and in seconds had flipped her onto her back, pinning her beneath him. "So, the young miss is a dangerous wench. You shall pay dearly for your attempt on my life."

Feigning fear, Darcie gnawed her knuckles. "Oh, pray sir, forgive me. Jealousy reared its ugly visage and quite soundly overcame my normal sweet self."

"Forgive? I fear not," Zack bantered, capturing one of her nipples between his thumb and forefinger. "Have a care, for your punishment shall be meted out at once."

Darcie caught her breath and her eyes closed with pleasure. She could hardly speak. "Then, please be lenient with a poor wretch of a girl."

His mouth swooped down on hers and his kiss was savage as his grip on her tightened. Tongues of fire raced across her bare skin as he slid his hand down her stomach to the light thatch of hair at the apex of her womanhood.

Zack's other hand was wrapped in her long honey-colored hair, imprisoning her beneath him as effectively as gilded chains. Plundering deep within her mouth, his tongue missed nothing. The kiss ended, his lips moved on to her breast, licking, sucking, and teasing while they traced cool trails along the silken skin until Darcie fairly burned with desire.

All around her, colors swirled as she was swept along with the ebb and flow of her swelling passion. Time after time, Zack brought her to the edge of release and skillfully controlled the tide of her emotions until she could stand no more.

"Now, Zack," she whispered, arching to meet his thrust.

"I love you, Darcie. I love you." Zack murmured the words close to her ear as he nibbled on its lobe.

His tongue again plunged deep within her mouth as his rhythm steadily increased, fanning their passions into an unending frenzy that refused to be quelled.

Darcie no longer controlled her body. Her head whipped crazily from side to side as she babbled words that urged him on. Animal passion now reigned between them, isolating them from the civilized world—and their rapture came, it exploded into a simultaneous gratification that left both of them spent and happy.

Zack rained kisses all over her face, neck, and breasts while he uttered sweet words to her. When the glazed look had left her eyes, he gazed lovingly at her. "We'll be together soon, my darling. Soon."

Darcie gave a start. She must have dozed off after Zack had made love to her. She giggled into her pillow with joy. He'd said they'd be together soon. Could she believe it? Dared she?

This time was to be the best, she'd promised herself. And it had been. Together they had soared higher than ever before, skimming the shimmering crest of rapture, tasting the ecstasy they both sought and gave so urgently.

Dawn sent fingers of gray and purple searching through the skies as Zack crept out Darcie's window and dropped to the ground. Watching as he paused to see if anyone else was up, she longed to call him back. Suspicions or no, Darcie wanted to go with him more than anything she'd ever wanted to do before.

In a few months, she and Zack could marry without her uncle's permission. Until then, well, she didn't know. She watched until he was gone and then returned to her bed to toss and turn for the remainder of her restless night—now made a precious memory by Zack.

During the next few days, Darcie spent a great deal of time with Madelaine and Gabriella. Many times, they arrived right after Margot left on some errand. At other times, they all drank tea and talked and laughed together. Occasionally they went shopping or on other outings. When Margot was away, Madelaine sent Gabriella out of the room several times, allowing for moments of privacy for her and Darcie.

She often spoke of Darcie's engagement. Just as often, she directed the conversation towards Zack.

Each time Madelaine spoke of Zack, Darcie felt a catch in her breath. She hadn't seen him since that awful night of her welcoming ball when Uncle Talbot had announced that she was betrothed to Simon.

Simon always seemed to be underfoot. On several occasions, he'd tried to kiss Darcie, always ending with a cheek scorched by a resounding slap. More and more, Darcie kept to her room to avoid him—until she thought she would become batty.

One morning soon after her betrothal ball, a messenger came with an invitation to the Empress Eugénie's New Year's Day reception and ball. Madelaine and Margot immediately began to plan Darcie's gown, and before the morning was out had dragged her off to select the fabric and pattern.

Darcie was excited to have received the invitation, which also named her. Ever since she learned that she was coming to France, she wanted to see Tuileries and the Empress. Of Napoleon, she had heard little except that his government mimicked that of his famous uncle. But of Eugénie, she had heard great things. A charitable woman, she set about her vast social work. Word of her kindness and concern had reached Charleston.

Christmas was coming. The house took on a festive air once again, but Darcie couldn't seem to catch the spirit of the season. During her outings, she bought presents for everybody—including Zack. She hid his present away, hoping to see him again before Christmas Day.

But she didn't. His present remained in her armoire, wrapped in a bit of tissue and velvet ribbon. The tiny pin, a stickpin, was to be used to hold the new fashion in cravats. The gold pin with the tiny pearl cost her most of her remaining money, but she didn't care. This gift would be one that Zack would look at and remember her by. It had to be special.

One afternoon, Darcie was sitting in her small parlor thinking about Zack when Mimi announced that she had visitors. Pausing to check her appearance, Darcie smoothed a curl into place and then hurried down the stairs to the sitting room.

Aunt Margot was there already, chatting amiably with Barclay and Em. "Ah, here she is!"

"Em! Barclay! How delighted I am to see you." Darcie accepted Barclay's light kiss on her hand and then hugged Em. "Are you enjoying Paris?"

"Oh, Paris is wonderful," Em gushed, her eyes glittering with pleasure. "I wish you could explore with us, but I suppose you can't."

"I don't know why not," Darcie answered, a bit puzzled by Em's supposition.

"Well, your uncle has said that—"

"Mother, I heard that—" Simon bolted into the room. "Oh. *Pardon.*"

"It's quite all right, Simon," Margot cooed to her son. "I believe you know everyone."

"Of course. I'm glad you could visit with us. How is your stay in Paris? Is your hotel comfortable?" he asked solicitously, kissing Em's hand.

Em smiled shyly. "Everything is wonderful. Such a lovely city."

A little amazed, Darcie watched the interplay between her friend and cousin. She smiled inwardly. Simon is falling in love with Em, and it looks as if Em is equally attracted to him. *Too bad Uncle Talbot doesn't know,* she thought. Perhaps he'd release her from this ridiculous marriage contract.

Darcie sat down near the fire and listened to the excited conversation among the small group. She was distracted, and had little to say. Aunt Margot left the room to check with the housekeeper about plans for dinner.

When the door closed behind her aunt, Darcie sighed restlessly. As much as she loved Em and Barclay, she was eager for them to leave. Barclay's glowering face irritated her almost as much as the torture she felt at having to watch two people fall in love while her own love was away.

She thought of nothing else. Zack was a part of her life as no other person had ever been. Her every waking moment was filled with thoughts and dreams of him, of their stolen time together, of the joy that had sought her out that afternoon when he had released her shawl from the clutches of her garden gate. Barclay's touch on her shoulder startled her from her reverie.

"Darcie, I understand that you are angry. You have every right to be." He knelt beside her knee, glancing at the other couple.

Neither of them appeared to be paying attention to anyone else, and Darcie was glad. Why couldn't Barclay understand that she couldn't marry him? She glared at him. "You're making a spectacle of yourself."

"I am. I shall until you come to your senses." Barclay took her hand. "Simon doesn't love you. He loves Em. I'm sure you are confident about his devotion, but he's been seeing Em almost every day."

Darcie stared at Barclay in shock. "Every *day?* How can that be?"

"Not jealous, are you?" he taunted.

"Jealous? Of course not. Why should I be jealous of Simon?" she answered with clipped words.

"Good. I shall speak to your uncle at once." Barclay stood and looked down at her. "Today—if he's here."

"Barclay, no! You can't!" Darcie jumped to her feet, ignoring the two startled faces from across the room. "I forbid it!"

"Don't worry, my dear. I shall take care of everything." Barclay strode from the room.

Darcie knew better than to argue. He had convinced himself that he could talk Talbot into accepting his suit, even though Darcie's engagement had been announced.

Picking up her stitchery, Darcie sat down again. Since Em had come here, presumably to visit with her, she could hardly leave the room. She glanced up from her sewing. Simon had Em's hand clasped to his heart. *What joy these two could give each other,* she thought.

"Darcie," Margot called from the doorway. "Some parcels have arrived for you. Mimi needs your advice on where to store your purchases."

"Em, forgive me," Darcie said, glad for the distraction. "I'll see you again soon."

Almost running from the room, Darcie breathed deeply. She couldn't have endured another moment of the sweet scene that had been playing out before her. Her heart ached for Zack, but she didn't know how to find him.

After telling Mimi about her purchases, Darcie tarried a few minutes before heading downstairs. She hadn't been gone as long as she expected, so she decided to return to the parlor. Perhaps Simon would be gone and she could talk with Em.

She opened the door and found the parlor empty. Relieved, she returned to her sitting room, where she could be alone with her thoughts.

Christmas Eve finally arrived. Even though Darcie had moped around for the past few days, the season inspired her to be cheerful, in spite of the fact that she hadn't seen Zack in weeks.

Small gifts were exchanged among the family members and then the servants were presented with their gifts. For Charity, Darcie had bought a French lace handkerchief. And, for Mimi, she had found an ivory-colored woolen scarf.

Uncle Talbot and Aunt Margot gave her an exquisite mantalet of black lace, so lovely that Darcie cried. From Simon she received a box of writing paper and a new fountain pen.

Later in her room, after Mimi had left, Darcie sat down before the fire and wondered why she hadn't heard from Zack. It had been more than two weeks since his nocturnal visit and Darcie had begun to worry about him.

Sighing, she rose and walked to her bed. Lovely as her gifts were, she found no joy in the season without having seen Zack. She lay down and blew out her lamp, leaving the glow of the fire as her only light.

Tears in her eyes, she finally fell into a fitful sleep complicated by nightmares. Some sound woke her. As still as a frightened sparrow, Darcie opened her eyes and glanced from side to side without moving her head. She saw nothing out of the ordinary in the dim light.

Raising her head slightly, she looked around again. She almost cried out when she saw a man sitting by the fire. Her movement caught his attention and when he turned, she recognized Zack's profile. "Oh, Zack! How you frightened me!"

For a moment, he didn't move. When he did rise, he limped over to the bed and kissed Darcie passionately.

"Zack, what has happened . . . Sit down . . . Let me see what is wrong with you . . . Are you hurt badly?" Darcie touched a damp spot on his thigh and he flinched. "Who did this?"

"Zounds!" Zack jerked away and fell down beside her. "Trying to kill me?"

Darcie moved over and threw back the covers. "Here. Let me look at that."

"It's a scratch." Zack reached for her head and pulled her down into a kiss. "Forget it. I came to wish you a Happy Christmas."

"Don't be ridiculous. Let me see that scratch before I become violent." Darcie reached over Zack and turned up the lamp. She could see the spreading damp circle on his trousers. "Oh! What happened?"

Wincing with pain, Zack stretched out his leg and lay back on the pillows. "I ran into an Italian knife."

"An Italian knife?" Darcie looked at him curiously. "Whatever is that?"

"A sharp blade wielded by an Italian," he explained patiently. "Now come here and kiss me."

"Zack, don't be a goose. Let me bandage that wound."

Shaking his head, he said, "No, Darcie. I can stay but a moment. Others can bandage wounds. For a moment, just lie with me."

On the verge of tears, Darcie complied with his wishes. As they lay there, he kissed her gently at times and at others, merely rested against her.

After a while, he reached in his pocket and pulled out a small box. "I've carried this for some time now. It's yours for Christmas, since you're bound not to marry me."

Darcie jumped from the bed and ran to the armoire. Fumbling through a pile of boxes and shoes, she found her Christmas gift for Zack. Returning to the bed, she replied, "I have something for you, too."

Exchanging boxes, they both opened their presents. Zack got his open first. He removed the stickpin and stared at it.

Darcie stopped trying to open her gift and gazed at Zack.

"It's for your cravat. The man in the store says you cross the ends of your cravat and pierce them with this pin."

"It's wonderful. I can't wait for a ball so that I can wear this." He glanced at her. "Did you give Simon a pin like this?"

Darcie stuck out her tongue at him. "Of course not. I found it just for you."

"Go on. Open yours."

With shaking hands, Darcie finally opened the box. It contained a ring. Zack took it from her and slid it on her fourth finger. "To match your eyes."

Darcie looked at the sapphire, its facets casting glittering shapes on the wall. "Zack! I can't accept anything so expensive from you. Oh, but it's lovely. I could never—"

"You can and you will." Zack pressed her palms together and held them in his. "This is your betrothal ring."

Chapter Nineteen

Darcie gazed at the ring long after Zack was gone. It had been her betrothal ring—until Uncle Talbot announced her betrothal to Simon.

Staring at the sapphire, she wondered if Zack could be telling the truth this time. As she thought about it, she realized that she wanted him to be telling the truth, that she hoped he could do something to stop her marriage to Simon.

Why did she have to wait on him? She could do it herself. Once she told Uncle Talbot that she had slept with another man, he would dissolve the engagement. Resolving to do just that as soon as he awoke, Darcie fell asleep wearing Zack's ring.

New Year's Day dawned clear and cold. Darcie slept late after staying up to see the New Year born and half-expected Zack to materialize. But he hadn't.

The afternoon was spent getting ready for the ball. Darcie had tried to relax, but Margot's constant buzzing about finally drove Darcie to her room. Mimi, too, was excited, but Darcie managed to calm her down enough to assist with her dressing.

When at last the carriage arrived in front to take them to

Tuileries, Darcie's hair shown like spun gold laced with sapphire-colored ribbons. Her matching gown of sapphire-studded silk, the palest of blues, was simple, much more simple than Margot and Madelaine had wanted. Madelaine had been surprised by Darcie's insistence on the simplicity, but had to admit that the graceful bell-shaped skirt was far lovelier than she could have imagined.

"All those gewgaws will only take away from the tiny sapphires sprinkled about the bodice and skirt," Darcie insisted, finally convincing the two ladies that she would refuse to budge from her position.

"Well, Darcie, you know best, but I insist that you wear my sapphire necklace," Madelaine said, giving up her argument. "With that daring neckline, they will be quite the thing."

The necklace had been delivered this morning and now Darcie looked at herself in the mirror. Everything was perfect. The sapphires set in the gown were not really gem quality, but they twinkled like much more expensive baubles.

Her gaze fell to her hand. Zack's ring sparkled brilliantly on the third finger of her left hand. If anyone noticed, they would probably assume that Simon had given it to her. If Simon, Aunt Margot, or Uncle Talbot noticed, Darcie would explain that it was her own.

Mimi held Darcie's velvet burnous which matched the blue of her sapphire while Darcie slipped it on. The effect was lovely. Darcie's eyes glittered as gaily as her jewelry.

The trip to Tuileries was gay. Aunt Margot told Darcie of the wedding of the Emperor and Empress. What a lovely surprise the Spanish Countess had become. Paris was now considered as elegant as during the reign of Louis XVI.

"No," Margot chattered on, "we haven't been invited to Tuileries before. This is our first time. Although I've heard a great deal about it. The Empress has redecorated the entire palace and it is splendid," she declared.

Darcie stared at her aunt's neck for the first time this evening. Aunt Margot wore Darcie's mother's necklace—one that had been stolen by the pirates! How could that be? Was Uncle

Talbot involved with Zack and his bunch of cutthroats? Had her uncle staged the robbery and sinking of her ship to obtain the jewels? It seemed strange that they were on board when the attack occurred. Darcie was more confused than ever.

As the carriage drew closer to the palace, the night sky was ablaze with light. Carriages and cabs of all description lined the drive and elegantly dressed gentlefolk hurried up the walk seeking refuge from the cold air.

When Talbot handed his invitation to the doorman, a quiet conversation ensued between the doorman and a lackey standing behind him. "A moment, please."

A list verified the invitation and Talbot beamed with pride. Darcie realized that being noticed by the Emperor and Empress could do much to enhance the shipping business. As they moved past the doorman, he stopped them again.

"Please, the Empress wishes Mademoiselle Gaynor's company in the Salon Rose. She will rejoin your company in the Salle des Mare'chaux." The young lackey led Darcie away.

Blushing for being singled out, Darcie shrugged slightly and followed. They reached the Salon Vert where the ladies-in-waiting awaited Eugénie's presence.

Darcie was introduced to Mlle. Bouvet, an assistant reader especially close to the Empress. "Come with me."

Mlle. Bouvet escorted Darcie through a lovely green room. An enormous painting of a basket of flowers dominated the ceiling and the over-doors were painted with brightly colored birds.

They reached the Salon Rose. Darcie was immediately struck by the scent of flowers. All about the room, huge bouquets of flowers arranged in Sevres vases were everywhere. Paintings of flowers dominated the ceiling, panelling, and over-doors.

"The wonderful painting on the ceiling is the *Triumph of Flora* by Chaplain. Wait here." Mlle. Bouvet tapped lightly on a doorway and then entered.

Darcie turned slowly around, caught in the majesty of the room. In addition to the wonderful florals, the walls were covered with paintings of beautiful women.

Behind her, the door opened again and Darcie whirled around in time to see Mlle. Bouvet step through the doorway. "The Empress Eugénie."

A thrill passed through Darcie and she curtsied to the lovely auburn-haired Empress. Eugenie strode regally across the room, reached down, and lifted Darcie's chin. "You are as beautiful as he said."

Who could she be talking about? Darcie wondered and stood up straight. "I am honored to meet you, Your Royal Highness."

"And I am delighted to meet you." Empress Eugénie's blue eyes sparkled in the candlelight as she gazed at Darcie. "My friend, M. Manville, speaks highly of your beauty and your wit."

Darcie gave a start at the mention of Zack's name. "I am sure he exaggerates."

The Empress laughed. "And I am as sure he does not. Mlle., please take Miss Gaynor to join her guardian. And, Miss Gaynor, would you join me in my box at the Opera later this month?"

"I should be honored to do so, Madame." Darcie curtsied again and the Empress left the room.

"Come. We go to the Salle to join your aunt."

Darcie followed the young woman through the ornate halls to the Salle. Before she could locate Aunt Margot, Zack emerged from a group of men and caught her hand. "Dance with me." He looked at Mlle. Bouvet and said, "Thank you, mademoiselle."

Zack and Darcie whirled into the midst of the other dancers, and it seemed that both of them were afraid to break the spell. Tucked neatly into Zack's cravat was Darcie's gift. Obvious on her finger was Zack's ring.

He spoke first. "I see you found the courage to wear my ring."

"Yes," Darcie admitted, glancing at the gift she treasured above all others. "My gown was designed to go with the ring."

"You are by far the loveliest of the ladies here, in all of Paris, in fact." Zack smiled down at her, wishing that he had insisted that Eugénie allow him to meet Darcie privately before the ball. However, Eugénie was one for formality in most instances and he hadn't argued with her. "And, if I am not mistaken, those are my mother's sapphires caressing your adorable neck."

Darcie closed her eyes and swayed to the music. She wanted the night to never end. In Zack's arms, she felt so alive and happy that time meant nothing to her. "I see you are as observant as ever."

"Make no mistakes. I miss nothing about you. I memorize every facet of your personage to recall in my moments alone." Zack bowed briefly. "Here, let's look at Paris."

"But what of your injury? You seem to have recovered nicely." Darcie's gaze dropped to his thigh, but she could see nothing that indicated he'd been hurt.

"A mere scratch, as I told you."

They stopped dancing by the windows and gazed into the night. Across a lovely garden, Darcie could see an obelisk in the distance.

"La Place de la Concorde," Zack said. "Such a stunning sight. The place where kings and queens were beheaded, now immortalized forever in cold stone."

Hardly able to remove her gaze from the sight, she whispered, "What a stunning view."

Darcie felt a part of history for the first time. Louis-Napoleon and Eugénie would be famous for reviving the elegance of France, and Darcie was right in the middle of it. She had met the Empress personally—in fact, had been commanded to meet the auburn-haired beauty—and she would never forget the moment.

"Quite stunning."

Darcie looked up into Zack's eyes. He was staring at her, rather than the view from the window. Fresh color blossomed in her cheeks.

"Come. Let's leave the crowd for a moment."

Darcie followed him along a narrow passageway to an intimate room some distance away. The strains of music were barely audible here.

Once alone inside the room, Zack took her into his arms. "How I've missed you, my love."

Breathless, Darcie whispered, "I have missed you, as well. I thought you might have come to my room last night."

"I wanted to, but I could not get away," he explained. "I have been out of Paris for several days—since Christmas, in fact."

"Where have you been?"

"I have been on the business of the Empress. Beyond that, I cannot say." Zack kissed her again. "Come, let's sit here."

He led her to a sofa and waited for her to sit down. Darcie arranged her voluminous skirts around her and smiled up at him. "The Empress invited me to attend the opera with her."

"And you accepted?" He seemed surprised.

Darcie studied him thoughtfully. "Yes. Why should I not?"

"You are aware that several attempts have been made on Napoleon's life," he reminded her. "While we were crossing the Atlantic, another attack occurred. You should not go until this matter is settled."

"Not go?" Darcie's hand went to her throat in horror. How could she refuse the Empress's invitation, especially after accepting it. And why should she? So far, nobody had been killed.

"This Italian is mad. He'll stop at nothing." Zack's words were clipped.

"But, Zack," Darcie protested, "I've already told the Empress I'd go. I can't renege on my promise now."

Zack comforted her as he would a child. He knew how much this meant to her. He had, in fact, asked Eugénie to invite her to this ball, knowing that Eugénie would adore her as he did. Eugénie's influence would be needed if he were to be able to extricate Darcie from this gross fraud perpetrated by her uncle. "Louis-Napoleon has been warned. I'm sure he will post guards to assure everyone's safety."

"Do you really think he'll strike again?" Darcie asked, feeling a little uncertain about going with the Empress.

"I'm sure of it. But it will probably be at an event less public than the opera," Zack conceded.

Together they stepped into the corridor and walked back toward the ballroom. His hand rested lightly on her waist, and before they reached the Salon, he stopped and turned her to face him. "I am to be gone for a few days. I do not know if I shall return by the night of the opera, but I shall try."

Gazing into his eyes, Darcie smiled. "Please do. I would feel much better if you were there."

"Darcie," he began, and wondered if he should bring up her uncle's duplicity again. "While I'm away, beware of your uncle. Something is wrong. I don't know why he's announced your betrothal to Simon, when he knows full well you are engaged to me by agreement of our fathers."

"Father?" Darcie asked, staring in amazement at Zack's concerned face. "My father agreed to our marriage? How do you know? Did you know him?"

"Wait, allow me to answer one question before you toss out another." Zack laughed and kissed her nose. "You are such a darling. Our fathers were bitter rivals, as you know. Our crews ravaged your ships; your ships ravaged ours. There were no winners, only vast losses to answer for the carnage. Talbot arranged a meeting."

"Uncle Talbot?"

"Yes. He arranged a meeting between your father and mine. They agreed to a truce between the two companies." Zack held her close, fighting the desire to drag her off down the hall to his chamber. He knew that Eugénie would be appalled if he did, so out of respect for both ladies, he did not. "As a token of honor, each man offered his most prized possession—you and me. Our betrothal is documented in the truce. I have not found my father's copy, but he told me of it before he died."

Considering Zack's words, Darcie looked at him with sudden understanding. "Then my father may have had a copy."

Nodding, Zack held her against him, feeling desire rise in him that would refuse to be quelled if he continued to press her body to his. "Both had copies."

Darcie leaned against him, gathering courage from his strength. She would confront Uncle Talbot. He would admit to his lies and consent to their marriage. Within the last few days, Darcie had decided that she and Zack would marry as soon as she rid herself of the albatross hung on her neck by Uncle Talbot—Simon.

"We had better return to the Salon, or I cannot answer for my actions," Zack teased, kissing her deeply and inhaling her wonderful fragrance. "We may be too late already."

"Too late for what?" came a lilting voice from behind them.

"Your Highness!" Zack whirled in surprise, clasping Darcie to him protectively.

"Yes, you cad." The Empress stopped beside them. "What a bad boy you are, taking advantage of this lovely girl. I should send you away."

"Please, do not," Darcie pleaded. "I . . . I love him. My uncle refuses to allow me to see him."

"Who is this uncle?"

"Talbot Neville. He is my guardian," Darcie explained.

"Ah, yes, Zacharie and I have spoken of him." She turned to Zack. "Have you found proof of your allegations?"

"I have not." Zack bowed his head. Eugénie was fair, but she was never rash.

"Then her guardian's claims must take precedence."

"Eugénie, please allow me some time." Zack grimaced and gazed at her pleadingly. "Don't allow this miscarriage of justice."

"I shall prevent this marriage from happening until April." With a look of dismissal for Zack, she took Darcie's arm and moved toward the ballroom. "A fine man. Don't worry, my dear, he'll find the proof we need."

Darcie didn't see Zack for the remainder of the evening. She felt as if he'd left the palace immediately after the interview with the Empress.

When she returned home with her aunt, uncle, and cousin, Darcie was strangely quiet. Her thoughts were on the proof she needed to convince the Empress that Uncle Talbot had lied.

Odd, she thought. *Here I am trying to find proof of a document that will bind me to a man I suspect of causing the attacks on my ships.*

Darcie was extremely tired. The excitement of the evening had left her lusterless, almost spiritless. She wanted nothing more than to climb into bed and sleep for days.

"Oh, Darcie, my dear," called her uncle from the library. "I would like to speak with you a moment."

"Now, Uncle?"

"Please."

Darcie followed him into the library and watched him close the heavy door. "Yes? I'm really tired and—"

"This will only take a moment. Sit down." He motioned to a chair and waited for her to be seated before he continued. "I have noticed your . . . affection for this man, Zack Manville."

Blushing, Darcie opened her mouth to respond, but nothing came out. What could she say? She didn't know what her uncle wanted to talk about, and the conversation might turn out well for her without her having to tell him of their true relationship.

"You are young. He is a handsome, persuasive man." He paced the floor for a moment, leaving footprints in the freshly beaten Aubusson carpet. "Do not allow him to seduce your mind. You and Simon are to be married. I have decided that the wedding will take place as soon as possible."

"No, Uncle," Darcie began, wondering how she could tell her uncle this sordid story without hurting him. "I cannot marry Simon. I love Zack."

"Love? And what do you know of love?" He sneered, opening a box and removing a cigar before slamming the box shut again. He paced for a few moments, chewing on the end of the cigar. "Love? Hah. Your marriage was arranged by your father."

Darcie knew then that her uncle wouldn't be swayed. She'd have to tell him everything. "I love Zack. He says that we are betrothed from the date our fathers signed a truce."

For a moment, Talbot studied her face and then her figure. "You are a lovely young woman, Darcie. Do not be fooled by this man who talks with eloquent words."

"I am not fooled. I believe him."

"You believe him?" Talbot threw the unlit cigar on his desk and propped both hands on the mahogany top. "You will do as I say. In one month, you will marry Simon. He will sign your company over to my management, leaving the two of you to enjoy your lives together."

"He'll sign my company over to you? What gives him that right?" asked Darcie in horror.

"The law." Talbot Neville sat down and stared at Darcie. "I forbid you to see Zacharie Manville again. You may go to bed."

"You forbid?" Darcie felt her temper rise along with the bitter taste of bile creeping into her mouth. She leapt to her feet. "You have no right to forbid any such thing. I shall see Zacharie whenever I choose. You cannot stop me. Furthermore, I refuse to marry Simon. That boy is an imbecile and unfit for marriage. Besides, he loves Emilie Rhett."

"Sit down," her uncle roared. "Listen well, my dear. You will not see Zack again. You will marry Simon the moment it can be arranged."

"I will not marry Simon." She pointed her finger at him and glared as she sat back down. "You and nobody else can force me."

Talbot stared at her hand. Her left hand was extended between them in anger. Glittering on her finger was the sapphire ring given her by Zack. Talbot jumped to his feet and rushed around the table.

Before Darcie could understand his intent, he snatched the ring off her finger. "Where did you get this?"

"Give that back. It's mine." Darcie scrambled to her feet. "Give it back, I say."

Talbot held her at bay and compared the setting to the necklace she was wearing. Darcie's hand went to her throat. Zack had recognized his mother's sapphires, and now Talbot had. He held it out of her reach. "I asked where you got this?"

"It's mine," she lied.

"You didn't have it when you came to us. Where did you get it?" His voice rose and a steely glint came into his eyes. He raked one hand through his graying brown hair and stared at her. "Well? Did Manville give you this? Have you seen him without my permission?"

"I do not need permission from you to see him." Darcie stood toe to toe with him defiantly. "I am betrothed to him by my father on a document signed years ago. You have deceived me, and I will not tolerate it."

"I see your wild nature coming to the fore. Listen to me for I shall say this but once more." Talbot placed his hand on her shoulder and pressed her back into the chair. "You will not see or speak to Zacharie Manville ever again. You will not leave your room without permission from me. You will marry Simon as I have stated."

"Let me up. I refuse to remain in this house any longer." Darcie struggled to rise, but found his strength superior to hers. "Leave me be. *You* ordered the attack on my ship. *You* stole my jewels."

"You are distraught. It was done by Manville. That man is a liar. He is a pirate." Talbot squeezed her shoulder and his face came closer to hers. "You will agree to my conditions now, or I shall be forced to lock you away in the attic."

"You wouldn't dare. Zack would kill you." Darcie wriggled and fought as Talbot tucked the ring away in his pocket. "Let me go this instant. Give back my ring. I couldn't marry Simon even if I wanted to. I have already slept with Zack."

Talbot Neville drew back and slapped her with the front and then the back of his hand. Darcie had never been slapped in her life. Her own dear father never disciplined her with force, but reasoned with her instead. Looking into Talbot's eyes, Darcie knew real fear for the first time as she touched her swelling lip and looked at the blood on her hand. Regardless of what he pretended to be, Talbot Neville was a crook, and Darcie wouldn't bet that he wouldn't commit murder to attain his desires.

For the moment, she had to pretend to go along with him for her own safety. If she continued to fight him, then he'd imprison her in the basement and all hope would be lost. "All right, Uncle. I'll do it."

"That's better. Come, my dear, I'll escort you to your room." He held his arm out to her. "I expect that you'll feel so badly tomorrow that you won't even come down for meals."

"No, Uncle."

They stopped outside her door. "I'll see that M. Manville gets his ring back with your regrets and a note asking him not to call anymore."

"Yes, Uncle." Darcie turned to go into her room, anxious to see the damage to her lips and eye, which was swelling considerably.

"Oh, and Darcie, my dear."

"Yes?" She looked back at him, scared of what he might say or do next.

"Beginning tomorrow, I believe that we could let Simon stay here with you. I won't disturb him tonight, but I believe tomorrow will do."

"Whatever you say, Uncle." Darcie stepped inside her room and heard it close behind her. The bolt shot across and she knew Talbot had locked her in. She waited a few minutes, trying to decide what to do. Her degradation would be complete if Uncle Talbot let Simon sleep with her. She knew how the maids talked.

How had Zack gotten in? The first night, he'd remained behind when all their other guests left, but the other times, he'd climbed in somehow.

Darcie ran to the armoire. She dug down and found her bag. She'd taken everything out but the papers Horace had sent for her uncle. She'd forgotten to give them to him. Working quickly, she stuffed undergarments and sleepwear on top of the papers. Feeling awful for crushing the silks and velvets, she rolled three gowns and pressed them inside, along with their matching shoes. Last, she placed her jewelry bag on top and closed the bulging case.

She was running away. At the moment, Darcie didn't know where, but she had to go. Looking out the window, she realized that Zack was much more athletic than she. Even if she had been in much better physical condition, she would have had trouble climbing down without falling.

Her only recourse was to tie her bedlinens together and shinny down as gracefully as possible. After tying the linens together securely, she anchored them to the heavy four-poster bed. She dropped her bag out the window and started down.

Before she reached the bottom, Darcie thought her arms would be wrenched from their sockets. In addition to her bruised mouth, she would have sore arms and shoulders for several days.

Chapter Twenty

At first, Darcie didn't know where to go. She had decided to go straight to Tuileries, but the distance was too far for her to walk, and the hour too late for admittance to the Empress's chamber.

Her only other option was to walk the short distance to Madelaine's house and hope that no one saw her. The night was cold and Darcie hadn't stopped to slip on her burnous. Even through her slippers, the icy ground numbed her feet. *What a fool I am,* she thought as the wind bit at her cheeks and nose.

Snow began to fall. Darcie's first reaction was delight. Charlestonians saw little snow, being in such a temperate climate. The prospect of Paris blanketed in white cheered her somewhat, even though the damp snow melted beneath her feet and seeped into her shoes.

The wind swirled the snow all around her, and for a while Darcie thought there might be a blizzard. When the snow had melted, some poor unsuspecting citizen would find Darcie frozen to death in his yard.

When she reached the darkened house, she hesitated briefly

before raising the heavy brass knocker and slamming it against the door. The resounding bang echoed all around her.

Her teeth chattered uncontrollably as she stood shivering, waiting for someone to answer her knock. It became apparent that nobody had heard her. Mustering all her strength, she banged the knocker louder and waited again.

What could she do if nobody answered the door? She hadn't thought of that. Darcie wasn't familiar enough with the city to trudge off in search of an inn. Lacking sufficient clothing to maintain her body temperature, she knew that she'd be dead before she reached the river.

Suddenly from above her head she heard a sound and looked up. Madelaine Ortiz leaned over the balcony and peered down at her.

"Madelaine, I'm sorry for being such a bother, but—"

"Darcie! Is that you?" Madelaine asked, squinting to see better in the dim light. "By thunder, it's snowing. Wait a moment. I'll let you in. Gracious, what a night."

Waiting for what seemed like hours, Darcie simply stared at the brass knocker. *Thank heaven,* she mused, *that she has a knocker. If I'd had to rap with my fingers, I believe they would have shattered.*

The door swung open and Madelaine snatched Darcie's bag from her hand and pulled her through the door. "Come up to my room. My fire is still lit."

Linking her arm through Darcie's she half-dragged the young girl up the carpeted stairs. By this time, Darcie could hardly speak.

"I . . . I th—thank—"

"Oh, stuff and nonsense. Wait until you can speak before you try to explain." They reached the landing and moved toward Madelaine's sitting room.

Once inside, Madelaine pulled on a bell cord and then placed Darcie on a chair by the fire. "Sit here. I'll get something for you to drink." She glanced at Darcie and stopped still. "Gracious! What happened to your face? Never mind. We'll talk later."

She dropped the baggage by the door and waited for Beauchamps to appear. "Beauchamps, I'm sorry to trouble you at this hour, but as you can see Mlle. Gaynor has just arrived and is chilled to the bone. Bring me a bottle of rum . . . no, make her a toddy. Rum, sugar, lemon . . . you know what I mean. Quickly now. Can't you see she's freezing?"

Beauchamps left without further ado. While Darcie held wrinkled and icy hands toward the fire, she tried to talk again. "Oh, Madelaine . . . I . . . I . . . th-thank you. You c-c-can't i-m-m-magine—"

"Darcie, my darling, remain silent. Concentrate on warming —" The door swung open and Beauchamps hurried in. Madelaine took the rum toddy and handed it to Darcie. "Ah, thank you, Beauchamps. Start a fire in the guest room . . . no, bring a truckle bed in here for Miss Gaynor. And, fetch extra blankets."

"No, please," Darcie protested, wrapping her cold hands around the warm cup. "Don't do anything extra for me."

"Don't be silly. We've got to warm you up." Madelaine nodded to Beauchamps who left the room. "That woman is a wonder."

"I'm so sorry, Madelaine. I wouldn't have come, if I'd had any choice." Tears welled in Darcie's eyes as she thought of her narrow escape. After tonight, she would never have been left alone.

After a few minutes, Beauchamps returned pushing a bed on wheels laden with extra blankets and pillows. "Anything else, madame?"

"No. Thank you for your assistance." Madelaine waited for the servant to leave the room and then turned back to Darcie. "Now, let's start at the beginning. I want to know everything."

Since she had nowhere else to go for the moment, she needed a true friend, someone to trust. Madelaine and Margot were best friends, but Darcie didn't know how Madelaine felt about Talbot. Darcie started her story with Zack's arrival in Charleston. Madelaine pulled the truckle bed closer to the fire and then turned to Darcie. "Before you begin, let's get you in some dry clothing."

She pulled a nightgown of heavy cotton from the back of her armoire and laid it across the bed. "Here. Take those wet things off."

Darcie did as she was directed. Minutes later and clad in Madelaine's nightgown, she was tucked into bed and the feeling began to return to her fingers.

Then she began to talk. For most of the story, Madelaine merely nodded and listened. She occasionally shook her head. By the time Darcie revealed tonight's events, Madelaine's face resembled storm clouds gathering on the horizon.

"That worm . . . that lily-livered, lying thief. Hanging is too good for him." Madelaine paced back and forth in front of the fire. "I should send for the authorities right away."

"Oh, no. Please don't. I couldn't stand to answer questions about my . . . about Zack." Darcie's eyes sparkled with tears once again.

Madelaine shook her head and waggled her finger at Darcie. "All right, my dear. I won't, if you say not to, but it's no more than Talbot deserves. The nerve of that fool. When Zack hears of this . . . when he sees your face, Talbot won't be safe on this earth. That shall be his reward."

"Oh, Madelaine, I am humiliated. Everyone in Paris will know about my . . . my indiscretion." Darcie hadn't left anything out—not even her affair with Zack. "And, if people here find out, word will have reached Charleston by the time I do."

"Well, you'll just have to marry Zack. It's time someone snatched him from the marketplace." Madelaine laughed. "You know, at one time I considered trying to interest him in Gabriella."

"Gabriella?" Darcie looked surprised. Gabriella seemed such a quiet girl and so young, too young to be husband hunting.

"Yes. But the moment I saw the two of you together, I realized that she had no chance of winning his love." Madelaine leaned back in her chair. "Ah, Darcie, I saw the love that surrounded the two of you . . . that passed between you with each look. You didn't have to tell me the story of you and Zack. I'd already figured that much out. But I thank you for trusting me enough to tell me."

"I have liked you from the moment we met, Madelaine," Darcie admitted and leaned up on one elbow so she could see her friend better. "I wanted to tell you before, but I couldn't bring myself to . . . reveal our relationship to anyone."

"What do you intend to do, Darcie?" Madelaine asked simply.

"I don't know. I . . . I thought I might stay here until I could seek an audience with the Empress." Darcie sighed. With all that she had heard of royalty and heads of state, obtaining an audience might take months.

For now, she would have no money, no clothes, no residence, and no way of obtaining any of those things. Uncle Talbot would find her soon enough and then she would have to deal with him.

"Zack could help."

"Do you think so? I know that the Empress likes him." Darcie leaned forward and raised her eyebrows. "Did you know he calls the Empress by her name?"

"Oh, yes. The two of them are as close as a sheep and its wool," Madelaine agreed thoughtfully. "We'll go to the palace tomorrow. Perhaps we can work something out."

"I'd hoped we could do that." Darcie smiled for the first time since she'd reached Madelaine's house. "And, Madelaine, what are we going to do about Aunt Margot and Uncle Talbot?"

Madelaine considered the situation for a moment as she moved toward her own canopied bed. "What Margot knows, Talbot knows. We simply can't tell her."

That made Darcie feel even worse. Aunt Margot had been especially good to her and Darcie didn't want to repay a kindness by making her worry. But there was no help for it.

Morning came much sooner than Darcie had expected. Her eye was swollen nearly shut and her lip bulged disgracefully.

"Oh, Madelaine," she cried. "I can't go to see the Empress looking like this. What will she think?"

"She'll think that Talbot is a crazed fool." Madelaine sipped her chocolate and studied Darcie's face. "If your face doesn't convince her that Talbot has no business as your guardian, then there is no hope of it."

"Can't we wait until the swelling is gone down and this dreadful color disappears?" Darcie leaned closer to the mirror and tried to open the eye further.

Madelaine shook her head. "No. Now, get dressed. We're leaving as soon as the carriage arrives. You can wear my burnous. The color is all wrong for you, but it will hide your face."

For the entire length of the carriage ride to Tuileries, Darcie tried to talk Madelaine out of going. Even as they entered the palace, Darcie pleaded with her once more.

"We seek an audience with the Empress," Madelaine stated to the guard at the door.

"I'm sorry. There will be no audiences today," he replied as if he'd said the same words one hundred times already.

"Thank you," Darcie whispered from beneath the hood and turned to leave.

Madelaine caught her hand. "If we could see Mlle. Bouvet, we would seek a moment of her time."

The guard turned to a footman and said a few words. The footman raced off into the palace, his footsteps echoing on the marble floor of the entrance.

A few minutes later, he returned and led the two ladies to Mlle. Bouvet's sitting room. He left them huddled together next to the fire.

Madelaine placed her arms around Darcie's shoulders and tried to reassure her. "Here, Darcie, take off that burnous. You'll warm faster."

"No. I . . . I can't. I don't want anyone to see me like this." Burying her face even further in the hood, Darcie leaned against Madelaine for comfort.

"Don't worry. Everything will be—"

"Sorry to keep you waiting. I understand there's a matter of some . . . oh, my. What happened to you Miss Gaynor?" Mlle. Bouvet's mouth gaped open.

If she hadn't felt so foolish, Darcie might have laughed. She was sure that someone who exuded as much confidence as Mlle. Bouvet never allowed anything to change her practiced smile. "I apologize for shocking you, and for asking to see you without proper—"

"You have no need to apologize, Miss Gaynor. I rather think someone else owes the apology," she said and motioned for them to be seated. "What can I do for you?"

Darcie sighed as she dropped into a chair by the fire. How much did she need to tell Mlle. Bouvet in order to be granted an audience with the Empress. "Again I apologize. We have come to speak with Her Highness. The guard informs us that she is granting no audiences today. Since my problem is a delicate—"

"One moment. I shall speak to her and ask what her wishes are in the matter." Mlle. Bouvet walked to the door. "In the meantime, I'll send for tea. Or would you prefer coffee, Miss Gaynor?"

"Noth—"

"We'll have coffee," Madelaine interrupted in her brusque way. "We are both chilled from the carriage ride."

"Of course. I won't be a moment." Mlle. Bouvet disappeared.

"Oh, Madelaine, I feel so foolish. I look so foolish," Darcie lamented, closer to self-pity than ever before.

Madelaine rested comfortably on the sofa and closed her eyes. "Don't be absurd. We'll get this matter straightened out today if possible."

Time passed slowly for the two ladies staring into the crackling fire. Darcie felt restless, and at every sound jerked around to see who might be coming in behind her. Uncle Talbot's brutality had made her nervous.

"Darcie!"

"Zack!" Darcie jumped to her feet and ran into Zack's open arms. Though she tried hard to prevent them, tears misted her eyes as she cuddled against him for strength.

He gazed into her face and his own visage contorted with

anger. Glaring through eyes glazed with rage, he held her at arm's length and stared. "Who did this?"

"Zack, I—"

"Mother! How came you to be here with . . . never mind." He turned to Mlle. Bouvet. "Bouvet, tell Eugénie that this is an emergency. I wish to speak with her before I leave this morning."

Mlle. Bouvet nodded and left once again. Zack led Darcie to the sofa and sat down with her carefully tucked under his arm. For several minutes, he simply held her close, fearing that the rage that rankled within him might upset her more.

He glanced at Madelaine. "Where did you find her?"

Madelaine shrugged. "She found me."

"Darcie, can you tell me what happened? Tell me who did this awful thing to you." His arms were around her consoling and comforting, but the muscles rippled with his anger.

"I . . . No, Zack. I cannot tell . . . You're too angry and I don't want . . ." Darcie couldn't tell him, she couldn't say that she was in this condition because of her defiance of Uncle Talbot's ruling.

"M. Manville, the Empress will see you and Miss Gaynor." Mlle. Bouvet turned to Madelaine. "If you will wait here, I shall return and we will have tea."

Zack lifted Darcie in his arms and strode from the room. At the moment, he was so angry he felt as if he could lift Tuileries without difficulty. When they reached the Empress's apartments, he tapped on the door without putting Darcie down.

The Empress herself opened the door. "Bring her in, Zack. I've asked for tea and coffee."

Zack carried Darcie to the couch and sat her down. "I'm sorry to interrupt this morning. I know we hadn't planned to meet, but when I saw her face, I couldn't just leave."

"Of course not." The Empress sat down beside Darcie. "Now, tell us what has happened to you since we saw you last night."

Darcie related the story slowly. There were times when she thought Zack would fly through the door and find Uncle Talbot right then. Before she could finish, she was interrupted by a rapping on the door.

A servant brought in a tray and left without speaking. Behind her, a man came in carrying a leather bag. "My honor, what has happened to this child?"

"Doctor, please see if anything may be done to make her more comfortable." Not taking time for civilities, the Empress spat the order. "Zack, move aside. She can live without you for a few moments. Come here. We'll pour our tea while they speak."

Zack left Darcie's side reluctantly. All the time the doctor worked, Zack stared at him.

"Zack, your tea is getting cold."

"Damn! Why would anybody want to do a thing like this?" Zack jumped to his feet and walked back and forth behind the Empress. "Only a demented person would inflict wounds like these for no reason."

"Of course you're right. But do sit down and wait until the doctor is finished. Then Darcie can have her coffee and tell us the rest of the story," the Empress reasoned. She caught his arm and whispered, "Zack, I do believe you're making her more upset. Please calm yourself."

The doctor announced that there was little he could do beyond prescribe something to help her rest. The wounds were superficial and would heal soon enough of their own accord.

The Empress Eugénie watched the door close. "Now, dear, continue your story. Take your time and try not to let Zack upset you."

"I feel so awful for causing such a disruption in your household, madame. Please forgive me." Darcie had taken the medication the doctor left and began to relax.

Continuing her story, she told of Uncle Talbot's angry reaction to her revelation that she and Zack had been intimate. If the Empress was shocked, she said nothing. She told them everything, just as she had told Madelaine.

"After he locked me in my room, I packed a few items and climbed out the window." Darcie sighed, feeling the effects of the medicine heavy on her eyelids. "Then I walked to Madelaine's. Fortunately, I was able to rouse her. It was snowing. So cold. So cold. No coat. Forgot cloak. Dancing slippers."

Darcie fell asleep before she saw the rage return to Zack's eyes. Her head fell to one side and her breathing became shallow and slow.

"Damn the man for the cad he is. I'll kill him." Zack pounded on the table. "I swear, I'll kill him."

"Zack, please calm yourself. Think of Darcie's well-being. We need to develop a plan." The Empress helped herself to a small cake. "Here, have one of these. Never plot on an empty stomach."

When Darcie awoke, she was in a strange room. For several seconds, she tried to open her eyes, but found herself unable to open one of them at all. Remembering why, she touched the eye and felt the swelling. Her fingers paused at her lip, testing the amount of puffiness there, too.

Stirring slightly, she peered through her good eye at her surroundings. She remembered being at the palace, of telling her story to Zack and the Empress. Darcie propped herself up on one elbow. Was she still at the palace? Where was Zack? And Madelaine?

"Ah, miss, you are awake," a lilting feminine voice said behind her.

Darcie turned slowly to see who had spoken, but didn't recognize the woman. "Yes, thank you. Where am I?"

"At Tuileries," the woman answered and then left the room.

Trying to sit up, Darcie glanced around. Her room was sunny and beautiful. A fire crackled cheerfully in the fireplace and a pleasant scent permeated the air.

When she looked down, Darcie realized that someone had undressed her and put a lovely nightgown on her. Her bed was ruffled with flounces of lace and ribbons, and the furniture was white and gold. She sat up a little more and put her feet on the floor. The door opened and she looked up as the Empress entered the room.

The Empress had a lovely, warm smile. "How nice to see you sitting up, my dear."

"Your Highness, I feel like such a burden." Darcie tried to stand, but felt a bit shaky.

"Do not worry about anything. Zack and I have made elaborate plans to trap your uncle in his own devious plot." The Empress laughed. "It's been a long time since I played matchmaker to lovers such as you and Zack."

Darcie looked up at her in astonishment. "I don't understand."

"Well, Zack will be staying here when he returns to Paris. I don't know exactly when that will be, but soon." She laughed and sat down beside Darcie. "I expect the most circumspect behavior from each of you."

"Oh, yes, ma'am," Darcie answered quickly, reverting to her Charleston accent. "I would never do anything to embarrass you in any way."

"Good. And, please, when we are alone, call me by my name." The Empress stood and walked toward the door. "When you feel well enough, you may join my ladies-in-waiting in the Salon Vert. Until then, your every need will be seen to here."

"You are too kind, ma'am."

Again she laughed merrily. "Nonsense. Oh, don't forget our opera date. On the fourteenth. There will be several carriages in my entourage."

Darcie spent the next several days in her chamber. She was fed and clothed as if she were a permanent member of the household, rather than an uninvited guest.

If Zack returned, she didn't see him. On the evening of the opera, Darcie dressed quickly with the help of a young woman who had been assigned to her. She wore a gown of emerald taffeta accented with gold braid. In her hair, she wore satin roses in the center of a low chignon. Her above-the-elbow gloves were of gold kid that matched her slippers.

When she asked about the gown, the servant said that it had been made using the size of one of Darcie's gowns and that was all she knew. A young man knocked at the door and escorted Darcie to the portico where all the ladies-in-waiting were gathered.

Her carriage was the third behind the Emperor's and she was accompanied by Mlle. Bouvet who filled her in on the details of her wardrobe. "Yes. The Empress sent for her seamstress to make several gowns for you. I think you'll be pleasantly surprised."

"What of the cost? Until the matter of my guardian is resolved, I have no money," Darcie explained.

Mlle. Bouvet smiled. "I'm sure that is no problem. Do you know where we are going?"

"No," Darcie admitted, and peered out the window.

"We are going to the Opera in the Rue Lepelletier. Our outing was almost canceled."

"Canceled?" Darcie asked, looking at her companion with renewed interest. "Because of that Italian?"

"No," Mlle. Bouvet answered and laughed. "The Emperor and Empress will not be denied this chance to go among their people because of an irate Italian."

"What then could have caused the cancellation if not physical danger?" Darcie marveled at the strength the rulers of France possessed. How brave they were.

"Do you recall when you came to us? The doctor who saw you had been here to visit the Empress. She had a severe cough." Mlle. Bouvet laughed and shook her head. "Word even reached her sister, Paca, and the Empress had to write and console her. Paca thought the Empress was deathly ill."

Darcie shook her head in wonder. "I never had a sister, so I don't know much about their relationships. But I surmise that they can be quite meddlesome."

"Oh, yes. Particularly when they are close as Paca and the Empress." Mlle. Bouvet peered out the window. "I see the first of our carriages is pulling into the private carriage way. I do so enjoy—"

Her sentence was interrupted by an explosion. Their carriage was rocked as two more explosions were heard and felt. The horses reared and stumbled in panic, and cries could be heard from all around. For several seconds, Darcie and Mlle. Bouvet huddled together for fear of other blasts.

"The Empress. Let's see about her." Darcie opened the carriage door and jumped to the road. She never looked back to see if her companion followed, but reached the Emperor and Empress's carriage and flung open the door. "Ma'am, sir, are you injured?"

"Darcie, we are hardly touched. And you? Bouvet?" The Empress patted Darcie's hand reassuringly.

She marveled at the Empress's composure. "Ma'am, we are well. Here, you are bleeding, take my handkerchief."

The Empress Eugénie accepted the handkerchief and smiled as Bouvet's face appeared behind Darcie's. Napoleon's nose was cut slightly, but he said that he was fine. The other door was wrenched open and Darcie's eyes widened in horror as she thought the criminals might have eluded the guards that were hunting them down.

"Are either of you injured, Your Highness?"

"Only slightly," Napoleon answered.

Glancing around to make sure that no other attempts were likely, Darcie thought she saw Uncle Talbot. His face was obscured by a hat, but she was almost sure he was there. When she looked again, the man was gone.

Darcie and Bouvet were moved out of the way as the street filled with police and a throng of curious Parisians. The Emperor and Empress stepped down from the carriage and surveyed the damage. "Don't bother about us, such things are our profession. See to the wounded."

All around, people were screaming. Many appeared to be injured, either by direct hits from the three bombs or from broken glass. Darcie shivered as she looked into one bloody face after another as she tried to help.

When it appeared that they could not help, Darcie and Bouvet followed the Emperor and Empress into the theater foyer, and there in the light, Darcie could see blood splattered over the Empress's white gown. Eyes wide with admiration for the Empress's calm during the assassination attempt, Darcie waited while the Empress organized her group and then went in to sit down.

During the intermission, the Emperor and Empress left the box to stand in the outside balcony. The street was full of citizens who were concerned about their Sovereigns. After waving to reassure their people, Napoleon III and Eugénie returned to their box for the remainder of the performance.

Darcie could hardly keep her mind on the performance. Everywhere around her, people were whispering behind fans about the incident.

Giuseppe Mazzini and the "secret societies," as they were called, orchestrated the attempts from his exile in England. Felice Orsini hired the thugs who actually threw the bombs. Much was made in the coming days of England's harboring of known criminals. Every gathering included gossip about the crime and the criminals.

Darcie hesitated. Several days had passed since the opera and she had done nothing except lie around and read. This was her first dinner with Eugénie since Madelaine brought her here. Opening the door, she found Mlle. Bouvet about to knock again.

"Ah, you're dressed," she said and stepped to one side of the door. "I came after you because the Empress thought you might be more comfortable with me than anyone else."

Darcie smiled, grateful once more for Eugénie's thoughtfulness. "Thank you for coming. I'm a bit nervous."

"You look lovely. I wouldn't be concerned if I were you." She led the way down a gaily lit hallway to a small salon. "Wait here. I've got a quick errand to run before dinner."

"Aren't you staying?" Darcie whirled to face her companion, forgetting about the enchanting decor.

"I'll meet you in the dining room if I'm late. Don't worry." Mlle. Bouvet hurried out of the room before Darcie could speak again.

Darcie sauntered past a thick tapestry and sat down on a delicate chair before the roaring fire. Across the mantel were several small sculptures and a pair of silver candelabra, complete with long white tapers. Staring into the flames, Darcie thought of her uncle's treachery and how close she'd come to succumbing to his lies. If only Zack could find the proof they needed by April.

The door behind her opened and she leapt to her feet, whirling about to curtsey to Eugénie. *"Zack!"* Darcie exclaimed and ran across the richly colored Aubusson carpet. "Oh, Zack, I didn't know—"

"Shhh." Zack took her in his arms and lowered his lips to hers, effectively silencing her words.

Through the power of his kiss, Darcie recognized Zack's hunger and she opened her mouth to him. His steel embrace defied any movement she might want to make, but she was content in his arms.

When he finally released her, he gazed deeply into her eyes. "How I've missed you, Darcie my darling."

"And I you," Darcie whispered, afraid that any noise would break the spell of the moment. He was dressed for dinner and looked elegant in black with the white silk waistcoat. Her eyes went to his cravat, crossed and pierced by the pearl stickpin she'd given him for Christmas. "You're wearing the pin I gave you."

"Yes, don't you think it adds a little elegance to this old sea dog's appearance?" he teased.

"I say, 'old sea dog.'" Her gaze fell to the bare finger where she'd worn Zack's ring. Tears stung her eyes. "I wish—oh, Zack, Uncle Talbot has my ring and he'll probably sell it or something, and I'll never see it again."

Anger rose in Zack. The ring meant nothing compared to Darcie's happiness and well-being. He held her close, kissing the top of her head. "It's all right, darling. I'll get it back for you. I promise."

Suddenly filled with questions, she looked up at him. Would he answer her? She wondered and decided that he probably wouldn't. "You have . . . you've been absent from the palace for some time."

Zack stared into the glittering depths of Darcie's eyes and saw her concern. "Fear not, love. I am safe."

A door opened opposite the one they had entered and they jerked apart. A servant announced that dinner was to be served in the adjoining room.

Darcie hoped that dinner would be a quiet affair with the Empress, but her hopes were dashed when they entered a salon filled with the hum of conversation. Despite her dismay, she glanced around the room, noticing all the lovely ladies-in-waiting. Eugénie's friend Merimee, a writer, and Gustave Flaubert, another, conversed in a corner among a small group of men.

A few minutes passed and Eugénie entered, commanding everyone's attention. Darcie's place at the table was beside the Empress, while Zack's was at the far end.

The sumptuous meal barely caught Darcie's attention. She might remember the succulent venison with the fine dark sauce or the roast duck, but of the remainder of the fare, she knew nothing. She ate little, dividing her attention between talking to the Empress and watching Zack. It seemed that they sat at the table for hours—an eternity.

When Eugénie stood, she took Darcie's hand and led her to Zack. *"Zacharie,* my friend, I fear we may have exhausted poor Miss Gaynor. She hardly ate a bite of dinner. Please escort her to her room and see that she wants for nothing."

Zack didn't miss the gleam in the Empress's eye as she patted Darcie's hand softly. "Your wish is my command, Your Highness." Zack bowed deeply. "With your permission, I'll retire as well. I must leave early tomorrow."

"Of course. Goodnight, dear Darcie. Sleep well." Eugénie squeezed Darcie's hand and turned again to Zack. "And, Zack, take . . . take extra care to return to us as healthy as you are tonight."

"I shall." His smile was warm and personal. "Beware, Eugénie, of . . ."

Eugénie's visage was regal as she watched the concern play across Zack's face, but her laugh was a little artificial. "Go on.

Don't trouble me this evening with tales of intrigue. I'll see you in the morning before you leave. Have Bouvet wake me."

Darcie and Zack left the room without further words. When they reached Darcie's door, she expected him to leave. Instead he followed her inside.

"Zack!" she exclaimed, staring at him in disbelief. "What are you doing? I'm here out of the Empress's kindness. Don't do something that will—"

Zack kissed her, interrupting her flow of words. The kiss was sweet and gentle. He drew back and looked down at her. "Nonsense. You're here because she likes you."

"But, she said that my behavior must be above reproach while I remain—"

"Don't worry. Everyone is in the salon, drinking wine and telling lies. Nobody will disturb us this evening." He removed his coat, waistcoat, and cravat, placing them on the back of a chair. "I'm leaving early tomorrow. I don't know when—"

"Shhh," Darcie interrupted. She didn't want to know about the realities that nibbled away at their stolen moments together. "Love me, Zack."

Without speaking, he swept her off her feet and carried her through the door that connected with her bedroom. He closed the door behind them and locked it securely. Piece by piece and ever so carefully, he removed her clothing, taking care that the rustling taffeta gown hung without wrinkles across a chair.

Before long, Darcie stood before him, her ivory skin glowing like honey in the light of the fire. She waited, her skin singing with anticipation, while he took out the pins from her hair and let it tumble in a glorious cascade of curls across her shoulders. Lifting her once again, he carried her to the bed and deposited her on the satin comforter. Cupping her face in his hands, he leaned down and kissed her gently.

When he stood straight again, Darcie reached up and began to unbutton his shirt. Her fingers trembled when they reached his waist. She glanced up at him.

Looking down at her, he saw her hesitate and he removed his trousers. He blew out all the candles, leaving only the flames from the hearth to cast dancing shadows on the wallpaper. He strode to the bed and eased down beside her.

Darcie sat there motionless. The courage that had allowed her to unbutton his shirt abandoned her, and she felt like an untried maiden again. Inhaling deeply, she reached over and touched his chest. She flattened her palm against his skin and rubbed gently across his breast and flat stomach.

He gasped as she ventured further down, and she glanced at him in alarm. "Is something . . . did I do something wrong?"

As his gaze met hers, he recognized all that he'd hoped for when he'd first met her. Their life together would surpass his dreams. "No, my darling, you've done nothing wrong. Pray continue."

Darcie's eyes followed her hand as it traveled down his stomach into the thatch of curly hair, her fingers disappearing in its thickness. Then she felt him stiffen. His arousal, hardly noticeable before, became conspicuous as her hand closed around its silken length.

"For the love of sailing, Darcie—" He bit his lip and groaned. "If you don't stop, I'll . . ."

Her gaze flew to his face in dismay. "You want me to stop? Oh, I *have* done something wrong."

Zack laughed lightly. "No, it isn't that."

"What then?"

He pressed her back against the bed and kissed her. Her lips melded with his and she forgot what she had been doing. As his fingers traced little tingling pathways down her body, her breasts jutted up, nipples like hard candy eager to meet his touch.

Raising up, he slid her back on the bed until her body was nestled in satin and her head cradled in the crook of his arm across a pillow. Zack nibbled at her ear, kissed her neck, and whispered, "I have other things in mind tonight. We'll save the lessons in lovemaking for a more leisurely time."

"But, Zack, I want to . . . to give you the same pleasure you give me," she protested half-heartedly, succumbing to the gentle tug of his mouth on her nipple.

And then she forgot everything except the enchantment born of their union. Writhing beneath him, Darcie parried with each thrust of Zack's until she shuddered with exquisite rapture, gasping for breath as he finally rested beside her.

Zack couldn't get enough of her. He felt like a doomed man, grasping for the last pleasure he'd find on earth, and he intended to taste the sweetness of her love all night.

The fire waned and left nothing but glowing embers, embers that were very much like Zack and Darcie's passion. With a touch to fuel the flame, their passions would once again become a roaring holocaust.

Darcie slept easily in the crook of Zack's arm, her fingers splayed against his chest. Zack wanted to wake her, but didn't like the thought of a tearful goodbye, so he wrote a note and left it on his pillow.

When Darcie awoke, Zack was gone. Nothing remained to remind her of his visit except her exhaustion, until she spotted the folded paper on her pillow. She sprang from the bed and raced to the window to peer out. It was still dark, but dawn was edging its way up from the lifeless horizon.

Darcie lit a lamp and read Zack's letter.

> *My darling Darcie,*
> *My moments with you are the most precious of my life. I shall be gone for some time, but when I return our pleasure will be doubled. We shall be together forever, for I shall not return without the proof I need to make you truly mine.*
> > *With all my love,*
> > *Zack*

She could do nothing but wait and pray for his safety.

Chapter Twenty-one

Darcie was looking for a pair of earbobs that had somehow been misplaced and felt the papers Horace had asked her to take to Uncle Talbot. Feeling a little guilty for forgetting to give them to him for so long. *Well, it's too late now,* she mused.

Pulling the sheaf of yellowed papers from their folder, she started looking through them and forgot her earrings entirely. Some of the papers were bills of lading, inventory lists, passenger lists, accounting records, and other business forms.

But at the bottom, Darcie noticed a particularly old envelope. Her eyebrows creased as she tried to read the return address on the outside. It was from somewhere in France. Biarritz.

Opening the envelope, Darcie felt an odd sensation creep up her spine. She knew she shouldn't read these things that were none of her business—but they were. Gaynor Shipping was her business, not Uncle Talbot's as he would have liked.

The paper was thin and brittle, so Darcie handled it carefully. She read a few lines and then began to read faster, to scan the lines and paragraphs that made up the document. It appeared to be the truce that Zack had spoken of.

If it was, then there had to be a paragraph about her betrothal. Near the end, Darcie found it. She read the conditions and they were exactly as Zack had described. When the youngest of the two children reached age twenty-one, a marriage would take place between Darcie Jeanne Gaynor and Zacharie Etienne Manville that would unite the warring companies. A merger agreement followed.

Darcie scanned the remainder of the document. Her father and Zack's had foreseen a future for the two of them as co-owners of the world's greatest shipping line. Tears formed in her eyes, she wiped at them with the hem of her skirt and continued to read until she reached the two signatures. Her father's broad script was unmistakable.

From the moment she discovered the agreement, Darcie could hardly wait for Zack's return. Every day she walked down the stairs and asked if anyone had seen or heard from him and was invariably disappointed. She carried the old envelope in her reticule, primarily because once the document had been found, she didn't want to risk losing it again. But she wanted to pull it out and show it to Zack the moment he arrived.

For several weeks, she fought the urge to fling the document in Uncle Talbot's face. She thought it odd that he hadn't visited or inquired about her, particularly after having seen her with the Empress at the opera, but she put him out of her mind.

The Empress decided to leave for Biarritz sooner than anticipated and took Darcie with her. Their arrival at the Villa Eugénie on the Atlantic took place before Zack even returned to Paris.

Darcie missed him dreadfully. She didn't know what he had done about Uncle Talbot, but she didn't care as long as she didn't have to marry Simon. The Empress never mentioned their "plot" as she called it and merely smiled when Darcie brought it up.

The Villa Eugénie was a lovely diversion after all the intrigue in Paris. Gala dinners and parties were a common event and the entertainments were numerous.

One evening the Empress surprised everyone with masks. A

masked ball was to be held. Darcie dressed in her finest new gown, a rose-colored silk made by Worth. His expertise and delightfully different styles had captivated the Empress's interest. Darcie puffed the bishop's sleeves and fluffed the froth of robin's egg blue lace that hung from just below the elbow to her wrists. The full twelve-yard skirt settled gracefully over her hoops, allowing the scalloped hem to expose ruffles of the same robin's egg blue lace as in the undersleeve.

Darcie spun around, laughing as she did. The gown was the loveliest she'd ever owned. Worth spent long hours designing it. His newest gown for the Empress was of varying shades of brown stripes accented with black. He said once the Empress wore such a creation, it would sweep Paris like the juiciest gossip.

Patting her hair, upswept tonight with six long curls hanging from the back, Darcie headed down the stairs. The air was warmer tonight, far warmer than the frigid temperatures of Paris, and Darcie inhaled the intoxicating aroma of the salt air. How she had missed it in Paris.

Once downstairs, the Empress took her hand and led her across the room. "Darcie, my dear, allow me to present my friend whom I call M. Michel. He will be your escort this evening. Now promise me that neither of you will tell who you are. After all, I want the unveiling at midnight to be a complete surprise for everyone."

Darcie smiled from behind her domino mask. The intrigue of this evening promised to be fun. Deeply tanned skin showed around the domino mask of her escort for the evening. His warm brown eyes were lively and gazed at her with rapt attention as they entered the carriages that lined the drive.

"Do you know where we are going?" Darcie asked, hoping to involve her companion in a conversation. Thus far, he had been quiet, too quiet.

He shook his head. *"Non, senorita."*

A Spaniard! Eugénie was full of surprises tonight. Biarritz was a small fishing village nestled in the Basque region of France and the carriage followed a narrow road into the hills above the village.

They reached a stopping place and everyone peered through the windows. "What's wrong? Why are we stopping? I see no villa here," Darcie questioned.

"I do not know," came the husky reply.

Darcie began to wonder if Eugénie had given this man into her care because he was a dullard and needed looking after. He appeared to be young and healthy, but he had nothing to say.

"I believe the others are getting out." Darcie continued to gaze out the window, reminded of that awful night in January when the Italian had made an attempt on the Emperor's life. Since the Emperor had not journeyed to Biarritz with them, she doubted if there would be danger tonight.

Darcie decided that remaining inside with this strange man was worse than whatever had stalled their progress. She reached for the door, only to meet the hand of her companion.

"Allow me." He opened the door, jumped down, and then turned to help her. He held her waist and let her feet touch easily on the rocky ground. "Have care."

With his hand resting on her waist, he guided her past the carriages in front of theirs until they arrived at a lighted grotto in the side of the mountain.

"It's a cave!" Darcie exclaimed, laughing gaily. "What a treat."

From their vantage point on the lip of the cave, Darcie looked down. Below her, perhaps fifty feet, the Atlantic undulated gently in the moonlight, reminding her briefly of Charleston Harbor. Several hundred yards out to sea, a ship lay at anchor, bobbing on the rhythmic waves.

"Oh, isn't this the loveliest place on Earth?" she asked, peering like a child at everything she saw. "Look there, isn't the moon wonderful. It's like that in Charleston. You'd almost think you could walk across its path on the water. For a moment, I almost thought it was a Carolina moon."

"It is the same moon. French or Carolina. The same," M. Michel replied, shrugging.

"Not exactly," she disagreed. "Let's go in."

They entered the grotto and found a banquet table worthy of the finest in Paris. Illuminated by numerous torches, the grotto was bathed in a golden glow that made everything seem like a dream. Darcie sat down to eat and found that she was ravenously hungry.

Down at the end of the table, Eugénie kept watching her as if she expected her to do something. Darcie turned to ask her escort if he knew why they were here and found his gaze on her as well.

"Is something wrong?" she asked, feeling a bit impatient with this man who seemed to have no manners whatsoever.

"Yes. Something is wrong. Come with me." He rose and pulled out her chair for her to rise.

When they walked a short distance toward the back where the cave began to slope, Darcie stopped. "Where are we going?"

"Trust me."

A shiver crept up Darcie's spine. She looked more carefully at her escort. Those deep brown eyes, the black hair with the errant curl in front, the sun-kissed skin—it had to be Zack!

Her eyes sparkled in the glimmering light, but before she could say anything, she found that they had been followed. Eugénie was easy to spot in her new gown of brown and black stripes. Several others trailed along after her, two more reluctantly than the rest.

"Come, Darcie, don't dawdle." Eugénie took her hand and led her further into the cave.

Excitement teased a smile onto Darcie's face. The man must be Zack, he must be. Once again she looked up into his eyes and found a smile on his face. An almost imperceptible shake of his head prevented her from saying anything.

They reached a large room, filled with casks and kegs, maps and nautical instruments. *A pirate's treasure,* she thought. So Zack was about to tell her the truth finally.

Her gaze scanned the kegs and she saw nothing that gave her reason to believe any of Gaynor's treasure had been stored here.

"We may unmask now." Eugénie removed her domino first, followed by Darcie.

The two men who had lagged farthest behind removed their masks next. When Darcie saw their faces, she gasped aloud. "Uncle Talbot! Simon! And, you!"

The second man was the sailor about whom Captain James had warned her. His expression implied that he would rather be anywhere else but here. Darcie noticed that Uncle Talbot seemed to have several bruises on his face, one particularly nasty one below his left eye.

"Eugénie, tell me what is happening? Why are they here?" Darcie gestured toward them and then turned to the remaining unmasked figures. One by one the masks were removed. "Poule! Madelaine!"

Darcie hugged the sailor gently. "What are you doing here?"

"Hello, darling," Madelaine answered, smiling. She embraced Darcie. "You don't think I'd miss this, do you?"

"Good evening, miss." Poule blushed and looked down at his feet. "I'm here, well, I'm just . . ."

"I'll tell her, Poule." The last man to unmask was Zack, as she had known it would be.

She didn't know the others and soon found that they were officers of the palace guard. Darcie didn't care about anyone except Zack at the moment. Their embrace was warm and loving and prolonged.

"Excuse me, Zack, but I believe we need to complete our business so that we may get on to the pleasure of the evening," Eugénie reminded him quietly.

"Zack, before you say anything, I have something I want you to see." She opened her reticule and pulled out the envelope. "It's the truce! My father's copy."

Zack picked her up and swung her around. "What a detective you are. Where did you find it?"

"I had it all along. Uncle Talbot had requested some forms from Horace. It was among them. I forgot to give them to my dear uncle." Darcie glared at her uncle from the safety of Zack's embrace.

"Well, that settles a part of the controversy," he said. "Now, what about the piracy that you suspect me of?"

Darcie blushed. Somewhere there was a logical explanation, but she didn't know where. She tried to piece the puzzle together in her mind. "I . . . I suspected you because Captain James saw this man." Darcie pointed to the sailor in question. "I assumed that he had worked for you all along."

"Yes, I recall your questioning me about him. He had worked with young Dupuis before. You killed him, didn't you?" Zack asked.

"That's it!" Darcie exclaimed. "I saw them together several times, once just before poor Carson's body was discovered."

For a moment the sadness of the young man's death returned to Darcie. She clung to Zack for support and then stared at her uncle. "You. You ordered the attack on my ship. You knew I would suspect Zack. Especially when I found my mother's earring."

"What earring?" Zack asked.

"I found a diamond fleur-de-lis in your desk on the ship. It was wrapped in a handkerchief." Darcie sighed, now that the answers seemed to be coming freely. She pointed to the sailor who hung his head. "You planted it there. That's why you were on Zack's ship."

Talbot Neville looked increasingly uncomfortable. He glanced behind him and found his escape route cut off. "Darcie, look, this Manville is nothing. He's a smuggler. He's . . . he's a friend of the Emperor. France could be so great without *royalty*."

Darcie was stunned by the nasty tone of Uncle Talbot's words. "It was you I saw the night of the bombing. You knew I would be along. You helped those Italian criminals. You were trying to . . . to assassinate Napoleon and Eugénie."

"Hah! I knew of the attempt, but had no part in it."

Uncle Talbot's denial seemed to be a moot point after his prior statement. Darcie felt horrible.

"How can you stand there and lie? Everyone here heard what you said about—" Darcie began.

"No, my dear. I have no real interest in the Emperor and Empress." Talbot stared at the ground a moment and then glared at Darcie. Hatred seemed to pour from his eyes. "It was you I was after. You ruined everything for me. You refused to marry Simon. Barclay, the American, was easy enough to chase off. He and his sister left town immediately after I spoke with him. I didn't want to do it, but you forced me. I can't live without the income . . . my debts are huge. I'd be forced to live in poverty if you married this . . . this pirate."

"Kill me? You would have killed me?" Darcie felt her legs give way beneath her and she clung to Zack for support.

Burying her head in Zack's embrace, Darcie fought back tears. For the past weeks, the Empress of France had cared for her like her own child, and all the while, Darcie's uncle was involved in a plot to murder her, not to mention his theft of Darcie's property.

"Oh, Eugénie, what can I say? I have brought this . . . man into your life when you would have been much better off without either of us." Darcie felt the tears sting her eyelids.

"No, Darcie. You have brought me joy." Eugénie hugged Darcie's shoulders. "I shall miss you."

"Miss me?"

"Yes, my darling. I have rescued your ring from your dear uncle." Zack slid the ring back on Darcie's finger and kissed it. "If you consent to be married so soon, our guests are waiting. Poule will stand up for me, and Eugénie has consented to serve as your attendant."

"Here? Here in a cave?" Darcie asked, staring up at Zack.

He laughed. "Not exactly here. Outside in the moonlight, that wonderful intoxicating Parisian moon that I ordered especially for you . . . for our wedding."

"I have two questions." Darcie stopped and looked from Eugénie to Zack. "How do you come to be such close friends?"

"Allow me to answer, Zack," Eugénie said and held up her hand. "Zack's family has been close to my family for years. You see, when my father was, shall we say, out of favor, the Manville Trading Company smuggled in necessities and news to my mother. Our lives were entwined before we were born. Zack and his father before him use the title Prince of Smugglers."

"I shall have to keep a close watch on you then, sir," Darcie teased. "Now, why is Simon here?"

"He's here to apologize to you. And to tell you he's going to Charleston to marry Emilie Rhett."

Darcie hugged her cousin. "I'm glad."

Darcie, Zack, Eugénie, and the priest who had been standing in the shadows walked back to the ledge overlooking the Atlantic. The scent of jasmine was strong and Zack handed her a small bouquet. "Just for you."

She looked down at the Atlantic, at the undulating path of moonlight, and at the ship. "Is that *La Mer Magnifique?*"

"No, that's the *Darcie Manville,* waiting to be christened." He smiled down at her. "We're leaving as soon as our wedding feast is over."

"Where are we going?" she asked breathlessly.

Zack drew her into his embrace and kissed her deeply. Darcie forgot that they had an audience. The jasmine blossoms dropped from her hands and her arms encircled Zack's neck and she returned his kiss fervently. After a short time, Darcie heard noises that seemed intended to distract them and she opened her eyes. The entire party had gathered around them, and smiles and winks abounded.

"Where are we going?" she repeated.

"Home," he answered succinctly. "To Charleston."